****

Peacekeepers

Book Two of the Falling Empires Series

**By
James Rosone and Miranda Watson**
****

Published in conjunction with Front Line Publishing, Inc.

Disclaimer

This is a fictional story. All characters in this book are imagined, and any opinions that they express are simply that, fictional thoughts of literary characters. Although policies mentioned in the book may be similar to reality, they are by no means a factual representation of the news. Please enjoy this work as it is, a story to escape the part of life that can sometimes weigh us down in mundaneness or busyness.

Copyright Information

©2019, James Rosone and Miranda Watson, in conjunction with Front Line Publishing, Inc. Except as provided by the Copyright Act, no part of this publication may be reproduced, stored in a retrieval system or transmitted in any form or by any means without the prior written permission of the publisher.

ISBN: 978-1-957634-16-6
Sun City Center, Florida, USA
Library of Congress Control Number: 2022904115

Table of Contents

Chapter 1: O Canada 5
Chapter 2: Humpty Dumpty 26
Chapter 3: A Thief in the Night 33
Chapter 4: A Nation Divided 47
Chapter 5: Operation Spark 55
Chapter 6: Southern Front 66
Chapter 7: Bishop for a Pawn 84
Chapter 8: Escalation 101
Chapter 9: Thucydides's Trap 127
Chapter 10: Paukenschlag 136
Chapter 11: First Strike 167
Chapter 12: Man Down 197
Chapter 13: Occupation 225
Chapter 14: Operation Payback 240
Chapter 15: Stunned 258
Chapter 16: Partisans 289
Chapter 17: Desperate Plea 300
From the Authors 311
Abbreviation Key 314

Chapter 1
O Canada

December 1, 2020
Ottawa, Canada
Lord Elgin Hotel
Grill 41

Newly promoted Brigadier General Ryan Jackman sat across the table from the governor of New York, Tim Shank. Jackman had a broad smile on his face and optimism in his heart as he admired the small box that contained two silver stars, the rank insignia he had just accepted. He would now be the combat commander to lead the recently established New York Civil Defense Force, or NY CDF.

Jackman tried not to think about what he had given up for those shiny stars. This move had cost him his position in the New York Army National Guard as Commander of the 1st Battalion, 69th Infantry Regiment, along with any loyalty he had previously held to the Pentagon under the command of President Sachs.

Governor Shank returned Jackman's smile. "Congratulations, Ryan, you're officially a general. How does it feel?" he asked.

"I've never been happier or prouder in my life than I am right now, Governor," General Jackman replied, with a voice that seemed to feign confidence more than demonstrate it. "My only wish is that I could have persuaded more of my soldiers to cross over with me," he said.

Shank shrugged off the comment. "Don't beat yourself up over it, General. The fact that you were able to help convince more than thirty percent of the state National Guard to mobilize and stay true to their state is a testament to your leadership."

The governor paused for a second as he leaned in and fixed the new general with a steely gaze. "We're in for some tough times ahead of us. It's obvious we're heading for a civil war, one that's been brewing for decades. After this meeting, you're going to be a fugitive, a hunted man just like me. There won't be any going back once you take this position. If you want to back out, I'll understand, but once you're in, you're in until we either win or lose. Is that understood?"

Jackman was a bit taken aback by the governor's bluntness. He paused to reflect on his options.

Heck, most of the state elected officials have already fled across the border to Canada, he thought. Several Democratic governors had done the same. General Jackman concluded that if these politicians could stand up to President Sachs, then so could he.

Returning Shank's unrelenting stare, Jackman replied, "This is my country too, Governor. We're going to win this fight."

Governor Shank let out a sigh of relief and visibly relaxed his shoulders. "So, what do you propose we do next now that you're in charge of the state's militia?" he asked.

Jackman's mind spun. He smiled as he dreamed of ideas of how they would bring the Sachs administration to heel, or at least keep them out of New York state.

****

December 5, 2020
Ottawa, Canada
Lord Elgin Hotel

General Guy McKenzie brushed the snow off his overcoat and handed it to one of the bellhops, who looked a bit royal in his black pants and red jacket with black and golden trim. The man added it to the cart with McKenzie's belongings and waited for instructions about where to take it.

McKenzie looked the lobby over with a critical eye. The dark wood panel columns gave the location a very rich appearance, but the bright tile on the floor with ornate patterns along the side made the hotel seem warm and inviting.

This will do, he thought.

When it had become clear President-Elect Tate would need to set up his transition government in Canada, his campaign had worked with the Canadian government and the United Nations to secure and rent out all 355 rooms and suites at the Lord Elgin Hotel. The hotel sat conveniently just down the road from the Canadian parliament building. It was large enough to accommodate the people who would be critical to Tate's government, and it had enough conference rooms that could be quickly turned into briefing rooms when needed.

While General Guy McKenzie was assessing the hotel's general appearance, he promptly noticed the visible presence of a sea of private security contractors. The guards appeared to be part of the Senaca Group, an Irish-based security firm that provides private security in hostile nations and caters to the protective detail needs of world dignitaries. They also had a paramilitary branch that handled the more difficult, dirty jobs often associated with the Middle East and Africa.

After passing through security, McKenzie was escorted to the elevator bank and shown to the floor and room where the newly elected American President would be staying. The security guard knocked on the door twice, then stepped back and made his way to the elevator, leaving McKenzie to the charge of the other security guards on the floor.

****

Marshall Tate heard the double knock on the door and got up from the chair where he had been waiting. He opened the door, smiling broadly.

"President-Elect Tate, it's good to see you again," said General Guy McKenzie warmly. The two shook hands. "I was told you needed to see me in person," he remarked in a lower voice.

Tate nodded, doing his best to maintain a solid poker face. "I did, General. Please, come on in. Let's walk back to the sitting room, where the others are."

McKenzie nodded and followed him inside.

"I hope you don't mind us meeting in here," Tate said apologetically. "It's more private and away from prying eyes. I'm still not one hundred percent sure how loyal everyone is that's come over to our side, so I'm trying to minimize who all is involved in some of the critical decisions that still need to be made in the coming weeks."

"I can appreciate the secrecy," General McKenzie replied. "I don't envy your position, and I know this has to be a terribly hard situation for you and your family."

Tate nodded. "It has been incredibly difficult for my wife and children, but at least the kids are grown and on their own. I'm confident we'll get through it, especially with men like you and others to help guide us."

After walking through the galley kitchen in the suite, they made their way into the sitting room. For privacy reasons, Marshall had the curtains blocking the floor-to-ceiling glass windows that would normally give anyone sitting in this room a spectacular view of the city.

Waiting for them on the steel-gray couches were Retired Admiral David Hill, who was going to be Tate's Secretary of Defense, and Page Larson, who was going to become his National Security Advisor. Page had previously been a senior figure at the CIA. She'd quit her post at the Agency once she'd been named the President-Elect's NSA. Both she and Hill brought a wealth of defense and intelligence experience to his national security team, something they'd need in the coming days.

"Ah, I see you have your military advisors here," McKenzie remarked. He made his way over and shook their hands, exchanging the usual pleasantries.

Tate waited for a moment, then cleared his throat. "General, what we need to talk about next is a military question. I'll be frank, McKenzie, I'm not a military man, and I don't understand the intricacies of our present situation." He paused for a moment as if searching for the right words to say. "I never wanted to be in this position. However, we're here now, and we have to deal with it. I truly thought President Sachs would step down once he saw the UN and many other world leaders side with us. I had hoped he would see reason and agree to just retire, but I fear he's only digging in."

He motioned toward his new NSA. "Page told me that some of her former colleagues at the CIA informed her that Sachs is preparing the country for war. She said the intelligence apparatus of our country is being turned loose on the countries that are allying against him and he's ordered the Pentagon to begin preparations to implement a military blockade of Canada. He's also preparing the military to meet our forces head-on if necessary."

Tate sighed involuntarily. He couldn't completely conceal that he was having second thoughts about all of this. "I believe our country is headed toward a nasty civil war," he stated solemnly. "I'm not sure what can be done to stop it. If we do have to fight, I also don't know how we win. If Sachs does use military force, it seems that the majority of the United States military will side with him—I'm not sure your UN force is going to be much of a match. At least that's what Dave here thinks," he said, motioning toward Admiral Hill.

General McKenzie grimaced. He'd been hearing some similar information but was not fully aware of the situation inside the American Pentagon. He turned to face Admiral Hill and Page Larson. "If you had to put a number to it, what percentage of the military do you believe is going to remain loyal to Sachs?" he asked.

Retired Admiral David Hill leaned in. "I still have ears on the ground in D.C., and things don't look good, that's for sure. The SecDef and the cabinet have rightly shown that this election was a fraud. While many people in the government and the military may not like or agree with Sachs and his policies, they are dead set against replacing him in this fashion. We're going to get probably close to twenty to twenty-five percent of people who'll cross over, but that's largely the core group of people who have openly expressed disdain for Sachs and want to see the country remade according to the vision President-Elect Tate has put forward."

McKenzie crossed his arms. "Look, I can respect that many people in your country dislike Sachs, but if these people are crossing over simply because of this personal distaste, even though they agree the election was likely a farce, how can we trust them or know that their loyalties are going to be with our cause?" he countered.

"Does it really matter, General?" asked Page. "At the end of the day, whether this election was legitimate or not, people are using it as a means of getting rid of Sachs. And frankly, that's all that really matters."

Marshall Tate shot her a mortified look and held up a hand. "Do you really believe the election was a complete farce?" he asked. "You believe what Sachs and his cronies have been saying about it being rigged is true? Isn't there even a slight chance that I actually did win legitimately?"

She tilted her head to the side. Her expression registered a mix of surprise and pity. "I don't mean any disrespect, Mr. President-Elect, but did you really think you won this election on your own?" she asked. Page shook her head dismissively. "Of course it was a sham. You honestly think all those things happening the last six weeks of the campaign were coincidence? It was a well-engineered coup d'état to get rid of that bloviating buffoon. And it worked—or it should have worked. He wasn't supposed to find out about the postal workers who'd been handing over absentee and mail-in ballots, and we certainly didn't think he'd try and challenge the election results like he did or impose martial law. He was supposed to just take it on the chin and retire to enjoy his billions."

Tate sat there in stunned silence for a moment, taking in what Page had just said. While he knew a lot of powerful groups and people had been working to help him defeat Sachs, he'd legitimately believed he'd won. He'd truly felt Sachs had been making all of this up as a means not to give up power. Her words were like a blow to the gut.

What have I done? he thought, staring blankly back at Page.

"You truly didn't know?" she asked incredulously.

Tate slowly shook his head. "I knew some of the details, but I was told it was best if I didn't ask questions."

"That figures," Page remarked. "I'm sorry they kept you in the dark, Marshall. I truly am. I wasn't involved in the plan from the beginning. Heck, I was only made aware of most of it in the last year of the campaign, and really only got seriously involved once things started to fall apart. At that point, there wasn't much I could do to help right it other than to keep tabs on what the administration knew and what they were doing.

"Regardless, Sachs had to be replaced, and the powers that be couldn't take a chance on a second electoral upset. Change had to happen, and it has. You just need to continue to take charge of things. There are more pieces of the puzzle being moved into position."

General McKenzie grinned. "Wow, you had me fooled. I thought you were aware of what was going on, Mr. President-Elect," he remarked before shrugging his shoulders. "It's OK. As Page said, a lot of pieces are in motion now. It'll work out in the end; you just need to stick to your position and continue to lead the country, or at least the parts that are loyal to you."

Turning back to face the admiral, McKenzie said, "You believe that a lot of the active-duty military appears to be siding with Sachs. What about the portions that are going to flip? Do you know who they are? You know, what units or commands do they control and what equipment will cross over with them?"

Retired Admiral Hill lifted his chin up. "I've spoken secretly with Rear Admiral Harold Ward, the commander for Carrier Strike Group 11. They're still finalizing some maintenance issues at the Bremerton Naval Facility before they move back to Naval Station Everett just north of Seattle. He told me the captain of the USS *Nimitz* and at least twenty percent of his officers and enlisted personnel will side with us. He's not sure yet how many other vessel captains will join him, but he's hoping he can convince at least some of them to cross over before they set sail to enforce Sachs's blockade."

McKenzie's right eyebrow rose in surprise. "You mean the captain of a supercarrier may join us?" he asked incredulously.

Smiling, Hill nodded. "Well, we have a few diversions that are going to be created to help with flushing the ships out of port before they're fully crewed. If the full crew were already on board, there'd be no way they could pull it off. The admiral's goal is to remove the ship from being used against us. We obviously can't crew it, and the ship won't have its airwing, so it's not like we can use it in any sort of military sense. However, removing the ship from being a part of a blockade or military function that could have been used against us will be a huge political win for our side. It'll help to show the public that even the military isn't falling in line with that dictator."

McKenzie sported a devilish smile, which suddenly turned sour. "If Sachs moves forward with this blockade, we could be in trouble. Will the current naval officers actually fire on our ships?"

Hill scratched his chin before he responded. "I'm not one hundred percent sure they'll fire first. I know if they're fired upon, they won't hesitate to fire back, but as to whether or not they'll fire on ships attempting to run the blockade, I don't know. If they were issued a direct order, I'd say it's probably fifty-fifty that they would."

"OK...what about the Atlantic side?" McKenzie asked.

Hill nodded. "The captain of the USS *Colorado*, which is a *Virginia*-class fast-attack submarine, is going to join our ranks. The captain and I were friends at the Academy many years ago. Like the captain of the *Nimitz*, his ship is supposed to be a part of the blockade in a few weeks. He's also going to put to sea in the early hours of the morning with the crew he knows is loyal to our cause."

Admiral Hill went on to tell them about a few more ships that might cross over. They wouldn't know the exact tally for a few more weeks, but he was cautiously optimistic that they might be able to peel away enough forces to convince Sachs that he should step down.

The more Hill talked about these naval units crossing over, the more Marshall Tate could sense the tension in the room decreasing. McKenzie was visibly more relaxed. "Well, that certainly does make the situation on the naval side seem more palatable," Tate admitted. "My bigger concern is the situation with the ground and air forces, though. What's our angle there?"

General McKenzie nodded. "When Sachs orders some of the Army's ground combat units or the Marines to head toward the US-Canadian border, how do you propose we handle that?" he asked Admiral Hill. "Are there other Army units that might also cross over?"

Hill shook his head. "I don't believe we'll see any direct units change sides. It's a lot harder for Army and Marine equipment to change sides en masse than it is a ship. A pilot or two might switch and just fly their fighter across the border, but we aren't going to see battalions of tanks do that. We'll probably see a trickle of soldiers start to go AWOL and stop showing up to their home units, but I wouldn't count on any big chunks of ground equipment."

General McKenzie nodded. He didn't seem that surprised or disheartened by the answer. "What about the militia forces?" he asked. "How quickly can we raise them and how reliable will they be?"

"The governor of New York just announced the formation of his state's militia unit. A former National Guard commander is going to take command of it. The man's done a couple of combat tours in Iraq and Afghanistan, so he's competent. From what I gather, close to thirty percent of the state National Guard is rallying on him. Once a general call for support is issued, I suspect they'll probably raise maybe ten or twenty thousand volunteers. These will be green recruits—some of them might have prior military service, so that'll help, but they will need training and equipping."

General McKenzie grunted. "I think we can handle the training at least," he asserted. "We'll get them carted off to the existing Canadian military training bases and begin to run them through a rough, shortened version of our basic infantry school. That way they'll be ready for combat much sooner than if we ran them through a standard training program."

"Excellent idea," Hill responded. "I'll make sure we get this coordinated with the governor. I think you may want to get things ready at those bases, though. Once the call goes out, I suspect the other governors are going to want to do the same. We could suddenly find ourselves inundated with fresh recruits from across the country as people make their way north to join up."

Marshall Tate tried to let the military experts handle this conversation, saying very little over the next few hours. The situation wasn't nearly as bleak when they left the room as when he had entered

it, but the next month and a half, all the way up to January 20th, was going to make for some interesting times, to be sure.
****

December 6, 2020
Quebec, Canada
Canadian Forces Base Bagotville

Just one day later, as General Guy McKenzie sat in the small room with a few of his key air squadron commanders, he felt like General Norman Schwarzkopf, trying to figure out how to attack the fifth-largest army in the world without getting his forces slaughtered. Preparing to fight the American military was no small feat, but if they were given the go order, then, by God, he was going to do his best to land some crippling blows and hopefully achieve their political and military goals before the Americans could get organized and pound his forces into the dirt.

After completing his review of the paper briefs that had been provided to him, General McKenzie kicked off the meeting in earnest. "Lieutenant Colonel Jean Pégoud, I was led to believe that your squadron is the best deep penetration squadron in the French Air Force. During a training exercise against the Americans in Europe, your squadron succeeded in penetrating their air space and carried out a mock attack against Ramstein Air Force Base, no?"

The lieutenant colonel didn't even reveal a hint of a smile. "That was a training exercise, General," he responded flatly. "This is a real mission you're asking me to plan. Do you know how hard it will be to penetrate American air space if they know we're coming? They will have fighters on top of us before we even know what happens."

"That's why I need you to begin running your squadron through practice scenarios straightaway," McKenzie countered. "You need to get them ready for a deep penetration strike through a heavily defended airspace. This mission shouldn't be any different than any of the previous deep strike missions you guys rehearsed with NATO against the Russians."

"With all due respect, General, those missions were also done in *coordination with* the Americans, not against them. You're a soldier, General. I'm a pilot, and a good one at that. I'm telling you bluntly, a mission like this will get most of my pilots killed, if not our entire squadron."

General McKenzie paused for a moment. He saw the man's point, but he also knew that if his other plans were to have any chance of success, Jean's squadron had to succeed.

"Colonel, if you're given the order to carry out this mission, then I assure you, there will be a massive air attack all across the American border. Our plan is to sufficiently distract them so that your group should be able to penetrate close enough to launch your missiles. What I need to know is if this type of strike is *possible*, and if it is, what type of support you'll need to make sure it works."

Jean nodded and then looked more closely at the map. His fingers traced a line to the target, then an idea seemed to take hold. He grabbed a protractor and pencil and wrote out some distances on the map. A slight smile formed as he looked up at the general.

"I think I have a way we can make it work," Lieutenant Colonel Pégoud announced.

McKenzie's lips curled up at the corners, almost mischievously. The two of them discussed the plan for the better part of an hour before they parted ways.

Once the general had finished talking with his French aviators, he walked down the hall to the tiny room being occupied by his Chinese People's Liberation Army Air Force liaison officer, General Xi, who'd been assigned to his staff now for three months. Xi possessed a very unique set of qualifications; his French and English were both excellent, and he was also a pilot, so he understood the aviation challenge McKenzie was facing.

They had a lot to discuss. While the Chinese were largely going to focus their efforts on a southern front through Mexico, the Chinese Air Force was still going to maintain several squadrons' worth of fighters and anti-air artillery squadrons with the European contingent in Canada.

McKenzie knocked briefly on the door to get the Chinese general's attention, and then he walked just inside the threshold.

"General Xi, do you have a moment for us to talk?" he asked.

Xi smiled and waved him over to sit down. "Of course, General. I always have time for the UN commander," he replied cheerfully. "How may China be of service to you?" he asked.

"Thank you, General," McKenzie replied. "What I want to talk to you about is rather sensitive. Can we please speak privately, just the two of us?" He surveyed the room carefully.

This elicited a curious look from Xi, who nodded. He grabbed a notepad and proceeded to follow McKenzie back toward his office. They both knew the Chinese Ministry of State Security probably had a bug in his office, if for no other reason than to keep tabs on him and his staff assigned to Canada. The Chinese and Canadians might be partners in this endeavor, but it didn't mean the two parties fully trusted each other either.

The two of them made small talk as they walked through the headquarters building to McKenzie's office. Once there, McKenzie guided them to a set of chairs next to a small table he had in his office.

As soon as Xi was seated, McKenzie began, "General, I'm going to ask some questions, assuming China has a certain type of capability. You don't need to confirm what I'm saying to you—I just need to know if China could handle a very specific mission if it was handed to you."

Xi's smile and soft demeanor changed and hardened a bit as he leaned forward. "General, you know my nation is committed to doing what we can in these troubled times. What is it you believe we are uniquely able to handle?"

McKenzie sported a crooked smile. "I need to know if your stealth bomber—you know, the one that doesn't exist—would be able to deliver a bunker-buster bomb."

Xi lifted his chin up and paused, as if considering his words. Finally, he responded. "We have an aircraft that could accomplish this mission, if it were given some initial support and it had the element of surprise on its side. But as to the bomb, our current bomb is heavy, so our 'bomber,'" he said, making air quotes with his hands, "can only carry two of them."

McKenzie thought about Xi's response. He knew they'd need at least four of these bombs for the mission he'd had in mind. Suddenly, he remembered something. "The Russians have a unique thermobaric bomb, and I believe it weighs 7,100 kilograms. Could your hypothetical bomber carry four of them?"

Xi rubbed his chin as he did some calculations in his head. A minute later he explained, "It could, but I'd need to see the specifications for the bomb. Do you have a specific target in mind? If you're thinking of going after NORAD, I can assure you, neither the Russian nor Chinese bombs will penetrate it."

General McKenzie chuckled. "No, we aren't looking at NORAD." He pulled out a map, and Xi's left eyebrow rose in surprise.

The two talked for about an hour about how the bomber would approach this target and what kind of support it would need to breach that far into American airspace. Xi wasn't sure he could get permission to use their "new" bomber for this mission, but he vowed to make every attempt to secure the go-ahead.

"General, this would certainly go down in military history as one of the craziest bombing missions ever devised," he asserted.

"I know," McKenzie acknowledged with a smile.

****

December 9, 2020
Ottawa, Canada

Johann Behr had flown out to meet with General McKenzie in person. There were some things that just shouldn't be discussed over any form of electronic communication.

When McKenzie had finished his brief, Johann felt his face contorting with the skepticism he felt. "How do you know it'll work?" he asked. "I mean, it looks like this would be a suicide mission."

"Going to war against America *is* typically a suicide mission, Mr. Secretary," McKenzie answered. "But if we are going to do it, then this plan gives us the best chance of chopping the head of the snake off and potentially ending this war before it really has a chance to get going." His demeanor betrayed a certain sense of annoyance.

"General, if this war really does have to happen, do you believe this plan will end it swiftly, or will it prolong it?" asked Behr. He was starting to second-guess his plans.

"That depends on whether we're successful or not," McKenzie answered. "If we succeed, then I think it ends it before it spirals out of control. If we fail, though, you will have essentially kicked up a hornet's nest, Mr. Secretary. You can bet the Americans will be after blood. They will attack our forces in Canada mercilessly, and my country will bear the brunt of this retaliation." He took a deep breath and let it out with a huff. "We'll be ready to execute the military option when you tell us to, but I do hope you're able to negotiate a peaceful solution to this problem."

Now it was Johann's turn to sigh. He looked at his general. "I'm not confident that a peaceful solution to this problem *can* be reached. My biggest concern right now is figuring out how we could neutralize the Americans fast enough so they don't destroy our forces or retaliate against Europe, Russia, or China for their involvement in this effort."

Leaning forward, McKenzie fixed Johann with an icy look. "Sir, we're about to declare war on the most powerful nation in the world. You have to accept that they're going to strike back hard against the nations that are attacking them. What matters now is that we capture a lot of land rapidly. We need to get the people on our side and get them involved in this fight. We have to tear America apart from the inside out. If they somehow unify and rally around Sachs, then we're going to be in for a very tough fight."

"All right, General. You've made your point. Then please proceed as if we are going to war with America. Plan for their counterattacks and do your best to mitigate them. As to this plan of yours…consider it a go. Oh, and General, if you shoot at the king, you'd better kill him…"
****

West Des Moines, Iowa

The more Pat looked at his Facebook feed, the more livid he became. He'd just finished watching a video showing his representative, Congresswoman Jessica Lane, giving a spirited speech calling the President a dictator who'd refused to accept the results of the election and leave. She openly supported the UN mission to remove Sachs, who she called the "tyrant in the White House."

Pat reached for his bottle of Jack and took a couple of long gulps, letting the liquid burn its way down to his stomach.

We have to do something about this, he thought angrily.

He heard a quiet ding, looked back at his computer screen and clicked on the messenger app. A smile crept across his face.

Finally. A meeting.
****

It was 8:46 p.m. when Pat pulled into the parking lot of VFW Post 9127. He put his truck in park and got out. He glanced up at the sky—just a sea of stars without a single cloud in sight. He walked toward the rear door of the lodge, his usual limp seeming more pronounced this evening for some reason.

As Pat pulled open the door and headed to the bar in the rear of the building, he quickly realized that there were only five guys at this meeting of the III percenters, including himself.

"Glad you could make it, Pat. Take a seat," said his friend Joel. "We were just about to talk about our little problem."

Pat smiled and pulled up the only chair left at the table.

"Congresswoman Lane crossed a line the other day," one of the guys remarked.

"She didn't just cross a line, she openly invited a foreign army into our country," Joel responded angrily. "She broke her oath to protect and defend the Constitution."

Pat already felt his anger welling up. He stood back up and walked toward the bar. "I need a drink. Anyone else want one?" he asked.

"Grab the bottle and some glasses," Joel said.

Pat selected a bottle of Tennessee Fire, then pulled a twenty out of his wallet and placed it in the register.

That ought to cover the cost, he thought.

He placed the glasses down and filled each of them about halfway up before sitting down.

After downing about half the glass he'd just poured, Pat demanded, "Are we just going to talk about this or are we going to *do* something?"

Some of the guys at the table seemed a bit hesitant, but Joel quickly answered, "We're going to do something."

"Exactly what do you propose?" asked Doug, one of the squeamish guys.

"We shoot up her office," Joel responded.

"What? When would you propose we do that?" Doug inquired, his face a bit pale.

"We do it at night," Joel explained. "That way, no one will get hurt, but it'll send a message."

"Coward," Pat retorted, venom in his voice.

"What are you talking about?" Joel asked, a bit pained. He seemed surprised that Pat didn't agree with him.

"Shooting up an office in the middle of the dark sends the wrong message. We need to take her out. She has a town hall in two days—I say we shoot her. That'll get it through the thick skulls of those politicians in Washington that if they want to invite a foreign army into our country, we're ready to take them on and defend our communities."

There was a long pause while the others at the table were silent for a moment. Pat wondered if all their tough talk in the past was just that—talk—or if they had the guts to actually do anything about it.

"Who would do it?" one of the other guys, Bob, finally asked. He gulped down the rest of his Tennessee whiskey.

"Certainly not you, Bob," Joel retorted. You look like you're about to pee your pants." He laughed and the others joined in. The tension in the room seemed to break a bit after that.

"I'll do it."

"Pat, come on. Be serious," said Joel. "If you kill a congresswoman, the feds will be all over you and the rest of us."

Pat shook his head. "I thought this was a group of action. I didn't realize everyone here lacked a spine. You all like to dress up and play army, go shoot some guns and talk crap about the government, but when the rubber meets the road, you guys shy away from getting your hands dirty. Don't you guys remember your oath of enlistment? 'Against all enemies, foreign and domestic.' Lane's clearly crossed the line. A foreign army is building on both our northern and southern borders, and you guys are concerned about the FBI?"

Joel held up a hand to calm his friend down. "Let's just take this one step at a time. We don't have to shoot her office up. If you want, we can firebomb it instead. The flames and damage will play well in the media. It'll send the message you're looking for. We can also show up at her town hall and pepper her with difficult questions. I can have my son record it so we can use it on YouTube."

Pat looked at the others, disappointed. He realized they didn't have the stomach to do what needed doing.

Fine, I'll go along, he thought, but he made his own plans for after the town hall.

"OK. Then let's firebomb her office tonight, before any of you chickens get cold feet."

Joel surveyed the cautious faces around him, then replied, "OK. Let's do it."

19

****

Three hours later, Joel and Pat pulled up just short of the back alley of the storefronts where Representative Lane's congressional office was located. Pat looked at his friend and pulled an electronic device out of the center console, turned it on and placed it on the dash of the truck.

"What the hell is that?" Joel asked.

"It's an electronic jammer," Pat answered, a bit condescendingly. "It'll interfere with the CCTV cameras and prevent them from recording us when we break in."

Joel nodded, clearly wishing he'd thought of the idea himself. "All right, then. Time to suit up," he replied.

The two of them donned rubber masks in the likeness of President Obama, then pulled on two layers of surgical gloves. Pat put his truck back in gear and began to drive down the alleyway. They drove past an H&R Block store, a law firm and an Allstate insurance office before coming to the back of the office for Congresswoman Lane.

"Make sure to take those two cameras out," Pat said. He tossed Joel a can of black spray paint.

"I thought you said the jammer already took them offline," Joel remarked, obviously confused.

"It did, but I want them to think it was the spray paint that kept them from seeing what happened, not the jammer," Pat explained.

While Joel headed off to take out the cameras, Pat grabbed a specially designed prybar and placed it next to the lock on the door. When he applied pressure, he saw the doorframe bend just enough for him to pull the door open without having to break the lock or the frame. With the door slightly ajar, Pat placed the prybar on the ground next to the door and then grabbed his can of gasoline and headed in. Joel would stay outside and keep watch.

Once inside the office, Pat doused the desks and all the cabinets with gas. He mainly focused on soaking the wood, chairs, and computers—he knew that once the fire started, the rest of the place would go up.

When he was done, Pat grabbed two propane tanks and placed them in the congresswoman's office. He opened them up slightly, so they'd start to leak, and closed the door. Next, he tossed a match on one of the

20

desks that had a pool of gasoline on it and watched with delight as a red-and-orange fireball erupted.

He couldn't stay long. Pat dashed out to the alleyway and grabbed the prybar. Once again, he applied pressure to the doorframe and closed the door. It was as if they'd never been there.

Of course, by now, the flames had grown large enough that the internal sprinkler system had started to go off, along with the fire alarm.

"Come on, Pat, we need to go," Joel said urgently as he climbed into the truck.

Once Pat was in the vehicle, Joel floored it. They got probably about two or three blocks away when they heard a thunderous explosion.

Joel looked in the rearview mirror and then turned his head around to see the carnage. "Holy crap! That entire place just blew up. What did you put in there?"

Pat smiled. "Oh, just a couple of propane tanks for good measure."

Joel shook his head. "I think we should go stay at my brother's farm for the night—get ourselves out of town for a day or two until that town hall meeting."

"I agree. Let's do it."

****

As Pat pulled into the parking lot of the Herbert Hoover High School, he could tell this town hall was going to be packed. After Congresswoman Lane's office had been destroyed, her staff had announced that her original town hall had been postponed, so there had been time for everyone to digest what had happened. The turnout clearly demonstrated how passionate people were about the events that had transpired.

Using his handicapped parking permit for the first time in over a month, Pat managed to find a space relatively easily despite the crowds. As he filed into the line to get in, it was easy to tell that the people around him were all pretty angry—some were mad that Lane's office had been bombed, while others were irate that Lane refused to acknowledge the mounting evidence of voter fraud. Pat felt that he could readily tell the difference between the two, regardless of whether they wore anything that gave away their political affiliation. He had personally opted to wear a Senator Tate ball cap, to make himself appear less of a threat.

Besides anger, the other palpable emotion of the evening was fear—the whole crowd was hopped up on adrenaline, one way or the other. To help compensate for the heightened tensions, the police presence had dramatically increased at this event. In the past, there might have been one or two officers at a town hall, but Pat observed no less than a dozen. And then there were the two men in very conspicuous navy jackets with standard yellow FBI lettering on them.

As the line moved closer to the door of the high school, Pat spotted a set of metal detectors inside. His heart skipped a beat. He quickly took a deep breath to calm himself.

They won't find it, he told himself.

The line continued to progress forward one-by-one marching toward the officers at the security check solemnly as a prisoner might approach his execution. Pat found himself walking through the metal arch. It beeped loudly.

One of the officers pointed for him to stand off to the side.

"You have any weapons or knives, sir?" asked the man with a polite smile.

Pat shook his head, then pulled his left pant leg up a bit to reveal the prosthetic leg that resided where his real one used to be.

"Thank you for your service," the police officer responded. Then he waved Pat through without doing any further checks on him.

Works every time, Pat thought, holding back a smile.

He glanced over to the auditorium—it was already starting to fill up. Pat turned and headed toward the bathroom instead. He made his way over to the handicap stall, locked the door and sat down. He pulled his pants up a bit and took his prosthesis off. Then he removed the gel padding where his limb stump sat. Underneath, he had hidden his P238 Spartan subcompact pistol, which he now removed. It was a little gun, but the .380-caliber bullets it fired would still get the job done.

Holding the gun in his hand, Pat ran his fingers across the Greek phrase *Molon Labe* engraved on the side of the slide action.

Come and take them, he thought with a smile. He'd been ready to die for his country in Afghanistan—hell, half of his leg was still over there—and in that moment, he realized he was ready to die for his country again.

He placed the subcompact into his weather-worn jacket, reattached his prosthetic leg and pulled his pants down. Just then, a couple of men walked into the restroom, talking excitedly with each other. Pat flushed the toilet and stood up. He pushed the stall door open and walked up to the sink, going through the motions of washing his hands. As he did, he looked at his face in the mirror.

I can do this...I must do this...

Pat finished drying his hands, then made his way into the gymnasium. Despite the fact that it was filling up already, he was able to take advantage of the reserved seating for the disabled near the front. The woman next to him bantered with him briefly before she became distracted by her smartphone.

Before long, Congresswoman Lane walked in, flanked by a couple of her aides. Chaos erupted. Some of the audience cheered her arrival, others booed, and still others loudly hurled questions at her.

Seemingly unflapped, Lane made her way over to a table with several chairs and sat behind it. There was a microphone set up on the center of the table, as well as two other wireless microphones, presumably for a Q and A at the end of whatever it was she was about to say or do.

Since she didn't take anyone's bait, the crowd eventually calmed down and everyone took their seats. When they did, the congresswoman grabbed one of the wireless mikes and stood, walking in front of the table to be closer to the crowd.

"Good morning, everyone," she began. "First, I want to thank you all for coming here to listen to me speak. I also want to thank the FBI and the Des Moines Police Department for providing some additional security for this event. What happened the other day to my congressional office is frankly tragic. Fortunately, no one was there when it blew up and no one was hurt—but let's not forget this was a premeditated attack on a duly elected representative to Congress. We cannot resort to violence when we disagree with each other. That's what we have elections for. Sadly, our current President won't recognize the results of the last election."

Half the crowd immediately booed.

"The election was a fraud!" shouted one man.

A woman yelled, "Sachs was right—it was rigged!"

Somehow, above the raucous crowd, Pat could still hear another man scream, "When are you going to recognize the FBI and DOJ findings of election tampering?"

23

For her part, Congresswoman Lane blew off those cries like a practiced politician. Eventually, as she spoke, the crowd settled back down. She slowly drifted toward Pat's side of the room.

He'd heard enough. His right hand was already in his pocket, firmly in control of the pistol. He pulled the gun out slowly and calmly and then raised his right hand up in a fluid, practiced motion and fired three shots. Two shots hit her chest and one connected with her head before she even knew what had happened. The three pistol shots reverberated loudly in the gymnasium.

Pat retracted his arm, ready to point the barrel at his own head—he'd already decided he'd rather off himself than be captured. However, his right hand only made it about halfway back before he was tackled from behind and thrown forward into two other people.

The heap of bodies all landed on the floor with a thud, followed by the pained moans of the man on the bottom of the pile. Then a cacophony of shouts and screams grew in a steady crescendo, echoing off the walls of the gymnasium.

Pat desperately tried to regain control of his arm so he could finish the job, but a second set of hands grabbed at his right hand, wresting control of the gun away from him. Then his left hand was yanked behind his back. He felt the sensation of cold metal grasping his left wrist as the man on top of him quickly attached a pair of handcuffs. His right wrist was restrained seconds later.

Everything had happened so swiftly. He'd succeeded in killing the congresswoman, but he'd been unable to end his own life in the process.

Why didn't one of the police officers or FBI agents shoot me? he wondered.

As he lay there on the floor with a knee in his back, Pat overheard police directing people to exit the auditorium a certain way. Someone else called for an ambulance for the congresswoman, but Pat already knew she was dead.

A reporter who'd hung back shouted out, "Why'd you do it?"

Pat bellowed, "To honor my oath to defend this country!"

"Shut up! Don't say another word!" one of the police officers yelled at him.

"It won't be the last. This is only the beginning!" Pat managed to shout. Then one of the officers kicked him in the gut, knocking the wind out of him.

"Come on. Let's get this lunatic out of here," directed one of the FBI agents.

Gasping, Pat yelled, "Today is just the beginning!" Another officer punched him in the gut and then he was dragged out of the auditorium, kicking and doing his best to make his message heard.

Despite the chaos of rabid reporters shouting questions at him and the officers who were manhandling him, Pat noticed a man who had approached their little gaggle from the parking lot. When the man came within ten feet of their crowd, he pulled a handgun out of his jacket and fired half a dozen bullets into Pat and the police officers holding him before he himself was shot and killed by one of the FBI agents.

****

From the Associated Press:

> A shocking scene unfolded at Congresswoman Jessica Lane's town hall in West Des Moines, Iowa, as one of the attendees managed to smuggle a gun into the event and fire three shots at her, killing her instantly. After the assassination, the police and FBI were about to transport the attacker, now identified as Patrick Shay, into federal custody, when a man in the parking lot opened fire on Mr. Shay, who died instantly. Two of the police officers nearby were also injured but are now listed as being in stable condition. The police and FBI returned fire and killed the second attacker, now identified as Paul Whittaker. This left three dead and two injured in less than ten minutes.

From *Reuters Online*:

> The assassination of Congresswoman Jessica Lane seems to have inspired multiple copycat attackers. There have been more than three hundred killings in the span of a week that have been identified as clearly being politically motivated. Police across the nation are urging calm during this period of heightened tensions, and multiple political leaders have issued statements reminding the public that vigilante attackers will be prosecuted to the fullest extent of the law.

Chapter 2
Humpty Dumpty

December 10, 2020
Washington, D.C.
White House, Cabinet Room

FBI Director Nolan Polanski and Patty Hogan from DHS exchanged a nervous glance before returning their eye contact to the President.

"I don't think you fully understand how bad the situation is getting, Mr. President," Polanski said cautiously. "We've seen an enormous uptick in political and hate crimes being committed against both sides of the political aisle. It's completely overwhelming local law enforcement and my own agency. We need help, and we need it now, Mr. President."

Turning to face his Attorney General, the President asked, "How about it, Malcolm? What do you recommend we do?"

The AG shifted uncomfortably in his chair. "You've already declared martial law and activated the National Guards in all fifty states, sir. It's going to take time to get them all shifted around the country to their new assignments."

SecDef McElroy nodded. "Mr. President, we're also running into the problem of AWOLs inside the Guard units, as well as in the reserves and active military," he asserted. "Close to twenty percent of the units across the board aren't showing up. We don't know yet if they're just opting not to participate with the deployments or if they're truly crossing ranks to join the UN and militia forces forming up in Canada."

Sachs shook his head in frustration. "This whole situation is spiraling out of control faster than we can react to it. We have to do something to return order to our streets and stop the violence. I need answers, solutions—not more questions and problems, gentlemen," he insisted, his voice slowly rising to a near yell. He took a deep breath and let it out with a huff, then eyed his AG again. "Now, what more can we do to help local law enforcement?" he asked, his voice back to its normal volume and cadence.

"We should move forward with Patty's idea of increasing the Federal Protective Service force," Malcolm insisted. "They have, what, roughly 1,200 uniformed officers and another 14,000 contractors?" he asked, nodding to Patty.

"That's correct," she confirmed. "At this moment, their duties are to protect all buildings owned and operated by the General Services Administration. They're essentially mini police departments on some of our larger facilities. My proposal is that we turn the 14,000 contractors into federal workers, and then we move to rapidly expand that number to 100,000 people over the next six months. We can use this force to help augment our local law enforcement officers and FBI agents throughout the country."

The President let out a soft whistle. "That's a lot of new cops to essentially create overnight. How do you propose we do that?" he asked skeptically. "Especially when we have a ton of civil unrest happening now as it is."

"We use the draft," Patty proposed. "We work with the Selective Service, and we place a requirement for them to fill it. Of course, we'll also promote it externally and try to get folks to volunteer, but we use Selective Service to fill in the gaps."

Leaning forward, General Austin Peterson added, "If we're going to use the Selective Service, then we should also go ahead with temporarily increasing the size of the military. We're clearly facing a national emergency. We have a foreign army starting to amass on our borders, and we have a high percentage of desertions. I'd like to recommend that all soldiers currently in basic training be turned into infantry soldiers and that we go ahead now and begin the process of drafting at least half a million young men into the military."

"What about the other military specialties?" asked the SecDef, his left eyebrow raised to an uncomfortable looking height.

Turning to look at McElroy, General Peterson replied, "We can let some of the critical ones continue on to receive their advanced MOS training, but by and large, we're going to need a lot of infantry soldiers. My gut tells me if there's a conflict with this UN force to our north, it's going to be brief and bloody, not a long, drawn-out fight."

Sachs nodded. "I agree, General. I think the days of a prolonged battle are probably over, at least when it comes to a conventional force-on-force scenario. Go ahead with your plans and let's get the Selective Service involved. It's December tenth—I'd like the first round of the

draft completed by Friday, December 18th, with a report date of no later than January third. We need to get this force created and going."
****

Havana, Cuba

The weather was absolutely gorgeous as the wind blew some warm, moist air in across the hotel room through the open window. Vice Admiral Hu Zhanshu looked one more time at the disposition of his ship deployments for the Pacific, the Gulf of Mexico, and the Atlantic. This plan was years in the making. It was either going to succeed beyond his wildest beliefs, or it was going to utterly flop and doom his country. For his part, Admiral Hu was either going to be hailed a hero of China or lined up against a wall and shot for his failure.

"This is an audacious plan, Admiral," stated Major General Semyon Lobov. "Are you confident it will work?"

Admiral Hu stood even straighter than normal, trying to stretch his frame to maximum stature. "It'll work so long as your missile batteries are able to keep the American Air Force at bay," he replied, both taunting and appeasing his Russian counterpart.

For this plan to work, the Chinese and Russians had to work together hand in glove. It wasn't possible to take down the world's dominant superpower without a lot of coordination and twisting the arms of many smaller, less powerful nations to get them to go along.

"The Americans have spent the past eighteen years fighting Islamic extremists," General Lobov said dismissively. "Last time I checked, the Taliban doesn't have an air force. We've tested our systems against their aircraft in Syria. They'll work when the time comes."

"You've tested your radars and electronic jamming—not your missiles," Hu asserted. "It's going to be imperative that your force be able to drive the American Air Force nuts in the southern half of their country. If you can keep their Air Force and commercial aircraft grounded for even a month, you'll have bought our forces in Mexico enough time to tear the American Southwest apart."

"You ought to be more concerned with the Europeans in Canada," Lobov insisted, tossing aside the Chinese admiral's concern. "We Russians know how to fight. We've spent most of our history in one war or another. It's the Europeans who buckle under the weight of a conflict."

Admiral Hu snickered at the retort. "You may be right on that account. We'll see if the Germans and French are truly able to fight or if they're just a paper tiger."

Pulling a packet of cigarettes out of his breast pocket, the Russian tapped it against his palm briefly before he pulled one of them out. He bent over slightly and lit it with a gold-plated Zippo lighter he had been given by President Romanoff himself. He held the pack out to Admiral Hu, who looked at the cigarette disapprovingly before he grudgingly took one. General Lobov lit it for him, and the two of them stood there in the hotel room, looking at the map on the table before them.

General Lobov leaned over the map and examined it before he returned his gaze to Admiral Hu. "You realize, if we are successful in this endeavor, America will never be the same?" Lobov asked, almost rhetorically. "We will have altered the world balance for generations in China's favor."

"Even if we fail, America will never be the same," Hu shot back. "And, yes, the world balance will shift in our direction, but that is the direction it's been heading for more than thirty years. If we are successful, General Lobov, Russia will prosper along with China. The Europeans will have spent themselves trying to go toe to toe with the Americans."

Lobov grunted. "And all it will have cost Russia is half of our air force, most of our navy and half of our surface-to-air missile platforms."

Crinkling his eyebrows at the glum proclamation, Admiral Hu exclaimed, "General, be real. What you are sacrificing is old, outdated equipment that is costing your country more to maintain than it would to just replace it. You may believe you're throwing this equipment away, but what you're going to gain in return is something far better."

Lobov snorted at Hu's dismissive comment. "It's not the equipment loss that bothers me, Admiral—it's the trained men that we'll be losing with that equipment. China may be a nation with more than a billion people, but Russia is not."

"Your country is being well compensated for its participation in this grand UN endeavor, General," Admiral Hu asserted. "This effort is going to succeed; you wait and see."

Over the next couple of hours, they finished discussing the defensive plans for how Russia was going to turn Cuba into a massive surface-to-air missile swarm on the Americans. With dozens of S-300 and S-400 missile systems being set up in strategic points around Cuba, the Russians were going to make it nearly impossible for US aircraft to fly over Florida, Georgia, Louisiana, Mississippi, Alabama, and parts of Texas. With the American Southeast essentially tied down and the Northeast otherwise occupied, that would leave the Chinese to contend with the American Southwest. If they could succeed in removing the American Air Force from the equation, then the UN's ground force should be on an equal footing with the United States Army, and that was a horse race they believed they could win.

****

When General Semyon Lobov left his meeting with the Chinese, he turned to his deputy, Colonel Ivan Smirnov. "I don't trust the Chinese one bit," he admitted. "Mark my words, Ivan—they'll betray us if it suits them, or if they can profit from it."

Colonel Smirnov looked surprised. "Why do you say that, sir?" he asked.

Since it was only the two of them in the vehicle, Lobov turned to his deputy. "Because China is greedy," he answered candidly. "China is also an untested military. They've never fought a serious war where they were looking defeat in the eyes. If they get their nose bloodied, they'll likely back down. I don't trust them, and I think we should make our own preparations in case they double-cross us."

Smirnov nodded. No other response was needed.

He's a good little soldier, Lobov thought with a smile.

****

Orlando, Florida

Seth Mitchell had planned his family trip to Disney's Animal Kingdom with his usual military precision. The truth was, ever since returning from Yemen, he wasn't that great with lines, so he'd organized the outing to minimize the amount of time spent waiting. They'd arrived promptly at 8:30 a.m., so they were some of the first people to make it into the park when it opened at 9:00 a.m. Then they'd made a beeline for the new Pandora section of the park, which tended to have the longest wait times.

His wife, Dana, was sort of used to Seth's idiosyncrasies at this point and had downloaded the app to keep up to date on exactly how long each line was, minute by minute. She'd already put the expectation out there with the kids that they probably wouldn't be able to ride the Avatar Flight of Passage ride—even for her, the wait for that ride was usually too long, and fast passes had been snatched up way in advance. So, when she saw that the line for the Navi River Journey was remarkably short, she'd hurriedly steered the family in that direction.

Seth found himself somewhat distracted by the beauty of his surroundings. Normally, waiting in lines and sifting through large crowds made him feel like he was about to break out in hives, but in this lush setting with greenery and streams, he almost felt like he was being transported to the scene of the movie *Avatar*. Then he heard some words that jolted him back to reality.

"The Navi River Journey is currently down for maintenance. We aren't sure exactly how long it will be down, so we are recommending that everyone go to a different ride."

Realizing that he shouldn't swear in front of his kids, Seth managed a weird sort of growl instead. However, several people vacated the line right after the announcement, and then there were only about forty people between him and the entrance of the ride.

"I think we should ride this one out, Dana," he told his wife.

"Really?" she asked incredulously.

"Yeah. Why don't I take Lily to get her face painted at that stand over there while you hold the line with Eric? If we finish and there's no movement, we can trade out."

"OK," Dana said, smiling.

Seth walked his daughter over to the nearby kiosk, and soon he was willingly paying over twenty dollars to have his daughter's face decorated in fancy paint that would glow on the ride. Normally, he was a bit of a tightwad, but today, all that really mattered was the smile on his daughter's face. She was so ecstatic. He tucked the memory of her delighted cheers into the back of his mind, hoping that what was going on in the world wouldn't mean that this was the last of such happy occasions.

Just as he and Lily rejoined the line, a crew of drummers showed up and started a performance twenty feet away from where they were waiting in line.

"Aw, cool!" Eric exclaimed. "Dad, can you take me a little closer until the line starts moving?"

"Sure thing, bud," Seth answered. Truthfully, he didn't like loud music anymore, but for his son, he would deal with the heightened level of anxiety and the elevated heart rate.

Five minutes later, he felt his phone buzz. He checked the screen—it was Dana.

"Zip your way on back here fast. We are moving," she announced.

Seth grabbed his son's hand and they joined the herd that was lurching forward toward the line entrance. Soon, they were meandering through a maze of rope lines. To their right and left were many different lanes that could be opened when the waits grew long.

Thank God we didn't have to sit through all that, Seth thought.

They kept moving along at a rapid clip until they lurched to an end right before everyone boarded the boats. They had totally lucked out waiting for this ride. It was pretty much the best-case scenario.

Seth had to admit—it was pretty cool watching his daughter's face paint light up with all of the other luminescent displays. However, the slow boat ride wasn't all that exciting for an adrenaline junkie like himself.

I'm so glad we didn't burn a fast pass on this, he mused.

The day continued along in an almost ideal dreamlike state. His wife did shoot him a look when he bought the kids those enormous lollipops, but he calmly squeezed her shoulder, winked, and whispered, "It's Disney, babe."

Truthfully, it was hard for Seth to stay mentally present. He kept thinking about where he was going to be sent next and whether or not he would come back home to see his wife and kids again.

What's going to happen to America? he wondered. Then he shook himself back to reality. *Keep smiling*, he told himself. *Give them one perfect day.*

Chapter 3
A Thief in the Night

December 15, 2020

It was nearly 0230 hours as the last lines were being cast off from the USS *Nimitz*. Captain Terry Pearl's heart raced—he'd been preparing for this day for some time. There was only a skeleton crew aboard, since Pearl had given shore leave passes to those he thought might not side with him. Generally, everyone left on the *Nimitz* viewed Sachs as an illegitimate dictator.

Captain Pearl smiled. It was as if Mother Nature had seen fit to assist them in their scheme. The area was being blanketed in a shroud of fresh snow, which severely cut down on visibility around the carrier. This gave them extra time to get the ship disconnected and have the tugs start pulling away from the pier before anyone else even noticed that anything out of the ordinary was happening.

Slowly and steadily, the ship pulled away until it became safe for the captain to have their own propulsion help to get them moving. Now it was a race against time. They needed to travel up Puget Sound to the Canadian naval base CFB Esquimalt, roughly one hundred miles north.

Captain Terry Pearl kept scanning the horizon for where he knew the main gate to be, watching and waiting somewhat patiently and somewhat afraid that the plan had fallen apart. Then the sight he had been waiting for manifested before him—one explosion broke the dark night sky, then another, then two more. Four mortar rounds had smashed into the area, three of them landing near the piers where some of the destroyers were tied up. The officers on watch on the remaining ships would scramble and put the ships to sea, hoping to protect their vessels from further attack. They'd come back to fetch their crews later.

Pearl laughed, realizing that the reaction was a bit inappropriate, but he didn't care. *Right on time*, he thought.

The captain lowered his high-powered binoculars and turned to one of his radiomen. "Send a flash message out to the destroyers and to the base," he ordered. "Tell them we're putting to sea to protect the ships. Ask that they arrange for the Coast Guard to come to our assistance, in case there are additional attacks being organized against the fleet."

And just like that, our little coup d'état will slip away under escort to the Canadian side of the border, Pearl thought with a mischievous smile.
****

Arlington, Virginia
Pentagon

Secretary of Defense McElroy reached for his smartphone as he climbed into the armored Suburban for the quick ride to the Pentagon. He'd been woken out of a sound night's sleep ten minutes ago by the watch officer at the National Military Command Center, or NMCC, who'd told him that a mortar attack was underway at Naval Station Bremerton.

At first, McElroy had thought it was a dream, but when the duty officer had told him his security detail was being instructed to bring him to the Pentagon, the SecDef had realized that the situation was all too real. Acting hurriedly, he'd thrown some clothes on and rushed out the door to find a vehicle already waiting for him.

"What the hell is going on?" McElroy barked into the phone. The Suburban sped away from his home with its lights on to help cut through the early morning traffic.

The voice on the other end replied, "The base has received two separate mortar attacks, sir. The first one consisted of four mortar rounds and started about fifteen minutes ago. The second attack consisted of sixteen mortars and just finished."

"Do we know who launched the attack? Or what type of mortars were used? Was anyone hurt?" McElroy peppered the poor man on the other end of the call with questions. He grabbed for the handle above the passenger door as his driver briefly swerved around a car that had pulled out in front of them.

As he sat there listening to the report, McElroy's stomach tightened at the realization of the damage sixteen mortars had probably done to the base. It appeared they had been trying to target the ships tied up at port in an effort to damage or disable them before they could put to sea to enforce the President's naval blockade of Canada.

A few minutes went by and then his vehicle pulled up to the executive entrance of the Pentagon. His door was held open for him by his security detail. McElroy stayed on the phone, being fed information as he weaved his way through the maze of the building down to the NMCC.

As soon as he walked into the massive room, McElroy zigzagged through the busy beehive of desk clumps over to the duty officer.

"Colonel, how the hell did this happen?" the SecDef yelled. "Did any of our ships get damaged?"

"The USS *Stockdale*, one of the *Arleigh Burke* destroyers, took a direct hit to the forward missile magazine during the second mortar attack. The round caused one of the warheads to detonate, which caused a series of secondary explosions." The officer shook his head as he explained. "It completely ripped the ship apart, sir. They don't think anyone survived the explosion."

Damn it! thought McElroy.

"Did they hit the *Nimitz*?" the SecDef asked.

The officer shook his head. "No, sir. It appears the captain was able to get the ship underway fast enough that when the second wave of mortars hit the pier area, they were already out of the way."

"Thank God," McElroy said in relief. "That would've been an even bigger disaster had they landed a few rounds on the carrier. What other damage has the base sustained, and what about the other ships that were there?"

"Several of the other destroyers took some damage when the *Stockdale* blew up, but they're all underway and, for the moment, out of harm's way. As to the damage to the rest of the base, they're currently assessing it. They alerted the Army over at Joint Base Lewis-McChord, and they're scrambling a quick reaction force to head over to the naval base. The base commander also placed Bremerton on high alert and is getting a number of their helicopters airborne to make sure they don't fall victim to the same type of attack."

The Secretary of Defense shook his head in disbelief. "I want to know who carried out this attack, and I want them found!" McElroy shouted in a voice so loud, the walls seemed to shake. The President would be demanding answers any minute now, and they needed to have something to tell him.

****

Joint Base Lewis-McChord

I Corps HQ

Lieutenant General Andrew Biggs looked at the status of his forces in a depressed state. Two hours into the base-wide recall and two and a half hours after the mortar attack, the individual readiness numbers were still showing less than eighty percent. A sick feeling started to settle into the pit of his stomach.

What if that remaining twenty percent isn't coming because they've switched sides? he worried.

That was the last thing on earth he needed. The SecDef had called him personally to rally up his command and prepare them to defend the naval facilities in the local area, along with his own base, should they be attacked again. That was quite possibly the most unpleasant phone call of his life, and he wasn't interested in seeing what would happen if McElroy became even more displeased.

Biggs calculated his options in his head, then found the man he was looking for, Major General Scott Stevens. "General, I want you to start getting your Stryker battalions rolling to the naval facilities immediately, before we start running into the morning rush hour," he ordered. "Secure the naval facilities in the JB Lewis-McChord area. Live ammo is to be issued, and the use of deadly force has been authorized by the Secretary of Defense."

"Yes, sir," Stevens replied. He began issuing orders to his various unit commanders. Tentative rules of engagement had been disseminated, and they all began working like a well-oiled machine, as if this were just another drill.

As they headed out, General Biggs hoped that this attack at Bremerton hadn't been the precursor to something more nefarious. The country was already at such a precarious tipping point. As it was, more than two hundred naval personnel had been killed already, and twice that many injured.

****

USS *Nimitz*

It was now 0742 hours, and the light of the new day was starting to brush aside the darkness, though the sky was still overcast with snow flurries that were supposed to continue for another hour or so. Rear

Admiral Harold Ward joined Captain Terry Pearl out on the flying bridge.

"Are we ready?" asked Ward.

Captain Pearl nodded. "I sure hope this works, sir. Otherwise, they'll hang us for sure."

Admiral Ward sighed. "Removing the *Nimitz* from the chessboard will hopefully cause the President to see reason. He needs to know that the entire military is not drinking his Kool-Aid. A reset needs to happen."

"I know," Captain Pearl responded. "I just hope history judges us kindly." His mood was remarkably more somber than it had been earlier in the day. He paused for a moment as he looked out at the Canadian coast. They'd be turning to head toward the Canadian base soon. "You heard the *Stockdale* took an unlucky direct hit to her missile compartment?" he asked.

A look of sadness appeared on Ward's face as he nodded. "I did. God, I wish those guys had been more accurate with those mortars. They were supposed to hit in the *vicinity* of the piers, not strike the ships that were tied up."

"I have a feeling this whole situation is about to turn real ugly, sir. What'll we do if the President orders a SEAL team or the Marines to try and recapture the ship?" asked Pearl. "We don't have a big contingent of people on board that can defend it."

"Once we cross into Canada, I've been told the Canadians, Germans and French have some soldiers and sailors that will come aboard. They'll help augment our missing sailors and Marines for security," Admiral Ward responded.

****

Joint Base Lewis-McChord
I "Eye" Corps HQ

Lieutenant General Andrew Biggs was on a secured video teleconference with the Pentagon when an aide walked into the room and brought him a note. He quickly read it and then looked up at the messenger, asking, "Has this been verified?"

The man nodded and then slipped out of the room, leaving those in attendance wondering what had just transpired.

With all eyes turned toward him, Biggs cleared his throat. "Um, I just received a flash message from one of the Coast Guard ships and confirmed by one of the destroyer escorts who was racing to catch up to the carrier. They were escorting the *Nimitz* out to sea to get them out of danger." He paused awkwardly for a moment. "I don't know how to say this, so I'm just going to spit it out. Instead of continuing out of Puget Sound and into the Pacific, the *Nimitz* turned and crossed into Canadian waters. They're currently taking up station outside the Canadian naval base CFB Esquimalt. It would appear the carrier has turned on their defensive weapon systems."

A collective gasp filled the room. Then a voice came across the video call. "Everyone except Biggs and his key staff—vacate the room immediately."

There was a scuffle as everyone grabbed their belongings and exited the room without a word. Then a silence fell over the room. The President was front and center on the videoconference, visibly simmering. His nostrils were flared and his face was flushed—Biggs wondered if he was about to punch something.

Sachs took a couple of deep breaths, as if to steel his nerves. "General, do you still have control of your base and the men and women of your command?" he finally asked.

General Biggs sat up even straighter. "I sure as hell do, Mr. President. I've ordered the base to be placed on lockdown, and I have multiple Stryker battalions en route to the various naval bases in the area as well as the Air Force bases. I have helicopters armed and circling our facilities, ready to attack anyone that attempts to carry out a similar type of attack. My command stands ready to execute any combat orders you wish to issue."

Letting out a sigh of relief, the President nodded. "I didn't mean to insult you, General, but I needed to know if another shoe was going to drop. Thank you for getting your units spun up and ready to deal with whatever may be coming next. Right now, I need you to start identifying potential threats to your facility and the state of Washington from this UN force." He paused briefly. "I also need to know what forces you need shifted over to help you defend the state, should it come to that."

"I'll have my staff send over a request for any additional support we'll need to the SecDef," Biggs replied. "Presently, Mr. President, my primary concern is figuring out who launched the attacks on Bremerton.

It could have been Special Forces units from one of the UN member state militaries across the border, or it could have been a rogue National Guard unit.

"My other worry is that according to most recent reports, roughly twenty-two percent of our soldiers haven't responded to the recall. I have no idea where they are, but they're currently listed as AWOL. I fear they could be in the process of crossing over to the other side."

Several groans filled the room.

The President shook his head, then turned to face his SecDef, McElroy. "You need to check with our other ship commanders and our Air Force base commanders and make sure we don't have any other major capital assets deciding they want to fly off to Canada," he ordered. "I also need an assessment of what you all think they're going to do with that carrier. Are they really intent on using it against our forces, or are they just trying to neutralize it from being used against them?"

"Uh, yes, sir. I will personally call all of the carrier strike group commanders and the carrier commanders immediately," McElroy stammered. He seemed to have been caught off guard. He cleared his throat, then continued more strongly. "I'm also going to get with the Marines and make sure they're solidly with us, and then make sure they're keeping an eye on their Navy counterparts."

The Attorney General, Malcolm Wright, added, "We need to issue arrest warrants for these sailors and make it known that they have betrayed their oath of office. They've committed an open act of treason against their country and will be held accountable."

The President nodded in agreement. "Make it happen," Sachs ordered. "And make sure it's widely publicized too. We need this to be a deterrent. Oh, and make sure to terminate the paychecks of those officers and enlisted personnel. I'm not about to keep paying them. If their families don't have money, then they should have thought about that before they committed treason."

****

Mount Vernon, Washington
I-5 near Fish Creek

"Hurry up! We don't have much time to get those charges ready. That convoy is less than ten minutes away," yelled Lieutenant Willie Yank.

The two soldiers underneath the bridge did what they could to speed up their process. They were nearly done attaching their blocks of C-4 to the undercarriage of the I-5 bridge that crossed Fish Creek. Their experience as an engineering unit in the Washington State National Guard was finally being put to good use, along with all the weapons and explosives they'd snatched before jumping out of their guard unit to join the Washington CDF.

Lieutenant Yank looked around nervously. The snow was starting to let up, which meant that the convoy of soldiers heading toward them would be able to spot them from much farther away.

"It's done. Let's get out of here," one of the soldiers announced. He slid on his butt and feet down the side of the bridge embankment to the frozen creek below.

"Back to the trucks. We've got two more bridges to drop before the Army catches on to what we're doing," Lieutenant Yank ordered. His motley crew of four guys raced down the frozen river to their pickup truck roughly half a mile away. Despite the fact that they slipped and slid through the snow and ice, they managed to make it back before the convoy got to them.

When they got to their vehicle, Yank climbed into the bed of the truck and stood up for a better view. One of his other soldiers held a radio-controlled detonator in his right hand and a pair of binoculars in the other hand. "Here they come," the soldier announced. "I'm going to let a couple of vehicles cross before I blow it—that way we'll nail a couple of them."

Lieutenant Yank took a couple of deep breaths, realizing his comrade was counting the Strykers as they crossed over. Even without his binoculars, Yank could tell that there was also a fair bit of the normal civilian traffic on the bridge. He felt a twinge of sadness as he realized that some innocent bystanders would inevitably be killed in the blast.

"Hurry up and do it, we need to get out of here," he barked anxiously, not wanting to be there any longer than he had to. He didn't like the idea of killing non-soldiers, but he reasoned that this was war, and in war, people died—even civilians.

The man holding the detonator depressed the red button, and in a fraction of a second, a short-burst message was sent to the receiver attached to the blasting caps.

BOOM.

One loud, enormous explosion went off, throwing a Toyota Camry some twenty feet into the air along with chunks of the bridge. One of the Strykers fishtailed from the shockwave of the explosion before rolling over on its side. Another Stryker couldn't stop in time and flew right off the missing portion of the bridge, only to crash down onto the frozen creek below.

The remaining vehicles on the bridge slammed on their brakes, tires screeching loud enough to echo all the way to their vantage point. However, at the speeds they were traveling and with the roads still a bit snowy and wet, these evasive maneuvers weren't enough to stop another twelve civilian cars and semitrucks from sliding off the bridge. Two more military vehicles also crashed into the icy waters below.

"Good job, guys! Now, let's go drop the next bridge," Lieutenant Yank announced. He jumped down from the bed of the truck and walked over to the passenger-side door.

****

JB Lewis-McChord
I Corps HQ

"Here are the latest casualty reports, sir," a captain announced as he handed Major General Scott Stevens a document. "Fourteen soldiers were killed in the crash, another eighteen injured. Eighteen civilians were also killed in the subsequent pileup, along with another thirty-two injured."

"Send a message over to the battalion commander," General Stevens ordered. "Tell him to get the rest of his troopers back on the road to Whidbey Island. We need to make sure that facility is fully secured. Also, send a flash message over to the base commander at Whidbey— tell him someone dropped the I-5 bridge at Fish Creek and hit our convoy. He needs to send out whatever forces necessary to secure the bridge crossings at Deception Pass Bridge, or his base will be cut off. Understood?"

41

"Copy that, sir. I'll make sure they know what's happening," the young man replied. Then he rushed off to get in touch with the naval station.

General Stevens felt a burning pain in his chest, accompanied by a twinge of nausea.

Damn reflux is acting up again, he thought. Stress always seemed to make it worse. If he didn't take care of it now, the pain would just keep getting worse until it felt like he was having a heart attack. He opened up the top drawer and rummaged around until he found the roll of Tums he was searching for. He popped three and hoped for the best.

Someone knocked on the door to his office. He looked up to see commanders of the 16th Combat Aviation Brigade and the 201st Expeditionary Military Intelligence Brigade. He'd been waiting for their arrival. Stevens smiled. "It's good to see you, Bob, Justin—come on in," he said, motioning for them to come sit down.

"Sorry it took us a while to get over here, sir. We've had some maintenance issues that needed my attention. Plus, I appear to have a pair of Apaches and a Chinook that have gone missing," Colonel Bob Barr said angrily as he took a seat.

An aide walked in with a fresh pot of coffee and a couple of extra mugs. He placed them on the table and retreated, closing the door behind him.

"Before we go any further with what I need to put out to you guys, tell me about the three missing helicopters. What's going on?" asked General Stevens. He decided against drinking any coffee at the moment but made a motion to offer some to his guests.

Colonel Barr sighed. "I'm not going to sugarcoat it, General—I think they took their helicopters and went AWOL. These weren't even the same crews that normally flew together. When the alert went out, they were already at the flight line, like they knew in advance that it was going to happen. They jumped into their helicopters and were armed and airborne in record time. At first, we thought it was because they were the duty crew that was on alert, but they weren't. They claimed to have been in the area when the alert went out when they reported in, and with all the stuff going on, no one thought anything unusual about it. They jumped in their helicopters and just took off.

"In the beginning, the two Apaches and a Chinook full of soldiers looked like they were heading over to Naval Air Station Whidbey Island to provide them with support. However, they flew right over the base and just kept going north. They flew up to the Canadian naval base and set down there."

"This isn't right, sir. I think this must be an inside job. Someone helped to coordinate this entire thing," Colonel Justin Bryant added angrily. "They engineered an attack at Bremerton that would flush the ships out to sea, so they could just cross right over into Canadian waters without anyone being the wiser. Then these pilots and soldiers just happen to be in the area when the alert goes out, so they're the first ones in the air and then they cross over? Throw in this group of saboteurs dropping part of the I-5 bridge over Fish Creek, preventing our QRF from getting over to augment the naval air station or Customs and Border Protection station at the border, and it just doesn't add up, sir."

Great, I have a coup in my own ranks, thought General Stevens indignantly.

"Colonel Bryant, I need a frank assessment. You're my intelligence arm, my eyes and ears for what's happening around us. Is the base under threat?" Stevens asked. "And if so, what kind of force are we being attacked by? Is this some sort of militia group? Rogue elements of our own force? Or are these foreign troops from that UN force across the border?"

Bryant paused momentarily, seeming to search for what to say. "I'm not sure. I've tasked my intelligence guys with talking with the local police and anyone they can think of off base and in the surrounding area. They're trying to kick the bushes and turn over some rocks to see what they can find. Some of the local police and sheriff groups are more helpful than others. Until we get lucky and either capture some of these guys in the act or catch a break in the case, I'm not going to have a lot of those answers."

General Stevens turned to his aviation commander. "Barr, I need you to get your surveillance drones up. Have them patrolling the major highways. Pay special attention to the bridges," he ordered. "Also, start getting some surveillance up along the border. I want to know what's going on up there. We need to stay frosty and be ready for whatever may be coming our way."

He tapped his pencil on his desk while he contemplated next steps, then suddenly blurted out, "Let's start to issue weapons and live ammo

to everyone. I want the base fully armed and ready in case there's another attack. I'm not going to lose soldiers because they weren't prepared."
****

Washington, D.C.
J. Edgar Hoover Building
FBI Headquarters

Director Nolan Polanski sat in the briefing room outside his office, looking over a collection of data points, social media posts, and various cyber-intrusions, trying to understand what it all meant.

Assistant Deputy Director Ashley Bonhauf pointed to one of the documents. "Mr. Director, as you can see from this post, whoever is behind this is doing exactly what we saw happen during the October 24th attacks. They're taking one or two situations and recasting them as something different than what they really are, then they're using social media to propagate it through various newsfeeds and groups that people follow. They're essentially taking an otherwise unknown situation, something no one would have cared about, and weaponizing it for different groups of people to rile them up into taking an action they otherwise wouldn't take."

Polanski furrowed his brow. "So, you're saying that whoever is behind these social media campaigns is manufacturing fake outrage in order to gin up real outrage?" he asked incredulously.

Ashley nodded her head. "That's exactly what I'm saying. Someone, or some group, is using social media to stir up passions in people to get them to bring about an outcome they want. Let me show you something else," she said as she pulled a couple of other papers out with some different posts on them. "This one here," she said, holding it out for him to look at, "is targeted at a conservative audience. It says that Senator Tate is working with the UN to take over our government, that they're going to come and take our guns. This post is being boosted and propagated via bots, specifically targeting individuals who are members of the NRA or have expressed views that indicate they're a part of a group that supports the Second Amendment."

Polanski held a hand up to slow her down. "Whoa, how exactly are they doing that? And how are they able to identify information on that granular of a level on individual people?"

"Through Facebook, Google, Amazon and other major websites. All these groups have been collecting data on every single person in the US—and really, the world—for *years*. All that data is then used to build a social profile of each individual person. Through behavioral analytics, marketers can engineer ads that are specifically tailored to exactly what you'll respond to. They're targeting both liberal and conservative groups with these posts—I have to surmise that the goal of all this is simply an attempt to divide the country and turn us on each other in a violent fashion."

Polanski grunted at the synopsis. "I'd say they've succeeded in doing exactly that." He let out a sigh, then turned to look at his deputy. "Joe, what's your take on all of this?"

"I was skeptical at first, but to be honest, after seeing all this put together and looking at past posts and messages being boosted by some of these groups, I think Ashley is on to something. I had some people look at where a lot of these posts are coming from—you know, backtracing the IP addresses and messages. Oddly, a lot of them are being pushed by either shell corporations or people who appear to be Americans, but in reality are foreigners."

"What?" Polanski asked skeptically.

"They come from a variety of places," Joe answered. "So far, we've managed to track the IPs to Russia, Germany, Norway, France, Macedonia, Greece, Cypress, and of course, China. The NSA and the CIA are trying to narrow it down to specific people but have yet to firmly land on anything. It's only a matter of time, though. From what I was told by our Agency rep, they have dozens of their Special Operations Group teams carrying out raids and snatch-and-grabs all over the globe right now, trying to find out what the heck is going on."

Polanski shook his head in frustration. "Look, this whole thing is a mess. What I need you guys to do is figure out how to best explain this in layman's terms, with some charts or pictures or whatever you need, so it can be easily digested by the average person. We need to get this over to the AG and the White House ASAP. We have to get this information distributed throughout the government and the military, and eventually out to the public—so we can nip this in the bud before the entire country fractures. I fear we may already be too late, but we as the FBI owe it to the President and the American people to present what we know."

With his marching orders issued, Joe and Ashley left to get to work on putting together the information they had up to this point for the DOJ and the White House.

As they left, Director Polanski ran his fingers through his hair and then sat with his face in his hands, resting his head as he pondered the situation.

I just hope we aren't too late, he thought.

Chapter 4
A Nation Divided

December 17, 2020
Washington, D.C.
White House

Looking into the cameras, the President did his best to remain calm. He looked at the teleprompter and saw the words for his speech, ready to be delivered to the nation and the world. In another moment, the lights would turn on and they would signal to him that they were live.

Three…two…one…

"My fellow Americans, the last six months, and in particular, the last eight weeks, have seen an unprecedented level of violence, disinformation and outright manipulation of our nation. In a few minutes, the Director of the FBI, the Director of the CIA and the Attorney General will outline what can only be described as an all-out attack on our nation.

"For decades, special interest groups and wealthy donors have sought to influence the levers of power in our government. This manipulation and control first started with campaign contributions. However, as we entered the twenty-first century, money became less influential. The new currency became data—information about each individual in our country, including you."

He paused for a moment to let that last part sink in before he continued. "Through a herculean effort by the FBI, CIA and NSA, we have uncovered a plot by foreign actors to leverage the power of social media against you and our government. They've used carefully created, extremely detailed personal data profiles of Americans to turn us against each other. The FBI will explain in detail exactly how that has happened, and the CIA and NSA will follow up with an analysis of the groups and nations that have been involved in this conspiracy against the American people.

"What I can tell you now is that we as a country have been duped and coerced into fighting against each other, when we should be coming together as one people to stand against these outside factions that are striving to destroy us.

"America has been a prosperous and generous country that has continually stood up for freedom and been a beacon of hope to the hopeless. In the twentieth century, we stood firm against the destructive forces of fascism and communism. Now, in the twenty-first century, we must stand together against those who are looking to divide our nation and loot our wealth and our people.

"Sadly, there are forces within our own government who are part of this conspiracy. Some who were even part of my administration who have sought to undermine our government and have aligned themselves with these outside groups. Most of you are aware that Rear Admiral Harold Ward, the commander of the *Nimitz* Carrier Strike Group, along with roughly five hundred sailors, betrayed our country and their oath of office and sailed our carrier off to join this UN peacekeeping force. Sadly, a small portion of our military has also aligned themselves with this group of traitors and fled to Canada to join the growing UN army."

The President looked down, more in disappointment than for any prerehearsed reason. After a brief pause, he returned his gaze to the cameras. "The bottom line is that a foreign power has manipulated us into fighting each other, and I'm asking all of you not to fall for it. I implore you not to take up arms against your fellow Americans."

With growing conviction, the President added, "To Senator Tate and those Americans who have chosen to fight against our country—I'm offering you a forty-eight-hour amnesty proposition. If you turn yourselves in during these next two days, you won't be tried for treason or prosecuted for sedition. However, after these forty-eight hours have passed, any American caught taking up arms against the federal government will be labeled an unlawful enemy combatant and an enemy of the state. You will be prosecuted. Going forward, any American joining this UN force in Canada will be labeled an unlawful enemy combatant. Your personal property and finances will be seized by the IRS, and you will be prosecuted by the Department of Justice upon your capture.

"To the governors who have recently created their own militia forces—disarm and disband. I don't want to order the military to have to battle these groups, but I will, and they will be destroyed. We are a republic of fifty states; we aren't going to break apart over political differences of opinion or because of outside manipulation. I will fulfill my duty to hold this country together, and we will hold a new presidential election when it is safe."

Sachs paused for a moment. "Many people have insinuated that I have become a dictator, an emperor answerable to no one. I am not. I have not suspended the Constitution, nor have I suspended the rule of law. I have ordered the Senate to rapidly begin deliberations to fill the Supreme Court with new justices, and in the absence of Congressman Borq, who has fled to Canada to side with this UN peacekeeping force, I'm asking the newly confirmed Speaker of the House to set a new election date. Because Senator Tate has invalidated himself as a presidential candidate by taking up arms against our country, I'm proposing that the new election be held in November of 2022 to allow enough time for a new challenger from the Democratic Party to be chosen. To further show that I am not a dictator or seeking to take over the country, I am also announcing that I won't seek reelection. My term will end following the new upcoming election. This is my last plea for peace. I ask that Senator Tate and his cohort accept my amnesty terms, so we can defuse this situation before it turns to war.

"To the UN Secretary-General, Johann Behr, the UN military commander, General Guy McKenzie, and to the member states who have contributed soldiers to this force—I warn you, if you attempt to interfere in our internal affairs, the United States will treat it as a foreign invasion. We *will* attack you, and we will destroy you. I won't allow foreign troops to operate on our soil. This is your last chance. If you don't heed my words, your forces will feel the full impact of American military might."

Turning to look at the directors of the FBI, NSA, and CIA, the President gestured for them to join him at the podium. It was their turn to speak. "I now leave you in the capable hands of our senior law enforcement and intelligence officials to outline the case of this foreign interference and influence campaign that has brought our country to this dangerous precipice."

As the other officials came forward, the President briefly nodded toward them and headed to one of the side exits, out of the empty briefing room. The President didn't want any press in the room while he gave this monumental speech, and he didn't want his directors harassed by the press while they gave their portions of the brief. This presentation was meant for the public, not the media.

If Senator Tate and the UN wouldn't take him up on his offer for peace, then in forty-eight hours, the country would shift its focus to preparing for war.

49

****

Four Hours Later
Washington, D.C.
White House, Situation Room

Ever since a military conflict had become a realistic possibility, the Situation Room had been slowly transformed into what looked like a war room of sorts. In addition to the TV monitors and electronic maps depicting the military situation, the walls were now covered in maps of the US-Canadian border, with little red and blue dots denoting various units. Little icons that looked like planes were pinned to red and blue squares, denoting airfields. On the side of the wall next to the map hung various clipboards that contained additional details of each of the units for quick reference. All this information had been collected and collated in a short span of time to show the men and women deciding the fate of the country exactly what they had to deal with and help them make the best decisions possible if hostilities should officially begin.

What caused the President the most alarm was how few combat forces they had arrayed near the border. While they'd placed many of the divisions on alert, they were already experiencing difficulties in getting them ready to move up north from the south. Then they had to contend with the National Guard brigades and divisions, which were having their own problems. In the past, the US could spend months shuffling units around while it got itself mobilized for war. Sadly, they didn't have months to get ready for whatever was coming.

Standing next to the Chairman of the Joint Chiefs, the President commented, "I think our Canadian border is a bit naked, don't you?"

General Austin Peterson just nodded. "I was thinking the same thing. We've had several of our divisions on alert for deployment for the past week. With your permission, I'd like to go ahead and order a full mobilization of our forces to the north. It's going to take some time to get our forces moved across the country, and I'd like to get that ball rolling. I also think if we make a show of force, we may be able to convince the UN to stand down."

"I have to agree, Mr. President," affirmed Secretary of Defense McElroy. "We can order the 10th Mountain Group to take up positions along the border while we mobilize the rest of our guys further south."

He pointed at a spot on the map in the Atlantic. "We also have a problem here."

"What do you mean by that?" asked the President, crossing his arms.

The Chief of National Operations, Admiral Chester Smith, interjected, "One of our submarines that was supposed to be supporting the blockade hasn't checked in. It's possible they crossed over to the other side."

General Peterson swore under his breath. "What type of sub is it?" he demanded.

"One of our newer *Virginia*-class subs."

McElroy shook his head. "Admiral, you've got to get control of your skippers. We can't have more of our capital ships defecting like this. What help do you need to make sure this stops?"

Admiral Smith straightened up. "I've ordered NCIS to start interviewing all of our admirals and senior captains right away. I've also spoken with the Commandant of the Marine Corps and I've placed his command in charge of making sure we have no more defections. He's placing Marines on every single naval ship and submarine going forward, with explicit orders to make sure this doesn't happen again. That particular sub had set sail prior to that set of orders, but there shouldn't be any further incidents."

"OK, guys, it sounds like the admiral here has put a decent solution in place to handle this problem, so let's move on," said the President. "His branch isn't the only one seeing defections. We've lost close to thirty percent of the National Guard units and roughly twenty percent of the active duty Army and Air Force, so this is cutting across all branches. Hopefully, this forty eight hour amnesty will convince many of them to return to duty. What units are we going to deploy to the border, and how soon can we get them there?"

General Vance Pruitt, the Army Chief of Staff, chimed in. "We're looking to deploy the 3rd Infantry Division to the Northeast. The 4th Infantry Division will go to the Dakotas and the northern part of the country, and the 3rd Cavalry Regiment will deploy to the upper Midwest. This will leave us the 1st Cavalry Division, 1st Armored Division, and the 82nd and 101st Airborne Divisions as a mobile reserve should we need to deploy them. Frankly, I'm hoping that once these UN peacekeepers see how much combat power we've shifted to the

Canadian border, they'll back down and call this whole thing off. My only concern is what may happen with these individual state civil defense forces—these CDF groups could pose a problem for us if they opt to fight."

"That's a good point," the SecDef replied. "Let's make sure we're coordinating our efforts with Homeland Security and the FBI. I'd like to largely let them handle these militia forces if they stay small. I'd rather keep the regular Army soldiers focused on staring down this foreign army for the time being instead of going after their fellow Americans."

Taking all the information in, the President weighed the different options and authorized the rapid deployment of active-duty forces from their home bases to the border. One way or another, they'd know in forty-eight hours if there would be peace or if conflict was inevitable.
****

Geneva, Switzerland
United Nations Headquarters

Secretary-General Johann Behr sat at the head of the long board table as he surveyed the representatives of the Security Council. The empty seat for the representative from the United States seemed to be talking to him. The US ambassador to the UN had been pulled back to Washington when it became clear the UN force was not going to back down from President Sachs's forty-eight-hour warning. Johann had also ordered the headquarters relocated to their alternate location in Geneva, to make sure none of the diplomats would be in any immediate danger from the coming conflict.

The British ambassador, Sir John Grant, shook his head in disgust. "This is utter madness. You're going to lead the world toward a needless war that will solve nothing and cost the lives of tens of thousands of people!" he shouted.

"What is utter madness is allowing that illegitimate dictator to remain in power over the most powerful nation on earth," shot back the German ambassador.

"Poland won't support this authorization for force," asserted Ambassador Duda. "You may think Sachs is politically wounded and weak, but he still commands the most powerful military in the world. He's already ordered many of their divisions to the Canadian border as we speak. If you go down this path, Mr. Secretary-General, you will destroy the UN." The American military forces that were normally on rotation in Poland had already been pulled back to America. Their loss had hurt the Polish economy and put a hold on a growing military relationship between the US and Poland.

"Enough! America has been a global bully for decades," retorted Ambassador Karlov of Russia. "They've waged endless wars across the world, deposing leaders they disagree with and looting the developing world of its natural resources in the name of profits. It's time the world unites together and deals with them once and for all."

"That's rich, coming from you!" shouted the Polish ambassador. "Especially considering that you stole Crimea from Ukraine, along with the eastern half of their country. America is the only country that kept you from invading the rest of Eastern Europe."

"The Crimea has always been a part of Russia," Karlov responded icily. "It was Ukraine who stole it from us when they opted to form their own country after the fall of the Soviet Union." The two men stared daggers at each other from across the table.

Ambassador Liu Jieyi of China slammed his hand down on the table. "Enough! We have a renegade president in charge of America who has turned the world upside down these last four years," he asserted angrily. The rest of the room bristled. This was a very unusual outburst of emotion, coming from Ambassador Liu. "We've been given an opportunity to rid ourselves of this buffoon with the support of at least part of their country and military. We need to seize this opportunity *now*. China is ready and willing to commit whatever financial and military aid is needed to see this through to victory."

Standing, Johann leaned forward, placing his hands on the table so it appeared like he was looking down on them. "Ladies and gentlemen, I'm not going to make any long-winded speeches or explanations for why the UN should act. These facts have already been explained. President-Elect Marshall Tate and many members of the American government are currently living in exile in Canada because they have been branded enemies of the state by President Sachs. We have support from at least thirty, maybe even as high as forty percent of the American people. We must act *now* to stop this madman from taking full dictatorial control of the most powerful military on earth. If we don't, the twenty-first century may be a darker period in human history than the last one. I formally put a motion to move forward with forcefully removing President Sachs to a vote." He sat down confidently.

It took roughly five minutes for the vote to be completed. When it was all said and done, only the UK, Poland and the Dominican Republic voted against the resolution. The UK, however, used its veto vote, preventing the motion from passing in the UN Security Council. Johann had already known that this would happen and had moved the resolution to the General Assembly for a final vote. That evening, the measure passed, with 130 nations voting in favor of removing Sachs while 63 members voted against it.

With the measure approved, Johann sent a coded message to General McKenzie to move forward with Operation Spark.

Chapter 5
Operation Spark

December 20, 2020
Rosslyn, Virginia
Key Bridge Marriott

"This plan had better work or we're all dead men," Joe said as he pulled the Javelin antitank guided missile launcher out of one of the black hockey bags. He immediately went to work on setting up the system.

Responding without so much as glancing at the man next to him, Lucky retorted, "Shut up and just make sure that thing is ready."

Joe Miller and James Cochran, a.k.a. "Lucky," were part of an eight-man team that had been directed to make a strategic hit. While they were all prior military, they were currently working for an Irish private military company that had been hired to protect President-Elect Marshall Tate.

"What are we going to do if they have an armed helicopter with them providing overwatch?" asked Joe. He finished setting up the anti-tank missile, then sat with his back against the lip of the roof. His legs were extended, the anti-tank missile sitting across them.

"Hey, you knew the risks when you signed up for this mission," Lucky replied. "If there's an armed helicopter, then we have to hope Delta Team is able to take them out. Chances are, they won't have one, not for this short of a trip. The target's just going from the White House to Langley. Plus, the government is closed for the week, so traffic should be light."

"I sure hope you're right, Lucky."

"I know I'm right. Now shut up, sit tight and wait. It shouldn't be much longer."
****

Washington, D.C.
White House

Agent Bill Cartwright had been assigned to the President's Secret Service detail now for more than four years. When it had become clear that Sachs was going to be the Republican nominee in 2016, his boss had told him he was being promoted and placed in charge of the candidate's security. While Bill was thrilled by the advancement in his career, he hadn't initially respected the man who he'd sworn to protect. In time, though, he had grown to like the President. He might not always like or agree with everything he said or did, but he had a certain appreciation for Sachs as a person. He was a straight shooter and typically told it like it was, and he was a staunch supporter of law enforcement, even when it wasn't popular. That certainly won him a lot of accolades from the LE community.

The past ten weeks had been rough—not just on the President and the country, but on the Secret Service as an organization. They'd had to field more threats against Sachs in the last ten weeks than they had during the past four years. Now the FBI and the NSA had alerted them that there was a credible threat against the President's life, and this time, it was being orchestrated from someone within the West Wing. That alarmed Bill—not because he was in charge of the President's security, but because someone he knew and worked with on a daily basis was actively planning to kill his charge. The challenge now was trying to flush that person out so they could deal with the insider threat.

"Are you sure this is going to work?" asked one of his fellow Secret Service agents.

Bill nodded. "Yes. The NSA has confirmed it. We know they're going to ambush the President along the route, and we know how they're going to do it."

He could see the looks of concern on the faces before him. These people routinely put their lives on the line to protect the President, but this was something different. He was asking them to be decoys.

Bill raised his hand to quiet them down. "OK, listen up. We know a private military contractor group is going to carry out the actual attack—that means these guys know what they're doing. This isn't some lone wolf crazy guy. These are former military or Special Forces guys who've been trained to do these exact types of missions, so stay sharp."

He paused for a second. "I know you're all nervous, but we need to find out who in the White House is orchestrating this whole thing. That means we have to go through with this plan so we can root them out. We've taken every possible precaution we can, but I can't guarantee that none of you will get hurt. This is a voluntary mission—if you want to opt out, this is your chance. No one will think less of you. But once we leave, we're committed. Is that understood?" Bill asked. He saw the men and women nod their heads in agreement, looks of determination written on their faces.

"All right, then let's saddle up and head out," he ordered. He lifted his sleeve to his mouth. "It's time to get Carnegie on the move," he announced.

A few minutes went by. The President's vehicle pulled up to the White House side entrance and a couple of agents unfurled some umbrellas to help block the view of the President leaving the building as he climbed in. Once POTUS was situated inside "the Beast," as his vehicle was commonly called, it made its getaway from the White House grounds.

As they drove past the main gate, the rest of the security detail formed up, and the small convoy drove down 17th Street until they hit Constitution Avenue and turned right, heading toward the on-ramp of the Theodore Roosevelt Bridge on their way to the George Washington Memorial Parkway. From there, it was a pretty easy trip to the CIA headquarters in McLean.

****

Fort Meade, Maryland
NSA Headquarters

"Got it!" shouted one of the SIGINT analysts who'd been monitoring all electronic activity happening on the White House grounds. The RQ-4 Global Hawk that had been loitering some 10,000 feet above D.C. had been specifically monitoring all signals emanating from the White House for the past few hours in preparation for this very moment.

"What do you have, Shelly?" asked Leah Riesling as she walked over to her terminal.

"A one-word text message to an unknown number in New York. When it reached that phone, that connection shotgunned the text out to ten different phones in Rosslyn, Virginia."

"Whoa, that was fast. What did the message say?" Leah asked. "Do we know who sent it, and do we have the locations in Rosslyn it was sent to?"

"Share the data with us. We'll track some of that down for you," called out another coworker. They all wanted to get in on the action—it wasn't every day you got to stop a presidential assassination.

Shelly looked at the cell phone number that had sent the call and raised an eyebrow. Without speaking, she motioned for Leah to come closer. Leah leaned in and looked at who the number belonged to and did a double take.

"Are you sure?" she asked.

"One minute. I'm going to look at the CCTV cameras we put in place. I'll know in a second."

Shelly and Leah watched as they pulled up the footage from the room the text message had been sent from and pulled it back to the exact time stamp of when the message had been sent. Once they'd narrowed it down, they zoomed in and saw the traitor—the person who had deliberately sent a message letting their co-conspirators know the President was in the vehicle and on his way to the ambush point.

Leah looked at Shelly. "Keep this between us," she said in low tones. "I'm going to get the Director. We need to alert the FBI and Secret Service as well."

"You got it, boss," Shelly answered.

"I've got the locations in Rosslyn now," announced one of the other analysts. "It appears several of them are located at the Marriott, and a few are at other points along the GW Parkway."

Using the drone's advanced cameras, they swiftly identified several attackers lying in wait with what appeared to be some sort of anti-tank weapons, ready to deploy when the President's motorcade arrived in the kill box.

The NSA Director had just walked into the room a moment before. "Alert the detail of the pending attack," he barked. "Have our agents move in now to apprehend the attackers. Take 'em alive if you can, but dead or alive, take them down."

He swiftly spotted Leah and made his way over to her. "I heard you found our traitor," he said quietly.

Nodding, Leah pointed down at the frozen image of the person holding the phone.

Shaking his head, the NSA Director replied, "I never would have thought. Let's make sure the President knows, and let's figure out how we can use that person to our advantage."

****

Key Bridge Marriott

Peering his head slightly over the lip of the roof of the hotel, Lucky still didn't see the President's motorcade yet. He reached down and looked at the time stamp on the text message.

That was five minutes ago, he realized. *Something's not right.*

"Did they take a different route?" asked Joe as he nervously fidgeted with the Javelin.

"I don't know. Let me check something," Lucky replied. He reached for his pocket binoculars. Placing them up to his eyes, he scanned further down the GW to see if he could spot the motorcade.

There they are...what are they doing? he wondered. Instead of turning onto the GW to head in their direction, the convoy had stayed on I-66 and now appeared to be parked along the side of the road, not moving at all. Suddenly, he had a sick feeling in his stomach.

"Drop the missile, we need to get out of here. It's a trap!" Lucky said in an urgent voice. He swiftly put the binoculars down and reached over for his pistol.

"I knew this was too good to be true," Joe responded. He released his grip on the Javelin and pulled his own pistol out.

The two of them got up and dashed toward the rooftop exit they'd left partially ajar. They got within fifteen feet of the door when it suddenly busted open. In the flash of an eye, several men clad in black body armor with yellow lettering that read "FBI" across the front of it appeared, guns at the ready.

Before Lucky could even say anything, Joe brought his pistol up and fired off a shot. Lucky watched Joe get hit multiple times in the chest before he fell backwards, riddled with bullets. Not wanting to share the same fate, Lucky threw his pistol on the ground and raised his hands as quickly as he could, all the while cringing in anticipation of his own death.

"Down on the ground!" shouted one of the FBI agents.

Lucky dropped to the ground, making sure his hands were fully extended and open. A string of gunshots went off a little further away, probably from one of the other ambush teams. More agents stormed the roof of an adjacent building in search of the other attackers.

An FBI agent ran up to Lucky and patted him down before throwing a set of handcuffs on him. In mere seconds, he found himself being led down the stairs to an uncertain future.
****

President's Motorcade

Sachs breathed a sigh of relief when the head of his Secret Service detail, Bill Cartwright, told him they'd successfully thwarted the attempt on his life.

This is getting out of control, he thought.

Just then, the secured phone in his vehicle chirped. The other agents in the vehicle, all heavily laden with body armor and weapons, watched him as he reached over and answered the phone.

"This is the President," he said in a voice barely above a whisper.

"Mr. President, this is Deputy Director Tony Wildes from the NSA. We have the assassins in custody, and we've identified the traitor. Before you ask, I have a proposition for you."

Sachs looked at the receiver quizzically. "First, tell me who the person is that betrayed us."

A brief pause ensued before Tony responded, "It's Deputy National Security Advisor Ava Marx. She's the one who sent the text message that you had left the White House. Once we knew it was her, we backtraced all her text messages, phone calls and any other piece of electronic data we could over the last three months. She's sent a number of encrypted messages, all to a person in New York. We're still tracking down who that person is, but right now, she's the mole."

The President let out a stream of obscenities.

Tony cleared his throat. "Sir, what I wanted to propose was—now that we know it's her, we could spin this," he offered. "We could selectively use her to leak misinformation to whoever her handlers are. This could give us a leg up on whatever is coming next."

Sachs thought about that for a moment. It might be an advantage to use her like that, but at the same time, leaving her in place to continue spying for whoever she was leaking information to could continue to hurt them.

God only knows who else is working with her, Sachs thought.

Returning his attention to the phone in his hand, the President replied, "No, have her detained. I want her interrogated. I know we could use her to leak false information, but I don't know that we can contain what she'll see and learn of our future plans—not in her current position. Let's find out what she knows, and maybe we can uncover some of her co-conspirators."

"I understand, Mr. President," Tony replied. "I'll let the FBI know of your decision. Stay safe on your way back, sir. Until we know who else she's working with, there may be other plots we'll need to look out for."

The call disconnected, and the President looked nervously to his Secret Service agents. "OK, boys, let's head back to the barn. Good job today saving my bacon, and yours as well."

His usually stoic counterparts allowed themselves to smile ever so slightly at that comment.

****

Three Days Later
Washington, D.C.
White House, Situation Room

The President and the National Security Council were still in a bit of shock at the revelation that there was a mole in their midst. They all knew Ava personally and had worked with her in the NSC for the past two years.

I still can't believe she was working to undermine me and my agenda the entire time, thought Sachs.

"All right, Polanski, tell me what you've got," the President said. He needed to wrap his head around what could have caused this woman to participate in an attempt on his life.

"Yes, sir," answered the FBI Director. "Well, during the interrogation, Ava revealed that she was initially approached around two years ago by three men. At the time, they were asking simply for information that could be used against you, mostly about trade deals with Europe. She says that she initially refused, but then they showed her pictures of her kids and told her that if she didn't comply, they would be kidnapped and returned to her one piece at a time."

"Has the FBI secured her family?" Sachs asked.

"We have," Director Polanski confirmed. "Once she saw they were safe, that's when she began spilling the beans on everything else she knew."

The President nodded. "So, what else did she have to say?" he inquired.

"For nearly a year, they'd ask her to provide details about trade deals with the EU and China, but that was about it. They would also occasionally send her a picture of one or both of her kids playing at a park, or in school, or at some restaurant to remind her that they were still watching her.

"When you found out about the election shenanigans, they tasked her with keeping tabs on what the NSC was doing and what your next moves were. They then told her to propose that you travel to Langley to give a pep talk to the staff there in preparation for what was about to come. She was told that once it had been arranged, she was to send a one-word message, 'Spark,' when you left the White House. After that was done, they promised her they'd leave her alone."

The President was torn for a moment between feelings of anger and betrayal and a sense of compassion for Ava. He was very grateful that the Secret Service had been tasked with protecting his family, and he couldn't imagine what he would do to protect the people he loved the most. His mind drifted down the rabbit hole for a moment, until Polanski pulled him back.

"Mr. President?" he asked.

"Uh, yes," Sachs responded. "So, tell me, Polanski, did we get any useful intel out of her?"

"Unfortunately, a lot of the names she's given us have already crossed over to Senator Tate's faction in Canada, so she's not providing a lot of new information. That said, we just identified the person she was sending the messages to in New York."

The President nodded and uncrossed his arms, hopeful that this might turn into a solid lead.

"The number was to a burner phone that was later traced back to a 7-Eleven store in Queens. We checked with the store, and it just so happens that this particular location has been robbed more than a few times over the past several years, so the store owner has all of his CCTV video backed up at a remote location. We acquired the data and reviewed all the people who bought burner phones over the last two months. It took us a while to crunch the data, but with some help from the NSA, we were able to identify eight individuals who bought burner phones from that store. We ran their facial images through the NSA, CIA, DoD and Homeland Security databases and turned up a hit to two of them from the DoD's records. The other six individuals were nothing of note."

"Please tell me we know who these guys are—it better not just be a match to some obscure piece of information the DoD collected," Patty Hogan asserted.

The President chuckled. Patty had made her opinion about the Department of Defense's biometric database well known in the past. He remembered her referring to the DoD as a "vacuum cleaner" that sucked up information without knowing if it might be valuable one day.

Brushing aside Patty's comment, Polanski continued, "As it turns out, the two individuals are active members of the German KSK, or Kommando Spezialkräfte—German Special Forces. They had apparently gone through a very specialized training program back in the early 2010s that US Special Operations Command Europe had been providing to selective NATO members."

"Whoa, these were *German* Special Forces? Exactly what kind of training did we provide them with?" asked the President. He leaned forward, his interest now piqued.

General Vance Pruitt, the Army Chief of Staff, replied, "Counterintelligence and kidnapping operations. Essentially, we trained them to do exactly what they did to Ava and her family. God only knows who else they've blackmailed and done this to." The general shook his head solemnly. This wasn't the first time US Special Forces had provided some very specific training to an allied force only to have that exact training turned and used against them.

"Where are they now?" asked Robert Grey, the man who'd first hired Ava to work on his staff at the NSC. The President looked at Robert and could easily detect that the man was broken—he obviously felt utterly betrayed by what had happened with his deputy.

"We have them under surveillance now that we know who we're looking for," Polanski explained. "We're not sure how they entered the country just yet or who else they're working with, but we'll know more in the coming days as we keep them under surveillance. Eventually, they'll meet up with someone else or make a phone call. When they do, we'll begin to see who else they're connected to."

Patty Hogan readjusted her ponytail. "Geez, if we have German Special Forces running long-term kidnap and counterintelligence operations on our soil, how many other European nations are doing the same?" she asked. "Hell, they may have other sabotage teams ready to carry out all sorts of attacks if given the order."

"Don't worry, Patty," responded CIA Director Nick Olson nonchalantly. "We've got our own teams all over Europe, Russia and China ready to execute missions of our own should it come down to it."

"That doesn't help us here at home, Nick," she retorted.

"It's called mutually assured destruction, Patty. It does help in its own way," he shot back.

Nick then turned to face Sachs. "Mr. President, one of my senior staff members, Page Larson, flipped to Tate's side right after the election. She's a wealth of information to him, and I'm certain she's been briefing their side on nearly every contingency plan we've put in place for something like this. I can't say for certain that she doesn't have friends still in the Agency providing her with information, so there is a good chance that Tate—and by proximity, this UN peacekeeping force—is learning everything we're talking about in these meetings or what we're going to do next. I know you've been trying to give all sides a chance to end this peacefully and return the country to some semblance of order, but we've moved past that point."

Nick paused for a moment as he surveyed the military members in the room. "We need to start cleaning house and preparing for war. We have to move rapidly to identify who's not on Team USA and purge them from the government. We also need to order the military to enforce the blockade of Canada and prepare to disarm this army on our northern border, by force if necessary. We also need to address these militias and stop them from getting any larger than they are."

Then he turned to look at the FBI Director. "I just read a report from Nolan's group that said more than five dozen new militia groups have sprung up across the country, with their membership numbers estimated to have swelled past 100,000 people. This is a brewing disaster, Mr. President. We can't have partisan militia units forming in our states. People are getting way too riled up from all the crap going on with Facebook, Twitter, and all these other social media platforms. I fear we're on the cusp of some really brutal stuff about to be unleashed on the country."

The President turned to his Attorney General. "Malcolm, what thoughts do you have about what we can do concerning these militia forces?"

"We continue to work with the local police departments to help us in identifying who these individuals are. We look through their social media posts and see what they're saying. If we spot them making threats of violence against any person, group, or the government, we use existing laws and we apprehend them, or at least temporarily seize their weapons under various red flag laws. It's about the best we can do without violating people's rights," the AG surmised.

Sachs nodded in approval. "Then see to it," he ordered.

The President tapped on the table. "Now, to the military situation—General Peterson, I want the military ready to protect the country and deal with this foreign threat as soon as possible. It's imperative that we're ready to handle whatever is coming next. I have a feeling we're about to get nailed by an unseen tsunami."

Chapter 6
Southern Front

December 24, 2020
Port of Manzanillo, Mexico

Slowing his walk to stop under a nearby tree, General Han Lei looked at the three Mexican officials giving them the tour of the port. The weather was stunningly beautiful this time of year in Manzanillo. It was eighty-two degrees with low humidity and a cool breeze blowing from inland instead of from the Pacific, which meant that the weather was a lot less humid than it might have been.

"The port will be ready to begin handling your container ships," the port manager told General Han and the small contingent of Chinese military men touring the new facility with him.

Han nodded approvingly. This site sure had changed a lot since his previous visit. Over the last ten years, China Ocean Shipping Company, also known as COSCO, had been investing heavily in developing deep-water ports all over the world to increase the accessibility of Chinese goods to various countries and regions around the world. One of their key investments in the last six years had been in Mexico.

COSCO had made a five-billion-dollar investment in expanding and upgrading the Port of Manzanillo and the Port of Ensenada. In addition to these ports, COSCO had also invested heavily in nearby railyards, bridges, and highways that helped connect the ports with various manufacturing centers in Mexico, bringing more Chinese products to market faster. They'd also helped to build out the Mexican oil and natural gas fields, something the Chinese economy was aggressively looking to expand anywhere in the world they could.

"What about the tent cities? When will they start to go up?" asked one of the Chinese soldiers, who was dressed in civilian clothing for this visit.

A Mexican soldier replied, "We begin setting them up tonight. Once we start, it'll be an around-the-clock operation. Within four days, we should have enough housing for roughly 10,000 people. Within a week, it'll double. By the end of January, the camp will be able to house roughly 50,000."

"What about the Port of Ensenada? Will it be ready for our ships?" asked General Han.

"Yes. We have tents already set up there, with more going up as we speak," answered another Mexican official from the Secretariat of Foreign Affairs Office. He was smartly dressed in a suit. "We received the shipment of tents and containerized housing units last month from you and got them all prestaged, just as you requested. The airports will also be closed starting tomorrow as you wished, to allow for your airliners to begin operations."

Han nodded. "In twenty-four hours, tens of thousands of my countrymen are going to arrive along with a Chinese Army group. The Americans are going to apply enormous political pressure to your government. Are you sure your president is going to be able to hold out against that pressure and will not cave to the American demands?" he asked sternly.

The Mexican official stuck his chin out with pride. "President Lopez wholeheartedly agrees with Secretary-General Behr. Sachs is a danger to the world that needs to be removed. Mexico will no longer be used as an American puppet."

"Excellent," General Han said, softening his expression. "Let us continue with the tour then." They resumed their walk around the new terminals and cranes. In the end, Han was satisfied. This site was already prepared to begin offloading an entire Chinese Army group.
****

December 27, 2020
Ontario, Canada
Canadian Forces Base Petawawa

The weather was still relatively warm, hovering somewhere around the high twenty degrees Fahrenheit, but threatening more snow. The weather forecast projected there to be a couple of inches of the wet fluffy stuff, but it should let up then for the next week or so before another front rolled in.

General McKenzie looked at the sky one more time before walking into the building. Soon, they'd have to move to the Cold War–era command bunker at North Bay. However, until the fighting started in earnest, they would continue to use their standard facilities.

McKenzie reached for the door handle and made his way into the headquarters building for the 4th Canadian Division. Each time he walked in, it was more crowded and busier than his last visit, but that made sense. This building had essentially become the de facto headquarters for the rapidly growing UN peacekeeping force that was steadily building up across Canada. Each day, dozens upon dozens of commercial airliners brought in thousands of soldiers from Europe and the other nations that were contributing forces to the UN.

General McKenzie made his way down the hall toward one of the two main briefing rooms. He was eager to get an update on what was transpiring both in the Atlantic and along the Pacific coast of Mexico.

One of the young officers saw McKenzie enter the room and shouted, "Atten-TION!"

The senior officers from the multinational command stood as he made his way to the center of the conference table. When he took his seat, everyone else took theirs and the meeting officially began.

"Where do we stand with regard to the American blockade?" McKenzie asked, placing his reading glasses on so he could see the PowerPoint slides more clearly.

A German naval officer cleared his throat. "The Americans are going to move their Carrier Strike Group 2, which consists of the carrier *GW Bush* and her escorts, to take up station in the North Atlantic. Our sources tell us the carriers *Truman* and *Ford* are also preparing to set sail for the Atlantic before the end of the year."

"How many ships are a part of the current strike group that's taken up position off the Canadian coast?" asked McKenzie.

"Aside from the carrier, they have the *Philippine Sea*, which is a *Ticonderoga*-class guided missile cruiser, along with the destroyers *Truxtun*, *Roosevelt*, and *Arleigh Burke*," the German officer explained.

One of the Americans, Captain Eli Tapper, interjected, "You can also bet that strike group is going to be traveling with at least two submarines, probably three, if I had to guess."

McKenzie turned to the man with interest. He knew the young captain had been passed over for a promotion after making some disparaging remarks about Sachs, but he needed to feel out his level of loyalty. "Captain Tapper, we're clearly headed toward a military confrontation with your country—one that is going to involve attacking some of your fellow naval officers. I would understand if you feel like you can't participate in that discussion."

Bristling a bit at the comment, Tapper just shook his head. "This is my country, and a madman has seized power. If removing him means I must wage war against some of my former colleagues…then so be it. I'll let history be my judge."

General McKenzie nodded. "Very well, then. If you were going to break this blockade, how would you do it?" He knew Captain Tapper had twenty-eight years of experience in the US military and had been working for the Chief of Naval Operations before he'd left Norfolk, so his opinion might provide a valuable key to scoring a quick victory that could end this war before it really got underway.

Leaning forward before he replied, Tapper asked, "What forces do I have available to work with, so I can make an educated proposal?"

The German naval officer answered, "Between the French, German, Italian and Norwegian navies, we have twelve submarines, fourteen frigates and destroyers, and two light carriers."

With a thick accent, the lone Russian naval officer added, "My country is also willing to commit our northern fleet and submarines to this grand endeavor. Even now, our ships are being made ready in Murmansk and will set sail as soon as the request is made."

Turning to look at the Russian, Captain Tapper asked, "What ships *exactly* are you willing to commit? I ask because, make no mistake, most of the ships in this fleet may get destroyed. However, I believe I may be able to help ensure that we also take out at least one American carrier and most of its strike group. That may not sound like a fair swap, but I can assure you, the one thing the American Navy is averse to is losing ships, particularly carriers. And they don't like to risk taking high casualties either."

The Russian officer snickered at the comment. "Yes, America does not engage in a fight unless it can be assured of complete victory. I agree with you, Captain—we may lose most of our combined fleet, but if we can sink a couple of carrier strike groups, it will have been worth it. I have been instructed to say that most of our northern fleet, sixteen surface warships and eighteen submarines, are available for this operation."

Smiles spread across the faces of the other naval officers when the Russians said they'd be willing to essentially commit the bulk of their

Atlantic fleet. They were by far committing more of their resources to this fight than their EU counterparts. Then again, they also had a lot more to gain from the destruction of, or at least heavy damaging of, the American Atlantic fleet.

Captain Tapper turned back to General McKenzie. "With a fleet this size, I believe we can bust through the American blockade and allow a substantial amount of supplies and reinforcements from Europe to make it to Canadian ports. However, once our combined fleet attacks, you need to make sure the supply ships move as fast as they can for the ports. They can't dawdle—if they wait too long, I can assure you the US Navy will hunt them down and destroy them. After the thumping we're about to give them, they'll be looking for revenge. I'd also make sure your ground forces are ready to move. Once the naval fight kicks off, I can almost guarantee you Sachs will order the Army and Air Force to begin their own attacks in retaliation."

The group continued to talk for another hour as the various officers went over some of their ships' capabilities with the American naval officer, calculating how they could best defeat the American blockade with the forces they had. It was going to be a tough battle, considering that it would be taking place in the winter weather of the North Atlantic. However, General McKenzie felt increasingly confident of their chances of victory, especially if American airpower was largely grounded because of inclement weather.

When General McKenzie had finished going over the naval picture, he took a walk further down the hall to the Army and Air Force group. They had been going over various possible battle plans for several days. Thus far, the militia forces inside the US had been providing them with near-constant reports and updates on what US Army units were moving toward the border and where they were setting up their camps.

They'd also been keeping an eye on where the Army was establishing some of its supply depots to keep their fighting force equipped. A big part of McKenzie's strategy was for his forces to take out these depots. If they could disrupt their supply chain, it would hinder their ability to respond to his force's movements. The militia units would also tie down thousands of soldiers as they sought to maintain law and order.

Part of the way into the brief, General McKenzie turned to look at his air chief, a French general. "How are we going to handle the onslaught of American bombers and cruise missiles that will be thrown at us once the war officially starts?" he asked.

"We have a plan to deal with the American aircraft, but as to their cruise missiles, we are not as confident. We've begun to set up C-RAM systems around some of our critical bases and other missile interceptor systems, but we have a limited capability to defend against such weapons. However," the Frenchman said as he gestured toward a Chinese general, "our Asian colleagues have a surprise waiting for the Americans once the war starts. He won't share all the details, but he's assured us that within the first day of the war, many of the bases housing the American bombers will be attacked and destroyed. If they're able to neutralize the enemy bombers, then we'll have a lot fewer cruise missiles to have to contend with."

"What about air defenses?" asked McKenzie. "The Americans are going to hammer us with F-22, F-35, F-16 and F-15 fighters like we've never seen. How are we going to defend against that?"

Clearing his throat, a Russian colonel responded, "Very easily. We've deployed multiple S-300 and S-400 integrated air defense systems. I assure you—this won't be like attacking Iraq or Syria. We've deployed the best air defense systems in the world. We'll see how tough the vaunted American Air Force is when it has to fight a tier one military and not some raghead Muslim extremist group."

A few of his Chinese and European counterparts chuckled at the comment, but McKenzie wasn't having any of it. He stood up and placed his hands on the table as he looked down at the officers.

"You all may think this is humorous, but let me tell you something—we're about to wage war on the toughest, most determined, most combat-hardened military in the world. If you think for an instant this is going to be an easy fight, you're in for a huge surprise. Don't forget, the Americans have been in a state of war for the past nineteen years. Their soldiers know how to fight, even if they've been fighting Muslim extremists. The average American soldier has seen more combat in a four-year enlistment than any of you have in your entire career. On top of that, their average citizen is armed, and while some may view us as liberators, many more will view us as invaders."

He sighed briefly as he turned away, then looked back at them. "Don't underestimate them," he warned. "When this war kicks off, they're going to hit us with everything they have. We'll be lucky if we still have an Air Force by the fourth or fifth day of this war if the Chinese aren't successful in blunting their bombers. Knowing this, I expect you all to plan for every contingency and be ready to execute at a moment's notice. We could be given the go order any day now. You need to be ready for when it comes."

When he'd concluded his speech, he abruptly left the room. He shook his head as he walked down the hallway.

We're going to get murdered when this war starts if these guys think it's going to be a walk in the park, McKenzie thought.

Just then, his secured smartphone buzzed. Looking down at the phone, he saw a short text message from Johann. *"What happened with Spark? We need to move to Omega."*

McKenzie was frustrated with the whole Spark plan. The Germans were certain it would work, but he wasn't so sure. It relied on using a private military company to carry out the assassination rather than one of their direct-action Special Forces units. Invariably, someone found out about the plan and they tipped off the American FBI and Secret Service. The media had a field day with the attempted assassination. In the end, all it had achieved was to add further anti-UN fuel to the fire brewing in America.

****

Pentagon
National Military Command Center

"What do you mean the Chinese just offloaded a combat brigade in Mexico?" demanded the Secretary of Defense.

The colonel who had just finished briefing them on what was happening down south shook his head.

General Pruitt interjected, "It's not just Mexico, and it's not just a brigade, Mr. Secretary. The last satellite pass just confirmed at least two brigades' worth of Russian equipment being offloaded in Mariel, Cuba, which is a medium-sized port fifty-six miles west of Havana. In Mexico, it appears that at least three Chinese brigades' worth of equipment has been offloaded in the last several days in Manzanillo and at least two brigades in Ensenada, which is just eighty-six miles south of San Diego."

"How in the hell did we not see this happening?" McElroy demanded. "And what kind of units are being offloaded?"

The colonel grimaced slightly. "Sir, most of our attention has been focused on what has been going on in Canada and along our northern border. We hadn't been paying nearly as much attention to what was going on in Mexico because the government down there has been staying silent on this whole UN peacekeeper army. They didn't have any forces participating in the exercise, so we'd focused our attention on the other nations."

"This is unacceptable," McElroy said, smacking the table once with an open hand. "We need better intelligence on what's going on down there. What is the size and scope of this new force? What units specifically have been brought in and what other units are en route to join them? What the hell is the Navy doing? How could they not have seen this massive convoy of forces being delivered just a few hundred miles south of San Diego?" McElroy angrily barked in rapid-fire succession.

I should have been getting briefs on this for weeks now, McElroy thought as he gave his intelligence professionals the stink eye.

The Chief of Naval Operations, Admiral Chester Smith, cleared his throat. "Sir, China and Mexico already conduct a large amount of trade between each other. So do Russia and Cuba. These countries already have a steady and consistent schedule of freighters and cargo ships moving between them. It appears that somewhere along the way, the Chinese and Russians swapped out a lot of the normal cargo with military equipment and troops—that's how they were able to move large swaths of forces completely under our nose. I can assure you, we're now fully aware of what they're doing and will move to intercept them if the President orders us to."

As much as McElroy would have loved to have the Navy begin searching Chinese- and Russian- flagged ships, he knew that wouldn't fly—at least not until hostilities started, and that was something all of them were desperately trying to avoid.

Seeing a break in the conversation between the SecDef and the CNO, the colonel providing the brief added, "I know no one wants to hear this, but it's hard to say what the full composition of the force arriving in Mexico is until more of the equipment is unloaded and deployed. What does concern us though, is that, in both Mexico and Cuba, it would appear the Chinese and Russians are offloading a myriad of advanced air defense weapon systems. Our satellites in Mexico are showing a number of HQ-19, HQ-26, and HQ-29 systems, which are essentially Chinese versions of the Russian S-300 and S-400 surface-to-air missile platforms. In Cuba, we're seeing multiple S-300 and S-400 systems intermixed with other tracked anti-aircraft vehicles. It would appear the Russians are looking to turn Cuba into a heavily defended surface-to-air missile platform."

"Good grief! They'll be able to threaten aircraft flying over the entire state of California and the southern half of the country—not to mention the entire Gulf coast," McElroy exclaimed angrily.

McElroy decided to shift to naval operations, hoping for some better news. "Admiral Smith, what is the status of the Pacific and Atlantic fleets?" he asked. "Are we ready to begin enforcing the blockade, and can we protect our coasts and port facilities?"

"We're obviously a carrier short in the Pacific with the defection of the *Nimitz*," the CNO replied glumly. "We also have two carriers down right now for maintenance, though we are doing everything in our power to cut that short and get them operational again. We're probably looking at four to six weeks before both of them will be ready for action, at least. That said, since we've pulled our ships out of Japan, we've relocated them to our San Diego facilities. Even with the loss of the *Nimitz*, we'll be ready to enforce a Pacific blockade. The Canadian Navy, along with the Chinese, aren't nearly strong enough to break the blockade. Even if they tried to incorporate the *Nimitz* into their plans, the carrier is missing its airwing and more than seventy percent of its crew. They may have the ship in their possession, but at the moment, it's an empty carcass."

"What are our options with the *Nimitz*?" asked Chairman of the Joint Chiefs General Peterson. "We clearly can't just leave it alone. Not with what's brewing."

The CNO cringed. "We've thought about that, and we do have some recommendations. I was hoping to go over them with you shortly, but we can discuss them now."

McElroy nodded for him to go ahead. "I have a feeling I know what you're going to say, so let's just dispense with the business none of us want to talk about but needs to be said."

Admiral Smith let out a deep sigh. "We need to take it back," he asserted. Then he held up a hand to forestall any questions. "Not only can we not just leave the ship alone to play neutral—we can't risk its technology falling into the hands of the Russians or the Chinese. It's also a massive military and political black eye, leaving the ship anchored in Canadian waters. Those crew videos they've been recording and airing on social media are having a huge negative effect on the rest of the Navy."

The SecDef let out his breath in a huff. He was frustrated as hell with the situation. Admiral Smith was right. Those videos had become a huge problem—not just inside the Navy, but across the DoD. It was causing a lot of folks to question orders at a time when they needed the military to stay unified.

"How heavily guarded is the ship?" McElroy asked.

Smith leaned in. "We have a source currently on the ship. The sailor is providing us with some good intel about who all is on the ship, and what kind of guard force they have. As of this moment, there are no Chinese or Russian sailors on the ship, but that could change. So far, a company of German marines and a company of French marines have come on board to provide ship security. Our source has said members of both of these groups have had access to the combat information center and the classified systems there within the CIC, so I can't guarantee that they aren't already sharing that information with their home navies or the rest of the UN naval task force. For all we know, the Chinese and Russians are already being fed information from the French and Germans."

Admiral Smith paused for a second before continuing. "The loss of the ship hurt our capabilities in the Pacific. However, the leakage of classified capabilities of the ship, our radar, weapons and communications systems is a far bigger concern. For all we know, the Chinese and Russians are already gaining access to what our full capabilities are. In reality, that's probably more damaging to our ability to fight and win than losing the carrier in a battle would have been."

McElroy shook his head in frustration. "I figured you'd say that. OK, if this is what has to happen, how do we do it in the least destructive way? Is there a way we can fly in an assault force and recapture the ship?" he asked.

The Marine general leaned forward. "The only way we could successfully land an assault force on the ship is if we can disable the carrier's air defense systems," he explained. "If we can't, then they'd shoot our helicopters down before we even had a chance."

Admiral Smith chimed in. "We *do* have a source on the ship—we could see if they would be able to disable the ship's defensive weapons systems. If they could, do you believe your Marines could take the ship?"

The Marine general thought about that for a moment, and a slight smile crept across his face. "It'll get messy, but I believe we could," he concluded. "It'd have to be a lightning-fast raid, but I think I know just the unit to handle it."

McElroy perked up at that comment. "OK, then, Admiral. I want you to find out from our source on the ship if they think they can disable the weapons systems. If they can, then I want your Marines ready to take our ship back."

With that decision made, McElroy moved on to the main threat that needed to be dealt with. "What's the situation on the other coast? What's going on with this UN naval force forming up around Iceland?"

Admiral Smith shifted uncomfortably in his chair. "It's brewing up to be a fight, sir. There's no way around it. The UN is clearly not going to back down. At this juncture, most of the world wants to see us knocked down a few rungs. As a consequence, they've bought into this UN lie and they've been sending warships to this growing fleet, believing they can do it. What's concerning is that the NSA has intercepted a flurry of messages between the UN force and the Russians. From what we've gathered, the Russians are committing most of their northern fleet to this fight. When you couple their ships with those of France, Germany, Italy and Norway, it's shaping up to be quite the force."

McElroy frowned. "So, what's your assessment? Do we wait for them to launch the first volley or do we hit them first?" he asked.

"Our standard military doctrine would dictate that we strike them first. The last thing we want to do is wait for them to sort themselves and force us to react to them as opposed to forcing them to react to us. My concern with Russia, though, is how will they react if we successfully sink a large portion of their Navy? I don't think they would opt to go nuclear, but you can never rule anything out when dealing with the Russians, and the same goes for China."

McElroy brushed aside the nuclear concern. "Look, these countries have been warned to stand down," he asserted. "The EU nations should know by now that when we issue a threat, we mean it. We told the Assad regime that if he used chemical weapons on his people, we'd respond with force. When they used chemical weapons, we hammered the air base that they were launched from. When they tested our resolve a second time, we hammered every facility in their country that was associated with their chemical weapons program. Likewise, we told the Russians if your forces got close to our forces in Syria or attacked our Kurdish allies, we'd attack them. When they disregarded our warning, we slaughtered two hundred of their paid mercenaries. Hell, we convinced that madman in North Korea to disarm and abandon his nuclear weapons program because we made it abundantly clear that if he didn't, he wouldn't stay in power for much longer. The EU, China and Russia know we're not messing around. I want you to go ahead and put together a plan to neutralize this force before they have a chance to attack us. We'll brief it to the President, and if he gives the go-ahead, then we'll execute."

The SecDef shifted his gaze to the Army officers. "We now have a new threat brewing on our southern border in addition to our northern border. How do you propose we handle this?"

General Vance Pruitt from the Army replied, "If we're going to launch a preemptive attack on this naval force, then I'd recommend that we launch a massive preemptive attack on the UN's ground forces as well. We could have the Air Force hammer them with a massive cruise missile strike and then quickly follow it up with an overwhelming number of air strikes. Once they've crippled the enemy's air force and hammered their ground forces, we'd launch a ground invasion of Canada and Mexico. We'd then move swiftly to crush the enemy force and then withdraw to our own borders. As long as we don't try to stay in Canada or Mexico and occupy any territory, we should be able to complete our combat operations within six to ten weeks at most."

The Air Force Chief of Staff added, "If we hit their air force and air defense systems fast with a preemptive strike, it'll reduce the number of aircraft losses we might otherwise take. We have to remember, a lot of the aircraft we'd be going up against aren't old Cold War airframes. These are tier one NATO aircraft. Many of these nations are fielding the same aircraft we're fielding. Shoot, the Canadians, Norwegians, Dutch and Italians collectively have eighty F-35s in Canada. The Russians and Chinese have also deployed several airwings of their most advanced aircraft."

McElroy nodded his head. "I know. All these countries apparently knew a conflict was going to happen and summarily moved in their tier one equipment to Canada in preparation for it." McElroy sighed. "It really pisses me off that so many of our European allies completely turned on us when they saw an opportunity to hit us."

No one really said anything for a few moments as they all sat there waiting to see what the SecDef would say or order next. The political situation raging across the country was having a huge impact on the men and women working in the Pentagon. Many of them had colleagues who'd crossed over to the other side, and many more had family members urging them to do the same thing. As Chuck McElroy surveyed the room, he could see the looks of concern and frustration written on many of their faces. He knew he should probably say something encouraging, but he just didn't know what to say.

Finally, he figured he'd just be honest and speak from his heart. "Look, I know no one is happy about what's going on, and neither am I. None of us asked for this. Outside forces have taken advantage of the situation and figured out how to manipulate social media and our own news services to turn us on each other. Every one of you has a top-secret clearance and has seen the intelligence on what's transpired. While many others in the public may not know the truth or want to accept it, you've seen the raw data. It's our responsibility to make sure these outside forces don't succeed in ripping our country apart from the inside. Do what you need to do to steel yourself for what's about to come, because it's going to get ugly before it gets better."

He paused for a moment before turning to General Peterson. "I want options to present to the President by COB today. That gives you guys roughly five hours. After that, I want everyone to take the next few days to be with your families. Enjoy the downtime with them, because when you get back, things are going to shift into high gear."

With his pep talk done, McElroy got up to head back to his office, leaving the Chairman of the Joint Chiefs to work out the details with them before they presented their plan to the President. Come January third, they'd begin preparations to end this standoff once and for all.
****

Bellingham, Washington

Jake Baine was engrossed in a fascinating documentary on the History Channel, called *The Men Who Built America*. He was at least halfway into the episode where Andrew Carnegie and John D. Rockefeller began their rivalry to see who could build the largest corporate empire and become the world's richest man when his wife, Marcy, called to him, "You want anything from Costco?"

Jake didn't hear her. When he didn't reply, Marcy snapped her fingers to get his attention. "Hey, zombie boy. I'm going to Costco. Do you want me to grab you anything?"

Jake paused the show, put the remote down and stood up. "Actually, I think I'll come with you. We can get dinner while we're there if you'd like."

She shook her head and sported an amused grin. When they were dating, they used to eat there rather often when they wanted to have a cheap date. In Jake's mind, nothing quite beat Costco's dollar-fifty hot dog and drink combo.

"Really? A Costco dinner? We're not broke, you know—we can afford McDonald's," she said sarcastically.

Jake laughed. "I know, but I like their pizza and those fresh-made churros."

Marcy rolled her eyes, but then she smiled. "OK, fine. You twisted my arm. We can have dinner there. Get your shoes and jacket on."

The two of them headed out the door and climbed into his Ford-150. It wasn't too far of a drive—only about ten minutes from their subdivision. As they traveled down the lightly snow-dusted road, Jake gave the dash a little pat.

"Man, I love this truck," he remarked quietly.

When he'd gotten back from his deployment to the Middle East at the end of 2016, Jake had spent a month shopping for a new truck until he'd found his F-150 Lariat on a DEA auction block down in Seattle. He'd made a few inquiries with some of his law enforcement contacts in the city and was able to bid on the truck. Fortunately for him, he'd won and snagged the truck for a song. He'd purchased the two-year-old truck, which would normally retail for around $30,000, for $21,000. Of course, it had a few bullet holes that needed to be patched up and some bodywork that needed to be done, but Jake didn't mind. It was the truck he'd always wanted.

"You think it's going to snow much?" Marcy asked.

Jake turned on the windshield wipers to push the melting snow from the window. Not taking his eyes off the road, he replied, "Not sure.

I didn't see any news alerts about a snowstorm, but I could have missed something."

As they drove down the road, Jake's eyes were constantly on alert, checking and double-checking everything on the sides of the road and looking for anything that might be out of the ordinary. When they'd approach a parked car on the side of the road, he'd inspect the rear tires and the back of the car to see if they were sitting lower than the rest of the car. His eyes darted about, searching for signs of a new patch on the road or garbage that looked out of place. He might have returned home from the war, but his mind and his instincts were still very much in the thick of the combat that had nearly killed him several years ago.

When Jake and Marcy drove into the parking lot, Jake noticed how packed it was. "Is there a sale going on or something?" he asked.

She laughed. "No. It's always this busy on Saturdays."

He felt his forehead scrunching up involuntarily. "I guess I'm usually at home when you make these Costco or Wal-Mart runs," he remarked.

Jake hated the feelings of anxiety he'd get when he was around large groups of people, or the fact that he couldn't control any of the situations happening around him. Aside from his job with the county, he usually only ventured outside his house to go to church, visit the VFW lodge a couple times a month, and make his once-a-month journey to the rifle range with a couple of old Army buddies.

Jake found an empty handicapped spot and pulled in. He made sure his placard was in the window so he wouldn't get a ticket. He and Marcy got out of the truck and walked over to grab a cart. Marcy showed the greeter at the door her membership card and was waved in.

As they walked past the giant TVs on sale, the two of them saw a news program playing. "Hostilities between the US and UN forces seem almost inevitable at this point," one anchor commented. A small group of people gathered around the television set, speaking to each other in hushed tones and glancing at each other with nervous looks.

Jake decided not to linger. They made their way down the main walkway toward the meat department and the bakery. Jake had his eyes set on some New York strip steaks for tomorrow's dinner.

As they headed deeper into the store, Marcy touched him on the shoulder. "I know this isn't what you want to hear, babe, but I'm glad you aren't in the Army anymore," she remarked. "Not with all these talks of a possible war with the UN."

The Army was still a sore subject for Jake. He'd spent ten years on active duty as an explosive ordnance disposal guy before deciding to get out, burned out after all the deployments to Iraq and Afghanistan during the height of those wars. When he'd returned to Washington, his mother had suggested he get a job working for Whatcom County, where she worked. There was an opening for an assistant city planner, and since he did have a BS in civil engineering, he was very likely to get the job. Sure enough, he'd applied, interviewed, and gotten the position. While he liked working for the county government, it had been boring him to tears. He'd gone from defusing IEDs on the side of roads to navigating endless red tape just to get a pothole filled or a new children's park built.

Three years after leaving active duty, Jake had decided he didn't want his ten years of federal service to go to waste, so he'd joined the Washington State Army National Guard, which also had an EOD unit. Three years into his stint with them, he'd been deployed to support Special Forces in Iraq and Syria fighting ISIS. During the last month of his deployment, Jake had been nearly blown up trying to disarm an IED. The explosion had sadly cost him his left leg just below the knee, and he'd sustained a traumatic brain injury from the blast.

After four months at Walter Reed, he'd been sent home for continued care. Unfortunately, his time in the Guard had to end. He'd been granted a one hundred percent disability rating from the VA and had used some of the money to buy his truck. After that, he'd done his best to put everything behind him and focus on his job at the county.

Jake looked over at Marcy, who nearly had tears in her eyes. "I know, babe," he answered. "I'm glad I'm out of the military as well. I am concerned about this UN army invading our country, though. You know, our city will fall behind enemy lines pretty quickly if a fight does happen."

When they entered the bakery section of the store, Marcy grabbed a container of the freshly made butter croissants and placed them in the cart along with some assorted muffins.

"Hey, what's with all the pastries?" Jake asked.

"Um, because it's our small group's turn to bring snacks to church tomorrow," Marcy answered, chuckling.

"Oh man. I forgot about that. Thanks for remembering."

As they continued through the store, Jake saw a lot of people stocking up on water bottles and other bulk items one typically associated with preparing for a long winter storm. Marcy asked, "Do you think we should buy anything in case stuff does go down between the US and the UN?"

"Are you telling me you're concerned too?" he said playfully.

"I'm just trying to be prepared, that's all," she shot back.

Jake shrugged his shoulders. "Sure. We can stock up on some items, but they aren't going to be the type of items you'd normally think of," he replied. He took over pushing the cart and headed down a couple of aisles that didn't have a lot of people in them.

First, he grabbed two types of coffee—a couple of brands of instant coffee, and about twice as many bags of the regular coffee you make with a filter. Next, he grabbed a couple boxes of coffee filters.

Seeing that the cart was nearly full, he told Marcy, "I'm going to go grab another cart. Be right back."

She gave him a quizzical look but didn't say anything. This was his wheelhouse and she knew it. A moment later, he returned with one of those large flatbed carts.

"Whoa, cowboy. What are you doing?" she asked, flabbergasted. "I said we could get a few items, not stock up like it's the end of the world."

He laughed at the comment. "I'm not stocking up for the end of the world. I'm just rounding out my stash of goods I already have."

"With what, like ten years' worth of coffee?"

"Hey. What you don't know about coffee is that it's one of the most tradable luxury items you can have. You have to think about bartering, babe. You need something of value that people want. That my dear, is coffee, along with a few other goods we'll be grabbing."

"Uh-huh. Well, I'm glad we brought your truck, then."

For the next two hours, they wandered through Costco, stocking up on a host of dry goods and canned items that Jake knew they could trade for other goods should there come to be a shortage. When they left the store, he loaded everything up and told Marcy, "I need to make one more stop at the liquor store next to the building before we leave."

He returned with several cases of hard alcohol and a box of their favorite red wine.

82

"Tradable goods…right," Marcy said sarcastically. Clearly, she wasn't buying it.

Shrugging his shoulders, Jake finished loading up the back bay of his truck and hopped in.

"Seriously, what's with all the booze?" she pressed.

"Alcohol can be used for a lot more purposes than just getting drunk," he explained. "You can use it to disinfect a wound or help cut down on the pain if you have to stitch something up. Heck, you can even use it to run a generator if you have to. Besides, it *is* a valuable trading item."

The rest of their drive was relatively quiet. The further outside of town they got, the less traffic they encountered until they came to their little subdivision. It wasn't anything fancy, but at least the houses weren't stacked on top of each other.

Jake drove the truck around to the back, where he'd had a small two-car garage shed built. It was his unofficial man cave and workshop. He'd also had a false floor built inside, which led to a buried twenty-foot shipping container he had turned into his "end of the world" supply bunker. That was where he stored most of his valuable prepper gear, along with his rifles and ammunition. Inside the garage, he maintained five shelves of dried goods and a small supply of ammo, to give the appearance that this was his main stash, but in reality, it was meant to act as a ruse should anyone actually try to search the place. Jake figured if he gave up something they might be looking for, they'd assume victory and leave.

Chapter 7
Bishop for a Pawn

Kingston, New York
New York Army National Guard

Captain Jay Peeler was anxious as they turned down North Manor Avenue, near the National Guard armory. The 1st Battalion, 87th Infantry Regiment had been tasked with securing the various National Guard armories around the state. The last thing the federal government wanted was for these weapons and equipment to fall into the hands of the New York Civil Defense Force. They were already having a problem with close to thirty percent of the National Guard members going AWOL.

"We're coming up on the armory now," announced the vehicle commander. A moment later, he abruptly let out a stream of obscenities. "Hey, I think we've got a problem, sir."

"What do you mean we have a problem?" asked Captain Peeler.

The vehicle then came to a halt, and the driver called out, "What do you want me to do?"

"Stand by while we figure it out," the vehicle commander ordered.

"Sir, it looks like they've moved one of their Guardians to block the entrance to the armory," the driver observed.

Captain Peeler looked at the monitor and promptly realized this was going to be an issue. "Give me the radio, would you?" he asked.

A soldier handed him the handset.

"All Warrior elements, prepare for possible contact. Break." He released the talk button for a brief moment. "I want Warrior Four to pull alongside my vehicle. I want Lieutenant Drake and Master Sergeant Willis to come to my vehicle. Out."

Captain Peeler handed the radio back to the soldier next to him, then he looked at the soldiers sitting in the back of the Stryker vehicle. Their faces betrayed their nerves.

"Listen up, soldiers," he told them. "We've been given orders to secure this facility and make sure the weapons and equipment don't fall into the wrong hands. We can't afford for the New York militia to take these weapons and vehicles. If they do, they'll most likely use them against us at a later date. I need you all to stay calm but ready for action.

If those National Guardsmen decide to fire on us, then you guys need to return fire and try to end this swiftly, OK?"

The soldiers reluctantly nodded, unsure of what might come next.

The vehicle commander lowered the rear hatch, which let in the cold winter air. While there wasn't snow on the ground yet, it was certainly cold enough for it. Master Sergeant Willis and Lieutenant Drake both walked up to him. At least two squads of soldiers had dismounted from their vehicles and were now milling around behind them.

"Drake, Willis. I'm going to walk up there and try to sort this whole thing out. If by some chance they shoot me or try to shoot at us, then I need you to take over, Drake. Listen to Willis here and seize that armory. Go ahead and send one of your squads around to the rear of the building. We don't know how many Guardsmen are there or what their intentions are. For all we know, they could have deployed that vehicle to guard the place against possible militia units, but we need to find out."

"Sir, if you don't mind, I'd like to move Warrior Three in place of your vehicle," asserted Master Sergeant Willis. "It's equipped with the cannon. If they shoot at you with that vehicle, then I'm going to tell our gunner to take it out."

Nodding in agreement, Lieutenant Drake added, "I think he's right, sir. With Warrior Three and my own vehicle, that gives us the 105- and the 50-cal, if we need it."

"OK. Do it while I get some sort of white flag rigged up to walk out there," Captain Peeler replied. "Make sure we send at least one squad, if not a platoon, around to the rear of the armory. I don't want them to try and stall us while guys are running out the back with weapons in hand."

The next couple of minutes were tense. They saw several Guardsmen come out of the building and take up defensive positions, which made the 10th Mountain guys nervous that this might actually turn into a shooting match.

Meanwhile, one of the platoons took off at a trot into the nearby woods. They'd move a few hundred meters into the woods before they turned north to get themselves tucked away behind the armory. It being winter, there wasn't a lot of underbrush to keep them hidden, so they had to move further away than they wanted to before they turned to head north.

At this point, a lot of civilians were coming out of their homes to see what all the commotion was. The soldiers shooed them away, telling them they needed to stay indoors. One of the women said she was calling the cops.

Captain Peeler finally got a white oil rag they had in the truck tied to one of their spare radio antennas. When he walked outside the back of the Stryker, he heard a police siren. A police cruiser approached but stopped maybe a hundred yards away from them.

I'd probably stop too, if I saw sixty or seventy heavily armed soldiers and ten Stryker vehicles, Peeler thought, holding back a chuckle.

"Captain, you want to deal with this before you head up to the armory?" asked his first sergeant.

Peeler sighed, then walked toward the rear of their position. When he got to the last Stryker vehicle, a second squad car had shown up. The four officers got out of their car, guns drawn but not aimed at the soldiers, at least not yet.

The fact that the police officers had their guns out of their holsters and in their hands caused a platoon's worth of soldiers to bring their weapons to the low ready. If these cops thought they were going to order them to vacate the premises, they had another thing coming.

Walking towards the police cars, Peeler called out, "I'm Captain Peeler from Fort Drum. We're not here to cause you guys any trouble, but I'm going to need you to stand down."

Out of the corner of his eye, he saw at least one civilian with their smartphone out, probably recording everything that was going on.

Great, all I need is for this to get posted to YouTube, and God knows where else, Peeler thought.

"What are you guys doing here?" shouted out one of the police officers.

"We're here to secure the weapons and vehicles at the armory. We're not here to cause any trouble."

One of the officers called out, "The governor said those weapons and vehicles belong to the people of New York."

Almost laughing at the statement, Peeler replied, "Really? Because last time I checked, those are military vehicles and military-grade weapons. They belong to the US Army, not the State of New York. Now, we're going to go up there and secure the armory, and you guys are going

86

to leave. If you opt to interfere with our operation, we'll be forced to disarm you and hold you until we're done."

A couple of the cops looked nervous. One of them looked super agitated and angry. That officer said something to his fellow officers before he raised his sidearm toward Captain Peeler.

From somewhere behind Peeler, a shot rang out and the officer dropped dead from a bullet directly to the head.

As soon as the officer was shot, two of the other officers instinctively raised their own sidearms. They were both cut down by a series of shots fired by Peeler's men before he could even yell out for everyone to remain calm.

The last police officer dropped his pistol and raised his hands high, obviously hoping he wasn't about to get ripped apart by these soldiers.

Captain Peeler could hear several urgent calls taking place over the radio as the soldiers near the front of their little convoy called out to find out what was going on. Then, out of nowhere, he heard the unmistakable sound of a 50-cal heavy machine gun, firing a dozen or so rounds.

Turning around, Peeler yelled out, "Who fired those shots?"

Before anyone could respond, the Stryker equipped with the 105mm cannon fired, piercing the air of this quiet neighborhood, probably unlike any noise they'd ever heard before.

Boom.

The Guardian vehicle exploded, further rocking the neighborhood. Then rapid gunfire ensued as at least a dozen soldiers began firing at the Guardsmen around the armory.

The shooting lasted for maybe two or three minutes before someone called out for them to stop. Several of the Guardsmen who hadn't been killed threw their weapons down and held their hands up. The soldiers advanced on them as they moved rapidly to secure them and the building.

Captain Peeler walked past one of his Stryker vehicles and saw that it had sustained a fair bit of damage from the Guardian's fifty-caliber machine gun. Then he turned his attention to the Guardian and discovered a burning wreck. Five or six dead National Guardsmen lay dead on the ground nearby, and a handful of his soldiers were grouping the remaining Guardsmen together and zip-tying them.

This is a freaking disaster, Peeler thought to himself as he made his way into the armory.

He started barking orders to his men to start securing the weapons, military vehicles, radios, night vision equipment, and any other military equipment at the armory. While his guys were busy doing that, he grabbed his smartphone and placed a call back to battalion headquarters. He needed to let them know what had happened here. It wouldn't be long before this was blown up all over the internet.

Why did that cop have to try and shoot at us? Peeler thought in disgust. The Guardsmen had probably fired because they thought his men were firing on them. *What a mess.*

****

December 30, 2020
Fort Stewart, Georgia

Major General Robert Dickman had his hands on his hips as he watched the M1A2 Abrams main battle tank get loaded onto the last railcar. A handful of soldiers and contractors guided the driver as he deftly maneuvered the 71-ton monster onto the flatcar. Once it was strapped down, the long line of railcars transporting the 2nd Armored Brigade Combat Team would begin their journey across the country to Syracuse, New York.

The destination had been chosen because it had a major railhead and it would place the division close to Fort Drum, which was near the Montreal-Ottawa side of the Canadian border. Another group would go to Buffalo, which was closer to the Hamilton and Toronto side. These were the two most likely routes where the UN peacekeepers would try to cross into the US and where most of their military buildup was taking place.

Turning to look at the train engineer standing beside him, General Dickman asked, "How many days did you say it'll take to get to Syracuse?"

The engineer briefly looked down at his clipboard before he replied, "Day and a half. We'll pretty much be driving nonstop. I was told you guys have a crew up there ready to handle the offloading."

Dickman nodded. "Yeah, we sent an advance party up there three days ago. They've been getting the camp ready."

The engineer sighed. "Well, if you don't have anything else for me, General, I'll head on up and make sure everything is ready. We should be underway within the hour."

"That should do it. Sorry you guys pulled this kind of duty," General Dickman said in a conciliatory tone. "Hopefully all this posturing will be just that—posturing."

The engineer snorted. "Well, if the UN decides they want to cross into *our* country, you guys give 'em hell. We don't need no foreign military in our country if you ask me," he said in a thick Georgian accent. He spat a stream of tobacco juice on the ground and then trudged off to do his checks before he got underway.

Dickman took one last look at the train before turning to head back to his vehicle. It was a short drive back to his headquarters, and he had opted to drive himself. There was no need to make a soldier drive him around. He was doing his best to give as many of his troopers as possible time off to be with their families before things got crazy and the rest of the division left the base. The current plan had them all boarding a series of commercial airliners, Air Force troop transports and trains the day after New Year's. The entire division would descend on Syracuse on January second. They had orders from the President to be ready to begin combat operations by January 15th, and he fully planned on being ready to roll when the order was given.

****

East Syracuse, New York
CSX Terminal

The CSX manager sat in his office with Colonel Jose Bender from the 3rd Infantry Division and two of his officers. "You know, we're catching a lot of grief from the state and local government for letting you guys use our facility," he said before he unwrapped a stick of gum and started chewing it with a smirk.

Colonel Bender was momentarily distracted by the view outside the window; the snow was starting to come down steadily now. He returned his gaze to the railyard manager. "I wish I could tell you something to ease your concern, Mike, but we're just doing what we're told," he said. "I do have the check your company requested. All $790,000 you guys said it'd cost for us to use your facility for the next five days. If we need more time, we'll let you know."

The CSX manager reached over and took the government-issued check, examined it to make sure it was for the agreed-upon amount, and then placed it in a desk drawer for his secretary to collect on Monday when she came in. Most of the workers at the railyard had been given the day off to be with their families, since the company had turned the holiday into a four-day weekend.

"I sure hope you all know what you're doing," Mike responded. "A lot of people around here aren't going to be happy when the rest of your unit shows up here in a couple of days. Not everyone agrees with the visible presence of the Army or the National Guard. You know, they sent our local National Guard unit down to Alabama and sent us a guard unit from Georgia."

When the governor of New York had attempted to activate the state's National Guard units, President Sachs had federalized them and sent them south. This was when thirty percent had broken off and formed the New York Civil Defense Force—that had been the catalyst for a whole series of events. A day later, the governors in several other states led by Democrats had begun to form their own militias, but that had been followed by multiple Republican governors doing the same. Tensions had risen nationwide, and there was a general sense among the population that battle lines were being drawn.

Colonel Bender just shrugged. "Well, we're here to make sure those UN peacekeepers know to stay out of our country. Hopefully, this whole mess will get resolved without anyone having to get hurt, and we can go back to normal."

With their business done, the colonel signaled for his men to leave. As they got up and headed out into the wintery mix, one of the other officers asked, "Do you think the governor's militia force is going to cause us some problems?"

"You mean the New York Civil Defense Force?" Colonel Bender asked, crossing his arms. "No. They're a bunch of untrained, underequipped, poorly led ragtag civilians who are pretending to play at Army."

The officer who'd asked the question snorted but said nothing. They continued their walk through the snow silently. Soon, they climbed into their JLTV vehicle and headed out of the railyard to the makeshift camp their advance party had been working on establishing in a nearby forest, adjacent to the CSX trainyard. The clearing was a relatively wide-open area with a road that connected to the trainyard and was flanked on two sides by a nature conservation area. The only downside to the location was its close proximity to a high school and a middle school.

After a relatively silent ride down the road, they eventually came to the main entrance of their new camp. Rolls of concertina wire had been strung up around the perimeter to deter people from trying to check the area out. The entrance was also manned by five soldiers from the advance party, who did a quick check of Colonel Bender and his crew's IDs before they waved them in.

As Bender and his men pulled into the camp, they saw dozens of large tents that had been erected in the forested area. The soldiers were doing their best to situate the tents between the trees, keeping as much of the open area as possible cleared for the vehicles and tanks that were due to arrive in two days. Despite all the progress, they still had a lot of work to get this place set up and ready. The initial goal was to turn this place into a supply depot since it was close to the railyard, but a long-term camp was being put together outside the city, closer to Buffalo. The 2nd Armored Brigade Combat Team was a heavy tank unit, and tanks need room to maneuver, something they wouldn't have if they stayed in the city limits.

After parking their JLTV in front of the newly established command tent, Colonel Bender and his two officers got out and headed in to check on the progress of the other camp. Bender made a beeline toward a map board, which was hanging from some five-fifty cord along one of the tent walls.

"Parker, give me a status update on the new camp," he said briskly.

Captain Parker, one of his newly promoted captains, grunted and nodded. "Yes, sir. Major Corker from the 9th Engineer Battalion said his unit is getting the Camillus Forest Unique Area set up. He said to tell you they'll have the area ready to start receiving the brigade once they start to arrive. However, he also wanted me to tell you that they ran into a problem with the local sheriff."

"What type of problem did they encounter?" Bender asked cautiously.

"He said the sheriff wanted to pass them a warning. He'd apparently heard word that the local militia defense force had made some threats in town about possibly attacking any federal soldiers that move into the area."

Colonel Bender shook his head. "Did the sheriff say if he was investigating it, or was he just passing along the information?"

Captain Parker just shrugged his shoulders. "Major Corker didn't say. He did want to know if we could spare any additional soldiers to increase their guard force. He also wanted to know what his rules of engagement were, in case they were attacked."

Colonel Bender sighed at the question. "OK, listen up, people!" he shouted. "This is the last time I want to go over the rules of engagement. We've gone over this before, and I don't care if we're in Afghanistan, Iraq, Syria, or freaking New York City. The rules are the same. *If* someone is shooting at you, or is posing an imminent threat to your life or the lives of your soldiers or innocent civilians, you have been authorized to use deadly force. For better or worse, and whether we agree with it or not, the entire country is under martial law and has been for the last six weeks. The public has been made fully aware that they aren't to threaten or attack federal or National Guard soldiers. If they do, deadly force has been authorized and will be used. Period. No more asking me what the ROEs are—they haven't changed, so get used to them and enforce them!"

Bender popped his knuckles and then turned back to the captain. "What is the status of 1st Battalion, 67th Armor? Have their soldiers arrived yet?" he asked.

Parker nodded. "Yes, sir. Lieutenant Colonel Flute reported in a half an hour ago that they landed at the Syracuse Hancock Airport. They're working with the Air Force to collect their vehicles now that the C-5s have arrived."

Colonel Bender's expression warmed into a smile. "How much of their equipment is arriving on this first trip?"

Captain Parker looked down at the clipboard on the table next to the map board, then read off the first load: "Twelve Bradleys, sixteen of our heavy expanded mobility tactical trucks or HEMTTs and fourteen of our M113 tracked vehicles. The Air Force also brought about sixty of our standard 463L pallets—mostly food, ammunition and other critical items we'll need right off the bat to get started."

"Excellent work. Best news I've heard all day," said Bender with a nod. "Tell Major Corker that as soon as 1st Battalion has collected their equipment from the Air Force, they'll head his way to shore up his positions. We'll continue to work with our skeleton crew here until the rest of the main body starts to arrive in a couple of days."

The advance party would be incredibly busy over the next seventy-two hours or so, getting things ready for the pending arrival of 3,800 soldiers and hundreds of tanks. The one exception to the busy schedule Colonel Bender was making was his concession to allow all his soldiers time to visit the local Denny's or IHOP for a solid New Year's Eve lunch or dinner. They might be deploying for a possible fight along the Canadian border, but until that threat materialized, he was determined to allow his troopers to have a decent holiday meal on the local economy.
****

Watertown, New York

As he drove down Arsenal Street, Roy started to slow down. He flipped his right blinker on, then turned down Breen Avenue, driving past Pete's Trattoria. He went a little further down the road and then pulled into someone's driveway briefly so he could back out and turn around. Then he drove past a few houses until he stopped his truck near the front entrance of the fine Italian restaurant.

Not seeing a lot of cars in the parking lot, Roy began to think they might have come a bit too early. He knew he couldn't leave the truck running on the side of the street with his hazards on if they had to sit down and wait inside the place, so he pulled his truck into the parking lot. He made sure to back his truck into its space, so he could peel out of the parking lot when the time came.

Looking to his right, he saw Dillon, checking his Glock for what must have been the tenth time since he'd picked him up and given him the weapon thirty minutes ago.

"Stop fiddling with that thing. You're going to shoot yourself, not these soldiers," Roy snapped at his partner.

"Sorry, I guess I'm just a bit nervous, that's all," Dillon replied.

"Look, we've gone over this a couple of times already," Roy asserted. "We know that every night, there are several soldiers eating at this place, either by themselves or with their families. We're going to walk in there, find 'em and shoot 'em. Just like in *The Sopranos*, OK? This isn't any different. Now, let's get going and do this thing." Roy proceeded to get out of the truck, leaving it running so all they had to do was hop in and get out of Dodge.

Roy Cutter was the newly appointed CDF leader for Jefferson County, which included Watertown, the next-largest city adjacent to Fort Drum, home of the 10th Mountain Division. A couple of days earlier, Roy had been given orders to start assassinating soldiers from the base. They needed to send a message to the soldiers that they were not welcome in New York.

The two of them got out and walked towards the front door of the Italian restaurant. Dillon grabbed the door and held it open for Roy as he walked in. They stopped briefly at the hostess's stand and scanned the restaurant for any soldiers or people dressed in civilian clothes that looked like soldiers.

"Just the two of you?" asked the college-aged woman as she grabbed a couple of menus.

With his train of thought broken, Roy stumbled. "I, um, I'm sorry—what did you just say?"

Smiling, the woman repeated her question, to which Roy nodded. "Sorry. Yes, it's just the two of us. Can we sit at that table over there, by the wall?" he asked.

"Sure thing, sir. Just follow me," she replied.

The hostess guided them over to their table. "Your waitress will be here shortly with some glasses of water, ready to take your orders," she said.

When she left, Dillon asked, "What do we do now? I don't see any soldiers here."

Trying not to look angry or mad, Roy replied, "We wait. Just keep your gloves on. I'll order us an appetizer. If we haven't spotted any soldiers walking into the place by the time we're done, we'll go ahead and order dinner. I'm pretty sure we'll see someone walk in by then. If not, then I guess you just got a fancy dinner, compliments of the CDF."

Dillon laughed, but he was clearly nervous. He was starting to sweat. When the waitress brought them their water, his hand had a slight tremor to it as he grabbed the glass. The waitress didn't seem to notice. She took her order pad out. "What can I start you guys out with?"

Glancing down at the menu, Roy replied, "Can we get an order of your maple bacon Dijon scallops and an order of your tomato bruschetta?"

"Sure thing, luv. Do you gentlemen want a glass of wine or beer to go with your appetizers or dinner?"

"I'll take a standard martini," blurted out Dillon.

"I'll have a gin and tonic myself," Roy added as he gave Dillon a glare.

"OK, no problem, guys. I'll get your appetizer order in and bring your drinks over," she said. Then she whirled around and headed off.

Once the waitress had left, Roy leaned in and quietly tried to talk his partner down. "Dillon, close your eyes and take a deep breath. Pretend you're with that stripper from the other night. Put your mind somewhere else until it's time. You need to calm yourself down."

A few minutes went by and she brought them their drinks. Dillon practically downed his in one sip and ordered a second. Roy whispered to him to go easy on the alcohol. He didn't want him so drunk he couldn't help him out when the time came.

Just then, the door dinged as some more guests walked into the restaurant.

The waitress brought the two couples around to a table not far from them and sat them down.

"I think these are our targets," Roy said quietly to Dillon.

"They're in civilian clothes. How do we know they aren't just guys who have a short haircut? I mean, your hair looks the same," Dillon countered.

They both hushed up as their waitress brought out their appetizers and their second round of drinks.

They ate their appetizers and just listened to the conversation of the two couples a few tables down. Roy eventually heard them say something about their unit possibly being deployed soon. That was it—now Roy knew for sure they were soldiers.

"Dillon, this is it," Roy said. "I'm going to stand up and walk over to them. I'll shoot both of the men and then we'll walk out of here, OK? All I want you to do is stand up and be ready, in case someone else pulls a gun or tries to stop us." He pulled his own Glock out from his waistband.

Dillon just nodded as Roy stood up and walked toward the two couples. He got within a few feet of them before one of the men noticed him. The soldier had a look of surprise when he saw Roy stop next to their table. Then his facial expression changed—he must have sensed danger.

Before the man could react, Roy raised his pistol up and shot the man a few feet from him in the back of his head, splattering blood and brain matter over the couple sitting opposite them. The soldier on the opposite side tried to lunge at Roy, but he'd already shifted his aim and he fired two more shots, which both hit the man in the chest.

The two women at the table screamed hysterically at the scene unfolding before them. Roy realized that the second man had been hit by both of his bullets, but he appeared to still be alive. Roy aimed his pistol at the man's head and fired a third shot.

As he turned to head out of the restaurant, Roy saw that Dillon was practically frozen in fear. "Come on. We need to get out of here," he ordered. He ran past his partner to the front entrance.

Two seconds later, Roy was out the door and racing to his truck. Dillon was hot on his heels. They both swung open the truck doors and hopped in. The engine was still running, and Roy threw the truck into drive and raced out of the parking lot.

They could already hear the police sirens wailing in the distance as they turned onto Arsenal Street. Now it was a race to make it out of town to their safe house in the countryside.

Fortunately for Roy, several police officers in town had already pledged their loyalty to the CDF, so he knew they'd help impede any investigation into the shooting. He just needed to avoid getting caught during his escape. He made a series of elaborate turns, winding down some side roads that would take them through some neighborhoods as they continued to get themselves outside of town.

A couple of minutes later, Roy started to breathe a lot easier. He was pretty sure that he'd managed to lose his tail.
****

Fort Drum, New York

Major General George Hays was not a happy camper. Two of the soldiers in his 10th Mountain Division had been shot dead the night before while eating at a restaurant in town. Not only had the shooter not been caught, but the local police chief was doing nothing to track the people down. It crushed him that two of his guys had been killed around Christmastime, and they weren't even in a combat zone yet.

One of the majors walked over to General Hays and handed him a sheet of paper. "General, the scout platoon from the 1st Battalion, 22nd Infantry Regiment reports they're in place," he announced.

General Hays hastily read over the report, then nodded in approval. "Excellent. I'm glad the ground wasn't too frozen for them to get those seismic sensors in place."

"If we'd waited another month, the ground would probably have been too hard, that's for sure," the major acknowledged. "These sensors should give us a heads-up if that UN force is on the move or approaches the border," he added.

The scout platoon had crossed into Canada the night before and placed a series of seismic sensors along a number of the major approaches the UN force might take. Since the official border between Canada and the US had closed nearly a month ago, the vehicle traffic between the two countries had ground to a halt. Nearly all the traffic now consisted of small clusters of Americans trying to cross into Canada to join the renegade American National Guard units and militia forces.

"Is the rest of the 1st Battalion ready to deploy?" asked General Hays.

The major nodded. "Yes, sir. Just as ordered. They'll deploy the day after New Year's and begin setting up their various listening-observation posts along our area of operation. The battalion commander did pass along one question—he wanted to know what his guys should do if they encounter any persons trying to cross to either the American or Canadian side. In the past, we would have called the Border Patrol, but that doesn't seem like what we'd do in this instance."

Hays snickered at the thought of calling CBP if they spotted some enemy soldiers or Special Forces trying to cross into America. "Tell the commander he should detain them until the military police can fetch them. If they're Americans, then we'll let the provost marshal and the DOJ handle them. If they're foreign military—well, we'll cross that bridge when we have to."

Some of the soldiers in the ops center overhead his comment and a few nervous laughs erupted. Just then, the other general on the base, Hays's deputy, Brigadier General Don Wittman, came into the room with a serious look on his face. He rapidly made his way over to General

Hays. "Sir, this just came in from intelligence," Wittman announced. "They received a flash message from the NSA. I'm waiting for confirmation from the Air Force as well. They said they had a recon drone headed over to investigate, so we'll hopefully have confirmation one way or the other shortly."

Grimacing at what was probably bad news, General Hays looked at the report, then motioned for Wittman to follow him to his private office. He needed to talk with him where no one else could hear them. Not only was the UN force *not* heeding the President's warning, they were mobilizing their forces.

Once inside Hays's office, Wittman asked, "Sir, do you think this is just them trying to make a show of things, or do you believe they're actually gearing up to attack us?" Wittman had just been promoted to general after serving in the 82nd Airborne as a brigade commander. He was being groomed to take over a division command himself in a couple of years.

Hays sighed. "Don, I think things are about to get real crazy, real fast in a few days," he responded. Then he pulled his keys out of his pocket and walked over to the vault built into the wall of his office. He pushed the appropriate key in and turned it, unlocking the door. General Hays pulled out a folder that read "TOP SECRET/NOFORN/ORCON/" on it and placed it on the desk between him and his deputy.

"I wasn't supposed to show this to you until December 31st. I just received it via courier five hours ago from the Pentagon. It's been signed and approved by the President."

General Wittman looked at the folder. He hadn't seen a set of orders ever arrive at any military command he'd ever served in quite like this. After staring at it for a few moments without saying anything, he looked up at Hays. "Have you read it?"

General Hays shook his head. "Not yet. I was told to read it and acknowledge it by COB today. I still have another two hours, but I figure I might as well as look at it with you. I know the instructions said not to share it with anyone else until December 31st, operational security and all—but hell, I need some help deciphering all of this crap going on in our country."

"You and me both," Wittman replied. "It's like a switch was turned on in September and the country hasn't been the same since…"

Hays sat down, then broke the seal on the new set of orders and opened it up.

///////TOP SECRET/NOFORN/ORCON///////

BY ORDER OF THE SECRETARY OF DEFENSE, THE PRESIDENT OF THE UNITED STATES HAS AUTHORIZED *OPERATION FORTRESS*, THE AUTHORIZATION OF OFFENSIVE MILITARY ACTION TO BE TAKEN AGAINST UNITED NATIONS PEACEKEEPING FORCE AND ANY OTHER HOST NATIONS PROVIDING MATERIAL SUPPORT AGAINST THE UNITED STATES OF AMERICA. THE PRESIDENT HAS AUTHORIZED THE SECRETARY OF DEFENSE TO USE ANY AND ALL MEANS NECESSARY TO DEFEND THE TERRITORIAL INTEGRITY OF THE UNITED STATES.

BY ORDER OF THE SECRETARY OF DEFENSE, UNITED STATES NORTHERN COMMAND (USNORTHCOM) WILL ASSUME COMMAND OF ALL CONUS MILITARY FORCES EFFECTIVE 31 DECEMBER 2020. USNORTHCOM COMMANDER, GENERAL RAYMOND MOORE USAF, IS BEING REPLACED WITH GENERAL JOSEPH TIBBETS USA, EFFECTIVE 31 DECEMBER 2020.

ALL DIVISION COMMANDERS ARE HEREBY ORDERED TO MAKE READY FOR COMBAT OPERATIONS, ALL FORCES BY NO LATER THAN 15 JANUARY 2021. *OPERATION FORTRESS* WILL COMMENCE ON OR SHORTLY AFTER 15 JANUARY 2021 IF PEACE TALKS FAIL. DIVISION COMMANDERS ARE HEREBY ORDERED TO PREPARE THEIR FORCES AND FACILITIES TO REPEL ANY POTENTIAL ATTACKS OR INCURSIONS BY EITHER FOREIGN OR DOMESTIC FORCES, EFFECTIVE IMMEDIATELY. AUTHORIZATION FOR THE USE OF DEADLY FORCE TO DEFEND YOUR MILITARY ASSETS HAS BEEN AUTHORIZED.

WARNING ORDERS AND ADDITIONAL APPENDIXES ARE ATTACHED FOR IMMEDIATE IMPLEMENTATION.

General Hays and his deputy spent the next twenty minutes going over the rest of the orders and the attached appendixes as they contemplated how they'd go about implementing them. From everything they'd read, it looked as if a military confrontation was not only inevitable, but imminent. The talking heads on the various news outlets were certainly not on the same page as reality at the moment.

Chapter 8
Escalation

January 1, 2021
Whidbey Island, Washington
Naval Air Station Whidbey Island

It was ten minutes past midnight when Colonel Rob Coates walked up to the front of formation of 1st Battalion, Marine Raider Regiment. As he stood in the aircraft hangar, he surveyed the painted faces of the six hundred warriors standing before him. He couldn't be prouder of the men before him than he was at that moment. They were about to embark upon perhaps the most audacious mission in the Raiders' short history. Looking to his right and left, he saw that all three companies were ready for war.

"Marines, today marks day one in taking back our country and putting down this rebellion," Colonel Coates bellowed. "The past five days have been rough—we've been drilling hard on the decommissioned *Kitty Hawk*. That training is now going to be put to the test. I know many of you are wondering what's going on and why we've been transferred over here to Whidbey Island. By order of the President, we've been ordered to seize back control of the *Nimitz* from the renegade crew that stole her two weeks ago."

Colonel Coates heard a soft murmur of whispers from the men as they exchanged a few comments with each other. Colonel Coates raised his hands to calm them before he continued. "What these naval officers did, regardless of *why* they did it, was treasonous. They betrayed their oath as officers, and worse, they've placed our nation's most guarded secrets and technologies in the hands of foreigners. As such, we've been directed by the President to seize the ship and return it to US control."

He paused for a moment as he looked down at his watch. "As I speak to you, a SEAL team is preparing to surreptitiously board the *Nimitz* to disable their weapons systems. When the air defense weapons are disabled, an enlisted person who's still loyal to America will disable the carrier's radar systems to blind them just long enough for us to air assault in."

A few of the Marines whistled as they realized just how dangerous the mission was. If any of the carrier's close-in weapons came online while they were on final approach, they'd be dead before they even knew what happened.

"Alpha will lead the initial assault," Colonel Coates said, pointing toward the company. "Your objective is to secure the flight line and capture the tower. Following Alpha's insertion, Bravo and Charlie companies will land and immediately begin to search and clear the ship. Take prisoners if you can, but we have been authorized to use deadly force to secure the ship.

"Following us in will be three pairs of Cobra gunships. While we are confident our man on the inside and the SEALs will be able to disable the ship's air defense weapons, the gunships are our insurance plan. As you collect prisoners, I want them brought to the flight deck. We'll look to evacuate the prisoners via helicopter as we can to get them out of your hair. When the ship's secure, we're to fly in some crew members who'll be able to get the ship underway and back to US waters.

"This is going to be a tough fight, gentlemen," Colonel Coates added. "Intelligence says at least two hundred French and German marines are on board to provide security for the ship, so expect a confrontation once they see we're trying to board."

As he continued to speak, the helicopter blades of the attack force began to spin up outside the hangar. "Marines, in a few minutes, we're going to board our sky chariots and ride into history…I want you all to remember your training and do your duty. Your country is counting on you, the Corps is counting on you, and I'm counting on you. I'll see you on the *Nimitz*." With that, Colonel Coates called them to attention and then dismissed them to the charge of their officers.

****

Salish Sea
Off the Coast of Victoria, British Columbia

SO1 Chuck "Blackjack" Black had just finished attaching the REBS magnetic climbing gloves and shoes to his hands and feet. The newfangled device would allow him to scale up the backside of the fantail of the *Nimitz* without having to use a grappling hook or ladder system. While those would be preferable, until he and his partner neutralized the guards on the back of the fantail, it just wouldn't work.

They'd be detected and killed before they could take the guards out. So, that meant they had to try and use this new and untested system.

Once the foot and hand pieces were secured to their bodies, his partner, "Chubby," who was ironically skinny as a rail, gave him a thumbs-up. After double-checking their night vision goggles, Blackjack and Chubby began a slow and arduous crawl up the back end of the ship, looking very much like Spider-Man. Each time Blackjack repositioned his hand, the strong magnet would almost slap itself against the hull of the ship. It took every ounce of strength he had to make sure he slowed down the magnetic pull of the REBS device. They needed to silently climb the ship, and a loud metallic thud every time they moved their hands or feet up the hull would alert the defenders that something was amiss.

Ten minutes into their climb, they'd made it up nearly thirty feet of the hull to the rear fantail and the balconies of the rear deck. Staying just below the lip of the balcony, Blackjack and Chubby detached their shooting hands from the magnetic hand devices and reached down for their sidearms. Unsnapping his holster, Blackjack pulled his Walther P22 out. While the P22 shot a small .22 LR bullet, when used with a silencer, it was truly silent. This meant they could take the guards out swiftly with a well-placed headshot and get on board quickly. Stealth was far more important in this case than hitting power.

Seeing that Chubby also had his P22 ready, Blackjack nodded, and the two of them slowly raised their bodies above the lip of the fantail. It was pitch-black on the balcony; no lights lit the area. Despite the darkness, their NVGs illuminated six guards. Two were located on each end of the balcony. They appeared to be milling around the edge of the balcony rail, oblivious to the presence of the SEALs. In the center of the fantail balcony, two more guards were lounging on a pair of chairs. They had their rifles sitting across their legs and looked to be doing their best to stay awake.

Lowering themselves down below the railing of the ship, Blackjack and Chubby put their guns back in their holsters for a moment, then silently worked out who they'd take out first using hand signals. They decided to shoot the two guys in the chairs initially—since they were already sitting, they wouldn't make any noise when they were killed. Then they'd move swiftly and take out the two guards on either side of

103

the balcony. Once they were cleared, they'd attach the rope ladder and the rest of their team could climb aboard.

Blackjack nodded to Chubby, and the two of them raised their bodies once again above the lip of the balcony. They each raised their silenced P22 and took aim at the seated guards.

Spit, spit.

Both of their shots hit the guards directly in the forehead, right between their eyes, killing them instantly. With the two guards in the center down, they shifted to face the other guards along the side. They were roughly thirty feet away, so it wasn't a terribly long shot. In seconds, the remaining guards were neutralized, dropping to the deck like sacks of potatoes.

With all of the hostiles now dead, Blackjack and Chubby both climbed all the way over the rail and got themselves situated on the balcony. While Blackjack rushed to double-tap the six guards, making sure they were in fact dead, Chubby pulled his rope ladder off his back and got it attached to the rear of the fantail.

The next five minutes of waiting felt like an eternity, but soon the other four members of their team had joined them on the *Nimitz*. In the meantime, Chubby and Blackjack had grabbed the dead bodies of the guards and dragged them over to one side of the fantail so they'd be out of the way. They positioned two of the corpses so they would appear to be still standing watch, while the two in the chairs remained where they'd died. This way, if anyone stuck their head out of one of the hatches to check on them, it would look like they were still alive and doing their duty.

Lieutenant Tebo walked up to Blackjack. He leaned in and whispered, "Good job taking those guards out. Take point and let's go take those guns offline."

Nodding, Blackjack pulled his silenced P22 out and proceeded to open one of the bulkheads. He kept his HK416 slung behind his back, ready in case he needed the added firepower of his compact assault rifle. As soon as the door was ajar, Blackjack realized the hallway was lit, so he flipped his NVGs up on his helmet. He then led the way down the hallway with his pistol extended, ready to shoot anyone that happened to enter his field of fire. They needed to hurry to get to the Phalanx system.

The three of them progressed down the hallway, stopping briefly at each open door to make sure there wasn't someone inside that might spot them or need to be dealt with. It took them roughly ten minutes of moving through the corridors until they made it to the side hallway that would lead them outside again, to the balcony platform that contained the CIWS system and the Sea Sparrow launchers.

Moving up against the door, Blackjack flipped his NVGs back down. "One…two…three…," he said quietly.

He flung the door open and entered the balcony with his pistol at the ready. In the blink of an eye, a figure appeared near the CIWS system. The guard was caught by surprise and fumbled for his firearm.

Spit, spit, spit.

The sentry dropped to the ground, three small holes in his face. Blackjack turned to his right and fired off three more quick rounds, dropping another guard who had turned around to see what was going on.

"*Sonnez l'alarme, nous sommes attaqués!*" shouted a French marine. He raised his rifle and fired several rounds at the three SEALs on the nearby platform.

Bang, bang, bang.

"Four o'clock!" shouted Blackjack. He dashed to the side so one of the SEALs behind him could bring his HK416 to bear on the Frenchman.

Chubby and Lieutenant Tebo hit the French marine with a barrage of well-aimed shots, dropping him where he stood. Unfortunately, the warning Klaxon on the ship sounded, alerting the crew that they were under attack.

"Take the CIWS out! We're heading over to take the Sea Sparrow out," yelled Lieutenant Tebo.

Placing his P22 back in his holster, Blackjack swung his HK416 around to the ready position. When the LT and his other teammate went back into the hallway to make their way over to the other platform, a storm of gunfire erupted in the close quarters of the hallway.

Crap, this plan's falling apart, and we haven't even taken the first weapon system offline yet, thought Blackjack.

Sensing that they might not make it over the other platform, Blackjack raised his rifle and took aim at the radar pod that controlled the CIWS, firing off half a dozen rounds. He was rewarded with a flash of sparks and popping sounds from the electronics being damaged or destroyed. He then fired off the rest of his magazine into the missile pods on the Sea Sparrow, making sure he riddled them with bullets.

"Blackjack, we need your help! Hurry up and finish the job!" shouted the LT over the roar of more gunfire.

Stepping back to the bulkhead door, he raised his rifle with a fresh magazine and emptied half of it into the radar dome above the gun system. He then finished off the rest of his magazine into the control box next to the CIWS. Once he was sure the system wouldn't work, he dropped his empty magazine and jumped back into the hallway to help his comrades out.

Blackjack hoped the other teams had taken their targets out. They were going to need the cavalry to come bail them out.

****

USS *Nimitz*
Combat Information Center

Electronics Technician First Class Tiffany Aikman walked into the CIC at precisely 0213 hours with one purpose, to take the fire control system for the ship's self-defense systems offline so they couldn't function.

When the *Nimitz* had put to sea two weeks ago with only twenty percent of the crew, she'd found herself trapped on a ship with a crew and captain that had gone rogue. When the captain had announced over the ship's PA system that they were going to sail the *Nimitz* to Canadian waters and place the ship under the control of the United Nations, she had been appalled. However, when she'd been approached by one of the master chiefs and an officer and asked if she could still perform her duties in spite of what was going on, she'd replied that her loyalty was to the ship and its crew.

Later that day, though, she'd taken her smartphone and found a quiet place to make a call to the base NCIS office. Since they were parked next to a major naval port and city, she still had cell reception. In short order, naval intelligence had established a working process of sending information to her and allowing her to report back to them what was going on inside the ship. When they asked if she could assist them in disabling the ship's defensive systems, she had cooked up the idea of taking down the *Nimitz*'s fire control systems during a routine maintenance check.

A day went by before they sent her a message telling her the mission was a go. On New Year's Day at precisely 0230 hours, she needed to make sure the system was taken offline. Once that was done, she was to do her best to stay out of harm's way until the Marines were able to secure the ship.

As she walked into the CIC that morning, Lieutenant Junior Grade Miles smiled warmly. "Trying to get an early start on your shift, Aikman?" he asked.

Lieutenant JG Miles had a crush on Tiffany, and she knew it. She'd been flirting with him constantly the last week once the plan for her to disable the ship's fire control systems had been hatched, especially since she knew Miles worked the graveyard shift in the CIC. Normally, the CIC would be staffed by a dozen or more folks on a twenty-four-hour basis, but with only twenty percent of the crew present on the ship, it was down to just Lieutenant Miles and two other enlisted personnel during the graveyard shift.

"Chief Yonker asked me to do my calibration during the graveyard shift so it wouldn't interrupt their operations. For some reason, he figured tonight would be a good night, so here I am," she said coyly with a wink.

Miles blushed slightly at the attention. "Well, I'll have to thank the chief in the morning for giving us some company. It can be rather rough in here on the night shift."

"Doesn't anyone else come in here?" she asked, raising an eyebrow. She walked toward the computer terminals she needed to work on, just like she had any number of times before.

"Yeah, one of the guys from the mess deck usually brings us some coffee and a snack every couple of hours. I think he does that more because he's bored than trying to keep us awake. We sometimes listen to the local radio station or catch an episode of *The Daily Show*," Miles replied.

"Oh, *The Daily Show*," she said with a smile. "I love that show. Hey, if it's on, can you tune the TV to it while I work on doing my checks?" she asked, hoping to distract him while she disabled the fire control systems.

"Yeah. LT, turn it on for us," one of the enlisted guys responded. "There isn't anything going on. CFB Esquimalt would let us know if something was amiss."

Smiling, Miles stood up and walked over to the one TV monitor that would typically have ship announcements or AFN on. He fiddled with it for a second before he found the channel with the late-night shows on it. While he was doing that, Tiffany moved behind one of the control panels to begin running her system checks. She unscrewed the back of the panel to get to the circuit boards.

Poking her head around the panel with a penlight clenched between her teeth, she announced, "I have to turn the fire control system off for just a moment to run this circuit board through a quick systems check. OK?"

"No worries, Aikman. I just told the Esquimalt we're going offline for a systems check for the next ten minutes," said one of the petty officers. Then, looking to the LT for support, he said, "You do need to make sure you're done by then, though."

Still looking at the late-night show, Miles asked, "Do you think you'll be done in ten minutes, or will you need more time?"

Looking down at her watch, she saw it was only three minutes until showtime. She smiled as she responded, "No, that should be fine, LT. I should probably be done in a few minutes."

The guys then turned their attention to the TV. With the defensive systems now down, it was just a matter of waiting for the cavalry to arrive and rescue her from this madness.

****

Bridge of the *Nimitz*

The duty officer was standing watch with two other enlisted sailors, doing his best to stay awake. Being anchored off the shore with a minimal crew, the sailors were both tired from the long hours and extremely bored from not doing anything.

"We need some fresh coffee," grumbled one of the petty officers as he rubbed his eyes. He reached over and grabbed the ship's internal phone and dialed some numbers. "Galley, Bridge. Can we get some coffee and sandwiches brought up here?" he asked.

There was a short pause, and then he announced, "Coffee and sandwiches in ten mikes, guys!" with a smile and thumbs-up.

Just as they were finally starting to perk up, the darkness of the night was broken by a series of bright flashes and thunderous explosions coming from the rear of the ship and then near the front of the launch deck.

"Holy hell! What was that?" shouted the duty officer as he ran to the port side of the ship to get a better look at what was happening.

Pointing at the flames from the vicinity of the two catapults near the front of the ship, one of the petty officers yelled, "I think that was our CIWS blowing up!"

"Sound general quarters. We're under attack!" the duty officer shouted. He speedily donned his flak vest and helmet. The sailors immediately ran through their various checks just like any other drill; only this time, it wasn't a test.

The sound of semiautomatic and automatic gunfire broke the silence of the night, intermixed with excited shouts for help and cries of alarm.

****

USS *Nimitz*
Combat Information Center

Just as Aikman was about to freak out that things had gone awry and she'd have to turn the fire control systems back on, she heard a thunderous explosion through the metal skin of the ship.

"What the hell was that?" LT Miles asked.

Before anyone could say anything, the general quarters Klaxon sounded, letting them know they were under attack.

One of the petty officers shouted at Tiffany, "We need the system turned back on *now*!"

"Aw, crap! Hang on, I have to stop the diagnostic and get the circuit board reattached," she shouted.

One of the petty officers opened the outer door to try and see what was going on. Another used one of their exterior cameras to survey the scene. "Oh my God! Someone blew up our CIWS guns near the front of the ship!" he shouted.

The lieutenant and the other petty officer raced to catch a glimpse of the scene while Tiffany continued to fiddle with the system. When they had their backs turned to her, she stopped what she was doing and made a dash for the other door that led out of the CIC.

109

She had just closed the door when she briefly heard one of the guys yell out, "Stop!"

In that instant, she knew she needed to get away as hastily as possible. She ran to the next ladder well and did her best to slide down it at a rapid clip. When she hit the bottom, she turned and repeated the process down another level. Then she ran at a breakneck pace down the hallway to put as much distance between her and anyone trying to follow her as possible.

As she sprinted, Tiffany saw one of the men's bathrooms coming up. She opened the door and dashed inside. Luckily it was empty, and she rushed over to the stalls. She found one at the end and snuck in. Then she locked the door and lifted her feet up, so if anyone looked at the floor, they wouldn't see her feet. She said a little prayer that her disappearing act would work until the Marines landed and seized the ship.

****

500 Feet from the *Nimitz*

The CH-53E Super Stallion banked hard to the left as a string of tracer rounds flew where it had just been. The left side gunner fired a burst of fifty-caliber rounds right back at the attackers, trying to silence them while the pilot deftly maneuvered them in for a fast and hard landing on the carrier deck.

"Here we come!" shouted one of the crew chiefs. The Marines in the back of the bay readied themselves to get out of the chopper.

Ding, ding, ding.

Rounds hit the helicopter as the pilot pulled up on the stick, bleeding off the last remnants of their speed before slamming her down hard on the deck of the carrier. Within a fraction of a second of touching down, the Marines piled out of the helicopter with their rifles raised, looking for targets to engage.

Sergeant Strawman yelled, "Take that machine gun out!" Then he directed his fire to an enemy soldier who had appeared out of nowhere up on the control tower's flying bridge, holding a light machine gun. The enemy gunner was shooting into one of the helicopters as it tried to gain more altitude and move off the flight deck to make room for another to land.

The Super Stallion had gotten about ten feet off the ground and was moving to the side of the flight deck when one of its engines suddenly blew out flames and then began to smoke profusely. The helicopter slid sideways as the enemy machine gunner proceeded to walk his bullets from the engine compartment in the top of the aircraft to the crew compartment. A few seconds later, the helicopter tipped all the way over to the side and crashed into the water, right next to the carrier.

Several of the other Marines lit the enemy soldier's position up with their own rifles, until one of the H-1 Super Cobras swooped in and raked several decks of the control tower with its 20mm machine gun. Its brass casings fell on the Marines below as they sprinted to the doors that would allow them access to the control tower and the rest of the ship.

Sergeant Strawman rushed up to the door at the base of the control tower with his squad. They stacked up against the wall as one of the Marines readied a flashbang. Strawman nodded, and the Marine pulled the pin while one of his squadmates pulled the door open just enough for him to throw it in.

Several bullets slammed into the door just as they closed it, presumably from soldiers waiting on the other side. When they heard the flashbang explode, one of the Marines pulled the door open, and the first man jumped inside, his rifle at the ready. That first Marine was instantly hit by a barrage of bullets from the waiting attackers. His body fell backward into the second man right behind him. His friend bounced his falling body off him to his right and fired a quick burst at the hostile who had just killed his friend. The enemy soldier clutched at his chest as he fell.

The Marines advanced rapidly into the room. As soon as that first room was cleared, the Marines filtered into the rest of the control tower. They fanned out and made their way to the upper decks as well as down below decks, where the real fight would begin. As more enemy soldiers sought to fight the Marines in the tight confines of the corridors of the carrier, the Marines alternated between using flashbangs and riot grenades. They wanted to avoid using fragmentation grenades as they'd cause a lot more internal damage to the ship.
****

Lieutenant Grace Harper was the Combat Information Center Officer, or CICO, for Carrier Early Warning Squadron 116, the "Sun

Kings." Her comrades often pronounced her job title as "sicko," which seemed kind of appropriate since it was her job to manage the air battle of the flight group. Of course, her supervisor, Commander Grady, the Aircraft Control Officer, made sure she knew what she was doing. For Harper, this was only her second time being the sicko for a major operation. During their last deployment to the Arabian Gulf, Commander Grady had eased her into the sicko role as he sought to get her properly trained up to take his place one day as the lead officer in the back of "the bus," as they commonly referred to their E-2D Hawkeye.

"Remember to stay sharp, Harper," Commander Grady instructed. "When those helicopters move in on the *Nimitz*, you can bet the Canadian base and those Chinese ships may get involved. We've also got those Chinese fighters over in sector eight you'll need to watch." He sat in a nearby chair, staying close to her in case things really went to crap on this mission.

Harper nodded. "Thank you, sir. I've got this, though."

Smiling, Grady turned back to look at his own radar screen.

"The Marines are going in now," she commented. They watched as the first wave of Super Stallions swooped in on the carrier. Two pairs of Super Cobra attack helicopters were escorting them.

A few minutes went by as the attack got underway. Then she spotted some activity emanating from the Canadian naval base. A pair of ships started heading towards the carrier. She immediately hit the radio preset button that was set up to allow her to communicate with the gunships to warn them.

"Sun King to Viper Leader. You have two inbound Canadian gunboats. You are cleared to disable the boats and destroy them if necessary," she said in her cool, calm voice as she had been taught many times before.

"Viper Leader to Sun King. That's a good copy. We're moving to interdict the hostiles now," came the reply from the helicopter flight leader.

While she was talking, she saw that the two Chinese naval ships in the area had turned to head towards the *Nimitz* and appeared to be moving at an increased speed.

Seconds later, the two blips that represented the Canadian patrol boats disappeared. She was about to call the viper flight to find out what had happened when they radioed back, telling her that the gunboats had fired on them, so they had taken them out.

Before she could reply, the Chinese ships turned on their targeting radar and had a lock on the Marine helicopters. Moments later, several surface-to-air missiles were fired from both Chinese vessels at the group of Marine gunships and the transport ships ferrying the second wave of Marines to the carrier.

"Oh, it's on now!" called out Commander Grady. He hastily made contact with the F/A-18s that were loitering not far away, armed with a series of Harpoon anti-ship missiles in case this very scenario played out. Grady ordered them to engage the Chinese warships.

While he was busy handling the Hornets' attack run, Harper noticed that the two Chinese J-11s had turned towards the Super Hornets and fired off a series of their own missiles at the American planes.

Harper made contact with the Growlers on station. "Sun King to Cougar Six, start jamming the J-11s and the Chinese ships with your electronics package."

"Cougar Six to Sun King, that's a good copy," they called back.

Next, she called out to their F-35 squadron on standby in case the Hornets needed some air cover.

In the span of thirty seconds, all hell broke loose in the skies along the border between the US and Canada. The F-35s ghosted in undetected and took out the Chinese fighters before they even knew what had happened to them. The Hornets hit the Chinese warships with multiple Harpoons, though the Chinese anti-missile systems did manage to shoot down half of the Harpoons fired at them.

"I'm seeing a flight of Canadian fighters taking off from CFB Comox," Harper called out to Commander Grady.

"Got it. I'm going to try and hail them directly and advise them to stay away from this area. What's happening with the Hornets? Did they make it?"

Harper had almost forgotten about the missiles that had been fired at the Hornets. She saw several enemy missiles still streaking towards them. The F/A-18s were dispensing flares and other countermeasures as they sought to get away from the incoming threats. Just as she thought they were going to get away, one of the aircraft appeared to have been hit. The pilot sent out a quick mayday, telling them he was going to bail out. The other three Hornets appeared to have escaped with the help from the Growlers and their own electronic countermeasure pods.

"It looks like one is down. We need to get a SAR unit to fetch him," Harper called out. "Um...it looks like the second wave of Marine helicopters are landing. Oh, wait—it looks like one of them must have been hit by that volley of SAMs the Chinese frigates had fired at them. The third wave of Marines is turning around to head back to US territory."

"I've got a SAR unit dispatched to get our downed pilot," Commander Grady announced. "I just spoke with the commander of VFA-154 at Whidbey Station. He said he's scrambling the rest of his squadron armed with Harpoons to go finish those Chinese warships off."

"Oh crap! That Chinese ship, the *Wuhan*, is firing another batch of SA-N-12 surface-to-air missiles at our helicopters," Harper practically shouted in panic. Those were the same missiles that had already shot down two of the Super Cobras and one of the Super Stallions.

"Sun King Actual to Cougar Six. We have inbound SAMs from the *Wuhan* heading to attack our helicopters. You *need* to jam those missiles, or our Marines are going to get smoked!" barked Commander Grady angrily. The Growlers were supposed to be suppressing their targeting radars so they couldn't attack the air assault teams—clearly that hadn't happened.

Lieutenant Harper watched one of the Cougar elements, which must have lit his afterburners so he could swoop down to get right behind the enemy missiles. The aircraft did its best to get as close as possible to the enemy missiles and try to blind them with its electronic trickery before they could hit another four helicopters of the assault force. The other two Cougar aircraft began to fly in a tighter circular pattern around the two damaged Chinese warships so the strength of their jammers would be more effective.

It took only a couple of minutes for the Chinese missiles to close the distance on the helicopters. The choppers fired off some flares in hopes that the missiles would get confused and go after the distractions instead. The Growler that had swooped in behind them also did his best to jam the specific radar frequencies the missiles operated on.

Harper crossed her fingers, hoping the Growler could help to blind them before they hit their targets. As she watched her screen intently, three of the missiles sailed right over the helicopters, missing them entirely. The final missile hit one of the flares and exploded behind the helicopters.

Harper breathed a sigh of relief. "Splash all four SAMs. Our helicopters made it," she said over the crew net.

"Knights Actual to Sun King Actual. I've got six angry Hornets. Are we still cleared hot to sink these Chinese warships?" asked the commander in charge of the attack squadron.

Commander Grady jumped on the net before Lieutenant Harper had a chance to say anything. "Yes. You are cleared hot to sink 'em. They just fired another volley of four SAMs at our helicopters. We need that threat neutralized yesterday!" he practically barked over the radio.

"Copy that," came the quick reply.

Then the Black Knights began their attack run, swooping down from their higher-altitude perch. They lined up on the Chinese warships that were still in the Haro Straits, then each fired off two Harpoons. Harper watched as twelve new missile tracks appeared in front of the Hornets as they now broke away to head back to base.

While those missiles raced to the target, Harper observed that two of the F-35s had now crossed deep into Canadian airspace. They were headed towards the Canadian F/A-18s that had lifted off from CFB Comox, and they were probably no more than eighty miles from the Hornets. Just then, she spotted four new J-11s taking off from Comox.

"Commander Grady, I just detected four new Chinese aircraft taking off from Comox. They'll be over the battlespace in about fifteen minutes unless they light up their afterburners," she said over the crew net.

They had four F-35s on station. Two were loitering over the *Nimitz* and the Marine assault force, and two others had moved to intercept the Canadian aircraft.

Seeing that Harper had her hands full, Grady turned to the other officer in the back of the aircraft with him and asked, "What's the ordnance loadout of those F-35s?"

"Um, let me check," the young man replied as he looked for the ordnance manifest. After finding it, he replied, "They're only equipped for air-to-air. They each fired off one missile at the J-11s, so they have five missiles left each."

"OK. Let's hope the higher-ups are able to get the Canadians and the Chinese to back down," Grady said as they continued to monitor the situation.

Returning their attention to their radar screens, they saw the twelve missiles close in on the two Chinese ships. Some of them were taken out by the enemy's close-in point defense systems, but many more hammered the enemy ships. Chances were, they wouldn't stay afloat much longer.

The next couple of hours were tense as the situation escalated. However, whoever was working the diplomatic channels must have finally gotten through to someone in charge, because the fighters finally moved on.

****

USS *Nimitz*

Captain Terry Pearl was asleep in his quarters when he was violently woken up by a series of thunderous explosions that rocked the ship. He'd only gone to sleep about thirty minutes ago, after partaking in a wonderful New Year's Eve celebration at the Canadian naval base with a number of Canadian, French, German, and Chinese naval officers that were part of the UN maritime force. It had been a chance to unwind and celebrate a global holiday with fellow naval officers he normally never would have met—but now he was regretting what a great time he'd had.

Practically falling out of his bed when the general quarters Klaxon blared, he grabbed for his pants just as the phone in his room began to ring. He yanked the phone from its handle. "What the hell just hit us?" he barked into the receiver.

"Someone just blew up our air defense weapons," yelled the lieutenant on the other end in a strained voice. "It looks like we have intruders already on board, and now we're hearing a swarm of helicopters!" Alarm bells and other noises were going off in the background, adding to the chaos being played out over the phone.

"What? How did our self-defense weapons go offline?" Captain Pearl yelled. He took a deep breath and let it out in a huff, trying to force his mind to think more clearly. "Never mind," he said. "Get the flight deck lit up and tell security we're about to be boarded, Lieutenant. I'm on my way to the CIC. I want whatever defensive systems we have left up and running when I get there." He shouted into the receiver to be heard over the noise on the other end. As soon as he hung up the phone, he rushed to finish putting his shirt on and slide his feet into his shoes.

Just before he headed out of his cabin, he grabbed his flak vest and put it on, along with his helmet. He had no idea if this was the opening volley of an attack or what was going on just yet.

As Captain Pearl quickly marched down the hallways of the ship, he saw sailors running to their different battle stations throughout the ship. When he was halfway to the CIC, he heard a couple of smaller explosions and then the unmistakable sound of helicopter blades.

They're trying to recapture the ship, he realized. He picked up his pace to get to the CIC. They had to get those defensive weapon systems back online or they were going to be boarded.

Just as he reached the CIC, he heard a lot of gunfire and machine guns shooting at something above them.

Crap, we're too late. They're here.

As he entered the CIC, Captain Pearl saw two sailors trying to put something back together behind one of the computer terminals. The lieutenant JG who was the duty officer was on the phone with someone, panic and fear written on his face.

Pearl walked up to him and took the phone. "This is the captain. Who is this and what the hell is going on?" he demanded.

"Captain, this is OS2 Elias. We're under attack. Three Super Stallions just landed on the deck. What do you want us to do?" shouted the nervous operations specialist. Pearl could hear the roar of gunfire and angry voices in the background.

"Are those French marines engaging them yet?" demanded the captain.

More gunfire, now intermixed with the sounds of several light machine guns, rattled through the hand receiver. "Yes. They're trying to shoot at the helicopters. Oh, crap!"

That was the last thing he heard from the young sailor before they all heard the ripping sound of a high-powered cannon, the same sound Pearl would associate with the infamous A-10 Warthog's 30mm chain gun.

Turning to the lieutenant, who looked white as a ghost, the captain barked, "Sound General Quarters! All hands man your battle stations. Set condition Zebra and patch me through to the 1MC."

117

A second later, the warnings were being echoed throughout the ship for the crew to respond to the attack taking place. Then the lieutenant handed Pearl the internal ship intercom system's microphone. "This is the captain speaking. We're being boarded by US Marines. Prepare to repel the boarders. Seal and lock all bulkheads and recapture the flight deck."

A German Kapitänleutnant from the Bordeinsatzkompanie, the commander of the German marine contingent that was providing security for the ship along with a French contingent, burst into the room along with six other Marines from his group, fully loaded down with their weapons and body armor.

"Captain, the attackers have secured the flight deck and are, as we speak, attempting to secure the tower," the German commander said in a thick accent. "Several of the French marines who were providing security from the control tower have been killed, along with many other people. I recommend you move your command post to a more secured position in the ship. The enemy will most likely move to capture this position first."

Nodding, Captain Pearl agreed. He knew the Marines would hastily attempt to secure this room and the bridge in an effort to take control of the ship and its functions. Two of the German marines moved to the outer room that led to the CIC from the direction of where the breach was happening, and the other German marines prepared to defend the CIC.

The rest of the American sailors in the room made their way with Captain Pearl, several levels inside the ship. As they advanced further into the ship, they saw a few French marines booby-trapping some of the bulkheads and doors with hand grenades while they readied some other corridors for a much larger fight. Everyone's ultimate goal now was to hold out long enough for additional help from the nearby naval base to come and relieve them.
****

Sergeant Strawman's squad had just reached the corridor that led to the CIC when a string of bullets hit the bulkhead door just as they tried to open it.

"They've got it barricaded pretty good. What do you want us to do, Sergeant?" asked one of the lance corporals, sweat dripping from his face.

Looking behind them, he saw another squad of Marines begin to file into the room.

"How many grenades do you have?" he asked everyone.

Most of them had at least two or three. They had all started the mission with four riot grenades and six flashbangs.

"OK, here's what we're going to do. Whiley here is going to pull the door open. You're going to toss in one of your flashbangs and then Whiley's going to close the door. Once it goes off, he'll pull the door open again and this time I want you guys to toss a couple of riot grenades in there. Try to get them as close to the end of the corridor as you can before Whiley closes the door. Once they go off, we're going to bum rush their position and hopefully overwhelm them."

The Marines nodded, liking the plan. They all got their flashbangs and riot grenades ready for what was going to be a chaotic close-quarter fight.

****

Colonel Rob Coates stood next to the control tower on the flight deck of the carrier, yelling into the radio back to his command post. "Tell those helicopter pilots to turn back around and bring the rest of my Marines back. We need those reinforcements, and I have wounded that need to be evacuated!"

"Until the Chinese destroyers are dealt with, the helicopters can't risk flying back—not after the gunships were destroyed, sir," said the major on the other end.

Looking off in the direction of the two Chinese destroyers, Colonel Coates witnessed multiple small blasts in the air. This was quickly followed by several massive explosions, which he assumed must have come from the anti-ship missiles scoring some hits.

"Major, I just saw those two destroyers get nailed by our Harpoons. Find out if they're disabled, and if they are, get my reinforcements back over here!" Coates shouted. Then he handed the receiver back to his radio operator.

Turning to find one of his captains, Coates saw the outer door to the control tower open. Several Marines carried a couple of their wounded brothers out to the flight line. Navy corpsmen were rushing to their aid as they were laid down next to at least two dozen other Marines who'd been wounded. Lying next to them were also some of the wounded renegade sailors who had stolen the ship. A handful of wounded French and German marines were being treated as well.

When Colonel Coates heard Captain Pearl announce over the ship's PA system that they were being boarded and to prepare to repel the attack, his heart sank. He had hoped the captain would have seen reason and just given up. Forcing him and his Marines to have to clear the ship deck by deck, room by room was going to be costly in terms of lives and time.

We need to get into the ship's PA system and try to convince them to surrender, he thought.

Coates walked into the control tower and made his way up to the admiral's bridge. Of course, the traitor wasn't on the ship. When he walked into the room, he spotted one of his staff sergeants and a lieutenant fiddling with some of the electronics for the ship's communication systems.

"Is it up and running yet?" Coates asked impatiently.

"Almost, sir," replied the staff sergeant. "They initially locked us out from the CIC room, but I think we've found a workaround that will allow us to bypass what they did so we can use the ship's 1MC system." He spliced a few wires and then retied them together with a different set of wires.

The lieutenant grabbed the handset. "Dial tone. It's working," he said with a smile on his face.

Walking up to the lieutenant, Colonel Coates took the receiver. Then he paused for a second as he formulated in his mind what he wanted to say.

Depressing the talk button, he shouted, "Attention!" Despite the booming of his voice over the PA system, it was barely loud enough to be heard over the sporadic fighting taking place across the ship.

"Attention!" This time he practically screamed into the mic, which echoed his roar across the ship.

"This is Colonel Rob Coates, the commander of the United States Marine Corps Marine Raider Regiment. We have landed a substantial force on the *Nimitz* and are, even now, securing the ship along with a team of US Navy SEALs. I want to address Captain Pearl and the men and women who have rebelled against the US. I am ordering you to stop fighting. You are surrounded.

"We now have control of the bridge and the CIC, and soon we'll have control of the engine room. Even now, several tugs are preparing to tow the *Nimitz* back to US waters. This fight is over. Continuing to resist is only going to result in further loss of life with nothing to be gained.

"To the French and German marines, I ask that you stop fighting and surrender. There is no help coming from the mainland. US air and naval forces have secured the surrounding waters as we move the ship back to US waters. Continuing to fight will only result in the loss of your men and you will gain nothing. It's time to stop and save the rest of your men's lives.

"All US Marines—stand down for the next five minutes while we let the defenders think this over. If the defenders have not surrendered in that time, your orders are to kill everyone. No prisoners are to be taken; no quarter is to be given. Colonel Coates out!"

Several of the Marines around him nodded in approval, though they all clearly hoped the defenders would heed his words and surrender.

Over the next few minutes, several groups of German and French marines began to lay down their weapons and surrender. By the time the five minutes was up, calls throughout the ship were heard from American, French, and German defenders, letting the Marines know they were surrendering. The prisoners were rapidly disarmed and led to the top deck of the ship, where they were ordered to sit down at the end of the flight line while they waited for their helicopters to return.

Looking out the flying bridge, Colonel Coates saw several large fires burning off in the distance, just out of their line of sight. He suspected it was the Chinese destroyers that had fired on them. As he continued to survey the waters in the darkness, Coates saw a number of life rafts with their flashing strobe lights on to alert rescuers to their location; he realized that the two Canadian patrol boats the Cobras had attacked had finally gone under.

Somewhere in the distance, he could still hear some sonic booms from time to time as an aerial dance continued high above them. Slowly, then more steadily, they heard the rhythmic thumping sounds of helicopter blades. Knowing their rides were coming, Colonel Coates ordered the lights on the flight deck turned on now that the defenders had mostly surrendered. However, he still had small teams of Marines moving through the ship as they continued to clear each deck, room by room, to make sure they had all the defenders in custody and had fully secured the ship.

Colonel Coates had sent a message letting Whidbey field know the defenders had finally surrendered so they could also begin to ferry over some of the original crew that had been placed on shore leave. He needed sailors to get the ship underway and ready. While they did have a couple of tugs on their way, they weren't here yet, and Coates wanted to get the ship back to American waters as soon as possible. Their little raid was sure to kick up one hell of a hornet's nest, and he wanted to put as much distance as possible between him and the coming firestorm.

"Excuse me, sir," said one of the Marine captains as he entered the flying bridge. He had a young female sailor with him.

"What is it, Captain?" Coates asked, rather gruffly. He had returned his gaze to the prisoners being filed out of the control tower below and lined up on the back of the deck, and he was a bit overwhelmed at how many defenders they'd captured. There must've been two-hundred-plus French and German marines on board.

"Colonel, this is Electronics Technician First Class Tiffany Aikman," the captain announced. "She says she was the one who disabled the ship's defensive systems in the CIC."

Colonel Coates lifted an eyebrow as he turned to size her up. She wasn't a very imposing person, standing at maybe five foot four and a hundred and ten pounds soaking wet. "So, you're the one naval intelligence was referring to when they said they had an inside person," he remarked.

Lifting her chin up in pride, she replied, "I am. Those traitors betrayed our oath to the President and the Constitution, so I felt it my duty to try and stop them."

A wide smile spread across Coates's face when he heard the fight in her voice. Walking up to her, he placed a hand on her shoulder. "Aikman, you just saved the lives of hundreds of Marines and you helped recover an eight-billion-dollar supercarrier. I'm going to personally recommend you for the Navy Cross for your actions."

Tiffany seemed overcome by the gesture. "I was just doing my job, sir. I'm glad I was in a position to be able to make a difference."

Colonel Coates smiled and nodded. "Good job, Sailor. Good job."
****

Washington, D.C.
White House, Situation Room

"Is that it? We have the ship back under our control?" asked the President. He looked at his senior military advisor with a sense of apprehension.

Pulling the hand receiver down to his shoulder, the Chairman of the Joint Chiefs, General Peterson, nodded. "We just got confirmation. The Marines recaptured the ship. Most of the defenders surrendered."

Several people in the room spontaneously cheered, whistling and shouting as they celebrated the recovery of the *Nimitz*.

Smiling for the first time in hours, the President let out a deep sigh of relief. He was starting to think he was going to have a heart attack due to the amount of stress and worry he had been experiencing these past few hours.

Turning to his Secretary of State, Haley Kagel, Sachs asked, "Have you been able to get in touch with Secretary-General Behr or Prime Minister Martin yet?"

Secretary Kagel had been trying to reach both men since just before the raid had started. Her goal was to make sure they knew what was happening and convince them that this was a localized situation—America was not invading or attacking the UN or Canadian forces. The US was simply retrieving its ship, but it *would* defend itself if attacked.

Turning to look at the President, she lowered one phone. "I did get through to PM Martin and told him what we were doing. He told me he'd ordered his aircraft to stay clear of the area, but he couldn't guarantee that the other UN forces wouldn't intervene. He asked me to request that you please show restraint and not retaliate against his military facilities. He's trying to defuse the situation with General McKenzie and Secretary General Behr."

"He should have thought about that before he allowed his country to be used as a launchpad to attack our country," the President said, but then he paused. Shaking his head, he looked back at Kagel. "Tell him we'll do our best to avoid attacking his facilities, but he has to keep the UN from using them against us. We can't allow them to be used indiscriminately."

123

She nodded, then lifted the receiver back to her ear and relayed the message. She gave him a slight smile and thumbs-up. The warning had been delivered and received.

"Sir," one of the military aides said as he walked over to the President, "I have the Chinese Foreign Minister on the line." He held out an encrypted smartphone.

All eyes turned to look at the President when he took the phone. He placed the phone on speaker and then set it down in front of him so the others in the room could hear.

"Minister Wu, this is President Sachs."

"Mr. President, I was just informed that American forces savagely attacked two of our naval destroyers in Canadian waters and shot down four of our fighter planes in Canadian airspace. This is utterly unacceptable. This is nothing short of an act of war against the United Nations peacekeeping force and the People's Republic of China!" the Chinese Foreign Minister shouted angrily at him. His typically excellent English had become much more heavily accented as his anger got the best of him.

"Minister Wu, your ships attacked and destroyed four American helicopters that were attempting to recover our carrier from its renegade crew," replied Sachs angrily. "We only attacked your ships in self-defense and retaliation for the destruction of our helicopters."

"Those helicopters had crossed into Canadian airspace and were attacking a ship under control of the United Nations. You can't attack the UN and expect to get away with it."

"That ship belongs to the United States Navy, not the UN, and we are recovering our ship. If China, or any other nation, attacks our military forces again, I will order those military units *destroyed*. I highly suggest that your nation end this military buildup you're doing in Mexico, Panama, and Canada before it leads to war," the President shouted back.

There was a brief pause on the other end. The Chinese Foreign Minister was probably weighing what to say next.

"Mr. President, you have until January 20th to leave office, when your term as President officially ends. If you don't adhere to the United Nations' resolution, the world will remove you, violently if necessary. Your successor must take his rightful place as President. Good day!" he said and then hung up on them.

124

Vice President Luke Powers, who usually stayed silent in these meetings, remarked, "I think that went better than expected." That elicited a few snickers in the room, which helped to alleviate some of the tension.

The Vice President then looked at the Secretary of Defense and nodded, as if giving him instructions to say something.

Chuck McElroy looked at the President. "Sir, the Vice President and I, along with the Joint Chiefs, believe this situation is going to spiral out of control now that we have taken this military action to recover our ship. I believe we should move forward with initiating Operation Fortress."

"I have to agree with their assessment, Mr. President," Secretary Kagel said. "If we wait much longer, the UN is going to hit us. They're going to be screaming for blood after this raid."

Taking a moment to think about it, the President steepled his fingers and stared down at the notepad in front of him. He felt like the weight of the world was resting on his shoulders. What he said in the next few minutes would have a profound impact on the future course of not just his country, but the world at large. The Pentagon had initially planned to begin Operation Fortress on January 15th, if it genuinely looked like the UN would not back down. Now his advisors were telling him he should speed it up by a week.

Sachs lifted his head up to look at his Vice President. "Luke, you've been involved in all the same meetings I have. You've met with the congressional leaders, cabinet secretaries, and some of our key allies we still have left. Do you really believe a conflict is inevitable?" he asked.

Luke was typically a quiet, reserved man. He prided himself on listening more than he spoke. In a way, he was the polar opposite of the President, but that also made him a good VP. He was the yin to the President's yang, and that had served them both well. He took a deep breath and let it out, as if carefully calculating his response.

"I think the wheels leading to a conflict were set in motion a very long time ago, Mr. President," he began. "While I would normally advise that we just not play the game, that we sit on the sidelines and let the world sort out its own problems—we can't do that this time. For one reason or another, some outside force has conspired to take us down. It reminds me of what that Harvard professor Graham Allison said about the Thucydides Trap. When a rising power causes fear in an established power, it almost always escalates toward war as the rising power looks to unseat the reigning power. In our case, an alliance has formed to replace America as the established power, and for better or worse, we now have to deal with it."

He sighed briefly as he surveyed the others in the room. Everyone was clearly hanging on his every word. "I believe a conflict will happen, whether we attack them first or we wait to be attacked. If we seize the initiative, we can at least ensure we get the first couple of punches in, and that might be all that's needed to win this looming fight."

The President nodded at what seemed like sound advice. Then he looked at his senior advisors. "If we attack now, are our forces ready?" he asked. "Is everyone in place? Because once the missiles and bullets start to fly, it's going to be go-go-go. There won't be time to wait for more forces to show up. We're going to have to go with whatever forces we have ready and nearby."

Chuck looked at General Peterson, who nodded. "We had planned to initiate combat operations by the 15th, Mr. President. We could move that forward a few days, but not much more. We're waiting on having a few more brigades deploy near the border and further rebalancing our National Guard forces to key areas."

Sighing, the President looked at the two of them, examining their countenances. Then he shifted his gaze to the Secretary of State, who likewise nodded in agreement.

"All right, ladies and gentlemen. Issue the warning orders. Combat operations start on the 13th then. General, defeat this enemy force and protect the territorial integrity of our country. Use whatever force is necessary, short of nuclear war."

With the decision made, a burst of activity began. The generals issued the orders, and once these actions had started, the series of events would be all but impossible to stop. For better or worse, the nation was now moving to war. On January 13th, 2021, the world would be reminded once again why America was the most powerful military on earth.

Chapter 9
Thucydides's Trap

January 1, 2021

From the Associated Press:

> In a spectacular midnight raid, the US Marines and Navy SEALs carried out a heliborne assault last night to recapture the supercarrier USS *Nimitz*, anchored just off the coast of Victoria, British Columbia.
>
> It was exactly sixteen days ago when the captain, Terry Pearl, along with roughly six hundred members of his crew, defected with the ship to join the United Nations–led military force building up in Canada and Mexico. The Pentagon confirmed this morning that at least fifty-two Marines were killed in the assault, with many more wounded in the short but violent fight that ensued on the ship.
>
> The raid lasted roughly forty minutes before the remaining defenders were convinced to surrender. Rather than lose the rest of their men defending a ship that would ultimately be captured, the German Naval Commander in charge of the French and German Marines responsible for the defense of the ship surrendered to the US Marines.
>
> More than 110 French, German, and American sailors died while trying to resist the heliborne assault and capture of the *Nimitz*. The Pentagon confirmed that more than 160 French and German military personnel are now being held as prisoners at the US naval facility on Whidbey Island. The Navy has confirmed that they have detained all officers and enlisted members of the *Nimitz* that participated in the coup d'état, to include Captain Terry Pearl. Rear Admiral Thomas Ward, however, was not on the ship at the time it was raided and is believed to still be on Canadian soil.
>
> Responding to the events, the Chief of Naval Operations, Admiral Chester Smith, stated, "It's a sad and terrible day when we lose a sailor or Marine. It's an even greater travesty when those sailors are lost because of the misguided decisions of their

commanding officers. I can assure you, the Navy will be fully prosecuting the leaders of this coup d'état under the Uniformed Code of Military Justice. Regardless of their political disagreements, these officers and senior enlisted personnel not only betrayed their oath of office, they betrayed their country."

Admiral Smith also confirmed that during the heliborne assault, four US Marine gunships attacked and destroyed two Canadian Navy patrol boats that may have been trying to come to the aid of the defenders. During the confusion and melee that ensued, two Chinese Navy Luyang I–class destroyers operating under the guidance of the UN peacekeeping force fired multiple surface-to-air missiles at the Marine gunships. The admiral confirmed that all four Super Cobra attack helicopters were destroyed. There were no survivors.

In retaliation, and in defense of the ongoing heliborne assault, US Naval aircraft attacked the Chinese destroyers, causing significant damage to both ships and neutralizing them as a threat.

High above in the skies, four Chinese Air Force J-11 fighters attacked the American F/A-18 Super Hornets that had attacked the Chinese naval ships. The J-11s fired air-to-air missiles, shooting one of the American fighters down. The pilot was able to eject and was safely recovered. During this aerial engagement, all four Chinese J-11s were shot down by US Navy F-35 stealth fighters.

This marked the first time the F-35 has seen aerial combat. Following this brief aerial engagement, the Canadian government, along with the UN military commander, General Guy McKenzie, ordered all aircraft to stay away from the border area in an attempt to prevent the situation from escalating further.

****

From the *Guardian* newspaper:

President Sachs ordered an attack against UN naval peacekeeping ships in the Salish Sea, just off the coast of Victoria, British Columbia. Two Chinese naval ships were

> brutally attacked by US naval forces after they shot down four US Marine helicopters that were part of a much larger heliborne air assault to recapture the USS *Nimitz*, the American supercarrier whose commander had defected with their ship to join the growing Canadian peacekeeping force in Canada. It is unclear how the UN and the world will react to this hostile military provocation by the Sachs administration.

****

From the *South China Morning Post*:

> President Chen Baohua denounced the American attack on the UN naval ships as a blatant and premeditated attack on the world. President Chen said in a public address that "this wanton attack by President Sachs on the UN naval force and the downing of four People's Liberation Army Air Force fighters will not go unanswered."

****

Ontario, Canada
Canadian Forces Base Petawawa

Holding the phone tightly, General McKenzie tried to bite his tongue as Secretary-General Johann Behr demanded to know how the UN naval ships in Victoria could have been so brutally attacked and the *Nimitz* captured.

Politicians always think they know how to fight a war better than the generals and admirals, he thought in disgust.

"Sir, if you'll recall, I requested that we put our naval task force to sea and not stay in the confines of the Salish Sea. It was an indefensible position, and it left our ships vulnerable to attack," McKenzie responded aloud. He held the phone receiver away from his ear while Johann shouted about how this attack could ruin everything.

Once Johann had said his piece, McKenzie calmly replied, "This was not a one-sided disaster. We gained valuable information from the short engagement, and we can use this as the validation we need to start military operations. I'll agree the loss of those ships will hurt us militarily, especially out west, but again, this gives our forces the justification to begin military operations immediately. As a matter of fact, the Chinese are asking me for permission to start their part of this plan. Do I have your authorization to let them begin?"

A short pause ensued before McKenzie heard the answer he was waiting for. A smile spread across his face. Albeit they'd be moving their timeline up by a couple of weeks, but they could make it work.

When he hung up the phone, he had a coded message sent to the German and Chinese navies to begin Operation Paukenschlag, or Drumbeat in English. This was the secret mission that would permanently put a dent in the American Navy and Air Force before the war even started.

With his naval orders issued, it was now time to move the command element of the UN force to the former NATO command bunker at CFB North Bay. The Americans would be coming after him with a vengeance, and he had no plans to get vaporized by one of the bunker-buster bombs for which the Americans were so well known.

****

Bellingham, Washington

A week after his trip to the Costco, Jake Baine got a call from his old company commander from Iraq, Captain Al Slevin. It had been nearly three years since they'd seen each other. Slevin had been promoted to major in the time that had elapsed.

"I was wondering if you could stop by our old armory on Sunday after we're done for the day," Major Slevin invited. "A bunch of the guys want to have a few beers together and catch up."

Truthfully, Jake was very excited about the call and the invitation—he missed the camaraderie of his old unit. However, he sensed that there was something else going on. Rather than press the issue, though, Jake just responded, "Sure, sounds like a plan," and figured he'd decode the mystery when he got there.

The rest of the week went by expeditiously. There was an awful lot of chatter at work about the standoff between the UN and the President. Jake did his best to bite his tongue and stay out of it.

When Saturday rolled around, Jake spent most of the day out at his hunting lodge up in the nearby mountains. His great-grandfather had bought two hundred acres of land back in the 1940s, following the end

130

of World War II. He'd built a small house, which was originally a one-room log cabin but had been expanded over time into a four-bedroom retreat. When Jake's father had died last year, he'd inherited the property and built two small bunkers there to hide his emergency supplies. Jake didn't consider himself to be an over-the-top prepper, but he did want to make sure that he had enough supplies to make sure his wife and a few close friends could survive whatever happened.

Jake's original concern wasn't so much a civil war or foreign invasion as it was the world's electrical grid being wiped out by a solar flare or taken down by some rogue hacker group. He felt those were far more likely events. Even if the grimmest predictions of global warming came true, at an elevation of two thousand feet, he and his family were well above the danger zone of rising flood waters.

He and Marcy actually spent a fair number of their Saturdays getting the cabin dusted, cleaned, and stocked with goods they might need in the near future. Like the bunker in his backyard, Jake had a couple of shipping containers buried on the property. He'd gone to great lengths to make sure they would be hidden in plain sight. Marcy had created a vegetable garden over the top of one, and Jake had purchased an old, rusty, beat-up car to be placed over the other. Their entrances were connected by a third shipping container, which acted like a hallway between them. On top of that container was a smokehouse, which had the secret entrance allowing him to access his underground facility.

When Sunday afternoon came, Jake hopped in his truck and drove the fifty miles to his old National Guard armory to meet up with some old friends. By the time he arrived, it was dark, and they had dismissed everyone for the day. Jake walked up to the side entrance and pulled on the handle—sure enough, it was unlocked. Knowing the place like the back of his hand, he walked over to the room that acted as the bar.

He saw Major Slevin there, along with two of his other buddies from back in the day. There were also two other faces he didn't recognize.

"Jake, it's good to see you," said Major Slevin with a smile. He sauntered up to him and the two shook hands.

"You too, sir. I can't believe they made you a major," Jake joked good-naturedly.

"Yeah, well, you know what they say—if you stick around long enough, they promote you," Slevin responded with a smirk.

One of the staff sergeants piped up. "Hey, it's good to see you, Jake. I hear you're working for the county in one of them cushy government jobs." Jake suddenly realized how much time had passed; the young man before him had been a buck sergeant when Jake had still been in the unit.

"It's good to see you too," Jake responded. "Yeah, the office job is easy, but it's boring…so, why did you all have me drive fifty miles down here to see you on a Sunday evening? What's going on?"

"Let's go take a seat over here," Major Slevin said, ushering him over to the more comfortable seating area. "George, why don't you go lock the place up. Let's make sure no one else is lingering around who could possibly hear our conversation."

Eventually, they all found themselves sitting around one of the tables, sipping on a beer. "Look, a fight's coming and there isn't much any of us can do about it," Slevin began. "The governor wants the National Guard to side with him and this UN force. Meanwhile, big Army federalizing us before that could happen and putting us under their control. Most of the state's Guard units have already deployed elsewhere. We're one of the few that's sticking around. In either case, things are about to get messy. What many of us in the unit are trying to do is prepare to wage a guerilla fight once we fall behind enemy lines."

"So, why have you guys called me? You guys know what to do and how to fight," Jake said.

One of the sergeants explained, "We've called you because we know you, and you aren't part of the unit anymore. When this all goes down, most of us are going to stay loyal to the federal government, but some in our ranks are going to stay loyal to the governor, who's thrown his lot in with the UN. That means when equipment starts to go missing, everyone's going to look at the active members who are part of the unit as the ones who stole it."

"That's where you come in, Jake," asserted Major Slevin. "We all know you, and we can trust you. If nothing happens and this all gets resolved peacefully, then we can recover what we're about to give you. If disaster strikes, then we know you can hide everything for us until we can form up cells and start carrying out attacks against those invading our country."

Jake nodded. "So…what exactly what do you want me to *do* with the explosives I assume you're about to give me for safekeeping?"

Smiling, one of the sergeants asked, "How good are you at building IEDs?"

"Ah. I see," Jake responded. "Well, I probably should make a few discreet trips to some stores over the next couple of day, but yeah, I know how to make things that go boom, if that's what you're asking."

The others at the table nodded and smiled. "We're going to load your truck up with some stuff," Slevin said. "Don't tell us where you're taking it. Keep this radio safely hidden but accessible. If things really go to crap, use channel three to check in. We'll figure out a more permanent way to stay in touch and meet, but get whatever you need, get it ready now. Don't wait until the end of the week. I don't think we have very long."

When Jake left the armory, it was 8:20 p.m. As he drove back home, he spotted a Lowe's hardware store along the way and pulled into the parking lot. Once there, he loaded twenty pounds of nails into a cart, along with three boxes of hot glue tubes and forty pounds of nuts and bolts of various sizes. He paid cash for the items and swiftly placed them in the backseat of his truck. Jake hadn't opened the bed of his truck to see what his comrades had loaded there, and he wasn't about to do that in a Lowe's parking lot.

It was nearly 10 p.m. by the time he arrived at his cabin. Walking into the smokehouse, he turned on the outside light and then opened the back of his truck bed. His jaw dropped.

Holy crap. It's a good thing I wasn't pulled over on my way here, he thought. He had a moment of panic as he pondered what he would have said to a police officer.

****

January 10, 2021
Emmitsburg, Maryland
Carriage House Inn

Colonel Ethan Dawe scratched his shoulder over top of the black Land's End fleece pullover he was wearing as he reached for his glass of tea. It was a new fleece, and while he liked it, it was scratchy. He hadn't fully broken it in just yet. It probably needed to be washed at least one or two more times before it would have that homey feel to it.

Dressed similarly to him in a gray North Face jacket and sitting across from him at this quintessential American country diner was the German man he'd driven several hours to meet.

Why do Europeans like gray so much? Ethan thought in amusement as he sized his counterpart up.

It was dangerous for Ethan to travel these days. The Americans knew he was the operational commander for Canada's Joint Task Force Two because of the collaborative work he'd done with US Special Forces in Afghanistan, so he was a known commodity. Canada's Joint Task Force Two was the Canadian version of SEAL Team Six or the Army's Delta Force—that meant that anytime he set foot in the United States, he was a hunted man.

For the past three weeks, Ethan, like nearly his entire task force, had been infiltrating across the American border. He had advised General McKenzie against this harebrained plan, telling him it was too risky and the probability of success was far too low. However, in light of the botched assassination attempt on President Sachs in mid-December, a new plan to remove the man had been hastily put together.

Despite Ethan's protests, his orders had been given, and now it was up to him and his foreign SOF counterparts to figure out how to make it happen. Typically, a plan like this would take years to develop. They'd spend months surveilling the target, then they'd do their best to infiltrate the target with a human source and attempt to gather as much raw intelligence as possible. Unfortunately, the only actionable data they had to go on came from decades-old Russian Spetsnaz plans from when they'd intended to carry out this same type of attack during the Cold War.

Ethan cleared his throat. "So, from what you've been able to tell, has much of what the Russians have given us changed?" he asked quietly. "Is a perimeter assault still going to be our best way in?"

The German soldier took a long sip of tea. "You know, this is the second time I've eaten at this place," he replied casually in perfect English. "Their smoky bourbon salmon is exceptional, though you couldn't go wrong with the French onion soup either."

The German then placed the menu down on the table and leaned in slightly. "The perimeter is the least-guarded part of the facility. They've added some new security features to it, but I don't believe they will be a challenge to overcome."

Ethan nodded at the comment. "I had my eye on the Chesapeake crab dip and maybe a club sandwich," he said, just loud enough that if anyone nearby were paying attention, they would think the two of them were just discussing what they were going to have for lunch.

Ethan placed the menu down. In a much lower tone, he confirmed, "All the equipment is in place and ready."

Smiling, the German just nodded as he waved for the waitress to come over and take their orders.

The woman, who was probably in her late forties, came over and pulled her order pad out. She took a moment to make some small talk with them as she wrote down what they wanted, made a few suggestions, and then walked off to get their order going in the kitchen.

Raising his mug to his lips, the German paused for just a moment. "Is the mission still a go?" he asked, uncertainty evident in his voice. Then he proceeded to take a sip from his tea.

"Yes. Sometime tomorrow," Ethan replied. "We'll be sent a text message when the President's on the move. We'll be sent another message if he is, in fact, coming to our location. If he goes somewhere else, then we'll stand down and continue to wait." Then he casually looked at something on his smartphone.

Nodding, the German asked, "What about the second target?"

Ethan snickered quietly. "Yes. That's also a go," he responded with a smile. "Of course, if we hit the first target, we'll have to reassess and see what assets we still have left, but yes. We'll be expected to hit the second target later in the day if possible. If not, we'll have to hit it the following day."

The German sighed but acknowledged the order. It was going to be a busy thirty-six hours. Looking around, they saw there were still only six other tables in the restaurant with people seated at them. In another twenty minutes, this place would be hopping with the lunch crowd. At that moment, it was just loud enough to obscure their conversation, and just quiet enough for them to continue to pass critical pieces of information to each other. When they left, the two of them wouldn't see each other again until it was time to initiate their mission.

Chapter 10
Paukenschlag

Port Huron, Michigan

Luitenant-kolonel Maarten van Rossum of the Dutch 105 Commando Company continued to fall through the air. The wind buffeted his face mask as water molecules whipped past him. He was nearly through the dense cloud cover. Once he crossed through the 2,000-foot mark, he should start to see the land below him. The thick cloud cover was making this type of HALO jump incredibly dangerous, but it was also aiding in their infiltration of what was sure to be a hostile drop zone.

Suddenly, he was through the cloud cover, and he could see the city below as well as his primary target. Van Rossum looked at his altimeter and saw that he had just passed 1,200 feet. He knew that he was nearly ready to deploy his chute.

Five more seconds, he thought.

He took a deep breath and then grabbed his rip cord and yanked it. A fraction of a second later, his parachute deployed, and he grabbed his guide wires. As he got closer to the ground, he reached down and disconnected his drop bag from his harness, letting it fall to the ground moments before he landed.

Looking below, he saw the US Customs and Border Protection station with its thirteen traffic lanes. He smiled slightly when he saw the power for the facility go out.

Right on time, he thought.

Their cyber unit had found a way into the industrial control system that regulated the power to the facility a week ago. The planners of this particular mission had determined that when van Rossum's men crossed through the 1,000-foot threshold of their descent, the power to the facility would be cut. This would aid them in their quick capture of the critical bridge.

Craning his neck behind him, van Rossum caught a brief glance of the other team as they were preparing to land on the actual bridge span itself. Their goal would be to hastily disarm the demolition charges that had been identified by their previous recon of the bridge a day earlier. Van Rossum's team would move swiftly to take out the platoon's worth of soldiers and engineers who had set up shop at the CBP entry control point before they could either detonate their charges or call for help.

Once the objective had been secured, they'd send a signal to let the forces mobilizing on the other side know it was clear to begin crossing. Then the tough work would begin—securing as much of the surrounding area as possible and engaging the American 1st Cavalry Division, which was nearby.

At less than a hundred feet, van Rossum pulled hard on his guide wires to capture as much air as possible, as quickly as he could. This had the immediate effect of slowing his descent just as his feet and legs prepared to touch down on American soil. A split second later, his feet were on the cement traffic lane as he did a couple of short running steps before he hit the quick release on his parachute, which then collapsed on itself and fell to the ground in a heap.

With his chute off, he reached for his HK416 assault rifle and flicked the safety off. Then he did a quick scan of his immediate surroundings to make sure there was not a threat nearby that needed to be dealt with. With nothing sticking out as a danger, van Rossum ran to grab his drop bag and threw it over his back. Three more of his soldiers had also landed and collected their rucks. They came trotting up to him with their NVGs down as they, too, scanned the area for possible threats.

Nodding toward them, van Rossum used a couple of hand signals, directing them to proceed to the objective. The three of them were going to hurriedly clear the CBP building while the other two teams of four operators searched and cleared the various inspection booths. They needed to make sure there wasn't an engineer sitting in one of them, ready to blow the bridge. This mission would only be a success if they captured the bridge intact.

Moving with a purpose, the four them headed toward the main customs building in the center of the divided traffic lanes. As they approached the entrance, they saw one of the doors open. Two soldiers exited the building. In the cover of darkness, the American soldiers didn't spot them and turned to head around to the side of the building.

"They said the breaker box should be somewhere over here," one of the American soldiers said aloud to his comrade.

While the two of them were walking toward the breaker box, presumably to see if a fuse had blown, two of van Rossum's men slung their rifles behind their bodies on their single-point slings and drew out their knives. They silently crept up behind the soldiers.

Before either of the Americans knew what was happening, their mouths had been covered by strong gloved hands as their heads were pulled back, exposing their necks. In a swift and violent move, the two commandos slid their knives into the soldiers' throats, slicing through their jugular veins and their tracheas before pulling the blades out the front of their necks. The commandos held the soldiers briefly as they drowned in their own blood. The only sound they made was a brief gurgling noise before both their bodies went limp. Then van Rossum's teammates dragged the bodies, positioning them against the wall of the building.

They rejoined van Rossum and their other comrade at the door and nodded to them, letting them know they were ready to proceed. Not wanting to give up the element of surprise just yet, van Rossum swung his rifle behind his back and unstrapped his silenced Glock 17M pistol.

One of the soldiers grabbed the door handle and quietly gave it a turn. He then pulled the door open for van Rossum to lead the way with his silenced weapon.

Moving swiftly around the corner with his pistol extended in front of him, van Rossum activated the IR laser mounted below his pistol and stepped into the building. He silently advanced down the hallway toward where he heard other voices coming from. He spotted some light down the hallway in what he assumed must be the main room of the building.

With his NVGs still on, van Rossum saw four soldiers using flashlights to look at the internal circuit breaker.

"I don't see a blown fuse. I think someone may have cut our power off," one of the soldiers remarked.

"I don't like this one bit. This could be the start of an attack or something," another one said.

"Calm down, guys. No one's attacking us," another one retorted. "One of you guys get on the radio and call it in. Let's see what the captain thinks." Van Rossum figured that last voice probably belonged to the sergeant in charge since he sounded older. The group of soldiers headed toward a desk that had a couple of radios set up on it.

Before the soldiers could get to the desk, though, van Rossum waved his three comrades into the room. They silently creeped in, positioning themselves along the flanks of the wall, their rifles at the ready, waiting for the signal to open fire.

These guys don't deserve to die—not if we can take them prisoner, van Rossum thought.

In English, he called, "No one move, and we'll let you live!"

The four soldiers in the room froze, not sure who was speaking or what was going on, but the sudden sound of a commanding voice from behind them got their attention.

"Slowly, raise your hands. Keep them where we can see them or we'll light you up," he commanded, using some American vernacular he'd learned from his deployments in Afghanistan.

Slowly, the American soldiers lifted their hands. The two soldiers who were holding the flashlights raised the lights with their arms, which illuminated more of the room as the bright lights bounced off the white ceiling.

In Dutch, van Rossum ordered two of his men to move forward to disarm the American soldiers and zip-tie their hands. Another minute went by as the two Dutch commandos took their sidearms from them and then proceeded to secure their hands behind their backs. Then each soldier was placed against the wall and told to sit down, which they did.

Van Rossum kept his silenced pistol trained on the Americans. He ordered his other soldiers to search the room for the detonators to the charges and to finish clearing the building. While they were doing that, van Rossum broke half a dozen green chem sticks, releasing the chemical liquid that created an artificial green light. He placed a couple of them near the soldiers to help illuminate them and then hung a couple of them from the ceiling tiles in the room from some string. They needed some light to help them search for the detonators.

Squatting down on his legs in front of the four American soldiers, van Rossum said, "We know you have the bridge wired to blow. Where is the detonator?"

One of the younger soldiers spat on him in response. A steel-toed boot instantaneously connected with the soldier's gut, causing him to grunt before a Kevlar-knuckled glove punched him across his face.

"We don't have the bridge wired to blow," replied the soldier that van Rossum had pegged as their sergeant.

Van Rossum held one of the chem sticks in front of the man, examining him. His name was Sanders, and his rank insignia showed three chevrons and two rockers. Van Rossum couldn't remember the exact rank that made him, but he knew it meant he was a senior sergeant.

"We aren't fools, Sergeant," said van Rossum icily. "We've been watching you guys for weeks. We know for a fact that you placed dozens of C-4 charges on multiple bridge supports on the American side."

He paused for a second as he looked at the man, trying to gauge if he was going to cooperate or not. He sensed by the look of anger on his face that he was probably not going to help them, at least not willingly.

"Sergeant, I didn't have to take any of you prisoner. I could have just as easily killed you. Our fight isn't with you—it's with your government. Just tell us where the detonator is, and we'll let you guys live. You'll be able to go home and see your families when this is all over," he said, trying to reason with him.

"You won't get away with this," the American sergeant responded. "There's no way the four of you are going to take our garrison out." He defiantly stuck his chin out as if he were confident that help would arrive soon.

"If you're referring to your two comrades you sent outside to check on the external circuit breaker, I wouldn't count on them. They're both dead. And there are more than four of us here. Now, Sergeant—I'm going to ask you one more time. Where is the detonator?"

The American shook his head. He wasn't going to talk.

Van Rossum could see two of his soldiers were still searching through the room. Another team member was now moving down the hallway to check on the other offices. Standing up, van Rossum looked at one of the younger soldiers next to the sergeant. He aimed his silenced pistol at the soldier's leg and fired a single shot.

The young soldier let out a bloody scream as the bullet tore through his knee.

His other comrades and the sergeant cursed at him as they struggled against their restraints.

Van Rossum calmly walked over to the injured soldier and placed his boot on the wound, which was now bleeding heavily. As he applied more pressure, the soldier continued to scream in agony.

"Where is the detonator?" demanded van Rossum.

"You can't do this! You're a signatory to the Geneva Convention. You can't torture or execute prisoners!" growled the soldier through gritted teeth.

Laughing at the comment, van Rossum leaned down to the wounded soldier. "Those rules are for America, not the rest of the world. Now, tell me where the detonator is, or I'm going to keep shooting *all* your knees out, and then I will work my way down to your ankles."

Now the soldiers looked nervous as they glanced at each other. Finally, one of the soldiers yelped, "It's in the customs office a hundred meters beyond our building."

"Shut the hell up, soldier!" barked the sergeant angrily, but it was too late. He'd given up the goods.

Reaching a hand up to his throat mic, van Rossum lightly depressed the talk button. "Beta Team, the detonator is located in the customs building," he whispered in Dutch. A few minutes went by before they heard the first shots of the war.

****

The team approaching the customs office building ran into a roving patrol and was forced to engage them. With the element of surprise blown, the four-man team bum rushed the building. They broke through the front door and made a mad dash through the building, hoping to find the soldiers inside before they could blow the bridge.

When the sergeant leading that team entered the main room of the building, they were met with a barrage of bullets from the defenders. The commandos pulled back inside the hallway before one of them threw a fragmentation grenade in. That grenade was quickly followed by two more, and in seconds, they heard three loud explosions. The commandos rushed in, their rifles at the ready as they sought out the soldiers who'd been shooting at them. When they came around the corner, they spotted an American soldier lying on the floor, his left leg practically ripped off. Arterial spray shot out of the wound with each heartbeat.

One commando saw that the soldier had a devilish grin on his face. His left hand held the detonator while his right hand turned the crank. In that split second, the Dutch commando feared they had just failed their primary mission. But when he didn't hear a loud thunderous boom, he suddenly held out hope that maybe, just maybe, the other team that was on the bridge itself had found the charges and disabled them before they could be blown.

When the American soldier also realized that he hadn't heard an explosion, his expression completely morphed. He showed a mixture of sorrow and failure.

I kind of feel sorry for him, the Dutch commando thought. Not only was the man dying, but he had let down his fellow soldiers. Rather than leaving the man there to bleed to death, the commando fired a single shot to the man's head, killing him instantly.

The rest of the Dutch commandos hurried to establish a defensive position around the buildings they now controlled, while the main body of their armored force raced across the bridge to help them secure the area for the rest of their division.

It had taken the Dutch commandos all of ten minutes to capture the position and disarm the charges on the bridge. With the Blue Water Bridge now under their control, dozens of Boxer armored personnel carriers and CV90 infantry fighting vehicles rapidly transported the men and women of the 44 Pantserinfanteriebataljon Regiment into the American city of Port Huron.

Following hot on their heels was the 11th Airmobile Brigade, part of the joint German-Dutch Division Schnelle Kräfte. It was now going to be a race against time to get the division across the border to find, fix, and then destroy the 1st Cavalry Division in Michigan.

****

January 11, 2021
20 Miles off the Coast of Virginia Beach

Looking at his watch, Fregattenkapitän Ernst Hardegen saw it was now 0734 hours, precisely four hours and forty-two minutes after they'd received the coded message ordering them to begin Operation Paukenschlag. After spending days getting into position, they had finally been given the go order.

In a way, it saddened Hardegen that it had finally come to this. Like the other sailors and ship captains he had talked to, he had hoped the politicians would find a way to handle their disagreement without resorting to violence. Sadly, as he had been taught at the academy, war was just an extension of a political dispute—and this disagreement had been simmering just below the surface between the rest of the world and the American President for some time.

Shaking his head briefly, he couldn't help but smile at the operational name chosen for this mission. It was the same operation name used during World War II, when the German U-boats had aggressively sunk American merchant ships right off the East Coast. Now, some seventy-eight years later, his submarine, the *U-34*, was going to carry out the exact same mission.

It couldn't have come at a better time, either. While they had spotted a number of very tempting merchant ships they could quickly sink, Hardegen wanted to save the element of surprise and his limited number of torpedoes to attack a more valuable target. For the past two days, they had observed a number of high-value US Navy ships leave the port of Norfolk to make their way out into the Atlantic. These ships were forming up to create a more significant force that he knew would ultimately sail toward the rest of the combined UN naval fleet that had recently left Iceland to head toward America. It was shaping up to be the great battle for the North Atlantic.

German intelligence had sent him a coded message a day ago that the carrier *Truman* was getting ready to leave Norfolk to join the other two carriers already present in the mid-Atlantic. With this piece of critical intelligence, he'd positioned his sub in what he believed would be the most likely path the American carrier would take to join up with the rest of its fleet. He hoped he was right—they wouldn't be able to chase after the ship if he'd positioned them in the wrong spot.

Hours after they'd received their attack order, Hardegen had started growing impatient. A few days ago, they had watched the *Ford* and the *HW Bush* carriers head out to sea. They'd had to let them sail past as they hadn't yet received their attack orders. Now, with the orders finally in hand, it was eating him up as he sat there, silently waiting in anxious anticipation for the *Truman* to get underway and head toward him.

Just when he thought his sub had missed out on the opportunity to sink something of great value, they spotted it—the white whale.

"Sir—the drone shows the *Truman* passing Cape Henry Lighthouse as it heads out to sea!" exclaimed a very excited drone operator.

Hardegen smiled. They had launched their tiny little reconnaissance drone the day before—it was a huge risk to use it, but without it, he really wouldn't have had much warning of where the carrier was heading.

The Libelle or Dragonfly drone was a small submarine-launched UAV prototype that the German Navy had been developing for the better part of six years. It shot out of the small communications tube near the conning tower of the sub to the surface. Once the encased package bobbed up on the surface of the water, its protective shell casing popped open and inflated a small circular landing pad. The UAV's systems then turned on and its quadcopter wings unfolded and activated. Once the UAV had taken off and reached an altitude of fifty meters, a pair of short, stubby little wings on the bottom of the UAV unfolded to provide the quadcopter with additional lift.

More importantly, the little wings were covered in the most advanced solar cells available, which would ensure that the device's lithium-ion batteries stayed charged. Theoretically, the small drone could stay aloft on battery power alone for as long as sixteen hours, but only if it turned off its electronics. The theory was that the subs could use the electronic suite of the drone to help them better coordinate an attack during the day and then place the drone in a stationary hibernation mode during the evening hours to conserve its battery.

Trailing just below the water, the *U-34* had a small communications buoy that would drag just below the waves, just high enough to still receive microbursts of data from the Libelle. Hardegen felt his pulse race as he realized that this little device was going to be the key to helping him place his sub in the correct position to land what he hoped would be a death blow to the *Truman*.

Hardegen walked over to the drone operator's desk so that he could view the feed for himself. He saw the US warships fan out and form up their protective bubble around the carrier. He also observed four different anti-submarine warfare helicopters go to work. Like a sheepdog, these helicopters and destroyer escorts would do their best to keep the wolves like him away from their charge.

While he didn't want to view this opportunity as a suicide mission, Hardegen knew it was incredibly difficult to attack a carrier. Not because the ship was believed to be unsinkable, but because of the sheer amount of ASW support the ships tended to be protected by.

The German Navy didn't exactly have a lot of submarines to lose in a war with the US, nor did his crew want to die in vain. It was hoped these Libelle drones would be the game-changing technology that would aid them in doing what no other navy had done since World War II—sink an American aircraft carrier.

Weighing these options, Hardegen settled on a plan to let the American carrier essentially travel to within ten kilometers of their position. This way, they could guide their Seehecht torpedoes in toward the carrier at a slow speed to minimize their noise and, hopefully, their chance of detection. Then, when they had gotten in good and close, they'd cut the Seehecht torpedoes loose to run at full speed, in this case, fifty knots. This would leave the carrier with virtually no time to react, and the ensuing chaos of countermeasures and torpedoes would make it incredibly difficult to identify where the torpedoes had been fired from. If this worked, they'd be able to slip away to fight another day and celebrate their victory.

Seeing that the American carrier was still roughly thirty miles away and running through their zigzagging pattern, Hardegen knew they had time to get themselves in position. Slowly and steadily, using their air-independent propulsion system, as opposed to their diesel engine, they silently got themselves into the best possible firing position with the help of their UAV.

"Sir!" called out one very nervous-sounding technician. "Our towed array has detected a *Virginia*-class attack submarine no more than 10,000 meters to our port side, above the thermal layer."

For what felt like an eternity, they held their breath, waiting to see if they'd been detected before they were able to carry out their attack. When they didn't hear the sound of an American torpedo heading toward them or the sound of its sonar going active, they breathed a collective sigh of relief. They had now entered the carrier's protective bubble.

Ten more minutes went by as the carrier continued to zigzag in their direction, oblivious to the danger they were sailing into as they now closed the distance to just under ten kilometers.

"Captain, the carrier distance is 9,800 meters. We have a firing solution plotted for torpedoes one through six. We're ready to fire when you order," the subs weapons officer announced. Hardegen noticed that sweat had started to form on this man's forehead, despite the cool temperature of the room.

Everyone in the confined space of the control room looked at each other nervously. The tension was so thick you could cut it with a knife as the crew almost held their breath, waiting for the order that could very well end their lives.

Hardegen bit his lower lip and nodded at the information. His stomach was tied in knots as the stress of the moment continued to build and build. They had already opened the torpedo doors an hour ago in anticipation of this moment. He wanted them to be as silent as possible leading up to the actual launch. While they might have detected one enemy submarine, that didn't mean there weren't more out there, ready to pounce on them at the slightest bit of noise they made.

Looking at his weapons officer, Hardegen ordered, "Fire tubes one through five. Make your depth four hundred meters and come hard to port, forty degrees. Make your speed ten knots." Hardegen wanted to save one of the torpedoes just in case they still needed it.

Within seconds of their torpedoes being fired, the DM2A4 Seehecht torpedoes, Germany's most advanced torpedo ever, accelerated at a silent and modest speed of twenty knots toward the great white whale. For nearly two minutes, the weapons closed the distance between them and their unsuspecting prey. Then, it was like a switch was turned on. The carrier went from traveling roughly twenty knots in a zigzag pattern to accelerating to its maximum speed as it sought to put as much distance between itself and the newly identified threat.

"Bring the torpedoes up to full speed!" Hardegen ordered.

It was now a race against time to close the distance and hit the ship before it was able to run away from the threat. At this point, the carrier's best defense was to turn in the opposite direction and open its engines all the way up, which it did. With an operational range of sixty kilometers and maximum speeds of fifty knots, Hardegen was confident their torpedoes would win this race.

Once the carrier had gone to full speed to try and outrun the torpedoes, it deployed its Nixie torpedo decoy in hopes of being able to lure one or more of his torpedoes away. Hardegen walked over to the enlisted man guiding the torpedoes and watched as the man successfully steered them away from the decoy, keeping them locked on to the carrier.

The distance had now closed to less than 3,000 meters. At this range, the torpedoes went active with their own sonar as the targeting computer sought to get a picture of the hull of the ship it was heading toward. In seconds, this targeting computer ran through its stored data of known ships, identified the target as an American supercarrier and locked on to the most likely kill spot under the hull of the vessel.

When the Seehecht torpedoes got to within 2,000 meters of their target, the torpedoes' engines automatically kicked into their final stage and accelerated from fifty knots to sixty-five knots as they closed in for the kill. Hardegen held his breath.

Steadily, one by one, the five torpedoes made their way under the hull of the ship before exploding as they reached their marks. With each successive explosion, it sent a massive overpressure of water jets up through the lower two or three decks of the carrier. The ripple effect of the eruptions were so powerful, they briefly lifted the carrier a couple of inches up before gravity slammed the behemoth hard against the cavity of air and water below the hull of the ship, cracking the keel. When the *Truman* smacked into that vacuum below it, the carrier's hull fractured in dozens of places, ripping new fissures and cracks across nearly every deck of the ship.

For the briefest of moments, Captain Hardegen and his crew were elated as they listened to the massive explosions ripple through the water and the loud growing sound of the ship's hull as it began to break apart. They had succeeded in doing something no other submariner had ever done, hit an American aircraft carrier with a modern-day torpedo.

However, in their brief, albeit quiet celebration, they suddenly detected that an American torpedo had been fired at them.

"Enemy torpedo in the water!" shouted the sonar technician.

Unbeknownst to the crew of *U-34*, the *Virginia*-class submarine that had sailed past them earlier had detected them when they'd fired their torpedoes. The sub had turned around and closed in on their last known position as it hunted for them. While the Germans had been so intent on guiding their own torpedoes to the carrier, they had failed to detect the sub that had found them.

Before anyone in the German sub could react, the American torpedo slammed into their own hull, splitting the submarine in half. The last thought to pass through Captain Hardegen's mind before the control room was flooded with the icy water of the Atlantic was of his last family dinner with his beautiful wife and four children.

****

"Torpedoes in the water!" shouted a petty officer from the underwater threat station of the *Truman*'s CIC.

"Deploy the Nixie! Ahead flank speed and take evasive maneuvers," shouted the officer on the deck.

The battle station's Klaxon sounded as the ship's pilot announced emergency maneuvering. The carrier instantly turned hard to starboard while the engines jumped to one hundred percent. Despite the massive size of the carrier, its 260,000-horsepower engines spun its four propeller blades at such a rate that the carrier actually lurched forward as it moved from twenty knots to over thirty-five in less than a minute.

The captain of the ship, Brandon Reynolds, dashed into the CIC. "What the hell is going on?" he shouted. He grabbed for something to keep himself from falling over from the force of the sharp turn.

"Incoming torpedoes, heading 221, 11,000 meters and closing in quickly," shouted the underwater threat officer.

"Damn it! Get with our escorts and tell them to get a helo over to where those torpedoes probably came from and find that enemy sub," Captain Reynolds ordered.

If they could find and sink the enemy sub swiftly, they might be able to take them out before they could guide their torpedoes in for the kill—at least, so he hoped.

For the next seven minutes, the ship continued to race as rapidly as it could away from the underwater threats as they hoped and prayed the torpedoes would go for the Nixie. When the torpedoes blew past the Nixie, Reynolds knew they were in trouble.

A couple more minutes went by, and then the underwater threat officer shouted, "Brace for impact!"

The carrier briefly lifted several inches in the water before crashing back into the hole created below it. The bow of the ship dipped dangerously low to the waves before plowing through the water like a hot knife through butter.

The sudden jarring and impact from the explosion threw nearly everyone who wasn't seated or strapped into a chair to the ground. Many people injured their ankles, knees, or backs from the sudden impact.

Seconds after the violent tumult, the lights flickered briefly before they went out entirely, throwing the CIC and the ship into complete and utter darkness. The emergency generators should have automatically kicked in, but they failed—either from the sudden jarring or something else.

As the ship slowed to a stop from the loss of the engines, the battery-operated emergency lights popped on, providing them with a modicum of light. Then they heard it—a series of loud groans as the hull of the carrier buckled and broke from the numerous fissures and fractures spreading across the structure of the ship.

"Give me a damage report!" shouted Captain Reynolds. He climbed back to his feet in a state of bewilderment and shock at what had just happened. Never in his thirty years in the Navy had he experienced anything like this. He still couldn't believe his ship, his pride and joy, had just been torpedoed.

"Systems are still offline. I'm trying to reboot the computers now!" shouted one officer in reply.

"Captain, I have engineering on the phone!" yelled one of the senior chiefs. He held out the receiver to the ship's internal phone system.

"How bad is it, Scottie?" asked Reynolds as he grabbed the receiver. He said a silent prayer that the ship could be saved.

Commander George Scott, or "Scottie" as he was often called, had been the chief engineering officer on the *Truman* now for three years. He was one of the most senior engineering officers in the fleet, and he was definitely the guy you'd want in charge if there were ever a major disaster or accident.

Scottie's gruff voice yelled above the alarms going off in the background. "It's bad, Captain. The lower decks are flooding rapidly. I don't think we're going to be able to stop the water pouring into the engine room." A short pause ensued as Scottie yelled out some orders to someone nearby. Alarm bells continued to blare relentlessly.

"One of the torpedoes hit the propeller shafts and ripped them apart, sir," Scottie reported. "The explosion broke all the seals from the external shafts, all the way back to the engines. With those seals gone, we've got a massive flow of water rushing through them without a way of stopping it. I'll know more in a few moments if we'll be able to stop the flooding, but if we can't get it under control soon, we may lose the ship."

Captain Reynolds was horrified. Never before had a modern aircraft carrier been hit by a twenty-first-century torpedo. There wasn't a lot of data on how to deal with a hit like this because it just hadn't happened before.

"Just do what you can, Scottie," Reynolds ordered. "Call me back if things get worse." He handed the phone back to the senior chief. He then turned his attention to the other damage reports that were finally starting to flow in now that their computer systems and sensors were back up and running. The other damage control parties around the ship were also beginning to call in their reports.

The situation they were painting across the ship was bleak. They were currently dead in the water. To make matters worse, the leaks in engineering were becoming unstoppable as the magnitude of the damage was becoming known.

Twenty minutes after the torpedoes hit the *Truman*, it was determined that she was most likely going to sink. The driveshafts for the engines had been torn apart, and they had four large holes in the ship that couldn't be sealed off. To make matters worse, the cracks and fissures that had developed throughout the ship meant that once-watertight spaces and bulkheads were now leaking water faster than their pumps could expel it. As more water flooded into the ship, the pressure on the already damaged portions of the *Truman* caused more leaks to appear.

When Captain Reynolds realized there was a good likelihood the ship was going to go down, he ordered what helicopters they had on the flight deck to promptly begin evacuating the wounded to the other ships in the strike group. Likewise, the other destroyers and cruiser escorts used their helicopters to help offload the wounded from the carrier and begin ferrying as much of the crew over as possible. Since the ship was roughly twenty-six miles off the coast of Virginia Beach, they sent an emergency message to the Coast Guard and to Norfolk for immediate assistance.

Soon, dozens of helicopters from Norfolk and the nearby Coast Guard facilities were landing on the carrier deck, picking up the hundreds of wounded sailors and Marines. Several of the destroyers had also come nearby, and they did their best to assist in getting the injured and other sailors off the ship while bringing over additional people who could try and help control the flooding.

The first shot of the third war of the Atlantic had been fired, and it looked like the UN forces had drawn first blood.

****

Pacific Ocean
200 Miles South of Hawaii

"Captain, we're receiving a flash message from INDOPACOM. They're ordering us to go to Condition One. We're being told to prepare for an imminent attack," announced the communications officer.

Captain Ian Grady of the USS *John C. Stennis* walked up to his comms officer and grabbed the flash report to read over what it said for himself. Then he acknowledged the order, proclaiming, "Sound general quarters. Bring us to battle stations!"

The general quarters Klaxons blared, and the crew of the ship mechanically ran through their various procedures and processes that had been drilled into them from the first time they'd ever boarded a ship.

A couple of minutes after the alarm started, the strike group commander, Admiral Leslie Parker, walked in to see what was going on. She spotted the captain and made her way over to him.

"What is it, Grady?" she asked with a look of concern on her face.

Admiral Leslie Parker had just taken over command of the strike group ten days ago. She had transferred in from the CNO's office when the Pentagon had begun to prepare the entire armed forces for combat operations. She'd been one of the first female captains of a supercarrier, and now she was the first female strike group commander. By all accounts, she was a hell of a commander. She'd earned her chops as an F/A-18 Super Hornet pilot, flying combat operations in Afghanistan and Iraq. She'd worked her way up the food chain the old fashion way, through grit and determination.

Captain Grady was usually happy to see Admiral Parker, but he just shook his head in disbelief and handed her the flash report.

"It's the *Truman*. They were apparently ambushed twenty-some miles off the Virginia coast. The report doesn't say how many torpedoes they were hit with, but it looks grim," he replied.

Rear Admiral Parker didn't waste any time. "I want to know immediately what ships are within a two-hundred-mile perimeter of our fleet," she announced. "Send a flash message to our destroyers and let's make sure we don't get sucker punched by a similar attack. I want all our ASW helos airborne *now*."

With her initial orders issued to the fleet, she turned to look at Captain Grady. "I recommend we get some strike fighters ready in case we come across some targets of opportunity. If this UN force attacked the *Truman*, you can bet whatever ships they have in the area are probably looking to attack us as well."

Grady nodded, then turned to his Commmander, Air Group. "CAG, we need to get the ready alert fighters in the air," he ordered.

As soon as he'd finished his sentence, one of the radar operators yelled to get his attention. "Captain, I've got something!" he shouted.

Grady and Parker made a beeline for the chief petty officer, who was manning one of the surface-radar stations. The man was pointing at a cluster of ships on his radar screen.

"What do you have, Chief?" asked Grady.

"I show two Chinese Navy destroyers escorting what appear to be three massive freighters. They're roughly 140 miles away, so well outside our threat bubble, but they just turned on their targeting radars a few seconds ago. They're actively painting the strike group," the man explained. The nervousness in his voice was evident.

"I don't like it," Admiral Parker remarked. "Not after the attack on the *Truman*. Come to think of it, how did we not see them sneaking up on us like this?" she asked, the pitch of her voice rising higher.

"It's not that they snuck up on us, ma'am," replied a lieutenant who'd clearly come over to make sure his chief wasn't being unduly picked on. "They've only just now come into our search bubble. We hadn't expanded our perimeter yet. It does appear that they've turned to head toward us. The last time we had spotted them, they were roughly 160 miles away, and that was several hours ago."

Turning to look back at Grady, Admiral Parker ordered, "Get a strike group airborne now. I'm going to try and get permission from 7th Fleet commander to sink them. While I'm doing that, I want the strike group up and ready for action."

Captain Grady nodded and turned to get to work on his new task while Admiral Parker worked on trying to get through to the 7th Fleet commander.

****

Aboard the DDG-155 *Nanjing*, Senior Captain Ding Yiping watched the targeting radar screen with keen interest as the information started pouring in. They had already deployed two of their smaller surveillance and reconnaissance drones, which had helped them find the strike group a few hours ago. As the supercomputers on their destroyer crunched all the data coming in, they fed the results to the targeting computers on the CJ-10 cruise missiles they were about to fire.

Unbeknownst to the rest of the world, the People's Liberation Army Navy had converted a number of these massive freighters into floating missile platforms. It was a modern-day merchant raider fleet, just like the Germans had done during World War II. In place of internal cargo compartments, the ship's cargo holds had been redesigned and fitted with vertical-launch pods.

To add to the ruse, the tops of the cargo ships were covered with containerized shipping pods. These were all specially mounted on a rail system that could be opened up when it was time to fire off their missiles. After their missiles had been fired, the rail system would move the shipping pods back over the top of the VLS system, once again concealing them from the prying eyes of satellites and reconnaissance drones.

After the Chinese Navy had finished the conversions, a single cargo vessel now held fifty CJ-10 land-attack cruise missiles, providing the ships with a potent standoff weapon. These missiles were very similar to the American Tomahawk cruise missiles in range and payload. The ships also held one hundred of the vaunted YJ-18 or CH-SS-NX-13 anti-ship missiles. These missiles had a maximum range of 540 kilometers and gave the ships the ability to legitimately challenge the US Navy. The missiles cruised at speeds of Mach 0.8 and had a terminal velocity speed of Mach 2.5 to 3.0 when zeroing in on their prey. The warheads consisted of an armored tip for deep penetration of a ship's hull and a 300-kilogram warhead of an advanced explosive mixture, designed purely to cause maximum damage to a ship.

The Chinese had turned these floating behemoths into twenty-first-century battleships. Their overarching goal was to use them as a first-strike weapon against the US Pacific fleet, and either sink or disable the American carriers. With the US's carriers taken out of the equation in the Pacific, the Chinese could move forward with a multitude of operations to cement their hegemony over the Pacific.

One of the targeting officers who'd been manning a radar screen flagged Captain Ding down. "Sir, it would appear the Americans are launching additional fighters. Do you want us to order the raiders to begin their attack?" he asked.

"Find out if the raiders are ready to launch. Tell them they need to hurry up—I believe our cover has been blown."

"Yes, sir," he replied, and he rushed off to make the call.

A moment later, he came trotting back. "Captain, the raiders told me they need just a few minutes as they ready the VLS systems to fire."

"Very well," Captain Ding answered. There wasn't anything he could do now but wait.

As the minutes went by, they observed several of the American destroyer escorts moving into a screening position, placing themselves between the carrier and the Chinese ships. Six additional aircraft also joined the four fighters that were already circling the carrier. Two fighters, F/A-18 Super Hornets, headed toward the Chinese fleet. They were still a little more than 120 miles away, so the Chinese ships had time to get themselves sorted and ready to begin their attack. One thing was abundantly clear, though—the Americans suspected something and were preparing to deal with them.

Suddenly, a few alarm bells sounded in the CIC of the *Nanjing*.

"Sir, the Americans' targeting radars have painted our ships," a radar technician announced.

Despite this proclamation, the captain and the rest of the crew didn't seem too concerned just yet. The American Harpoon anti-ship missiles only had a range of 67 miles, or 124 kilometers. Unless the American ships started firing Tomahawks at them, they were well outside the Americans' range.

Ding's executive officer walked over to him, demonstrably excited. "Captain, the raiders are reporting they're ready to begin launching their missiles. They said it should take them approximately five minutes to carry out the first volley. The captain recommends we begin firing soon so we can keep the American warships at arm's length."

Taking in a deep breath, Captain Ding slowly let it out before issuing the attack order. They were about to show the world that China was officially a blue water navy, capable of projecting power well beyond its territorial border.

"Order them to begin firing volley one," he said confidently. "Have them begin preparations to fire volley two on Hawaii. We need to make sure we neutralize the next threat."

154

Within a minute of issuing his first order of this new war against America, the three merchant raiders made history by firing off hundreds of anti-ship missiles at an American carrier. It would take them close to five minutes for the firing sequence to complete. Then they'd begin the next firing sequence, which would look to hammer the American naval and air facilities on the Hawaiian Islands, roughly two hundred miles away.

****

One of the air defense officers aboard the USS *John C. Stennis* yelled out, "Vampires, Vampires, Vampires!"

Over his shoulder, Captain Grady watched as the radar screen suddenly filled up with dozens upon dozens of anti-ship missiles. "Where the hell did they come from?" shouted Grady.

"It's those cargo ships, sir," replied another air defense officer. "It appears the missiles are emanating from them."

Captain Grady felt his jaw hang open in shock, and he couldn't respond for a moment. He looked at Admiral Parker—she was similarly speechless.

"The missile count is now surpassing fifty!" shouted another petty officer excitedly.

The radar picture of the area was now being shown on the big board in the CIC. What they saw was terrifying. The small cluster of five Chinese ships was suddenly emitting missiles at an astonishing rate. A missile every two seconds was appearing from the cargo ships while the two destroyers were focusing their efforts on going after the fourteen aircraft the *Stennis* had managed to get airborne before the attack started.

One of the communications officers held a hand receiver out to Admiral Parker. "The *Antietam* is requesting permission to take over the strike group's air defense effort and begin engaging the enemy missiles," she said.

"Permission granted!" shouted Admiral Parker. "Order the rest of the fleet to engage those Chinese ships with our Tomahawks. We need to take them out before they can keep pummeling us with missiles. God only knows how many of them are packed in there."

The UAV operator waved his arms to get the captain's attention. "We're starting to get some images from the Triton. Holy hell! Look at this!"

Captain Grady rushed over to him. The drone operator had moved the UAV to get in closer to the Chinese ships and used its advanced optics to get them detailed visuals of the ships.

Before Grady could say anything, one of the master chiefs commented, "I don't know how they did it, but it sure looks like they covered the entire cargo hold of those ships with vertical-launch system pods. They probably packed them with hundreds of missiles, turning them into massive floating missile platforms."

Captain Grady found himself feeling simultaneously impressed with the idea and irate that they hadn't thought of it first.

Turning to the UAV operator, the master chief added, "Make sure this video is getting sent back to INDOPACOM. We need to spread the word of this new threat to the rest of the fleet ASAP. God only knows how many more of these ships they've got prowling the Pacific right now."

Captain Grady looked over at Admiral Parker, who'd followed him over. She definitely didn't appear to be her usual stoic self—she poked at the bun on her head as if it were about to fall off, and one vein in particular on her forehead was suddenly very visible.

Grady understood the reaction. The missile count was continuing to climb, now breaking through the two hundred mark. Many of those missiles would start to come into range of the strike groups anti-missile defense bubble in another three to five minutes. In ten minutes, the missiles would be in range of their point defense systems.

The captain heard Admiral Parker mumble, "Well, if you haven't found God, now would be the time to pray that our defensive systems do their job and protect the fleet."

****

Captain Ding was feeling good and optimistic about the attack underway against the American strike group until their radar screens showed a series of new threats. Tomahawk cruise missiles were being fired by the carrier's destroyer escorts, while the two guided missile cruisers went to work on engaging their anti-ship missiles.

The first wave of Chinese and American missiles were nearly ready to collide with each other as the YJ-18 missiles' AI systems took over and began to maneuver their way through the barrage of missile interceptors streaking toward them. Slowly, then very rapidly, the volume of missiles heading toward the strike group shrank.

"Begin engaging the American Tomahawks with our own interceptors," instructed Captain Ding. "Order the raiders to start launching their second wave of missiles."

The *Nanjing* shook as her own forward and rear missile magazines started firing their interceptors. In minutes, the two Chinese destroyers had launched twenty interceptors. As long as the *Nanjing* or her sister ship stayed operational, they'd be able to help guide the merchant raiders' missiles. If both of them were taken out, then the merchant raiders would have to rely on their own, less sophisticated targeting radars to go after the American ships.

"Captain, the first volley of missiles should be entering the carrier's point defense systems now," exclaimed one of the targeting officers.

Looking at the radar screen on the large wall-mounted monitor, Captain Ding saw that of the first two hundred missiles that had been fired at the fleet, only forty-two had survived to get within the American strike group's point defense systems.

Within two minutes, the group of forty-two missiles had been thinned out until there were just twelve left. Fortunately, four of them slammed into the carrier, while the remaining eight scored hits against the destroyer escorts.

"Prepare for impact!" shouted one of the officers.

Their own point defense systems engaged the American Tomahawk missiles. The loud ripping noise so synonymous with the CIWS gun system was deafening as the guns spat out a wall of 25mm tungsten projectiles. A loud blast erupted a few hundred meters away from the *Nanjing*, slapping the outer structure of the ship with shrapnel. One of the incoming missiles had detonated when it hit the wall of tungsten.

Then three enormously loud explosions rocked the ship. Turning to look at the CCTV cameras that provided them with an exterior view of what was going on outside the ship, Captain Ding saw that two of the merchant raiders had sustained multiple hits from the Tomahawks. Less than a minute after the missiles impacted, one of the raiders exploded in a massive fireball as the ship was literally ripped in half. The two broken remnants of the ship were ablaze and sinking rapidly.

The *Nanjing*'s sister ship, the *Taiyuan*, suddenly exploded in a brilliant display of flames and smoke as two Tomahawks slammed into the side of the ship. While the *Taiyuan* hadn't been torn apart like the raider, it was nearly completely covered in flames from the impact.

Turning to his XO, Captain Ding yelled, "How many Tomahawks are left?"

"We have ten more inbound," the XO answered nervously. "They're three minutes out. Our next set of missile interceptors is engaging them now."

One of the operations officers shouted, "Raider Three is firing their first round of land-attack missiles now! They're also firing another round of anti-ship missiles at the American strike group."

"What's the status of Raider One? Are they still able to fire missiles?" Captain Ding demanded.

"Not yet. I just spoke with their XO. They took a hit to the forward VLS pods. It took out their interceptors and temporarily disabled their targeting computers. They're working on getting them recalibrated and ready to fire. He said it'll be at least five minutes before they can resume firing."

"Five minutes?! We may not *have* five minutes if they don't get their missiles operational," Ding shouted.

****

"Brace for impact!" yelled out one of the *Stennis*'s targeting officers as they watched the next volley of enemy missiles enter their point defense systems.

Even from inside the CIC, Admiral Parker could hear the Phalanx CIWS guns start to fill the air with tungsten rounds as they sought to create a wall of protection around the carrier. The RIM-7 Sea Sparrow and RIM-116 rolling airframe missiles speedily joined the fray as they sought out the remaining missiles converging on the carrier.

Boom, boom, BOOM.

The enemy missiles began to be swatted from the sky.

Bang!

The carrier shook violently in a thunderous rumble as it took a direct hit from one of the missiles. Admiral Parker gripped her chair as if holding on for her life.

This is the one time we need seat belts, she thought.

158

Several of the crew members fell over, despite bracing themselves for the impacts. The process repeated five more times as a total of six missiles rocked the ship. After the last impact, the lights briefly flickered off before the auxiliary power kicked on and the emergency generators took over the load.

"Damage report!" shouted Captain Grady.

The damage report board showed a host of red alarms from a couple of the decks. The lieutenant commander who was manning the reports as they came in responded, "Sir, we've got fires raging out of control on the hangar deck. Apparently, one of the missiles scored a direct hit on a couple of the strike aircraft that we had been getting armed with anti-ship missiles—with all of that fuel and those Harpoon missiles aboard, the blast caused a series of secondary explosions to ripple through the hangar deck. It's a dangerous situation down there because there's the possibility of even more secondary explosions. Damage control parties are working to get it contained, but they're asking for help." After he finished speaking, the lieutenant commander immediately went back to other tasks—he needed to do his best to redirect personnel from other parts of the ship to where they were needed most.

"What's the status of those enemy ships? Have we sunk them yet?" barked Admiral Parker over the growing chaos in the room.

The petty officer who was watching the cruise missiles as they converged on the enemy ships answered, "The next wave of Tomahawks is arriving now. This should finish them off."

It felt like an eternity as the next two minutes passed and they watched, as one by one, the remaining Tomahawk missiles hit the surviving Chinese ships. Eight more missiles scored hits on the enemy, either blowing the vessels up completely, or engulfing them in fiery blazes that would ultimately consume the ships.

Looking at the big board, Admiral Parker didn't see any additional surface threats heading toward them. The strike group had successfully shot down the remaining enemy missiles from the second wave. It had been a much smaller cluster of missiles than the first one, so it was a lot easier to handle.

However, prior to her strike group sinking the last of the merchant raiders, the raiders appeared to have fired off twenty-two land-attack cruise missiles, which looked to be headed toward the Hawaiian Islands. Sadly, the missiles had gotten out of their range to intercept them. All

they could do now was send a warning to the US facilities on the island, letting them know they had a cruise missile attack inbound.
****

From *Reuters Online*:

> The world continues to wait to see if conflict will erupt between the United Nations and the US. The American's New Year's Day raid to recover the *Nimitz* and destruction of two Chinese destroyers have increased concern that further military action may be inevitable.
>
> In the last week, a host of meetings have taken place between the American Secretary of State and the foreign ministers of nearly a dozen countries. Sources reporting on condition of anonymity have confirmed that the goal of these negotiations is to dissuade these nations from participating in the UN military force. The success of these efforts is unknown; however, several leaders continue to publicly call for Sachs to step down as President.
>
> Within the United States, polling shows that more Americans currently back President Sachs than President-elect Tate. The majority of the country's population supports the plan for a new election in November of 2022. However, no new Republican or Democratic nominees have come forward at this time.

****

Arlington Virginia
Pentagon
National Military Command Center

The Secretary of Defense, Chuck McElroy, had just finished reading the latest signals intelligence report from the NSA. They had uncovered a burst of attack orders issued by the UN military headquarters at the Canadian Forces Base in North Bay, sending out all sorts of orders to their ground and air force units to begin whatever military operations they had in the works.

Fortunately, the NSA was steadily decoding the encrypted messages about where these forces were being ordered to attack. As targets were being identified, the NSA was sending flash messages to the bases and military commands of an impending attack.

"Do we need to activate the COG?" McElroy demanded.

General Joseph Tibbets, the commander of US Northern Command and now all US forces in North America, chimed in via teleconference. He was just about to move his entire staff into the mountain at NORAD when the attack had happened, so they were still operating out of Peterson Air Force Base.

"We're not tracking any missiles or aircraft to the capital region yet, so I'm not sure if we need to initiate the COG," Tibbets replied. "However, if these UN forces are able to break through our air defense of the region, I can't guarantee that they won't try and attack Washington. What I can say is this—General McKenzie knows that if he's going to fight America, he has to take us out of the battle quickly. He knows his forces won't be able to go toe to toe with us in a protracted fight. He needs to try and score quick political victories to maintain UN support. I'd be willing to put money on the odds that he'll try and launch an attack on the Pentagon and the White House."

With a look bordering on exasperation, General Adrian Markus, the Air Force Chief of Staff, interjected, "As soon as we heard about the attacks on the *Truman* and the *Stennis*, we scrambled our ready alert fighters out of Langley AFB and here at Andrews. We also rotated the 325th Fighter Wing to Joint Base McGuire-Dix-Lakehurst in New Jersey last week. They're scrambling their F-22s to meet this threat, but we need to get the President to ground all civilian air traffic ASAP. If an air attack is imminent, then there are going to be a lot of missiles flying around, and I don't want a commercial airliner to somehow get caught in the crosshairs."

Thinking for a moment, McElroy weighed his options while at the same time trying to keep himself from being overwhelmed by the sheer volume of data and decisions being thrown at him. Between NORAD and the intercepts from NSA, he knew there were a massive number of forces being made ready to attack the US ground and air forces in the Midwest and Northeast, but he still wasn't sure whether they should activate the COG.

The continuity of government plan had only been implemented a couple of times since it had been created. Most recently, it had been put into effect on September 11, 2001, when the country was unsure if there were more terrorist attacks still underway. The challenge with the COG was that, once it became activated, it put a series of plans into place that were hard to stop or unwind—such as evacuating all essential government personnel, including the Supreme Court justices, members of Congress, and other principal government workers, to various underground command centers. It also placed FEMA in charge of vast swaths of the government for as long as the President decided to keep the COG in place. On the other hand, if the UN forces were able to land a successful blow against the Pentagon, Capitol Building or White House, it could have a profound impact on the government's ability to respond to the attacks underway.

Turning to look at the Air Force General, McElroy asked, "Are there any strike aircraft in Canada that can pose a serious threat to the capital region?"

General Markus thought about that for a second before turning to one of his aides. "Give me a moment to find out, sir," he responded.

While the general was tracking down the information, the SecDef turned his attention to Admiral Smith. "What's the status of the *Stennis* and the *Truman*?" he asked. It had been nearly an hour since both strike groups had been attacked.

Admiral Smith grimaced at the question. "It doesn't look like the *Truman* is going to make it. She's slowly losing the battle to stay afloat. At this point, we've managed to get her tied to several tugs, which are going to do their best to drag her as close to the shore as possible before she goes down. Our goal at this point is to get her back into shallow water so she can be raised at a later date if the damage control crews are truly unable to save her. I mean, a miracle could happen, but she sustained five torpedoes to her underbelly. The hull's broken."

"I can't believe we got sucker punched like that," McElroy remarked, clenching his fist like he felt like punching someone. He let out a huff. "How about the *Stennis*? I heard we sank a few Chinese ships in that engagement."

Smith nodded. "We did. This attack was truly unique. We'd never seen anything like it. The Chinese Navy essentially converted several large freighters to become floating missile platforms. They hit the

Stennis strike group with 340 anti-ship missiles. Our ships were able to shoot down 302 of them, but we still took thirty-eight hits across the strike group. The *Stennis* took a number of them. She was hit with nine missiles. The carrier's still afloat and in no danger of sinking, but she's knocked out of the fight for the time being. Nearly half of her aircraft were destroyed when several missiles hit the hangar deck. Admiral Parker, the strike group commander, has ordered them to return to Pearl Harbor for repairs.

"Before we sank the enemy ships, they managed to fire off a number of land-attack cruise missiles at Hawaii. The naval facility and the airbase at Hickam suffered some pretty bad damage—nothing that can't be repaired, but it certainly put our forces in Hawaii on notice that the Chinese have the ability to hit them."

"What about San Diego?" McElroy asked. "I heard they hit us there as well."

"They did," Admiral Smith replied. "Apparently one of the cargo ships near the Port of Ensenada had *also* been converted into a missile platform. They hit our naval facilities in San Diego with thirty cruise missiles and the Marine base at Pendleton with twenty. I'm still waiting to get a firm casualty count, but I can tell you it's going to be high, probably in the thousands."

McElroy shook his head in disgust. "Admiral, you need to make sure your captains are getting their ships out of port and ready to handle whatever's coming next. I want you guys to start looking at all Chinese freighters within striking distance of our coast and naval facilities to see if any of them have possibly been converted into these floating missile platforms. For all we know, the Chinese could have them strategically placed along our shores and facilities. We could be on the verge of getting hammered with cruise missiles and not even know about it until it was too late."

The SecDef stopped for a second before shifting topics. "We also need to hit that UN naval force in the North Atlantic. I'm concerned that they have that out there as a giant distraction and they're about to sucker punch us from somewhere else.

"Also, the President is going to ask me this, so I might as well find out—what subs or ships do we have that are in striking distance of the EU or Mainland China? When the President gets over here in ten minutes, he's going to want to know what we can hit them back with."

Admiral Smith smiled and pulled a sheet of paper out of his notebook. "We've got two subs currently in the Med that could strike at targets in Italy or France, and then we've got three subs operating in the North Sea off the coast of England that have been monitoring the shipping between Europe and Canada. All five of these subs have a handful of Tomahawks that could be fired at critical military and port facilities, which would have an effect on their ability going forward to ship additional reinforcements to Canada. As to Asia—we have two subs between South Korea and Okinawa. There's a single sub near Taiwan and another sub down in the South China Sea. We could easily fire off forty or so Tomahawks at some Chinese ports or military air bases if the President orders. It won't hurt their long-term efforts, but it'll certainly let them know that we're in the area and can retaliate."

Clearing his throat, General Markus interrupted their discussion. "Sir, I've got that answer for you."

McElroy signaled for him to proceed, and the others waited to hear what the general had to say. His response would largely determine if they should advise the President to activate the COG when he arrived.

"Our latest satellite pass, along with our own signals intelligence, has confirmed that the French have two squadrons of Mirage 2000N and D strike aircraft at the Canadian Forces Base Bagotville in Quebec. These aircraft have a combat range of 920 miles when equipped with their two drop tanks. The fighters can carry one Storm Shadow low-observable air-launched cruise missile, which has a range of 300 miles and packs a 990-pound enhanced warhead. If these aircraft penetrate our northern air defense zone, they could hit Washington with these missiles."

General Markus held up a hand to forestall any questions. "In addition to the Mirage threat, the Russians have also moved two squadrons of Backfire bombers to the Canadian airbase at Goose Bay and Cold Lake. While these aircraft are old, they are still very capable bombers that could deliver a number of land-attack cruise missiles. There's also a rumor that the Chinese moved their two operational H-20 stealth bombers to Cold Lake. Our satellites haven't physically seen them, but a human source we have near there said they had spotted what appeared to be a black winged aircraft land at the base several days ago."

"Why am I just hearing about this?" asked General Pruitt angrily. "If your fighters can't keep these guys off our backs, they're going to hammer my brigades before they even find the enemy."

"Aw, that's it—we're going to recommend the President activate the COG," muttered McElroy. "The UN's already hit us in sneak attacks in the Pacific and the Atlantic. I'm not about to gamble that they may or may not hit Washington with cruise missiles." He felt his frustration levels rising—he'd hoped to hit the UN forces first, but now they were reacting to them instead of the other way around.

He sighed. "When's General Peterson getting here with the President?" he asked.

"Their helicopter just touched down. They're entering the building as we speak," said one of the operations officers.

"Good, keep the helicopters warmed up and make sure to alert our aviation assets that we're going to need to start evacuating the city of key personnel."

A few minutes went by as the Pentagon nerve center issued a batch of orders to the commands all across the country, alerting everyone of the pending attack and warning that the COG might be implemented very shortly.

****

Bursting into the room, President Jonathan Sachs made his way to the center of the table in the NMCC, flanked by the Chairman of the Joint Chiefs, General Austin Peterson, and his Secret Service detail.

"Chuck, what the heck is going on? Are we in any immediate danger?" demanded the President.

The Secretary of Defense sighed and then he explained the situation as they knew it up to this point. Everyone else in the room then rapidly briefed the President on what had happened in the Pacific and off the coast of Virginia Beach. They went over the signals intelligence that the NSA had acquired and what was probably headed toward the US in the next twenty to thirty minutes. When the President had been fully briefed, Chuck presented his recommendation to activate the continuity of government plan, to which the President reluctantly agreed.

With the COG initiated, the Secret Service and the Capitol Police now had a big task at hand. It was going to be a lot of work to get the designated people relocated to a number of secured military command and control bunkers until they could reasonably ensure they were safe.

Turning to look at his SecDef, the President remarked, "That's it, Chuck. I've tried to keep things civil and bring a peaceful end to this crisis, but it's clear that these groups—or whoever is behind all of this—are hell-bent on destroying and tearing this country apart.

"You all briefed me on several plans to deal with this UN force a few days ago, and I agreed to them. I want you to do two things now. First, I want you to defend the country and our military forces from further acts of aggression by any and all means necessary. Second, I want that UN force destroyed. I want them either wiped out or captured. No rules with this one, Chuck. General Peterson—I want this force destroyed as swiftly as we can. Use our bomber force, hit them with cruise missiles, whatever it takes, but defend this country and repel this invasion."

The generals in the room all nodded in agreement. With the orders given and the President's guidance clear, they reflexively went to work on defending the airspace of the country and preparing a decisive counterstrike against the UN forces.

McElroy turned to look at the head of the Secret Service detail and the President. "Bill, I think you should take the President to Raven Rock and avoid Air Force One," he suggested. "The skies are going to start filling up with aircraft and missiles, and while the air would typically be the safest place to be, it won't be today."

Bill Cartwright, the head of the President's Secret Service detail, simply nodded. He let the other Secret Service agents know the plan, and then they headed back to the helipad without delay. Site R, or Raven Rock, was a nuclear-hardened facility and the alternate Pentagon location. It wasn't too far from D.C. by helicopter. There was also a tunnel and tram system that linked it to the presidential retreat at Camp David, should it become necessary to evacuate the complex.

Now that the immediate decisions had been issued, the President, along with most of his senior military leaders, boarded a series of helicopters that had arrived at the Pentagon to head out to Site R, while most of the civilian side of the government would be dispersed to the Mount Weather facility and the Olney Federal Support Center, ensuring the government could continue to function even if Washington was attacked.

Chapter 11
First Strike

20 Miles off the Coast of Long Island

The sky was gray and dark, almost as if Mother Nature knew that today was a grim day—a day that would shake the world to its core. Lieutenant Colonel Jean Pégoud's flight of four Mirage 2000D aircraft from Fighter Squadron 2/3 Champagne were doing their best to slip undetected past the numerous American warplanes taking to the air. When they'd left Bagotville an hour ago, the war had been only minutes old. Now, the sky above the United States was filling up with fighters and missiles from both sides.

When his squadron had gone airborne, they'd broken down into six flights of four. While they sought to penetrate American airspace, the other UN squadrons looked to create as much of a distraction as possible for them. It had been hoped, at least amongst the leading UN military commanders, that if they could land a decisive blow against the American government, they could get the remaining leaders to agree to end this war before it really got out of control. If things went according to plan, this fight could be over by the end of the day. If not—well, then, it could drag on for a while longer.

Looking at his instruments, Pégoud confirmed that his altitude continued to hover around twenty meters above the water. Before they'd gone airborne, his flight had topped off their fuel tanks from a refueler. They'd dropped to treetop levels for the high-speed race across the American border to the ocean.

Their initial flight plan took them across wooded forests as they made their way to Portland, Maine. As they got closer to the city, they shifted further away from the developed areas as they sought to avoid being spotted by civilians. When they made it past Portland, they flew away from land and began their long flight over the North Atlantic. His flight of four planes continued to skirt the coast, staying roughly fifteen kilometers off the shore as they made their way down to Long Island, New York.

Once they reached Long Island, they'd be in range to launch their Storm Shadow missiles at the American capital. If all went according to plan, they'd land a handful of these missiles into several high-value targets all along the East Coast. In one strike, they'd either decapitate the Sachs administration or send a powerful message to the political parties that they could be attacked, even at home.

Forty minutes went by in relative calm. Their threat sensors hadn't detected any enemy aircraft or targeting radars being aimed at them. They'd detected a collection of search radars looking further inland, toward the Canadian border, but they hadn't been shifted to look out to sea. Presumably. the Americans didn't think the UN aircraft would attack from this angle, but those pompous Yankees were about to learn the hard way that they shouldn't underestimate the French Air Force.

As they approached Long Island, Pégoud saw that they'd just crept into range of their missiles. His flight of four aircraft was going to attack the American Capitol Building. His second flight of four aircraft was going to target the Pentagon, his third the CIA headquarters, his fourth the NSA at Fort Meade, his fifth, two known Department of Defense buildings in Crystal City, right next to the Pentagon, and the last two missiles of that flight would target the White House. The sixth and last group was carrying the French-made MBDA Apache anti-runway cruise missiles. These four missiles were being targeted at the F-22 fighter wing that was now operating out of the old McGuire Air Force base in New Jersey. These missiles would deploy a string of cluster munitions designed to disable the runways, thereby putting a severe dent in the American Air Force's ability to provide fighter cover for their ground forces along the Canadian border.

Seeing that they were now in range of their missiles, Pégoud sent a quick message to his flight mates. "We're going to fly another five minutes to get our missiles a little closer to the target before we launch. When you see me rise up to launch, follow suit. Once we release our weapons, follow me back to base on the flight plan we talked about earlier."

He heard three separate radio chirps, letting him know they'd heard his instructions. They were doing their best to keep their radio chatter to a minimum to reduce the likelihood of them being detected.

Five more minutes went by before Pégoud armed his cruise missile. He turned on its targeting computer and made sure it had established its satellite link and was ready to navigate its way to the target. Once he was satisfied that the missile was ready to fire, he pulled back on his controller, gaining enough altitude to release his weapon. The aircraft rose up; when he'd reached two hundred meters above the water, he fired his lone missile.

He felt the weight of the missile drop from his aircraft, staying at his current altitude just long enough to see the missile's engine ignite before it zoomed off to make history. With his missile away, he promptly dropped back down to twenty meters above the waves and turned to head back to Quebec.

A warning flashed on Pégoud's screen. A naval search radar had spotted them.

Damn. That's probably an AEGIS destroyer, he thought.

He didn't have much time to do anything about this new information. Less than twenty seconds later, alarm bells blared in Pégoud's cockpit. Several missiles were headed their way. He switched on his electronic warfare pod and crossed his fingers, hoping that it would successfully jam the incoming missiles.

"Light your afterburners and fly as close as possible to the water," he ordered. Maybe they could get the missiles to lose them in the ground clutter.

Another warning alerted Pégoud that the missile was now less than ten seconds to impact. He broke hard to the right and climbed in altitude as fast as his aircraft would allow. All the while, his Mirage 2000D spat out countermeasures as his defensive systems tried their best to shake and confuse the incoming missile.

Pégoud heard a loud explosion down to his right. One of his flight mate's planes had exploded in a spectacular fireball—he didn't see a parachute. Without any time to process what had just happened, he banked hard to the left and dove back down toward the water.

As he rapidly approached the water, he pulled up hard. His plane ejected a couple more countermeasures, and he felt the plane lurch forward a bit as one of the missiles that had been targeting him blew up behind him. Checking his gauges, Pégoud breathed a sigh of relief when it didn't appear that he had sustained any damage. The immediate threats to his survival were now gone, but that AEGIS system had reacquired him and fired off two more missiles in his direction.

I don't know if I'm going to make it out of this, he thought.

A few more minutes went by as the American missiles tried to locate him in the clutter of the waves below and eventually flew harmlessly past his plane. When his warning alarms stopped blaring,

Pégoud looked around to see how many of his comrades had made it out. Not being able to turn on his search radar meant he had to try and find them with his eyes. Eventually, he caught the glint of an aircraft off to his right and angled his plane toward it. It took him a minute, but he managed to locate his comrade. Sadly, the other two pilots appeared to have been lost.

I sure hope this was worth it, he thought glumly. Those guys were good friends of his. In solemn silence, he and his surviving comrade began their long trek back to Canadian airspace.

****

Washington, D.C.
Capitol Building

"What do you mean we have to evacuate the building?" demanded the newly elected Democratic Minority Leader, Jesús Perez.

When the former Speaker of the House, Harriet Miller, had been ousted by the more radical wing of her party, Congressman Timothy Borq of New York had taken over as leader. But when he, along with forty-six other Democratic congressmen and twenty-six Republican congressmen, had fled across the border to join the Tate administration in exile, the Democrats had elected Jesús Perez of Texas to take over as their new leader. However, with that many Democrats defecting, the Republican Party had regained control of the Congress by default.

Those that were left in Congress saw the looming possibility of a civil war, and in an uncharacteristic move for the House of Representatives, they had tried to foster a spirit of unity and cooperation. Jesús had vowed that his wing of the Democratic Party would work toward developing a peaceful solution to this political impasse, and both parties were doing their best to reach across the aisle to keep the nation from being torn apart.

Undeterred by his new position of power, the Secret Service agent who'd just explained the evacuation to him looked at Congressman Perez with a fierce determination. "Sir, the President has initiated the continuity of government. We need to get you to the helicopter *now*. We've been given orders to fly you, along with the other members of the government, to Mount Weather."

Perez shook his head. *That fool Sachs is going to get us all killed if this conflict doesn't get resolved*, he thought.

"Fine, I'm coming," he said with a huff. "Lead the way, Agent." He grabbed his overcoat and briefcase and followed the man out into the hallway, where he saw many of the other members of Congress filing out of the building. As he neared the outer doors, Congressman Perez heard a number of helicopters approaching. Once he was outside, Perez immediately observed that there were four Chinook helicopters landing at various positions on the park. Fortunately, there was no snow on the ground to make the already chaotic scene unfolding before his eyes any worse.

The Secret Service agent who had been escorting him lightly grabbed him by the arm and proceeded to guide him toward the closest helicopter. Dozens of congressmen and women were running like their lives depended on it to the waiting helicopters and the soldiers waving them on. Suddenly, a loud wailing sound could be heard throughout the city—D.C.'s emergency alarm system was going off. It was the same sound you'd typically hear if there was a tornado warning, only this was the middle of January.

Abruptly, the Secret Service agent yelled at him, "Take cover!"

The agent rushed them to the bottom of the stairs and then to the left, so they could get next to the lower wall of the promenade. Perez felt his heart race as he wondered what was going on. Then, over the roar of the helicopter rotor wash and the blaring emergency alarm, he heard the unmistakable sound of a rocket engine. As a Marine veteran who'd served in Afghanistan, that was a specific noise that he would never forget.

A fast-moving object slammed into the side of the building where his office was located and blew up. The Secret Service agent threw him to the ground and placed his body on top of his as the ground and everything around them trembled violently from the explosion. Seconds after the first thunderous boom rocked Congressman Perez's world, a second and then a third explosion shook their very beings.

In the flash of a second, the agent was back up on his feet, grabbing Perez by the back of his jacket. "Run to the helicopters!" he yelled.

Congressman Perez barely had any time to even look around, and his only overriding thought now was to get the hell out of there. Despite being tunneled in on his destination, in his peripheral vision, Perez saw that one of the helicopters had been hit by some sort of debris and had blown up. There were injured people strewn all over the place.

I can't do anything about that right now, he realized. Fortunately, he could see that some of the nearby soldiers were helping the wounded up and bringing them to the other helicopters that were still operational. More helicopters were flying toward them on the horizon to help with the evacuation.

When the Secret Service agent reached the back of the Chinook, he practically threw Perez onto the helicopter. Then he ran off to go help some of the other injured congressmen. Now able to look back for the first time, the congressman saw where the three missiles had slammed into the Capitol Building, blowing out large chunks of the iconic structure. Fire, papers and debris floated back down to the ground.

Sweet Mary…we have to get out of here before we all die, he thought in horror.

Turning to try and find the crew chiefs, Perez saw that they were still outside the big helicopter, loading more people onto it. He made a beeline to the front of the Chinook, where the pilots were. Sticking his head into the cockpit, he yelled, "I'm the Democratic Minority Leader. You need to get us the hell out of here before the rest of us are killed!"

The two pilots looked at him, fear and anxiety written on their faces. The older pilot just nodded. He must have said something over his radio, because a moment later, the two crew chiefs ran back on board and the helicopter engines picked up in speed. A minute later, the Chinook lifted off, not quite full. Perez didn't care. In that moment, he'd realized he was too important to stay there waiting for a few more people to get on board and risking the helicopter he was on getting blown up.

When the helicopter had gained enough altitude for him to see more of the city, his heart sank. Not only had the Capitol been hit, he saw large plumes of smoke emanating from the Pentagon and two buildings over in Crystal City. When the Chinook turned around, his view changed to show the White House. Miraculously, it looked like the building had survived unscathed with the exception of what appeared to be a direct hit to the Eisenhower Executive Office Building next door. A hole in that part of the building had thick black smoke billowing out of what was now a massive charred ruin.

Congressman Perez felt rage well up inside him as he wondered how those who'd defected could attack the country so blatantly. *Senator Tate's taken this too far*, he thought in horror.

The next sixty minutes went by in a blur and a state of shock for each of the members of Congress who had made it onto the helicopter. They had no idea how many of their fellow legislators had survived, but one thing was certain—whatever cajoling Senator Tate thought he could do to help oust President Sachs was over. The country would now rally behind the President.

****

20,000 Feet Above Buffalo, New York

Major Dieter Gräfe, of the German 74th Tactical Air Force wing, heard the warning alarm blaring in his ear for the fourth time in five minutes.

I can't think with that stupid woman yelling in my ear, he thought as the female voice warned him of another missile warning. He summarily switched the alarm off.

He banked his aircraft hard into another tight corkscrew as a missile streaked right past him. Then he hit his thruster and pulled hard into another turn just as a string of tracer fire flew right across his canopy. Then he did something remarkable and unexpected—he hit his airbrakes, dropping his speed until he was nearly in a stall.

If his pursuer was using his guns on him, that meant the guy was practically right behind him. A fraction of a second after he did his maneuver, the American F-15E that had just been on his tail moments before flew right past him. He could tell the American pilot was caught off guard, because he instantly lit up his afterburners, trying to add as much distance and speed between them as possible.

Closing his airbrakes, Dieter lit his afterburner. He switched from missiles to guns and depressed the trigger. A string of 27mm rounds from his Mauser BK-27 cannon reached out and slammed into the right wing and engine of the American aircraft as it desperately tried to get away from him.

The F-15's wing ripped clean off from the G-Forces of the tight, high-speed turn its pilot was trying to make to escape Dieter's cannon

173

fire. Next, its engine caught fire and the plane now spiraled into a flaming circle.

A second later, the canopy of the F-15 blew clear of the aircraft as the pilot and his backseater were blown out of the plane, their chutes deploying seconds later.

With the immediate threat neutralized, Dieter looked around for the next enemy aircraft and reset his controls. Seconds later, his alarm blared again in his ear. "Warning, warning, warning!"

Where did he come from? Dieter thought angrily. He cursed as a missile appeared behind him. Unfortunately, he had no time to react, and the projectile slammed into his Eurofighter.

Suddenly all of his instruments flashed red. The female warning voice now shouted, "Eject! Eject! Eject!"

Here goes the neighborhood, he thought. Then he pulled the handle. Fractions of a second later, his canopy blew off and he was shot out of his flaming jet, only to see it explode seconds later. His chute hadn't even deployed when his plane exploded below him. Had he waited even a fraction of a second longer to eject, he'd have been blown apart with his aircraft.

Looking around him, Dieter caught a glimpse of what appeared to be an F-22 as it zipped past him, seeking out more of his comrades to shoot down. Seeing that he couldn't do anything more to contribute to the fight, Dieter looked around to see where he was. At this altitude, he had a good view of the ground below—it looked like he was still somewhere over the city of Buffalo.

He did his best to angle himself away from the city so he wouldn't get tangled up in the tall buildings. He knew he was too far away to float back into Canadian territory; his best bet now was to land in a farm field and do his best to hide or make his way back to the border. For now, his part in the war was over, and that thoroughly frustrated him.

****

20,000 Feet Above Buffalo, New York

Lieutenant Colonel Jeb Trace of the 43rd Fighter Squadron smiled with satisfaction when he saw the German Eurofighter blow up. That was his third kill in the last ten minutes. At this rate, he'd be an Ace in a few more minutes.

Damn, if those Europeans aren't trying hard to kill us, he thought angrily. He couldn't believe that it had come down to this. Just six years ago, he'd been stationed at Spangdahlem Air Force base in Germany. He'd trained with many of the very same pilots that were now trying to kill him and his fellow countrymen.

Colonel Trace radioed back to his AWACs support a few hundred miles further back. Without his eye in the sky, the fighters of his squadron were essentially flying blind. "Badger One, this is Hornet One. I need a target," he said.

"Hornet Flight, be advised that we're tracking four potential F-35s heading toward your location," the battle manager responded. "We're doing our best to get a solid lock on them. We're going to start mirroring our radar screens to you now. We'll vector you guys in to get closer to them and then go active with your radars for missile lock."

A few seconds later, Trace's radar screen showed him four soft blips that were believed to be the F-35s. Since these were American-made fighters, they knew precisely what radar frequencies to use to get a better lock on them—however, they'd have to get within twenty miles before they could activate their own search radars. It was a risky move, but they needed to clear the skies of these threats. Otherwise, the EU F-35s would tear up the F-15 and F-16 fighters that were going after the enemy SAMs and providing ground support to the Army below.

"Listen up, guys," said Lieutenant Colonel Trace over their close-in communications system. "This is going to be a tough fight, but we have to clear the skies of these F-35s. We've trained against F-35s in the past, so let's put that training to good use and show these assholes that no one messes with America."

It took them five minutes to reposition themselves over southern Canada to get themselves prepared to launch their attack. When they'd gotten themselves to within twenty miles of the small group of F-35s, they turned their active radars on, and sure enough, within the first radar sweep, all four of them lit up like Christmas trees. Trace's flight of four F-22s fired off their AIM-120 advanced medium-range air-to-air missiles at their unsuspecting foes.

Their prey immediately took evasive maneuvers as their suite of electronic defensive measures went into overdrive, spitting out countermeasures and doing their best to jam their missiles. Several of their missiles flew after the countermeasures, and others missed their marks entirely from all the jamming.

Trace's flight of F-22s fired off another volley of missiles. This time they opted to use their AIM-9 Sidewinders as they had finally gotten within knife range of the F-35s. From further away, it was a fairly even fight, but that close, their F-22s could easily outmaneuver the F-35s.

Now that they knew their stealth cover had been blown, the Belgian fighters activated their radars and returned fire with their own missiles. For the next ten minutes, the two sides began a deadly aerial dance of firing missiles and shooting their onboard cannons at each other, both without a lot of initial success.

Soon, a second group of American F-22s showed up to join the fray. At that point, the tide definitively turned and all four F-35s were shot down. Unfortunately, they'd succeeded in downing two Raptors in the process.

The next several hours would see some of the most intense aerial combat of modern warplanes since the Battle of Britain, with both sides dueling it out with their fourth- and fifth-generation fighters. The United States seemed to be gaining an edge in the fighting, but they were certainly taking a beating.

****

Goodells, Michigan
Goodells County Park

The sky was dark and ominous. Gray clouds had crept in, obscuring what had looked like a beautiful day when the dawn had first broken through the darkness of the night. Now it looked almost like it might threaten them with snow, judging by the dark bellies of the clouds. Then again, it was January in northeastern Michigan, a part of the state that often received heavy amounts of snow in the winter—so this wasn't anything new.

Brushing aside his concern for what the weather might hold, Sergeant First Class Rylie looked to his right and left. He saw that his platoon of soldiers from 1st Squadron, 9th Cavalry Regiment was about as ready as they were going to be for whatever was coming toward them. They were spread out every couple of meters, sporting their winter camouflage outerwear over their standard-issue universal camouflage pattern uniforms. None of them were thrilled about being deployed to Michigan in the dead of winter, let alone the possibility that they might actually have to fight in the cold and snowy weather of the upper Midwest—but here they were, tricked out in their winter gear, doing their best not to overexpose themselves and preparing to ambush whatever enemy unit was heading toward them.

When they'd first reached this position roughly an hour ago, they were all still wrapping their heads around the reports that a German-Dutch military unit had crossed the St. Claire River. Then they'd heard the aerial dance of death taking place high above them as fighters from both sides fought for supremacy of the battlespace. There was no way to know from the ground who was winning that fight—but they certainly saw and heard a lot of explosions happening high above them. They even spotted a few parachutes descending back to earth as they watched some of the fiery wrecks spin out of control before exploding on the ground.

Despite their personal misgivings at what they were being told by their officers and NCOs, the fighting taking place in the sky above them made one thing abundantly clear—whatever hope there was for a peaceful solution had apparently been dashed. Now it was time to prepare to meet the enemy and send them back across the border.

Once his platoon and squadron had deployed to their blocking positions scattered on either side of Interstate 69, all Sergeant Rylie could do was sit and wait. Sixty long minutes went by as the tension and anticipation of the unknown wore on their emotions.

After what felt like forever, Rylie heard a sound that was unmistakable. The metallic clanking gave away a tracked vehicle as it traveled down the paved road in their direction. Steadily, the sound grew louder. His pulse raced as his blood was flooded with adrenaline; the sense of fear and excitement only continued to build.

While he couldn't see what was heading toward them yet, he felt the ground quiver a bit as the sound of tank tracks echoed through the barren woods and the surrounding area. The soldiers of Rylie's platoon all knew this sound well, and it could only mean one thing—an armored vehicle that wasn't American was heading toward them.

"Here they come!" shouted Sergeant Mendoza over the radio to the rest of the squadron. Mendoza and two other privates had set up a listening/observation post about fifty meters in front of their position, so they'd have eyes on the vehicles first.

Rylie signaled with his hands to the Javelin crew just a few meters away from him to get ready. The soldiers manning the anti-tank guided missile nodded in acknowledgment and looked through the optical sights, lining the missile up on the target they wanted to destroy.

"Steady...wait for it," whispered Rylie over the platoon net. He knew as soon as he yelled fire, all hell would break loose and it'd be game on.

Seeing the armored vehicle come around a slight bend in the road, he felt his stomach tighten with fear and excitement. This wasn't like Iraq or Afghanistan, where he had first cut his teeth in combat—this was a battle against a fellow professional army, one he had trained and fought with as an ally in Afghanistan.

When the vehicle finally reached their preidentified kill box, he depressed the radio talk button, talking just above a whisper. "Fire."

Pop...swoosh.

Two Javelin anti-tank missiles shot out of their tubes and instantly took off for their targets, a German Leopard II tank and the Marder directly behind it. The tank was the lead vehicle in a five-vehicle convoy; along with the tank and the Marder were three Fuchs armored personnel carriers. This was clearly a heavy scout element for a much larger force still further back.

Seconds after the dismounted American soldiers fired their missiles, the 30mm Bushmaster guns on their nearby Stryker vehicles fired a string of rounds at the three enemy armored personnel carriers. Each of those vehicles could carry ten infantry soldiers, so if they could take them out now, that would be thirty enemy soldiers out of the fight.

At lightning speed, the Javelins crossed the four hundred meters of distance and slammed into the Leopard and Marder before the drivers or their commanders even had time to respond to the attack. When the first missile hit the tank, the Leopard's reactive armor detonated as it was designed to do, barely saving the crew.

The driver of the tank fell back on his training and automatically popped their IR smoke canisters as he deftly gunned the engine and steered the tank off the road. They were clearly trying to get out of their line of sight before they got hit with another missile. As they drove off the road, past the ditch and into the wooded area to the right, the tank commander turned the turret in the direction of Sergeant Rylie and his men.

The Javelin that had been aimed at the Marder scored a direct kill shot. The shaped charge exploded through the reactive armor as the second charge blew into the troop compartment. The detonation of the second charge inside the vehicle caused a massive overpressure inside the sealed compartment, and the top hatches blew open, releasing a short jet of fire as the ammunition and anti-tank missiles inside cooked off. The vehicle ground to a halt in the middle of the road and then summarily blew up.

One of the German Fuchs APCs swerved to try and avoid getting hit with more rounds before it crashed into a tree on the side of the road. The Stryker continued to light the troop compartment up with 30mm rounds in an effort to slaughter its human cargo before they could get out. The other Fuchs saw what was happening and immediately drove off the road to the left and popped a series of smoke grenades to obscure the Americans' view. When the two remaining vehicles stopped, their human cargo of soldiers piled out of the rear and hunted for targets to shoot at.

"Light 'em up!" yelled Sergeant Rylie over the company net.

Rylie and his men opened fire on the unsuspecting Germans with their M4s and M240G machine guns, sending a wall of lead at the enemy soldiers. Red tracer fire raked the German positions as the Americans laid into them. The rest of the Americans' sixteen Stryker vehicles also joined the fray with their M2 fifty-caliber heavy machine guns, their 30mm chain guns and two Mark 19 automatic grenade guns, showering the enemy soldiers with an unbearable amount of withering gunfire.

Pop...swoosh.

A third Javelin flew out of their lines and went straight for the German tank that was doing its best to help its countrymen and kill the missile crews that were still gunning for them. The tank's main gun leveled at the center of the American lines for the briefest of seconds before it belched smoke and flame.

BOOM.

BAM.

A clump of trees, dirt and underbrush exploded when the nearby Stryker vehicle blew apart. Several other soldiers close to it screamed out in pain as they were hit by the hot shards of flying shrapnel and debris, adding to the chaos erupting all around them.

A second later, the Javelin crossed the distance between the two warring factions and slammed into the rear side compartment of the tank. This time, the warhead punched right through the reactive armor, shooting its jet of fire and molten copper directly into the engine and ammunition compartments of the tank. The fuel tanks and ammunition locker instantly ignited and exploded in spectacular fashion. Flame shot up into the sky as the ammunition locker's blowout doors released the force of its contents up and away from the crew compartment. The entire back half of the tank completely blew apart.

Shocked and disoriented, the Germans who hadn't been killed outright tried to return fire and organize themselves as best they could.

While the Americans thought they had the Germans pinned down, one of their Stryker vehicles exploded in a massive fireball, throwing several nearby soldiers to the ground and hitting many more with shrapnel. Then a second, third and fourth Stryker blew up before they even knew what was hitting them.

The remaining American vehicles didn't wait to find out where this new threat was coming from; they blew their own infrared smokescreens and started shuffling around for a better-concealed position while the four anti-tank crews swung their Javelins around to deal with the new threat.

****

On a hillcrest a couple of kilometers away from the ensuing battle, Lieutenant Colonel Jeremy Kilgore watched as one of his squadrons caught a German scout unit by complete surprise. As he observed the battle unfolding, the sounds of war saturated the area. The popping sounds of M4s, the heavy reports of the fifty-caliber machine guns and the ratatats of the M240G light machine guns were intermixed with the heavier bass sounds of the 30mm chain guns reverberating throughout the area.

Three hours ago, before the war had officially started, Kilgore's regiment had been deployed to a campground near the small town of Emmett, just off Interstate 69. This placed them somewhat close to the US-Canadian border without putting them in a city. Up until a few hours ago, everyone in the regiment had been of the mind that this was all a show of force—that somehow, some way, calmer heads would triumph and this UN force on the other side of the border wasn't actually going

180

to invade. The prevailing thought amongst his unit was that enough people would have seen the 1980s movie *Red Dawn* to realize that the heavily armed populous of America wouldn't tolerate a foreign army on its soil. Clearly that logic hadn't won the day.

When the first shots of the war had been fired, Kilgore's scout platoon had been watching the US-Canadian border in a state of anxious boredom. It had been a huge shock when they'd received word over the radio that a Dutch or German Special Forces unit had taken over the Blue Water Bridge before the platoon of engineers could blow it up. The whole capture had happened so fast, they couldn't do anything to intervene and soon a large column of German and Dutch armored vehicles and infantry soldiers had bum rushed the bridge. At that point, the 9th Cavalry Regiment was ordered to set up a blocking force on both sides of Interstate 69 around Goodells while the rest of the brigade moved forward to assist them.

Lieutenant Colonel Kilgore had been zeroed in on the action taking place below him when he heard a noise to his left. To his surprise, Kilgore saw a couple of civilian vehicles driving up the hill where he was situated. A group of eight lightly armed citizens wearing hunting camo got out of their vehicles and pointed in the direction of the battle unfolding in their sleepy little country town.

Before they could even walk over to him and his headquarters staff, Kilgore turned to his operations officer and barked, "Get those civilians out of here! Tell them to go back to their homes and hide their weapons. I don't want them needlessly getting killed."

He then turned his back on them and returned his attention to the battle still raging.

Just as he turned to look at his soldiers fighting it out with this lead German element, they heard a new sound pierce the battlespace—there was a sharp crack followed by the boom of a tank gun. The first sound was followed by three more in rapid succession. To his horror, Kilgore saw four German main battle tanks that must have been traveling along the frontage road of I-69 veer off the two-lane road and begin to race through an open farm field toward his troopers. A second volley of red-hot rounds raced from their tank barrels right for his troops, hitting them with devastating effect.

Colonel Kilgore turned to his radioman. "Get me our aviation support *now*!"

The young soldier handed him the radio handset a second later. "I've got them," he said.

Kilgore grabbed the radio. "Arrow Two-Two, this is Darkhorse Six. I've got four German tanks hitting my right flank. I need air support ASAP!" he shouted.

While he was talking, the German tanks fired another volley into his soldiers and two more of his Strykers went up in smoke.

In response, a lone missile flew out from one of the Javelin crews toward the enemy tanks. Two of the German tanks fired off smoke canisters to try and confuse the missile's IR tracking sensor, and they swerved to one side. The missile just missed its target at the last second.

"Copy that, Darkhorse. Arrow Two-Two is engaging now," replied the Apache pilot. Kilgore could hear his rotor blades and other electronics in the background as the pilot spoke.

In the distance, not too far away, Colonel Kilgore could hear the sound of helicopter blades getting closer. A second later, four Hellfire missiles streaked across the sky over their position on the hill toward the enemy tanks, flying right through the enemy smokescreen to slam right into the tanks.

Boom, boom, boom, boom.

All four enemy tanks blew up, and the attack on his flank ended as swiftly as it had started. Scanning back to where his soldiers were, Colonel Kilgore sadly saw eight burning wrecks that had once been Stryker vehicles. Looking toward the enemy positions, he also saw several new black smudges and a few new explosions as the Apaches now flew ahead of his position, engaging whatever enemy vehicles and units they spotted just over the horizon.

Go get 'em, boys, he thought.

Just as he was starting to feel good about the situation, or at least like they were getting the upper hand in this tug-of-war, both Apaches exploded in midair. A second later, a sleek-looking fighter plane with black Iron Crosses on it flew fast and low over their position before banking hard to the north as it sought to gain more altitude.

"Holy crap! They just took out our helicopters, sir," shouted the radioman incredulously, shock and horror written all over his face.

"Get me Brigade!" yelled Kilgore.

Changing to the Brigade frequency, the soldier handed him the hand receiver again.

"Stable Six, Darkhorse Six. I just lost both of my Apaches to a pair of German fighters. We need fighter cover from the Air Force now!" He hoped someone with more rank on their collar than him could get him some higher-level support. If the Germans had fighter support, they'd make short work of the rest of his regiment.

Thirty seconds went by before he heard a response. "Darkhorse Six, Stable Six. That's a good copy. I've relayed your request to our forward air controller. They've got fighters inbound to our AOR. I'm retasking additional helicopter support to you now. We've got a sizable German unit moving out of Port Huron toward you. I need you to hold your current position for a little while longer. Is that understood?"

Colonel Kilgore shook his head in frustration. He'd just lost more than half a squadron, and now he had an unknown German force headed toward him? He needed more information than that.

"That's a good copy. Be advised, I just lost half a squadron's worth of soldiers and vehicles. I need additional support if I'm to hold this position."

Another minute went by. Presumably, Brigade was looking at the bigger picture, trying to see what forces they had that could be shifted around to help him out. Then the radio crackled for a second and beeped as the SINCGARs finally synced. "I know you're in a tough spot, Kilgore, but we're getting hit all across our lines right now. The best I can do for support is shift a battery of guns from the 16th Field Artillery Regiment. Do what you can and report back if it looks like the Germans are going to break through your position. Out." And with that, Lieutenant Colonel Kilgore was on his own.

How big is this force heading toward us? he wondered.

Shaking his head, he looked at his radio operator. "Give me 5th Squadron."

A minute later, he had his tank squadron commander on the radio. "Hammer Six, Darkhorse Six. I need you to shift your tanks over to grid MI 5768 5786 and be prepared to deal with enemy tanks. We just got hit by a platoon of Leopard IIs. Stable Six said we have a large German force headed to our position along I-69. I need you to move ASAP and get ready to deal with them," he said.

"Copy that, we're on the move."

A moment later, Kilgore heard from one of the six scout units he had scattered in front of their positions. "Darkhorse Six, this is Watcher

183

Two. We've got what appears to be two companies' worth of tanks moving down either side of I-69 toward your position and those four tanks you guys blew up earlier. Estimate their arrival in ten mikes. We've also spotted another column moving up Lapeer Road to your north. We're relocating to alternate site Delta. Out."

Lieutenant Colonel Kilgore wished they could have had more scout units. *Maybe we could have spotted that first platoon of German tanks and called in helicopter support earlier*, he thought.

Looking at the map of where Watcher Two was located, he saw they were in a good position to call in some artillery support on at least two of the German columns. With the armored force still four miles away, he really wanted to start getting some steel on them quickly.

Seemingly sensing exactly what Kilgore was thinking, his operations officer opined, "We could try and call in an artillery strike on those positions—at least let them know we've spotted them. Maybe it'll cause them to advance a little slower and give us more time to get our own tanks in position."

Turning to look at the captain, Kilgore nodded. "Get back on the horn with Watcher Two and see if they can relay some coordinates for the artillery. See if you can't disrupt their movement while we wait on getting some additional gunship support from Brigade."

For the next twenty minutes, a near-continuous roar of artillery rounds flew over their heads toward the enemy, and then they heard counterbattery fire as the Germans tried to locate and take out his artillery support. The artillery duel continued until the whistling and rumbling of the rounds pounding the earth was joined by the metal clanking of his tanks and the German tanks traveling toward each other.

The two sides continued their long-range duel with each other as they sought to maneuver around each other for a better angle of attack. Interspersed with the artillery and tank fire was the growing crescendo of small-arms fire as the APCs and infantry fighting vehicles ferried the German infantry soldiers closer to his own.

As the battle grew, it became clear that Kilgore's men were most likely facing a substantially larger force than they'd first thought. More and more enemy tanks and armored vehicles continued to show up, probing around his flanks and looking for spots to punch through and encircle them.

The radio crackled and then beeped, letting them know the encrypted radio had synced. "Darkhorse Six, Stable Six. I need you to begin a tactical withdrawal to the Capac Rest Stop. It's roughly sixteen miles behind your current position. I've got most of the brigade moved up to that spot. We're going to try and organize a counterattack once you pass through our lines."

Finally, some good news, Colonel Kilgore thought, letting out a deep breath.

"Copy that. Out." He was more than happy to get out of Dodge.

With their new orders, Kilgore sent out the word to his squadrons to fall back to their new coordinates.

Now comes the fun part, Kilgore realized. Disengaging from an enemy that was determined to kill you was easier said than done.

****

Capac Rest Stop

Colonel Chris Compton of the 2nd Brigade Combat Team, 1st Cavalry Division, cursed at the situation he now found himself in. Somehow, he had to do his best to stop this German horde that had crossed into Michigan.

His intelligence group had said they were facing the 10th Panzer Division and elements of the division Schnelle Kräfte—these were the Germans' crack armor and airmobile divisions. This meant his meager brigade of 4,500 soldiers was stuck facing down 25,700 Dutch and German soldiers until the rest of the division came online.

Colonel Compton examined the map again and swore. *How the hell am I supposed to stop two freaking divisions of troops with a brigade?* he thought. If General Pots didn't get the rest of the division up there ASAP, he and his men were going to be nothing more than a speed bump.

The chaos around him didn't help him to stay calm. Even though the brunt of the fighting was sixteen miles to their front, the sounds of war still reached them. The nearly constant thumping of artillery rounds from the regiment of artillery to their rear was making itself known to the enemy. The counterbattery fire was forcing his artillery regiment to change positions every couple of shots. From time to time, a loud explosion could be heard as one of their M109 Paladin self-propelled vehicles or one of the ammo carriers took a hit.

185

High overhead, he heard the screaming of fighters dueling it out in the skies above them, adding to his anxiety of not even having solid air support to rely on. With a squadron of A-10 Warthogs, they could make short work of this German unit, but not with Eurofighters smothering the skies above them. He was lucky they weren't pounding his own positions yet.

"Sir, it looks like Kilgore's regiment is coming in," said Colonel Compton's XO. He handed him a pair of binoculars and pointed down the two frontage roads on either side of I-69.

Taking the field glasses, Compton looked down the road and saw Kilgore's ragtag force. Several of his tanks had their turrets facing behind them while their smoke generators were going. The tanks were doing their best to screen for the Strykers, Bradleys and other vehicles that were trying to beat feet back to his lines. Compton knew that not far behind them was a much larger armor force, ginning up for a fight. Kilgore's regiment had bloodied them up, but now they were looking for revenge.

Colonel Compton handed the binoculars back to his XO. "Send a message back to Warhorse Actual and ask him what his ETA is," he ordered. "Ask if he wants us to fall back to position Golf."

Five minutes went by as his XO went back and forth with Division, trying to figure out exactly where the rest of the other brigades were and if they should try and hold their position for a few hours or fall back now before they were fully engaged. Part of the problem with allowing a force to make contact was trying to break contact later on. Disengaging from a determined enemy was not an easy feat.

Before his brigade became bogged down, Colonel Compton wanted to know if help was only a few hours away or if they were looking at a day or two on their own. If it was the latter, then they'd carry out a fighting retreat rather than try and stand and fight. Maneuver warfare was the best option when outnumbered and outgunned.

****

Saginaw, Michigan
City Hall

Mayor Peter Russo stared at the police chief for a second as he tried to take in what he had just been told.

"You're saying the UN force across the border has not only invaded, but they've captured Port Huron?" he asked incredulously.

"Yes, Mr. Mayor. That is exactly what I'm saying. My nephew is a captain in the National Guard. He told me the regular Army is going to fight it out in Detroit, but aside from the city, they're going to conduct a fighting retreat south. That means the rest of us up north are going to have to fend for ourselves," Chief Ryan explained, clearly despondent himself.

The fire chief chimed in. "So, we're on our own, then?"

"It would appear so," the police chief replied glumly.

Mayor Russo knew the situation was serious, but a part of him felt like this might be his moment to shine. He remembered watching that movie *Red Dawn* about Cuban and Russian soldiers parachuting into a western town and trying to take it over. He specifically thought of the scene where the scared kids had stopped at one of their dad's sporting goods stores on the way out of town, and the man had given them all the rifles, ammo, bows and arrows he could. Russo knew he could do the same.

"OK, listen up, people," the mayor announced. His voice was loud enough that it caused everyone to pipe down and focus on him. "Here's what we're going to do. For the time being, we're on our own. But that doesn't mean we're defenseless. While some may welcome the UN as liberators, I, for one, do not. This is America. And we govern ourselves."

Mayor Russo pointed at Chief Ryan. "I want you to find all the records of people who personally own a firearm, either at the police station or the individual gun stores and sporting goods stores, and I want them destroyed. We're not going to let these so-called peacekeepers know who in our community is armed so they can arrest them.

"Second, I want all the gun and sporting stores to work with you on handing out all the firearms and ammo you can to volunteers to defend the city. If the Guard and the Army are going to leave us to fend for ourselves, then by God, that's exactly what we'll do."

As the group continued to talk about what they could do to defend their town, the police chief got an urgent call over the radio.

"Chief Ryan, this is Patrol Five. I've got a visual on eight military vehicles heading toward town. What do you want us to do?" called one of the police officers.

The radio crackled again before Ryan could respond. "Ah, yeah, this is Patrol Eight. I'm out near the airport and I'm seeing hundreds of paratroopers landing. I don't think they're Americans. What do you want me to do?"

The room suddenly became quiet as all eyes turned to the chief and the mayor.

"Order him to pull back to the edge of town," said Mayor Russo. "Everyone else, grab a firearm and let's set up some sort of ambush for them when they enter town."

Everyone but Ryan got up without hesitation and headed toward the door.

The chief depressed the talk button on his radio connecting him with the police station dispatcher. "Shirley, tell Captain Lacey to grab every rifle, shotgun, pistol and all our ammo and head over to city hall. We're going to arm our citizens with everything we have. If things work out, we'll ambush these foreign invaders and then we'll be able to steal their weapons."

The next twenty minutes were tense. The city government used the alert system that was normally activated for an Amber Alert to notify the citizens of Saginaw of the coming foreign attack. The message asked anyone with a firearm to report to city hall and requested that all others lock their doors and remain inside.

As the armored vehicles approached the outskirts of Saginaw, Chief Ryan began to receive reports from the field on his radio.

"Sir, the UN vehicles have stopped and seem to be surveying the scene. They've definitely spotted the roadblock." Several civilians had parked their cars and trucks across the main roads in an attempt to slow or stop the invaders.

"Stay the course," Chief Ryan ordered. A few minutes went by in anxious expectation.

"Sir, they're moving forward now."

The silent anticipation was broken by the sounds of gunfire.

"Chief, we've got several of the armed civilians shooting at the vehicles with their hunting rifles. Unfortunately, the bullets are bouncing off the armor."

"Well, at least they should be receiving the message that they aren't welcome here," Ryan replied.

"The armored vehicles have successfully pushed aside the roadblock, sir," his man on the ground announced.

The chief could still hear the occasional gunshot, but they seemed further away. The defenders must have retreated to the homes and vehicles nearby, just taking shots of opportunity as they were able.

"Sir, the convoy has stopped. They're dismounting their infantry."

The battle for Saginaw, Michigan, population 196,542, had begun, and so had the battle for the heartland of America.

****

New York/Quebec Border
Town of Chateaugay

Général de brigade Joseph Joffre hoped the politicians knew what they were doing. His brigade was about to cross the proverbial Rubicon, from which there was no returning. No nation had ever invaded America and come close to achieving any sort of victory. His superiors had told him that this was not an invasion, but a liberation with widespread support from within.

Well, we'll see if that's true in about five minutes, he thought.

The sky above them was silent, almost peaceful. However, the rumbling of nearly 1,200 vehicle engines that had just started broke through any sense of calm. The 8,000 French soldiers of the French 7th Armoured Brigade were ready to roll. The UN operation to remove President Sachs from power was no longer a tabletop exercise; it was now a real military operation with real lives and military equipment involved.

Intermixed with their armored force were roughly 2,000 New York Civil Defense Force soldiers. These newly created American militia units would help the UN force to support their narrative that they were not an invading army but rather liberators working with Americans to help remove a tyrannical dictator.

The militiamen's native English skills and knowledge of the area would serve Joffre far more than any limited military capability they might possess. As such, he had them thoroughly integrated with all his units to provide the public interface with the civilian populace when the time came.

****

As his column of vehicles moved across the border, Joffre had his scout units begin to fan out. Their intelligence unit said there was an American brigade operating in the area, so the French general sent his forty-two Panhard Véhicule Blindé Léger scout vehicles, or VBLs, to fan out and smoke them out. Truth be told, it was an American battalion, not a brigade. The American force was scattered across much of upstate New York and parts of Vermont, so Joffre wasn't facing a full American brigade. Nonetheless, he wanted to find them and destroy them quickly so he could advance down the state and liberate New York City, which was his primary objective.

Ten minutes after his first regiment had crossed the American border, his own command vehicle finally reached the Customs and Border Protection building. It was incredibly odd to see this usually busy location, where officials would regularly search vehicles and trucks crossing back and forth across the border, reduced to a ghost town. However, it occurred to Joffre that the structure could give him some strategic advantage, at least for the time being.

"Seize the building," Général Joffre ordered. "We are going to turn this into a forward command post, at least until the rest of our unit is further into the state."

Once the building had been cleared and secured, Joffre went to work making himself at home. One of the first orders of business was getting the maps set up with the various regiments' positions. Next, his reconnaissance unit began launching their scout drones to help in the search to find these vaunted American units. In a few minutes, his staff was able to make contact with the Air Force squadron assigned to support his force, making sure they had ground support should they need it.

Steadily, things were starting to shape up. It began to look as if they were going to have an easy go of capturing New York City. That was, until they received a frantic call across the radio.

Joffre's lead units had finally made contact with the enemy. Now it was time to fix them to their position and let the Air Force pound them while his armor shifted around their flanks and destroyed them.
****

Lieutenant Tom Boyette of the 2nd Battalion, 14th Infantry Regiment watched as the first enemy scout vehicle passed through their kill box. It took a lot of willpower not to open fire and smoke 'em, but his platoon sergeant had insisted that if they let the scout vehicle through, they'd be rewarded with a much more tempting target to blow up and save their element of surprise. It was one of the best tactical advantages they had. Even though it was winter in upstate New York, that didn't mean they couldn't conceal their positions well. They had various winter camouflage nets set up at different angles to break up the silhouettes of their vehicles, and at the moment, they were all but invisible.

Boyette and his platoon sergeant were under no illusion about their prospects in this fight. They had to hit the enemy fast and hard, and then do their best to pull a Houdini and slip away to fight another day. Their unit's orders were to carry out hit-and-run attacks on the French force until the rest of their battalion could maneuver around to meet them.

Nearly ten minutes went by before they saw their first real target rolling down County Road 11, a column of six VAB armored personnel carriers supported by four AMX-10 RC vehicles, which were light reconnaissance vehicles that packed a 105mm cannon. This group looked to be about a company-strength-level unit. It was precisely the type of target they'd been waiting for.

Turning to look at his platoon sergeant, Lieutenant Boyette nodded, knowing the sergeant would make sure the platoon did what they were supposed to do.

Boyette's platoon had set up four Javelin ATGMs, and two of their Stryker vehicles had been outfitted with their own 105mm cannons. Two of the four JLTVs they had with them were set up with the venerable M2 fifty-caliber machine guns, while the other two had the M240 light machine guns in their turrets. They also had the only 105mm cannon equipped Strykers in the company, which meant they packed most of their unit's firepower. For a small platoon, they packed a big punch.

Pop...swoosh...Pop...swoosh...

Boom, Boom.

The surreal scene of silence and peacefulness was instantly shattered as the Javelins shot across the three hundred meters of distance toward the French recce vehicles.

"Fire!" shouted one of the sergeants in the turret section of the Stryker.

BOOM, BOOM. Bam, bam.

191

The two Strykers fired their 105mm rounds right into two of the six APCs, blowing both vehicles completely over onto their sides and off the road as they erupted into flames. The crews in both Strykers scrambled to reload the 105mm cannon so they could take out the next two vehicles.

Several voices yelled out in French, barking orders to their men as they sought to react to the American ambush.

"Let 'em have it!" shouted Boyette over the platoon net.

The two M2 fifty-caliber machine guns on the JLTVs opened fire on the remaining French armored personnel carriers. Unfortunately, hitting them would be a little harder because they had popped off some smoke grenades to obscure the view and were doing their best to find a concealed position on the side of the road.

Around twenty of Boyette's infantrymen also opened fire on the soldiers that were spilling out of the two APCs that hadn't been hit.

Ten seconds after the fight started, two more cannons opened fire, hitting the last two APCs and turning them into charred ruins. The few enemy soldiers that survived continued to fire back at the Americans, doing their best to lay down covering fire for their own comrades.

Seeing their work there was done, Lieutenant Boyette yelled over the platoon net, "It's time to saddle up and bug out!" They needed to get out of there and fall back to their secondary position before reinforcements showed up.

****

Tampa, Florida
US Special Operations Headquarters

Lieutenant Colonel Seth Mitchell kissed his wife and his two kids goodbye, not knowing exactly how long he'd be gone. After a tumultuous deployment to Kosovo in late October and early November, he'd been fortunate enough to spend a couple of weeks on leave with his family. However, he'd always known that come January, the ops tempo at SOCOM was going to go through the roof.

During the month of December, the command had been charged with figuring out how they were going to disrupt and attack the UN forces operating across the border in Canada and Mexico. However, when close to twenty percent of the active-duty military went AWOL and crossed over to the rebel forces in Canada, the strain on the Special Forces community increased dramatically.

SOF was sadly not immune to the crossovers either. Fortunately, the percentage of Special Forces going AWOL didn't exceed ten percent, but the fact that ten percent of America's most elite warriors had joined the ranks of the enemy still stung. It didn't help that a former JSOC and SOCOM commander had joined the Tate administration as his new Secretary of Defense. His appeal to the SOF community had netted them a few thousand operators from across the four branches of service. Most of the SOF that crossed over had come from the ranks of the Naval Special Warfare groups, and some had been Marines.

When Seth had reported into work at 0700 hours the day after New Year's, he'd learned of the early-morning attack on the carrier USS *Nimitz*. He'd fully expected the UN forces to respond. A little over a week later, when the carriers *Truman* and *Stennis* had been attacked, General Royal, the SOCOM commander, had immediately issued attack orders to the various Army and Marine Special Forces units that had already crossed into Canada.

****

As Seth walked into the command center that morning, he saw his boss, General Royal, in a heated discussion with one of the operations officers about something and made his way over to see what was going on.

"What do you mean one of our teams has gone missing?" Royal demanded angrily. "Were they captured or killed, or did they just decide to go AWOL as a team?"

"We've tasked a drone with trying to get eyes on their last location," the colonel responded. "They had reported receipt of the attack order and were moving to proceed with dropping the US side of the Ogdensburg Prescott Bridge. It's possible the UN had their own SOF team on our side of the border, ready to interdict our guys. We know the UN had forces there, and they would need to capture that site if they were going to cross into upstate New York."

General Royal shook his head in frustration. "Tell me our other operations are at least going well," he demanded.

The colonel smiled and nodded. "They are. One of the A-Teams just ambushed a convoy of French soldiers headed to the Thousand

Islands Bridge, just north of Fort Drum. Two more teams engaged a German column trying to cross into Vermont from Stanstead, Quebec."

"What about the air bases?" asked Royal. "I've got the Pentagon all over us about putting them out of commission ASAP."

"Two of the ODA teams reported solid hits on the Canadian air bases at Trenton and Kingston," replied the colonel. "The bases won't be down for long, but it should give the Air Force enough time to hit them with a much larger strike."

"OK, good enough," said Royal with a sigh. "Tell the other teams to keep the pressure up and keep those intel reports coming in."

His conversation with the colonel complete, General Royal turned around to move to his next task and realized that Seth was standing next to him. "Your bags packed and ready?" he asked.

Seth nodded. "Yes, sir. Just point me where you want me and tell me what you want me to do. I'm ready."

General Royal signaled for Seth to follow him back to his side office. After a short walk, Seth closed the door and they both sat down.

"All right, Colonel, here's the deal," General Royal began. "I know you want in on the action now that we're in a shooting war with this UN force. However, I've been tasked with a special mission by Homeland Security and I've selected you to handle it for me. We're going to set up a training facility at the Florida Army National Guard base. The SecDef has directed us to work with DHS to help them get this new Homeland Security force up and running. So, we're going to use the Camp Blanding Joint Training Center to begin preparing it to receive new recruits so we can get this program up and running."

Seth leaned forward. There was a small part of him that thought he must be one lucky SOB to get to stay in Florida, but the Special Forces side of him was highly disappointed to have such an anticlimactic assignment.

"In light of all the civil unrest that's been spreading across the country, the DHS Director, Patricia Hogan, recommended to the President and the SecDef that they create this new national security force to augment the local civilian governments across the country. This was decided a few weeks ago, but we were just officially tasked with implementing it as of two days ago. This will free the National Guard units up for federal service, especially now that hostilities have started.

I'm going to task *you*, and a few other officers and senior NCOs, with getting this new force ready."

General Royal held a hand up to forestall any comments from Seth. "Before you ask—this mission has been specifically handed down to SOF. This is essentially exactly what we train indigenous forces to do so this makes it an ideal SOF mission. Right now, nearly all of our teams are deployed to support our conventional forces in the north and south of the country. That means I have to peel off guys from our headquarters group to meet this need. Now, I've been told Homeland wants to grow this force to around 100,000 personnel. I have no idea what they plan on using them for when the crisis has ended, but for the moment, we have too many of our National Guard units tied down with providing protection of critical infrastructure facilities and supporting local law enforcement. The regular Army needs their combat power, and we've been tasked with getting this force trained up so they can be freed for Big Army to use."

The general sighed briefly before he continued. "You're going to have about two days to get things ready at the base before your first batch of recruits will start to show up. They've already received seven days' worth of initial training, medical in-processing, uniforms and all that other admin stuff from the Federal Law Enforcement Training Center in Georgia. So when they do arrive, they'll be ready to begin your training without delay."

Seth finally interjected to ask, "What kind of training are we supposed to provide these guys if they're going to be used in a civilian law enforcement capacity?"

Grunting at the question, General Royal replied, "You'll be responsible for providing these guys with basic rifle and pistol marksmanship, and training them how to properly guard a facility and defend it against an attack. It's basically a shortened four week version of basic combat training with the exception that, instead of military history, drill and ceremony and other stuff we teach raw recruits, you'll be focusing on making sure they have the basic skills needed to defend themselves, their comrades, and whatever it is they're assigned to protect. There will be a detachment of Homeland Security law enforcement instructors who'll handle a lot of the classroom and admin functions for you. You'll basically have charge of the recruits for ten hours a day, seven days a week while Homeland has charge of them for six hours a day, seven days a week."

General Royal could see the frustrated look of disappointment on Seth's face at this new assignment. The general paused for a moment before adding, "It's a safe gig, Seth—away from the fighting. You did a good job for me in Kosovo, so I wanted to throw you a bone and help keep you out of harm's way; plus, I need some good officers to help whip this group into something useful."

Seth thought about it for a moment. He'd nearly been killed in Kosovo, and he was at the tail end of his career. No one wanted to get killed in their last year of military service before they retired if they could avoid it.

Seeing he didn't have much choice with the assignment, he figured he'd try and make the best of it. "OK, sir. I can handle this," he responded. "We'll get this group ready for whatever assignment Homeland gives them."

With his new marching orders, Seth got his affairs in order at work and back home before he headed off to Camp Blanding, which was located just south of Jacksonville in the northern part of the state.

Chapter 12
Man Down

Maryland/Pennsylvania Border
Camp David

Marine One turned hard as it swooped low, flying just above the treetops. The warning alarms in the cockpit blared as the pilots deftly maneuvered the helicopters to the nearby presidential retreat of Camp David.

"Why are we not heading to Raven Rock?" the President asked Bill, the head of his Secret Service detail. The helicopter circled the helipad at the facility and prepared to settle down.

Turning to face the President, Bill replied, "Enemy fighters are in the area. One of the helicopters that were carrying a group of staffers from the Pentagon was just shot down as it approached Site R."

The President's eyes grew wide as saucers as he realized how close they had just come to dying. There had to be close to a dozen helicopters heading to Raven Rock at that moment.

As the helicopter landed at the helipad, a contingent of heavily armed Marines ran forward and fanned out to set up a perimeter around Marine One as it landed and promptly turned its engines off. A second later, one of the Secret Service agents opened the side door and scanned the area to make sure it was safe. He then nodded to Bill, who guided the President out of the helicopter.

The group then made their way to the Aspen Lodge, which was where the President and his family would typically stay when they bedded down at the presidential retreat.

Walking into the lodge, the Secret Service agents spread out and secured the inside of the building while the Marines established an outer perimeter. They relocated small squads to various defensive positions around the camp while they tried to figure out what to do next—the camp wasn't exactly a defensible position where they could keep the President long-term, but with enemy fighters in the nearby area, it wasn't safe to move him via helicopter.

One of the Marine majors, who was the commander of the Marine contingent at the camp, made a side comment to Bill. Despite the fact that the President had begun a conversation with General Peterson, the

Chairman of the Joint Chiefs, who was being fed information by phone from someone at the Pentagon, Sachs could overhear the major say, "Sir, we could move the President to the tram and get him to Raven Rock that way."

Bill paused as he thought about that for a moment. Then he cleared his throat and approached the President and General Peterson. "Excuse me, Mr. President. We're going to go ahead and move you over to the camp commander's quarters. The entrance to the tunnel is inside one of the rooms there. We'll be able to evacuate you to Site R via that route. It's a more secured location than where we are now."

The Marine major interjected, "I've got a platoon of Marines heading over here quickly. I recommend we wait to move the President until they get here."

Even inside the lodge, they could occasionally hear the scream of aircraft high above. From time to time, they heard a distant explosion, signaling that a plane or missile had exploded. The man who always traveled with the President, who had the nuclear football attached to him, looked uncharacteristically nervous.

The President turned to face his senior military advisor. "I thought this place would be safe, General. We should have gone to the PEOC at the White House."

Turning deadly serious, General Peterson pulled his cell phone down to his shoulder. "Washington was just hit by a barrage of cruise missiles, Mr. President. I'm still trying to get some details, but from what I've learned, they hit the Pentagon pretty hard as well as the Eisenhower Executive Building next to the White House. It was good to get you out of D.C., sir. They were clearly trying to hit you with one of those missiles."

Turning beet red, the President felt his temper start to flare. He smacked his fist on the table so hard that it was a wonder nothing broke and let out a stream of obscenities. "Whose planes hit us?" he demanded.

General Peterson shook his head. "I don't know yet. It doesn't matter, Mr. President. We need to get you to the bunker, where we can find out what in the world is going on and organize a better response."

Just as the President was about to demand that they get a move on, the Marine major and Bill both put a hand to their earpieces as if they were trying to hear a message better. Bill's face became a bit pale as he looked at the Marine and just nodded.

Bill turned to General Peterson and the President. "We have to go now. We've got movement on the perimeter."

"What the hell? Do they know we have the President here?" demanded Peterson. He looked nervously over at the naval officer who was carrying the nuclear football.

"I don't know...let's get going," Bill replied. He motioned for the other agents to start moving.

The group headed for the door that led to the driveway. As soon as they exited the building, the President saw that two of their uparmored SUVs had just arrived. The vehicles would take them the short distance to the camp commander's quarters, where the underground tram was located.

BAM, boom, BAM. Ratatat, ratatat, ratatat!

Out of nowhere, a series of loud explosions shook the ground, and machine guns roared to life. The President felt as though his stomach dropped out of his body.

****

"Engage them now. Breach the perimeter!" shouted the German KSK commander, Oberstleutnant Rainer Hartbrod, over their secured radios.

Thump, thump, thump.

The mortar team started dropping rounds in the direction of the Aspen Lodge and pool area. Four separate squads of German Kommandos then rapidly advanced on the perimeter of the presidential retreat.

Several loud shots rang out as their snipers engaged the roving patrols of Secret Service and Marine guards on the perimeter. In seconds, the crescendo of gunfire picked up pace until it became a near-continuous roar of smaller popping sounds. Small-caliber pistols, American M4s, German HK416s, and the heavier chattering sounds of the German MG5 short-barreled light machine guns all added to the growing cacophony.

Shouts in German echoed through the barren woods as the various Kommando teams coordinated their firing lanes and covering maneuvers as they advanced on the small pockets of defenders at the perimeter.

Running to keep up with his forces, Oberstleutnant Hartbrod instinctively ducked just as a string of rounds flew right over his head.

199

Pieces of a tree rained down on him as a Marine rifleman laid into his position.

"Lay down suppressive fire! This position is under attack!" he shouted to several of his soldiers nearby.

They heard his orders and instantly jumped up with their rifles at the ready, charging the two Marines that had pinned him and one of his other soldiers down.

"Grenade!" one of them shouted. A few seconds later, they heard a bang.

"They're flanking us!" shouted one of the Marines. That yell was followed by a long string of automatic machine-gun fire.

Sticking his head above the fallen tree trunk where he had taken cover, Hartbrod brought his rifle to bear and sighted in on a Marine who appeared to be coordinating their defense. He depressed the trigger and swiftly sent several well-aimed rounds into the man's chest. The Marine fell backwards from the hit and didn't move or attempt to get back up.

"Fire!" he shouted as his guys bounded forward. Two guys laid into the American Marines, sending as much lead at them as they could, while four other guys advanced—two on each side of their flanks. Then those attackers fired a magazine's worth of ammo at the American positions while the guys in the center advanced.

In short order, the German Kommandos had finally breached the perimeter of the camp along Park Central Road, near the skeet shooting range.

Crump, crump, crump.

Hartbrod's mortar team fired off their third volley of mortars into the camp, hoping to cause further chaos and distract the defenders so they wouldn't know exactly where the main attack was coming from.

With his first team advancing through the skeet shooting range, Hartbrod sent a message to his second team to advance swiftly and follow through the newly created hole in the perimeter before additional help could arrive and box them in.

Hartbrod pulled a flare gun out of his trouser pocket. He aimed it high in the air and fired off the blue flare, signaling that they had breached the perimeter.

Seconds later, more gunfire erupted—this time from the opposite side of the presidential retreat. Hartbrod smiled. The Russian Spetsnaz team had started their attack.

The entire camp was now a chaotic melee of machine-gun fire, explosions and shouting in English, German and Russian as three highly trained groups of soldiers and Secret Service agents fought over the life of the American President and control of the nuclear football.

****

"Quickly! We have to move!" Bill shouted. He threw the President into the back of the uparmored Suburban SUV with a force that was almost violent. A handful of Marines ran ahead of the vehicle on either side of the road.

Machine-gun fire seemed to be erupting everywhere and nowhere all at once. The angry shouts for help in English and foreign languages and the noise of constant shooting echoed off the barren trees, intermixed with the sudden explosions that rocked the area.

"Holy crap, those are mortars!" shouted the driver. One of the agents jumped into the back of the vehicle with the President. Hot pieces of shrapnel bounced off the armor and splintered one of the passenger windows.

The naval officer with the nuclear football had been thrown in the chase vehicle, along with the Chairman of the Joint Chiefs. With everyone in the vehicles, the driver floored it and zoomed past the group of Marines who were doing their best to run ahead and clear a path for them.

Just as they rounded the corner in the road, placing them no more than one hundred meters from the building they needed to reach, a loud metal crunching sound overwhelmed their senses. A string of bullets had pounded the side of the armored vehicle.

Then the bulletproof glass of the windshield was suddenly turned into a series of spiderwebs. A cluster of bullets had pounded the brittle outer layer, shattering the outside of the window in circular patterns around the points of impact. So far, the inner layer of the windshield continued to absorb the energy of the impacts, but even the most bullet-resistant glass in the world would eventually reach a breaking point.

"Hold on!" shouted the driver. He instinctively ducked down a bit behind the steering wheel as he gunned the vehicle for all it was worth. The engine roared. Bill began to worry that the many bullets hitting the front of the vehicle would punch their way through the front armor and into the engine block.

As they zipped past whoever had been shooting at them, the side of their vehicle got stitched up by more rounds. Bullets peppered the armored doors and thudded into the bulletproof glass windows, partially shattering them but not yet breaching the vehicle.

Behind them, the squad of Marines that had been chasing after them down the road opened fire on the attackers, doing their best to provide covering fire for the Secret Service.

The vehicles came to a grinding halt less than twenty feet from the commander's quarters as their engine suddenly gave out and their tires were completely shot to pieces. Once the vehicle stopped moving, four Marines spilled out of the building, killing three of the attackers who were continuing to empty their magazines into the President's vehicle.

More and more Kommandos converged on the building, tearing into the Marines who were doing their best to create a perimeter.

The driver of the vehicle looked at Bill. "I'll cover you!" he shouted. "Get the President out of here!"

The man then pushed with all his body weight against the badly damaged driver's-side door and hopped out of the vehicle. He quickly brought his FN P90 submachine gun to his shoulder and sprayed two surprised attackers at near point-blank range. With those assailants down, the agent swapped out the magazine and sprinted to the other side of the SUV to help cover the President.

One of the Marines nearby yelled, "Frag out!" He threw a grenade in the direction of several enemy soldiers who were doing their best to flank their position and get at the President.

The enemy Kommandos broke cover as they sought to dive away from the grenade. That brief moment of weakness was all the Secret Service driver needed to get a bead on one of them and lay into the enemy soldier with a short burst of fire. The Kommando fell to the ground like a dropped doll.

"Get the President inside!" yelled one of the agents. Three more Secret Service agents spilled out of the chase vehicle along with General Peterson and the naval officer, who was clutching the nuclear football for all his worth. The man ran like an All-Star halfback as he clutched at the leather-bound case. Dirt, pieces of pavement, snow and ice kicked up all around him as he ran for the door to the building that had been left open by the Marines.

"Covering fire!" shouted one of the Marines. Three of them jumped up from behind their covered position. They proceeded to empty their magazines at the attackers while two of the Secret Service agents joined in. Bill and the remaining three agents did their best to run with the President to the open door, shielding him with their bodies.

The enemy soldiers must have seen what was happening. They increased their fire and aimed right for the agents who were rushing the President to cover. One of the agents was hit multiple times in the back and stopped running. The body armor he wore was no match for the armor-piercing rounds the assault teams were using. In a desperate last act, he tried to straighten himself up so his body would continue to absorb more rounds and prevent them from hitting the President.

A somewhat large projectile flew past them and slammed into the wall of the building, ten feet to the left of the door, and exploded. The force of the blast knocked them backwards to the ground, showering them with shrapnel and debris. A huge chunk of the building was suddenly a gaping hole as fire and wreckage rained down on the ground.

****

The group of Marines that had been running down the road behind them had finally caught up to them and opened fire on the attackers from the rear, catching them in a nasty crossfire from their front and rear positions.

One of the Marines saw the mass of bodies lying in the open area of the road, just in front of the building, and knew the President was among them, along with the Chairman of the Joint Chiefs. He ran toward them, firing his rifle the entire way.

When he reached the pile of bodies, he threw two of the gravely wounded Secret Service agents off the President. He looked down and saw Sachs. He had a wild and bewildered look of fear and anger on his face, blood streaking down his cheeks and from his ears. The Marine reached down and grabbed the President by his jacket, practically yanking him off the ground and to his feet. He shoved the President hard toward the door, doing everything in his power to get Sachs inside the safety of the building while making sure his body, which was covered in his body armor, was between the President and the Kommandos trying to kill them.

203

Bullets continued to whip all around the two of them as they ran the last twenty feet to get inside the commander's quarters. Another Marine from inside the structure jumped out and fired a string of rounds at an attacker behind them as he yelled, "Hurry up!"

The two of them jumped into the building and ducked down behind the wall as several bullets slapped into the structure, punching more holes through the wood. Suddenly, dozens of rounds hit the building, breaking the glass windows and showering them with chunks of broken glass and fragments of timber, plaster and drywall. The structure was being shredded by the relentless torrent of bullets.

"Where's General Peterson?" shouted the President as he finally collected his wits.

"Crap!" yelled one of the Marines. He stuck his head around the door to look back at the pile of bodies twenty feet away. "I see him. He's injured. Cover me!" shouted the Marine. He jumped back to his feet and ran at full speed for the general. Several of his buddies fired at the attackers as he rushed forward.

Bullets continued to fly at an enormous rate. A moment later, the Marine entered the door of the commander's quarters with General Peterson's arm over his shoulder. It was almost as if a guardian angel had somehow prevented them from getting hit during their mad dash back.

As soon as they made it back inside, they heard more shouting, and the volume of enemy fire seemed to increase. The attackers were clearly closing in on the building. Soon, they would breach it.

Crump. A grenade went off against the wall of the building, blowing even more holes in the structure and rattling them hard inside.

"We have to get the President to the tram *now*," shouted the only Secret Service agent who had made it into the building. He was helping the naval officer with the nuclear football move down the hallway toward the secret room with the tunnel.

"You men cover the door and the hallway. I'll help General Peterson," the President said. He pulled the man's arm over his shoulder and the two of them moved with a purpose down the hallway after the Secret Service agent.

"Hang in there, Austin. You aren't dying on me today," the President told his friend as they walked.

The three Marines left alive in the building were doing their best to shoot out of the windows at the attackers. The Kommandos had now made it up to the two armored SUVs, having killed the remaining Secret Service agents and Marine guards outside the building.

The group of Marines attacking from the rear section were doing their best to break through the attackers and get to the building, but they appeared to be heavily engaged and unable to get to their position. It was now up to these three Marines inside to hold the building long enough for the President to get away.

****

The lone surviving Secret Service agent reached the entrance of the secret room that led down to the tunnel. He entered a passcode, which unlocked the door. Once it was opened, the four of them went inside and the agent turned around and pulled the door closed. He hit another code and the entrance automatically latched shut—several cylinder locks dropped into the top and bottom of the metal door, making it nearly impossible to easily breach.

A motion-activated light system came on and illuminated a set of stairs. The four of them walked down, with the echoes of gunfire and shouting still audible through the door, adding to their sense of urgency.

Because of General Peterson's injuries, it took them a few minutes to get down to the bottom of the landing. When they walked into the next room, more lights turned on and they saw a tram-like vehicle sitting on a set of rail tracks. The inside had a total of ten seats. The Secret Service agent helped the naval officer with the football get strapped in while the President helped General Peterson. Then the Secret Service agent and the President took care of their own seat belts.

Looking at Sachs, the agent grinned and said, "Hold on, Mr. President. This is a very fast train ride."

With that, he turned the system on. The tracks in front of them lit up. The agent applied power to the tram, and in the blink of an eye, the vehicle shot off at a speed of seventy miles per hour down the long, dark, damp tunnel. It would take them less than five minutes to travel the seven miles underground to the Raven Rock facility, where they would hopefully be safe.

****

Standing outside the building the Americans had rushed the President into, Oberstleutnant Rainer Hartbrod saw bodies everywhere. He had to give the Americans credit—they'd fought like devils against his men. They'd killed far more of his comrades than he'd thought possible, considering how few Marines and Secret Service agents were at the camp.

"My men are still clearing the rest of the camp and the other buildings," said an imposing Russian colonel. "Did they get the President into the tunnel?"

Sporadic gunfire continued to ring out as the few remaining defenders were pinned down and finished off. Neither side was taking prisoners.

Smiling at the destruction their forces had just caused, Hartbrod turned to his Russian counterpart. "They did. It's time to get out of here. Mission complete."

The Russian Spetsnaz nodded in agreement. He spoke a few commands into his radio, letting his nearby vehicle team know it was time to come pick them up. Now they needed to do their best to fade away into the shadows and get ready for their next operation.
****

El Paso County, Colorado
NORAD Facility

General Joseph Tibbets was not having a good day. As he walked into the main command room in the NORAD facility, he saw his worst fear starting to play out. Rather than launching the first attack and seizing the initiative from the enemy as they had planned to do in forty-eight hours, the UN force, under General Guy McKenzie, had beaten him to the punch. The aerial picture across the northern border of the country was starting to fill with combat aircraft. Worse, they had just received reports from the Navy that one of their carriers off the coast of Virginia was under attack, and a second carrier in the Pacific was reporting that they were being assailed as well.

I wasn't even supposed to be here, Tibbets found himself thinking.

Just five months ago, General Tibbets had been on the verge of retiring after thirty-four years of service in the US Army. At that time, he had been tired and, more importantly, dejected after a tough assignment as the last ground commander for operations in Afghanistan and Syria as the US concluded those wars. He had felt like a lot of business had been left undone, but he'd also agreed that it was time to leave. There wasn't a winning solution to those wars.

When he returned from that overseas assignment, he had been assigned to Fort McNair and the United States Army Center of Military History. He was supposed to spend the last year of his time in the Army writing up the final lessons learned from the wars and postulating what could have been done early on and throughout the war to change the outcome. For millennia, philosophers had thought of war as an extension of a political disagreement; however, in the day and age of non-state actors, that belief didn't always hold true. Going back through all of his experiences honestly left him with more questions than answers, and he struggled with how to write or conclude his report.

General Tibbets's retirement had been set for November 11th— Veterans Day. He'd figured he'd end his military career on a day that honored the soldiers he'd fought with and led for the last thirty-four years. Then, the world around him had begun to implode as the nation he'd served so dutifully became rocked by terrorist attacks and marred by a coup d'état, and his retirement had been rescinded.

Shortly before Christmas, Tibbets had been summoned to the White House and found himself sitting in the Oval Office with the President and the Chairman of the Joint Chiefs. They told him what was happening and then asked him one simple question: "How would you defend the country against the forces arrayed against America?"

He'd spent the next two hours outlining his strategy and vision for how he'd handle the UN force and, more importantly, the Chinese. A couple of days later, he'd been informed that he would replace the US Northern Command, Commanding General and would be placed in charge of the defense of North America.

It was a daunting task, further complicated by the fact that he had very little time to get himself familiar with his new command and to get the forces needed to win ready. However, like many generals who'd been given an insurmountable task, he determined that he would do his best and let the chips fall where they may.

The red lights throughout the control room began to flash, and the missile launch alarms blared, pulling General Tibbets back to the present reality. One of the numerous screens zoomed in on a position just south of California, off the Mexican coast.

"What type of missile just launched?" he bellowed. He rushed over to the Air Force technical sergeant who was monitoring that particular station.

"It appears to be a ship-launched cruise missile, sir." There was a brief pause as he looked at more of the data. "The missile count is now rising above twenty. They appear to be heading toward our naval facility in San Diego."

The missile alarm blared again as a new launch site was identified.

"I'm showing a missile launch directed at the *Stennis* Carrier Strike Group from that cluster of Chinese ships there," announced an Air Force captain who was manning one of the other stations.

"Send flash warnings to those ships and naval facilities that we have confirmed cruise missile attacks heading for them," General Tibbets ordered.

Turning to Brigadier General Estrada, who was the watch commander for the floor, Tibbets ordered, "Bring us to DEFCON Two and alert the national military command center that we have confirmed cruise missile attacks underway against our capital assets and facilities. I want all alert aircraft across the country scrambled and additional air assets to get airborne. Send a flash message to the FAA that effective immediately, they're to ground *all* air travel across the United States until further notice. All inbound flights to the United States are hereby denied unless the aircraft doesn't have enough fuel to land somewhere else."

With all eyes now looking at him, he added, "For better or worse, people, our country is being invaded! It's time to strap in and get ready for the fight of our lives."

The official proclamation by the commander of all forces in North America clearly sent a shiver down the spine of everyone in the room. Not since the War of 1812, more than two hundred years ago, had a foreign power invaded America.

Fifteen tense minutes went by. The men and women in the command center watched as dozens upon dozens of US fighters took to the skies to meet the foreign aggressors, when suddenly, another missile alarm blared, this time alerting them of a missile attack off the coast of New York.

208

"Where the hell did *those* missiles come from?" demanded General Tibbets as he made his way over to the officer covering the East Coast.

Stammering for a minute, the officer replied, "They appear to have been launched from some strike aircraft."

"We're getting a flash message from the destroyer USS *Oscar Austin*. They're reporting contact with a group of Mirage 2000 fighters that just appeared off the coast of Long Island. They said the aircraft just fired off sixteen missiles. We're still trying to figure out where they're headed."

"Someone figure out what kind of missiles those fighters just launched and then start calculating what high-value targets are in range of those missiles," Tibbets ordered.

Then he turned to one of his Army officers. "Major, do we have any missile defense assets in the D.C. metro area, in case those missiles are headed there?"

After taking a deep breath, the major replied, "The only assets we have in that area are the localized ones at the White House and the Pentagon. But that system can only engage, at most, eight targets. It's really only meant to attack a single close-in air threat, not enemy missiles."

"Crap! What about any naval assets? Or do we have any fighters that can engage them?" asked Tibbets.

"We can have the alert fighters out of Langley Air Force Base see if they can engage them. Although they are probably only armed with their standard air-to-air missiles, so I'm not sure how much luck they'll have," explained the Air Force major. He then reached for a phone to call the base command post to see if they could get in touch with those aircraft.

A couple of minutes went by before one of the Air Force weapons analysts waved to get Tibbets's attention. He quickly marched over to the young woman, who seemed to be chomping at the bit to speak.

"Sir, I think I know what kind of missiles those are," she explained. "The *Oscar Austin* said the fighters that launched them were Mirages. So that means they're French fighters. The Mirage 2000D can carry one Storm Shadow cruise missile. The missile comes in three variants. One is nuclear, but since they fired sixteen of them, I believe we can rule out a nuclear attack as it wouldn't make sense to fire sixteen of them at the same target. That leaves the other two types. One is a conventional, enhanced high-explosive warhead, and the other is an anti-runway cluster munition."

"What about targets? The missiles have dropped down to wave top levels once they were fired. Where do you think they're heading?" he asked next.

She furrowed her brow. "If I had to guess, I'd say they're sending them to D.C. This whole UN mission is to remove the President, so what better way to remove him than to kill him while he's in the White House or a meeting at the Pentagon? It'd send a powerful message to the world if they could successfully blow up the White House or hit some other high-value targets in the capital." She spoke almost nonchalantly, as if she was describing the latest fictional thriller she had read and not a pending attack that was underway.

The sudden realization that the President might be the target of the missile attack caused General Tibbets to reach out to find something to steady himself. He looked around for his watch officer. "General, where is the President?" he asked, barely managing to get the words out.

Brigadier General Estrada walked over to find the red phone that connected them directly to a twenty-four-hour operator in the Secret Service office. That contact would know where the President was one hundred percent of the time. As soon as the person on the other end picked up, he handed the receiver to General Tibbets, who immediately snatched it.

"This is General Tibbets at NORAD. Where is the President right now?" he asked gruffly.

A short pause on the other end ensued before the voice on the other end replied, "This is Agent Lorain. He's in a meeting at the Pentagon. What's going on, General?"

"Agent Lorain, a cruise missile attack is headed to D.C., and we believe the President may be the target. You need to get the President out of the city now!"

He heard a stream of cursing on the other end before the agent asked, "Is it safe to get the President to Air Force One, or do we need to evacuate him to one of the other bunkers?"

"One moment, Lorain, while I find out what the air picture of the area looks like," Tibbets responded. He placed his hand over the lower receiver.

210

"Is it safe to have the President go airborne, or do we need him to go to ground?" he shouted out for anyone in the room to answer.

General Estrada looked at that threat picture and turned back to Tibbets and shook his head. His face was pale. "Sir, there are hundreds of enemy fighters crossing the US border now. They're either engaging American planes or forming up to attack. We can't guarantee one or more of those clusters of fighters wouldn't go after Air Force One if they saw it get airborne. It would be the prize of a lifetime to shoot it down."

"How would they *know* it was going airborne?" demanded Tibbets. He really wanted to get the President in the air so he could stay mobile.

General Estrada, who was from the Air Force instead of the Army like Tibbets, explained, "Sir, the enemy has their own AWACS aircraft up. Plus, you can bet they have some spotters watching Andrews to see if they can spot that big fat presidential plane taking off. I wouldn't have him go airborne, not yet."

Nodding at the logic, General Tibbets uncovered the mouthpiece to the phone. "Lorain, it's our recommendation that the President go to ground. Do *not* go airborne. Not yet. Can you get him to Site R?"

There was a short pause. "We'll scramble Marine One and get him to Raven Rock. Please keep us apprised if the air situation changes while we get him there."

With the President's immediate situation taken care of, Tibbets was ready to return his attention to the task at hand. Suddenly, one of the communications officers announced, "Sir, the Vice President is on an SVTC to speak with you. He's down at the PEOC."

Tibbets cursed under his breath. The last thing on the godforsaken earth he wanted to do was to get sucked into a meeting right then. He started walking over to the communications terminal where the video conference was set up.

Yet another alarm blared.

"Sir, we have a new missile launch warning...oh, crap, this one's in the Gulf of Mexico, sir!" shouted the same Air Force captain who'd been overseeing the missile warning screens.

"What kind of missiles are these? What's the target?" demanded General Estrada as he jogged over to the captain.

"They look to be cruise missiles, like the other ones we saw being launched at San Diego and the *Stennis*...one batch of missiles appears to be heading toward Texas. We'll have a probable target in another minute. Another batch is headed to Louisiana."

"Damn, they're going after our bomber bases!" shouted an Air Force technical sergeant.

General Tibbets ran his fingers through his hair nervously. The sergeant was right—the only military target of value in Louisiana was Barksdale Air Force Base, home of the 2nd Bomb Wing. Tibbets suddenly realized just how bad it would be if they lost most of those bombers on the ground.

"How long until those missiles hit?" General Tibbets demanded.

"If these are CJ-10 land-attack cruise missiles—which they most likely are—then they should reach Barksdale in roughly sixty minutes."

It was at that exact moment that Vice President Powers chose to ask him a question on the video teleconference.

I don't have time for this! he thought. He answered something that he almost instantly forgot, spitting out his words as rapidly as possible so that he could get back to issuing orders. The Vice President seemed to understand that he was in the thick of it and didn't press further.

Turning to look at General Estrada, Tibbets ordered, "Send a message to Barksdale and whatever bomber base they're most likely attacking in Texas. Tell them they have less than fifty minutes to get their bombers airborne or in a covered facility before those cruise missiles start to arrive."

While they were busy trying to deal with the various cruise missile threats heading toward their facilities, another Air Force officer, who had been monitoring the air situation over the Northeast, suddenly yelped, "We have a problem!"

"What's going on?" General Estrada asked. He hastily walked over to handle the next fire that appeared to be rearing its ugly head.

"We've got two pairs of Eurofighters that slipped past our air cover at Lake Erie. Our satellites are tracking them—they're currently flying probably about one hundred feet above the ground and headed toward Gettysburg, Pennsylvania."

In a flash, the general suddenly seemed to realize the significance of what that meant. "Get the Secret Service on the phone now! Tell them we have enemy fighters headed for Marine One and the rest of the helicopters evacuating the Pentagon to Raven Rock!"

"Dear God, get fighters over there to engage them now!" yelled General Tibbets, He realized there was a real possibility that the President and his entourage might be intercepted by these enemy planes.

For the next ten minutes they watched as a flight of American F-16Vs were diverted from an attack along the US-Canadian border to speed across the state of Pennsylvania to try and intercept the four Eurofighters that were streaking toward the small convoy of helicopters escorting the Pentagon staff and the President to the Raven Rock facility.

To their horror, they saw several missiles fired at the lead helicopters. Two of the choppers were destroyed before the fighters were engaged. The Secret Service immediately redirected Marine One to land at Camp David until the situation was resolved. They had a tunnel system they could use at Camp David to get the President to Raven Rock, so it wasn't like he was going to be left helpless at the presidential retreat.

The aerial battle above Raven Rock continued for another ten minutes as the remaining helicopters did their best to evade the enemy missiles and deliver the designated Pentagon staff to the command bunker.

General Tibbets could feel his jaw clenching involuntarily. With two of the helicopters shot down, God only knew which of the critical personnel had made it to the facility and which had just died.

"General Tibbets! We're getting an emergency message from the Marine garrison at Camp David. They are reporting that they're under attack by an unknown ground force. They're requesting a QRF from anyone in the immediate vicinity of the camp."

"WTF! Who could possibly be attacking them? Where are the closest assets?" shouted General Estrada. He rushed over to the airman manning the emergency switchboard.

"The nearest military force is a National Guard armory in Harrisburg," replied one of the officers.

"No! Call Andrews and tell them to saddle up the Air Force QRF they have on standby for Air Force One and get them on some choppers to Camp David *now*!" bellowed General Tibbets. "Tell them to drop everything they're doing and get help to the camp ASAP."

With the Army units at Fort Myer already tasked with the evacuation of the Pentagon and the rest of the capital, they had to find another military unit that wasn't already occupied—the Air Force security force's QRF seemed like the best option. However, the challenge now was whether they could get to Camp David fast enough to make a difference. Until then, the task of defending the President fell on a small contingent of Secret Service agents and a detachment of Marines at the presidential retreat.

The Vice President asked Tibbets another question on the SVTC. This time, he basically grabbed General Estrada and threw him at the screen so he could get back to work.

Eight minutes after they'd made the call to Andrews, and ten minutes after they'd received the call for help from Camp David, the Air Force told them they had two helicopters' worth of security forces airmen on the way to Camp David. Another four helicopters of airmen were being rounded up to head up there in another ten minutes.

"Sir, I just received a message from Raven Rock," announced one of the operations officers. "They said they just received a message from a Secret Service agent traveling with the President. They have him in the tunnel and they're on the tram heading to the bunker now."

When they heard the news, the room erupted in shouts of joy. A few of them exchanged high fives, relieved that the President had survived the ambush.

For his part, General Tibbets let out an audible sigh of relief. The thought of losing the President and the nuclear football had almost given him a heart attack. This new war wasn't even an hour old and they had nearly lost Sachs in a decapitation strike.

NUCFLASH – NUCFLASH – NUCFLASH.

The warning alarms blared. The satellites indicated a possible nuclear detonation had just occurred. The one screen on the side of the big board that was dedicated to monitoring such events was brought up as the main screen, and he zoomed in on the site of the suspected nuclear detonation.

"My God, they nuked Raven Rock!" someone shouted.

****

Washington, D.C.
White House, Presidential Emergency Operation Center

Vice President Luke Powers had been listening to the meeting happening at the Pentagon in the Situation Room when the Secret

Service busted in and demanded that he come with them to the PEOC bunker.

A sense of panic washed over him. As they briskly walked through the White House to get to the elevator, he saw staffers and others who wouldn't be going down to the bunker with him being guided out of the building, fear apparent in their eyes.

As they stopped in front of the elevator, he allowed some of his questions to spill out. "Where's the President? What's going on?" he demanded.

The door dinged, letting them know the elevator had arrived. The group piled into the elevator. It wouldn't be coming back up once they got to the bunker. They'd seal it off from the rest of the building and go into lockdown.

Turning to look at the Vice President, Rick, his head Secret Service agent, replied, "We received an urgent message from NORAD. Sixteen cruise missiles are headed to the D.C. area. They believe one or more of them are headed to the White House. The President's being evacuated right now with the rest of the senior leadership at the Pentagon to Site R."

"My God," he uttered, in a way that sort of seemed like a half-prayer. "Has everyone lost their minds? An attack on D.C.? You can't be serious."

Rick's normally stoic face betrayed some of his own personal anxiety at the situation. Vice President Powers suddenly remembered that the man before him had a wife and kids that lived in Arlington. Rick swallowed and cleared his throat. "I'm afraid this isn't a drill, sir," he answered. "It's probably a decapitation strike. We're fortunate NORAD was able to spot the missiles before they hit the city. They could have killed you or the President."

The door to the elevator opened and the agents in front of them stepped forward. Rick gently grabbed him by the arm and guided them out of the elevator toward the next set of doors. They walked through the massive blast doors and then stopped. One of the agents used a key on the elevator, keeping the door open and the elevator trapped down here with them. This way, no one else could use it to get down to them.

With that security measure complete, another agent entered a passcode and the large blast door behind them began to close. When the door was shut, the locking cylinders built into the massive door expanded out into their steel-reinforced holes as the hydraulic pressure behind the cylinders made sure they would stay locked in place. They were now sealed off from the rest of the world, and unless the White House took a direct hit from a massive nuclear weapon or a specially designed bunker-buster bomb, nothing was going to harm them.

They made their way down the hallway into a small command room that had a long boardroom-style table and chairs. The place was already bustling with staffers and military personnel who would operate the vice-presidential command post, ready to fill in should the President be taken offline or become incapacitated.

By the time Luke Powers took his seat at the head of the table, the military members already had the wall-mounted monitors up and running for a secured video teleconference. One screen was dedicated to United States Northern Command at NORAD, another displayed the National Military Command Center in the Pentagon, a third showed the alternate command post at Site R or Raven Rock, a fourth showed the congressional bunker at Mount Weather, and the final screen displayed the United States Strategic Command at Offutt Air Force Base in Nebraska.

Unmuting his speaker button, the Vice President spoke. "General Pruitt—what's the status of the President, and what's the status of the attack headed to D.C.?"

A flurry of activity could be seen on the monitor in the NMCC where General Pruitt was. He was clearly issuing orders to other people in the room before he returned his gaze to the Vice President and pushed the button to speak. "I'm sorry, Mr. Vice President," he apologized. "We're trying to get the building here evacuated, or at least get as many of our folks down to the bunker as possible. Could you repeat your question?" he asked. There was a lot of noise in the background, as well as a sense of organized chaos.

Powers nodded. He knew the man must be just as nervous as he was, and Pruitt wasn't sitting in nearly as hardened of a facility as the PEOC.

"General, where is the President, and how long until these cruise missiles hit the city?"

"We've evacuated the President to Raven Rock. He's on Marine One as we speak. As to the cruise missiles, they should start to arrive in"—he looked off-screen at something—"six minutes, give or take."

216

Please, Lord, protect us and protect this city, he prayed silently.

"Do we have anything that can intercept them?" Powers asked.

General Pruitt nodded. "We have two aircraft out of Langley moving into position to attack them now, plus the White House has four anti-air missiles. They'll attempt to engage whatever missiles are directed at your position, sir."

For a few tense minutes, they listened in as someone patched them into the radios of the pilots that were going to attempt to intercept the missiles. They could hear the pilots curse—the group of missiles they had been vectored to only had four of the sixteen that were headed to the city.

One of the pilots radioed that he had just fired off two of his AIM-9X Block II Sidewinder missiles. Thirty seconds went by before the pilot whooped over the radio. "Splash one…splash two. I say again, two enemy missiles down."

The other pilot had likewise fired off two of his own missiles. One missed, the other scored a hit.

Before any of them could celebrate, General Pruitt came over the video feed. "Prepare for impact!" he shouted.

Above the White House, all four of the Sidewinder missiles mounted to a launcher on the top of the building fired off at the incoming threats. They all missed. The incoming enemy missiles were now flying at their terminal velocity, which meant the room for error was so minute, the Sidewinders never had a real chance at hitting them.

While Vice President Powers couldn't hear or feel any impacts of the cruise missiles or the destruction of any of them happening outside the bunker, he did see the computer screen briefly shake and hear a thunderous explosion through the Pentagon's video monitor. The screen then went blank, followed by a "no signal" code.

"We just lost contact with the Pentagon, sir," announced one of the communications officers.

Turning around, the Vice President yelled, "Get us a video feed of what's going on outside! I need to see what the city looks like."

"Mr. Vice President, we just received a message from the command post at Raven Rock. The helicopters evacuating some of the Pentagon personnel…several enemy fighters jumped them," an Army colonel announced. "Marine One was able to escape and they've set down at

Camp David. They're going to move the President to the bunker via the tunnel at the retreat."

Vice President Powers was in a state of shock and bewilderment at the news. Everyone else in the room shared a nervous glance with each other before they all involuntarily stared at Powers. If the President became incapacitated or was killed, he'd have to step in and assume control of the government and the military.

Trying to shake off the implications of what the colonel had just said, Vice President Powers looked at the screen at NORAD with General Tibbets and pressed his talk button. "General, at the moment, we can't control what's happening at Raven Rock. I need to know what we're doing to respond to this attack."

General Tibbets, for his part, looked a bit frazzled. "Mr. Vice President, we're tracking multiple cruise missile attacks originating out of the Gulf of Mexico, directed at some of our military bases in Florida, Louisiana, Alabama and Texas. We have two cruise missile attacks originating in the Atlantic, headed toward our naval base in Jacksonville and Norfolk, and four additional attacks coming from the Pacific. Right now, we're just trying to get as many of our aircraft airborne and out of harm's way as possible. We'll start to respond to the threats as we get more of our fighters armed and airborne."

Sensing that his questions were only slowing the man down, Powers said, "I understand, General. Please keep us advised if anything changes or if you need me. I'll try to stay out of your hair while you get things organized."

The general gave a polite smile and then moved off camera, presumably to shout more orders and collect more information.

Looking at the men and women around him, the Vice President said, "I guess we just hang tight and wait."

One of the Air Force colonels was on the phone, talking to someone. Judging by the look on Colonel Brian Nagy's face, he was not happy with what he was hearing. Trying to overhear the conversation, the Vice President snapped once to get the attention of a couple of other folks nearby, then held his index finger to his lips.

"Are you certain it can't be something else?" Colonel Nagy asked desperately. There was a pause. "What about the Russian bombers? Where are they headed?"

Luke raised an eyebrow when he heard the words "Russian bombers," and so did a few others at the table.

Colonel Nagy suddenly realized everyone at the table, including the Vice President, had stopped talking and was now staring at him, listening to the one-sided conversation. "Hang on, Ryan. I've got an audience here in the room with me, so I'm going to put you on speakerphone." He hit the appropriate button, then placed the phone back in the cradle.

"Who all is in the room with you, Brian?" the voice on the other end asked defensively. "I need to make sure they have the proper clearance before we continue."

Raising his voice to be heard from the other end of the table, the VP announced, "This is Vice President Luke Powers. We're in the PEOC under the White House. Everyone in this room has a Yankee White clearance. Identify yourself and speak."

"I, um...yes, Mr. Vice President. I'm Ryan Montana from the National Reconnaissance Office. I was telling Colonel Nagy that we believe the Chinese Air Force moved their H-20 stealth bombers to the Canadian Forces Base at Cold Lake. I believe the Chinese are going to try and use those stealth bombers to hit Mount Weather and Raven Rock."

That last comment got everyone's attention, especially the Secret Service. They had just evacuated the President to Raven Rock, and with the COG now in full effect, most of the congressional leaders were either at Mount Weather, or they were nearly there.

Leaning forward in his chair, VP Powers asked, "Why do you believe that, and have you told anyone else this yet?"

"We've passed the information over to NORAD so they can try and figure out what to do with it. As to why my colleagues and I believe that—well, it only makes sense. The UN is trying to remove President Sachs and yourself. The elements of our government that support Senator Tate have already fled to Canada, and the senator has already set up a government in exile. The fastest and easiest way for the UN to install Senator Tate is to eliminate any political opposition he'd face in assuming control of the government in D.C."

Ryan quickly added, "Before you think I'm crazy, please hear me out. When the UN launched a cruise missile attack on Washington, they didn't just try to hit the Pentagon or the White House. They specifically went after the Capitol Building and the congressional office buildings.

219

They wouldn't do that if they weren't intentionally trying to kill congressional leaders. As to Mount Weather and Raven Rock—they know that when we institute the continuity of government plan, we'd evacuate the capital. They know we'd send the congressional leaders to Mount Weather and the military leaders to Raven Rock. If they could carry out a successful strike on those two facilities after we've initiated the COG, they could wipe out the military and political leadership of the government. It would make it that much easier for Senator Tate and his cohort to assume power."

"My God, what have we done?" murmured the Vice President.

Rick, the VP's lead Secret Service agent, interjected, "Sir, we sent some of the congressional leaders to the Olney Federal Support Center, just outside the capital. Another group of senators was dispatched down to our other facility in central Virginia, so they aren't all going to be at Mount Weather, if it really is going to be attacked."

The VP let out a breath hastily, at least somewhat relieved. If anyone knew where they had sent the congressional leaders, it would have been Rick.

While they were talking, the video feed to Site R came alive. "Mr. Vice President, we've just received word from Camp David. The facility there is under ground attack by a hostile force. We don't have a lot of information at the moment other than that they're requesting any QRF in the area to assist them. General Tibbets at NORAD is on it and assures us that additional forces are on the way to the camp. However, we need you to be ready to take over command, in case the President doesn't make it to the tunnel that'll take him to us."

Powers looked at the man on the monitor, not sure if this was some sort of joke.

How could things be going so wrong for them right now? he wondered.

He turned to look at Rick, who, upon hearing the news, had picked up a landline to place a call. A few seconds later, he nodded at the VP, letting him know the President's detail was indeed under attack.

Looking back at the NORAD monitor, Powers said, "General Tibbets, I know you're a busy man, but we just spoke with an individual at the NRO. He told us there's a high probability that the Chinese have one or more H-20 stealth bombers flying out of Cold Lake. He said the Russians and Chinese bombers may be trying to carry out a decapitation strike against our elected officials and military leaders. Is there any truth to that?"

Tibbets paused what he was doing for a moment. "General Estrada, please brief the VP on what's going on and what we're doing. I need to handle something," he said. Then he walked off the screen.

If they weren't in the middle of an unprecedented disaster unfolding before his eyes, Powers might have been pretty put off and probably would have ordered the general to stand fast and brief him, but he knew Tibbets was probably trying to organize some sort of defense of the nation, so he cut him some slack.

A brigadier general appeared in the seat where Tibbets had just been. "Excuse us, Mr. Vice President," he said apologetically. "We're trying to put out fires all over the battlespace. We haven't even dealt with the ground situation yet as we're trying to make sure our Air Force doesn't get wiped out on the ground."

My God—is the situation really this bad? Powers thought, practically unable to breathe from the strain of the circumstances.

"Can you answer our question about what the NRO told us?" the VP managed to say.

"Yes, sir. They're right about the bombers. We're tracking six Blackjack bombers that broke through our air perimeter less than ten minutes ago. We have faint blips of what we believe to be four Chinese H-20 bombers that just started appearing on our radars probably fifteen minutes ago."

"What?! Where are they headed and what are we doing to shoot them down?" demanded the Vice President, growing more and more exasperated with each passing minute.

"We just scrambled the Looking Glass and the TACAMOs in case these bombers are delivering a nuclear first strike. General Tibbets has already moved us to DEFCON Two. We're following procedures on this one. We sent a message to the Russians and to General McKenzie that if a nuclear detonation is confirmed on US soil, we will retaliate."

"Whoa—full stop, General. No one has issued authorization for nuclear weapons unless the President says so, or if he's incapacitated, then it needs to come from me. Is that understood?" demanded the Vice President angrily. He wanted to make sure the generals at NORAD knew there was still a leash on them.

"Yes, Mr. Vice President," answered General Estrada, in a tone that suggested he had his tail between his legs. "I didn't mean to imply that NORAD would authorize a strike. We needed to make sure that the aggressors in this situation know that we are ready to deploy our nuclear weapons if needed."

"Very well," Powers responded, much more calmly. "Where are these bombers headed, and what are you doing to shoot them down?"

General Estrada nodded. "Two of the Blackjacks are headed for this facility as we speak. We've scrambled a squadron of F-22s to go hunt them down. I'm fairly confident the Raptors will find them and take 'em out before they get in range of any weapons they planned on using. Unless they were going to hit us with a nuke, there isn't much that's going to put a dent in the mountain here. Two other Blackjacks are actually flying out of Cuba and heading for Eglin Air Force base. We're a little more concerned about stopping them, since most of our fighters are located along the northern border. I'll have more for you in about twenty minutes. The third set of Blackjacks is headed to Offutt Air Force Base. It would appear the Russians' main goal is to disrupt our command and control capability. It's very standard to the old Soviet playbook, so we believe we're ready to deal with it.

"As to the Chinese H-20s—we're not one hundred percent sure where they're headed just yet. Our last blip showed them passing over Pennsylvania. Again, we have some F-35s being vectored to their last known positions to try and see if they can't pick up the scent. There's a chance they'll find them as they get closer to them. The H-20s may be stealthy, but they aren't invisible."

Suddenly, Powers heard a lot of commotion over the video feed of General Estrada. Not sure what was going on, the VP looked at the other video feeds and abruptly noticed the one from Raven Rock had gone black and was displaying only the words "No signal," just like the one from the Pentagon.

"What's going on, General?" Powers asked.

Estrada was looking off camera at something, alarm Klaxons blaring in the background. Powers heard several people gasp, followed by a series of angry shouts. He could have sworn he heard someone use the word *nuked*.

"General, what's going on? We just lost the video feed to Raven Rock!" shouted the Vice President.

Returning his gaze to the video screen, an ashen-faced General Estrada replied, "Sir, we're trying to get confirmation, but right now, it would appear Raven Rock was just taken out."

The Vice President couldn't say anything for a moment. He realized his jaw had swung wide open in shock, and he snapped his mouth closed. "What do you mean it was taken out? That's a hardened bunker," he demanded.

There was a brief pause as Estrada conferred with people around him. "We're trying to get verification, sir, but the satellites are telling us the facility was just hit by what we can only describe as four tactical nuclear weapons."

Everyone in the PEOC suddenly became silent. A pin drop could have been heard as everyone took the information in.

"What about Mount Weather?" inquired the Vice President.

"It's still there. I think our F-35s in their vicinity may have found the Chinese bombers. They're moving to engage them now. We're vectoring some fighters over to Raven Rock to try and get us an independent visual. We'll know in a couple of minutes if they really hit us with a nuke."

The image of Estrada was abruptly replaced with that of General Tibbets. "Mr. Vice President—whether Raven Rock was hit by a nuke or a bunker-buster bomb, the facility is offline and unable to perform its duties. Our last report of the President's whereabouts was from the last Secret Service agent in his detail to make it to the tunnel alive. They were on the tram, traveling to the bunker. If they took that bunker out, it means the President may be dead. We're going to do our best to get confirmation of that over the next ten minutes, but we're going to need you to assume his role until that happens. Do you have your biscuit card for authentication?"

What? Dead? Authentication? Biscuit card? thought Powers in a jumbled mess. This was all happening too fast.

"Mr. Vice President, we need you to authenticate with your biscuit card," General Tibbets repeated.

"I...yes. I have my card," he finally replied as he reached inside his suit jacket and pulled his biscuit card out. He cracked the plastic enclosure around the paper card and pulled it out. He then read off his authentication numbers, which were verified by another officer at

NORAD and confirmed by Colonel Nagy, in the PEOC with the Vice President.

With the multifactor authentication complete, General Tibbets asked, "Sir, we're proceeding with you as the Commander-in-Chief until we can verify the status of the President. How would you like us to respond to this attack?"

Still in a bit of shock at what was happening, Powers looked up at the general and took a deep breath. "First, verify that we've hunted down those H-20s headed to Mount Weather and get verification that Raven Rock was in fact attacked by a nuclear weapon. If it *was* nuked, then we'll begin preparations for a limited counterstrike."

Leaning forward so his face looked a bit larger on the screen, General Tibbets said, "Sir, if I may—I'd like your permission to get at least four of our B-2s armed with nuclear weapons and airborne. We can place them in a holding pattern over Alaska until we determine if we need to use them. That way, we'll be able to rapidly move them to execute a counterstrike if ordered."

Pausing for a moment to think about that, Luke nodded. "OK, General. But also have a couple of B-2s loaded up with bunker-busters. If this turns out not to be a nuclear detonation, then I still want to go after the guys that did this with our own bunker-buster bombs."

Tibbets smiled and nodded. He said a few things off camera before he returned his attention to the acting President.

A million thoughts raced through Powers's mind. Even though he was a bit more involved than the average Vice President, he would definitely be drinking from a fire hose for the next several hours.

Chapter 13
Occupation

Augusta, Maine
Maine State Legislature Office

There was still snow on the sides of the road as the armored column turned off Interstate 95 to make their way to the state capitol building in downtown Augusta. Five hours ago, Lieutenant Colonel Sigurd Bruøygard's Norwegian Telemark Battalion had crossed into the northernmost US state with high hopes that they'd be able to capture the state in a bloodless coup.

They had been told that a large percentage of the American people wanted the UN to liberate them. The send-off speech they'd watched from President-Elect Marshall Tate led Bruøygard and the men and women of his battalion to believe that the American people would welcome them with open arms, that only a fringe element of hard-core Sachs supporters would give them problems. However, Bruøygard's battalion hadn't traveled ten minutes into America before they'd run into their first sign of trouble.

A group of civilians had created a blockade on I-95 around the small town of Island Falls. Not wanting to create a major incident, several of his men and some New York Civil Defense Force militiamen tried to talk with the truckers to convince them to move off the road. For ten minutes, the parties talked. Meanwhile, the battalion was getting backed up on the road.

Just when Bruøygard was about to order one of his tanks to bulldoze their way through the blockade, the truckers agreed to move. They were guided off the road and copies of their driver's licenses were taken. They were told if they caused any further troubles or attempted to delay any future UN forces from using the highway, they'd be arrested and detained.

An hour later, they came across another similar roadblock around the city of Howland, just north of Bangor. Seeing how they had been able to deescalate the last blockade, Bruøygard figured they'd try talking to the group and see if they could do it again. Five minutes into the impromptu meeting in the center of the road, someone from the roadblock suddenly fired a shot at one of his soldiers. In that instant, one of the truckers who'd been talking to one of Bruøygard's lieutenants pulled out his pistol and summarily shot the lieutenant in the face.

"Open fire!" ordered Bruøygard. He quickly crouched behind the door of the vehicle he was nearest to and started firing at the Americans, aiming first for the man who'd executed his lieutenant.

For the next five minutes, a running gun battle had taken place between his lead company and the two dozen or so truckers and militiamen manning the roadblock. Finally, one of the Norwegian Leopard II tanks fired a couple of rounds into the big rigs that were blocking them. The tank had then plowed forward, pushing the fiery wrecks off the road so Telemark Battalion could continue to Augusta.

After that brief but violent confrontation, Bruøygard put his head in his hands as he sat in the back of his CV90 infantry fighting vehicle. He was pretty sure at that point that they had been misled regarding the type of reception they would receive from the American people.

Our fight isn't with them, though, he thought. The government was the real source of conflict.

At that point, he hatched a plan and sent a small scout unit ahead of them on some of the less-traveled country roads that some of the NY CDF volunteers knew about. Their goal was to locate and detain the governor until they arrived with the rest of the battalion. Bruøygard wanted to personally talk with the governor and see if he could work out some sort of agreement with him regarding the occupation—the last thing he wanted his battalion to have to do was occupy the major cities in the state. If he could negotiate some sort of arrangement with the state government, then they might be able to get things back to normal without having to use a heavy hand to govern them.

Glancing down at his watch, Bruøygard saw it was now 11:05 a.m., nearly lunchtime. He shook his head in disappointment at how long it had taken them to go this far. He had hoped he would have been rolling into Augusta around 9 a.m., and they would have, if they hadn't had to deal with those two roadblocks.

He sighed. Realizing it wasn't going to help anything to dwell on the negative aspects of the situation, he found himself grateful for the company of tanks traveling with his battalion. Those sixty-eight-ton tanks would make for an invaluable intimidation factor if things didn't work out well with the governor.

Eventually, they began their drive through the downtown of the city of Augusta. Despite the chilly temperature, many people came out of their stores, offices, and homes to see his column of armored vehicles as they rolled through their city. Bruøygard made sure to have their Norwegian flag tied to a couple of the antennas of his vehicles, so they'd know they were part of the UN force.

Suddenly his vehicle lurched to a stop, and the vehicle commander announced, "We've arrived."

When the rear door opened, Bruøygard got out and stretched his legs and back. He'd been cooped up in that death trap long enough. While he performed a few basic stretches, he caught the eye of some of the civilians nearby. They didn't look friendly.

They definitely view us as invaders, not liberators, he realized.

One of the young captains who had arrived with the advance party approached him. "Sir, if you'll follow me, we have the governor and the head of the State Police and local police chiefs in a conference room waiting for you."

As he approached the Maine State House with its two tiers of columns in the front and copper-topped dome, Bruøygard had to admit, it was a beautiful building—not as old or ornate as the government buildings in his own nation, but impressive nonetheless. Eventually, he was led to a conference room that was being guarded by a handful of his soldiers. Bruøygard nodded toward them, acknowledging their presence. He took in a deep breath, held it for a second, and then let it out as he marched in to deal with the civilian government officials.

"Good afternoon, Mr. Governor," Bruøygard said in his best English. He held his shoulders back and stood as erect as possible, utilizing his imposing six foot five frame for all it was worth.

The governor, the head of the state police and the local chief of police all stood. However, none of them said a word to him or extended their hands to shake his. They didn't appear to be pleased to see him. He couldn't blame them, but he also didn't care. He just hoped he could find a way to cut a deal with them so his force could get back on the road—they had more objectives to meet. He simply motioned for them to take their seats, which they did.

"Well, my name is Lieutenant Colonel Sigurd Bruøygard. I'm a battalion commander in the Norwegian Army, part of the United Nations peacekeeping force. I understand that my presence, and the presence of my soldiers, may not be wanted or appreciated in your city, state, or country—but here we are. All of us are doing our part in this great play they call 'life.'"

Before he could say another word, the head of police cut him off. "Colonel, I don't want any of your men to die, so I suggest you take your force and go back to Canada before more people are killed."

Smiling at the bluntness of the man before him, Bruøygard replied, "Thank you for your concern. I do appreciate it. I, too, don't want any of my soldiers to die—nor do I want any of *your* citizens to be killed. Surely you heard about the two separate roadblocks my battalion encountered on I-95 as we made our way to Augusta?" He tried to read their faces to see how much they knew about the situation.

"I heard one of your tanks killed a handful of people north of Bangor," replied the governor angrily.

Bruøygard nodded. "You heard correctly. A small band of either militia or National Guardsmen—I don't know which they were—decided they would try and impede my tanks from using the interstate by blocking it with several trucks. While we were trying to negotiate with them, someone fired a shot and one of my soldiers was hit. Then they opened fire on the rest of my men, and we defended ourselves."

He paused for a moment. "I'm meeting with you because I'm seeking a way to avoid killing each other," he explained. "Will you help with that, Governor?"

The governor looked conflicted. When he failed to speak up right away, the police chief broke in. "If you want to avoid further bloodshed, Colonel, then I suggest you turn around and go back to Canada. Just because you've made it down here today doesn't mean you won't be attacked later tonight, tomorrow morning, or any other opportune time our citizens see fit. I don't think you Europeans appreciate exactly how many of our citizens are armed and ready to defend their homes and cities."

Bruøygard sighed softly; this was precisely what he wanted to avoid. He'd had his suspicions that invading America wouldn't work. Looking at the police chief, he replied, "Chief Wilkes, I don't like the situation any more than you do, but I have my orders. Now, I've been given a lot of latitude in how to handle things. I can mostly let you guys run everything just as you have before our arrival, *or* I can replace you with those who will accommodate my forces.

"Those who don't want to cooperate will be taken and placed in a separate holding camp until we can determine they no longer present a danger to themselves or those around them. Those individuals who are caught attacking or fighting my forces, or others of the United Nations peacekeeping force, will be summarily shot. We've been instructed to carry out public executions as a means of deterring future acts of aggression."

He paused for a moment as he saw the looks of horror and then contempt wash over their faces. "I think these orders are abhorrent, but they are my orders," he said. "I would rather not have to implement them. I'm asking for you to help me make sure I don't have to. If we're all lucky, this whole situation will be concluded in a few days, when President-Elect Marshall Tate is sworn in as your new President. Let's all try to work together and make sure everyone survives this turbulent time."

The governor looked like he was going to be sick. He mumbled to himself a few times as he shook his head. "I'll do my best to try and keep things calm, Colonel," he finally managed to say, "but you have to do your best to keep your soldiers out of sight and off the streets. The more military presence the people see, the more likely they are to do something stupid."

Bruøygard smiled. "Thank you, Governor. I knew we could work something out."

He turned his attention to the police chiefs. "I understand that your state and federal government keep a register of persons who own firearms. My captain here," he said as he snapped his fingers, "would like access to that list. We have a special unit that will start confiscating personally owned firearms straight away. We'll also be putting out an announcement that anyone who willingly turns in a firearm will be given a one-ounce gold coin in exchange for their weapon. If a person knows someone is illegally keeping a firearm and they turn that person in, they will get a one-ounce gold coin for each weapon confiscated."

Before Bruøygard could go any further, the head of the state police stood up and held his hands straight out in front of him. "You might as well arrest me now. Let me be the first person you arrest, because I won't surrender my personal firearms, nor will I willingly hand over a list of our citizens who legally own them. I can assure you of one thing, Colonel—no one in our state will willingly allow themselves to be disarmed like this. You'll unleash a torrent of violence the likes of which you can't even imagine against your soldiers.

"You may think you had it easy, waltzing into Augusta today, but rest assured, Colonel—today was the easiest day of this occupation you'll ever have. The citizens of my country are going to wage an insurgency on you like nothing you've ever seen, and I'll gladly be the first martyr to rally them to that very cause." He spoke with such vitriol and hatred it nearly caused Bruøygard to recoil.

"Cuff him and take him out of the building *now*," Bruøygard ordered. His men quickly complied.

This might be a bit harder than I first thought, Bruøygard realized.
****

From *Fox News Online*:

> Following the invasion of the northern states by the United Nations, the National Rifle Association sent out an email to their millions of subscribers, urging their members to be prepared to take up arms in defense of the country. "We are urging our members to seek out their local Army National Guard stations first and offer their services," they write. "If the local Guard unit doesn't need assistance, we recommend that all NRA members across the country band together to form militias to help defend the country from the coming foreign invasion."
>
> There has been no comment from the White House, Homeland Security, or the Department of Defense on this statement, other than to say they hope this situation can be defused and resolved shortly. In a related note, the Department of Defense has asked for all able-bodied men and women to report to their local military recruiter's office and volunteer for service in defense of their country.

****

Bellingham, Washington

Two days after the UN forces invaded the US, Jake Baine received a cryptic call on the radio he'd been given at the armory. He was supposed to meet Major Slevin at a park roughly twelve miles from his cabin.

Jake felt his hands sweating against the steering wheel; he was even more nervous than usual, knowing UN military convoys were using a lot of the roads nearby. So far, he hadn't run into any of them, but that didn't mean he wouldn't.

After an uneventful trip, Jake arrived at a park that was eerily empty. A fresh layer of snow had fallen the night before, and without another soul around, the stark scene seemed somewhat surreal. He parked his truck near Slevin's and walked over to the major.

"It's good to see you, sir," Jake said. He glanced around anxiously. It seemed too quiet here. "So, what did you want to meet about?"

"First off, don't call me sir anymore. Just call me Al."

Jake nodded, and the two of them began to walk down one of the marked trails. They didn't say much for the first ten minutes. They just moved deeper into the woods. When they reached a hill that Al seemed to be aiming for, he suddenly stopped.

"In another couple of days, half of the state will be under the control of the UN," he explained. "I hope you got those supplies."

Jake nodded.

"What I need to know is, how soon you can start building some IEDs for me?" Major Slevin asked.

Jake was silent for a moment as he calculated his answer. "That depends on what kind of IEDs you want. Do you want ones for blowing up some bridges or nicking a convoy? Or do you want to blow up some UN foot patrols?"

"For the moment, let's stick to the convoys. I don't want to risk civilian casualties if we can avoid it."

"Do you want command wire control, infrared, or remote control?" Jake asked next.

Slevin snorted at the question. "Man, I used to hate IEDs. Now you're asking me which one of those nasty little death devices I want." He ran his fingers through his hair. "Let's start with command wire first. As they adapt, we'll adapt. Let's not give away our toolbox of what we have available to us right away. This could be a long insurgency."

Jake smiled. "I agree. I'll make the bombs. When I make the command wire, I'll give you guys at least two hundred feet. I'll show you how to increase that if you want, but if I start making these half-mile-long command wire detonators, I'm going to run out of wiring."

Slevin nodded. "Not a problem. We'll get the wiring. Don't worry about a long command wire. Just give us fifty feet, and we'll rig them up the way we need them. How many bombs can you get us in a week?"

"Well, since you asked, I have four in my truck right now I can give you. They're each about two pounds of C-4, wrapped in about four inches of roofing nails, nuts and washers. Best I could come up with on short notice. I could crank out a lot more if you can get me some artillery shells or mortars, but if I have to stick to the C-4, there's only going to be so many I can dish out."

"Oh man, I knew you were the right guy for the job," Slevin said, slapping Jake on the shoulder. "OK, here's what I want you to do. We'll send you a coded message on Tuesdays at 1000 hours and 1700 hours. You'll either be told to bring the IEDs to a location on Thursday, or you'll be told to bring them to Miller's Quick Lube on Saturdays. You bring however many IEDs you're able to build, and we'll take 'em. If I can come across some mortar or artillery shells, I'll find a way to get them to you. Got it?"

"Sure thing, Al. Piece of cake," Jake replied nonchalantly. They both chuckled.

After stitching up some last-minute details, they spent the next ten minutes walking back to their trucks. Once the transfer had been successfully made of the completed IEDs to Slevin's truck, they went their separate ways.
****

Port of Balboa, Panama

Lieutenant General Song Puxuan of the 20th PLA Army Group stood in one of the control towers that overlooked the massive port. A broad smile spread across his face. Without a shot fired, his forces had captured the entire port, and even now, they were offloading his heavy armor and air defense equipment.

The capture of the Panama Canal was critical to their strategy of dividing the US Navy and clearing the Pacific of enemy threats. Now that the conflict had officially started, it was imperative that his ground force get offloaded and finish capturing the rest of the country. In the coming weeks, a steady gravy train of supplies would begin to show up, bound for Mexico and the US southern border.

One of his aides appeared next to him. "General, you said to let you know when General Loa arrived. His plane just landed."

General Song nodded at the news. He took one last look at the two roll-on, roll-off freighters being unloaded and then turned to head down the stairs back to the ground floor. A vehicle was waiting to take him over to the airport nearby.

As he exited the control tower, General Song felt the warm, moist air hit his skin. It was strangely comforting—certainly much more pleasant than the hostile winter weather he undoubtedly would have been feeling back in Beijing.

A lieutenant held his door open as he approached the blacked-out SUV. General Song directed his driver to take him over to the airport. He wanted to greet the air force counterpart who was going to be responsible for airlifting over many of his soldiers. With the war now raging along the American-Canadian border, it was a race against time to get his force assembled and ready for action.

When they pulled up to the Albrook International Airport, a pair of civilian guards saw their vehicle and the special placard they had in the windshield and waved them past the gate. Once inside the facility, they drove over to where several military transport aircraft were parked.

As they approached the large aircraft, General Song observed a lot of military personnel getting one of the Type 95 self-propelled anti-aircraft artillery guns set up. Another crew was hard at work getting a lone HQ-9 surface-to-air missile system unpacked. They'd hopefully have the system up and running in a few more hours. Although he didn't anticipate any immediate threats, Song wanted to have their air defense systems operational as soon as possible.

General Song continued to scan the area until he saw the man he was looking for, pointing toward part of the airport. "Driver, head over to that lean-looking man near the airport officials," he ordered.

Once they pulled up to him, Song's driver stopped and swiftly hopped out to get the door. General Song exited the vehicle and walked up to his Chinese Air Force counterpart. "General Loa, it's good to see you. How was the flight over?" he asked pleasantly.

Lieutenant General Loa turned to face him, sweat running down his anxious-looking face. "It was good, General Song, but we have much work that needs to be done. Has your equipment arrived in the port?"

Song nodded. "It has. Our equipment is being offloaded and made ready. Are the planes carrying my men still on schedule?"

"They are. They should start to arrive in the coming hours," General Loa answered. Then, as if he anticipated a question about how long all of this was going to take, he continued, "As you requested, the men from the 60th Mechanized Infantry Brigade will arrive first, followed by the air defense brigade and then the 16th Armor Brigade. Those are the soldiers slated to arrive today. The rest of your force will arrive over the coming three days. It's a long commute for our planes to have to make, General."

****

Perrysburg, Ohio

Adam Rutman sat in his recliner with his wife, watching the news in utter shock and horror.

We're really being invaded, he thought. He really couldn't believe it had come to this.

"Do you think Jimmie is up there?" asked his wife, Lucinda, with a fearful look on her face. "You know, fighting in Detroit?"

Lifting his beer to his lips, Adam finished off the bottle before he responded. "I don't know, honey. His unit was up in Detroit though, so I'd have to think he probably is."

"Oh, Adam. What're we going to do? What if they make it all the way down here to Perrysburg? What do we do then?" she asked, clearly fighting back tears.

Adam could understand why his wife was so distraught. Their nephew, Jimmie, had become kind of a son to them, and it now appeared that he was in harm's way. Unfortunately, Adam and Lucinda hadn't been able to have children themselves, but they'd been very involved in the lives of the three sons Adam's brother had had. Jimmie, the oldest of the three, had always said he wanted to be a soldier when he grew up and had joined the Army as soon as he'd turned eighteen. Now it looked like his unit was going to be turned into a mere speed bump between the UN army and the rest of the American Midwest.

"You should give Rich a call tomorrow," Lucinda said. "He'd know what to do." Then she got up and headed off to another room, clearly too distraught to watch the news any longer.

Adam sighed. He knew he needed to do something. He thumbed through his smartphone until he found the number he was looking for in his contacts.

Richard McVeigh was an old Army buddy of his. They'd been part of the same platoon in the 101st Airborne during the first Gulf War back in '91. Adam had gotten out of the military shortly after the war, but Richard had stayed in and made it a career. They'd kept in touch over the years, especially once Rich had retired from the Army and settled in about an hour away. His friend was a bit over-the-top at times as a prepper and conspiracy theorist, but Adam cut him some slack since his extreme views worked well with his business.

Richard ran a small outdoor rifle range outside of town. Perrysburg was just south of Toledo, so Rich maintained a lot of contracts with the neighboring cities' police departments. His business had become a full-service shooting range and training facility for local police and SWAT teams and gun enthusiasts. Rich's hard work had paid off well for him, and when he made his firearm and ammunition purchases, he mostly did so through Adam's store, which had been a godsend on more than one occasion.

The phone rang once before Adam heard his friend's voice.

"Adam, just the man I needed to talk with. I was literally just about to dial you," Rich said with a chuckle.

Joining in the laughter himself, Adam replied, "I think we need to talk. Can you stop by the shop tomorrow? Say around eight a.m.?"

"Yeah, I can do that," Rich answered. "Don't you open at ten, though?"

"Normally, yes, but I think we should talk before I open the shop. I have a feeling I'm going to be super busy tomorrow, if you catch my drift."

"You're telling me. I've had half a dozen people calling me tonight, asking what's going on, like I have some Batphone to the White House."

The two of them laughed again before they hung up. They'd talk more tomorrow in person.

****

Adam arrived at his storefront around 7 a.m. After letting himself in, he quickly locked the door and rearmed the security system. He made sure one of the AR-15s in the office was loaded and another under the front counter was also ready. He also put his level IV body armor on. He wasn't messing around today. He knew he'd have a lot of scared, concerned people coming in to buy him out of everything he had. He just wanted to make sure no one tried to rob him.

He double-checked his electronic payment devices to make sure they were still working. Thankfully they did, which meant he could still accept people's debit and credit cards. Steadily, he got the rest of his shop ready. Two of his other employees showed up early, just as he had requested. Adam had them doing an inventory of what ammo they had in the warehouse and how many rifles and magazines they had. He also had them each open carry a sidearm and wear body armor as well. When his other two employees arrived right before the store would open, he'd place them as guards outside the front entrance. He didn't expect trouble, but he sure wasn't going to sit around and allow an attack to happen either.

At eight o'clock, Adam got a call. Looking at the caller ID on his smartphone, he saw it was Richard. "Rich. You out back?" Adam asked.

"Yeah. Just got here. You do want me to come to the back door, right?"

"Yes. Knock twice, no more. I'll let you in. Is anyone outside yet? Do you see anyone else milling around?"

There was a pause for a second on the other line before his friend replied. "Not that I can see. Honestly, it's pretty quiet outside right now. That'll probably change in another hour as people start to hit the stores."

A minute later, Adam heard the two knocks. Before he opened the door, he disabled the alarm and then pulled his pistol out and had it ready. When Rich walked in, he held his hands up in mock surrender.

"Whoa, cowboy. You're the one who invited me, remember?"

Adam nodded and holstered his sidearm. "Sorry. You can't be too careful these days—not with all that's happening. Come with me back to my office."

He locked the back door, and the two of them walked to the other side of the store, where Adam's personal office was located. When they walked in, Adam closed the door and took a seat behind his desk.

"So, Adam, why'd you drag my butt all the way into town? I've got a ton of people coming out to the range later this afternoon."

Looking his friend over with a hard stare, Adam finally said, "Rich, I know you run in some hardcore prepper circles, and that's cool with me. I sell a lot of firearms and other stuff to that crowd."

Rich nodded.

Adam continued. "First, I want you to know that I'm going to be burning all the records of people who've purchased a firearm at this store—I'm not about to let them fall into the hands of the UN and their goon squads. So tell your people, if they bought a gun from me, they're safe. Second, I'm not doing any more background checks. I don't want any of that data to fall into the wrong hands when they get here. I'm not sure if you saw the news this morning, but it looks like our boys are getting their butts kicked around Detroit. That means it won't be long before they're on their way to Toledo."

Rich held up a hand. "I get it, Adam. We all do. We know what's coming. You want to know if you can help, right?"

Adam didn't say anything for a second, then he nodded. "What can I do?" he asked in a soft voice.

Rich leaned in and pulled a notepad out of the breast pocket of his jacket. "We're putting together a militia of folks that regularly shoot at the range. We don't really need rifles or even ammo, but there are other supplies we could use."

"If I have it, it's yours," Adam replied.

Smiling, Rich handed him the list of what they needed. It consisted of mostly camping gear, but there were some other interesting items on the unassuming scrap of paper—black powder, signal flares, two-way radios, and camouflage type netting. It was the kind of stuff you'd normally use to set up a deer or duck blind.

Adam almost breathed a sigh of relief when he realized Rich was essentially taking him in to whatever militia force they were going to create. He knew he wasn't the most physically fit guy, but he had enough stuff in his store to supply a small force, and he planned on doing just that.

"I'll find out later today what additional stuff we may need, but the one item I'd like you to hold back on would be some .22-caliber rifles and at least ten thousand rounds of ammo for them. We may need them for hunting and potentially trading in a few months," Rich explained.

"Make sure you keep the survival gear and batteries in the back. I know we'll need those, since we won't be able to get replacements once we fall behind enemy lines."

"What about ammo, my handguns, or other assault rifles?" Adam asked. "Should I hold on to those for your people?"

Rich waved a hand as if to swat away the question. "No. Our people all have their own rifles, and most of them have already stocked up on ammo. Let everyone else buy them. Besides, the more people that own them now before the UN shows up, the better.

"As to ammo—don't bother. We'll be able to take plenty off the dead, and if we have to, we'll swap out our weapons for theirs to make finding new ammo easier. It's some of the other consumable items, like batteries and those other items I gave you, that'll be hard to replace once the occupation settles in."

Adam smiled. "Thanks for coming down here, Rich. I wanted to help but I honestly didn't know how. Plus, it's a good thing you got here to claim what you want before I open—I have a feeling most of my store is going to get bought out today."

"Well if that's the case, make sure you raise your prices a bit," Rich responded with a chuckle. "No reason to have a sale. Besides, hopefully the profits will help cover the cost of everything we're going to need. I don't want to put you in a lurch financially."

Adam shrugged his shoulders. "That's what insurance is for. Once we get everything we need, we'll make sure the place is 'looted and firebombed' so we can file an insurance claim for a total loss."

Rich laughed at Adam's use of air quotes. "I'm sure we have some folks who can help with that to make it legit," he replied with a wink. He stuck out his hand to shake Adam's. "Welcome to the team, Adam. I know this is going to be a huge help to have you in the ranks. I've got your back on this one, buddy."

The two talked for a bit more until Adam's two other employees showed up. By noon, his place was packed with people trying to buy rifles, ammo, bows and arrows. It was a bonanza of a sales day.

Later that evening, Rich and some of his guys showed up with a few trucks. They drove around to the back of the shop and parked near the warehouse. They loaded up the stuff they'd agreed on and then headed out to their headquarters.

By the time Adam left the store that night, he didn't have a single firearm left in the place. He estimated he probably had maybe a quarter of his store shelves left with any items at all. He'd stay open another day or two and then close up for good. At this point, it looked like the UN forces might actually be in Toledo to their north in another two or three days.

Chapter 14
Operation Payback

Washington, D.C.
White House, PEOC Bunker

"Sir, it wasn't a nuclear weapon that hit Raven Rock," reported General Estrada from NORAD.

"Are you sure?" asked Vice President Powers.

"Yes, sir. The Chinese bombers hit the bunker with four Russian-made Father of all Bombs."

"Bunker-busters?" Powers inquired.

"Correct," Estrada confirmed. "They're essentially the Russian version of the American MOAB. The Chinese hit all four bunker entrances with these thermobaric bombs. They most likely penetrated the bunker and incinerated everyone and everything inside it."

"Have they found the President?"

"Not yet, sir. Due to the destructive nature of the bombs and the intense fire they created inside the facility, rescuers have been unable to get inside yet."

Powers sighed. "Well, update me if you have any new information on that front."

"Yes, Mr. Vice President," Estrada responded. He let out a deep breath. "Sir, the other entrance to the tunnel system at Camp David was also hit, and it collapsed. A team of engineers is hard at work, trying to open the tunnel back up and see if, by some miracle, Sachs and his small detail were somehow trapped in the tunnel between the two facilities during the missile strike. If that happened, there might still be a chance that they're alive…although, if I'm being completely honest, I wouldn't hold too much hope out for that."

"Understood."

They were now ten hours into the war. General Estrada and General Tibbets spent the next fifteen minutes briefing the new acting President on the information that was starting to filter in from across the armed forces. With each contact report and battle update, the big picture of where the enemy was attacking and what strategies they were implementing seemed a bit clearer.

Acting President Powers was starting to formulate a response in his head, but he still had so many questions. "General Tibbets, I'm still having a hard time wrapping my head around how the most powerful military on earth was caught so thoroughly by surprise. What in the world happened?"

General Tibbets sighed involuntarily. He obviously wasn't happy about the inquiry.

"Mr. Vice President, there are several reasons why this happened. Probably the most important reason is that, unlike previous enemies we've fought, this enemy got the first punch in. Per Sachs's guidance, we were going to hit the UN force on January 13th, once we had fully deployed a couple more combat brigades near our northern border. My guess—and this is only an assumption right now—is that someone in the military chain or the intelligence community who knew when we were going to carry out our attack tipped Senator Tate's camp off or told one of their former colleagues who'd defected. In either case, the enemy knew we were going to carry out a preemptive strike, so rather than wait for it, they hit us with their own."

Powers felt a rage billowing up inside him unlike any he had ever experienced before. He clenched his fists "How did the Navy get caught by surprise like they did?" he demanded.

"Sir, given how the events played out today, this plan to install Senator Tate has obviously been in the works for a very long time," General Tibbets explained. "There just isn't any other explanation. With regard to the Navy, it's simple. They had two things going for them. First, the Chinese apparently created a fleet of merchant raiders, similar to what the Germans did during World War II. We've gone over the satellite intelligence and videos from numerous reconnaissance drones and figured out how they did it. Let me share a video with you while I walk you through it."

A short video began to play on the screen, and Tibbets narrated while it played. "OK, sir, so we see here what appears to be a Kenyan-flagged freighter. On the deck of the ship is a single layer of cargo containers, which appear innocuous enough. Then, as you can see, half of the cargo containers on the deck slide to the side, like they're attached to a platform or something…and now we can see the string of vertical-launch missile pods. In less than one minute, the ship fires off fifty land-attack cruise missiles. Once the smoke clears, the UAV captures the cargo containers moving back over the top of the VLS system. And again, the ship appears like any of the tens of thousands of cargo ships that dot the earth's oceans."

With his mouth agape, the Vice President couldn't believe what he had just seen.

"That, Mr. Vice President, is how the Navy and the rest of us were caught flatfooted. It wasn't neglect or arrogance on our part. The enemy had apparently created a completely new weapon we hadn't seen or thought of yet and ruthlessly deployed it against us. As we speak, we're having the Coast Guard and the rest of DHS work with the NSA to try and figure out who owned the ships that attacked us and who owns those companies. These were Chinese-made CJ-10 cruise missiles, so we know these ships were operated by the Chinese Navy. What we're trying to do now is track down any shell companies that could have been carrying out these attacks so we can use that information to try and track down any additional freighters that may have been converted into merchant raiders."

Rubbing his face out of frustration and tiredness, the acting President looked at the general. "So, what are we doing to respond to this attack on our country and the government?"

"We have a couple of options: the first is political, the second is military. Let me go over the military first, as I think that's the more important action we need to address." When Tibbets saw that Powers didn't object, he continued. "With the ground war now underway, the UN force is going to burn through a lot of war stocks. They're moving their fleet in the North Atlantic to engage our Navy and attempt to break the blockade.

"What I'd like to propose is a cruise missile attack by our submarines against the EU's major port facilities in Canada, Europe and China. This will seriously degrade their ability to support their own naval operations and provide any logistical support to their forces in Canada. My goal is to starve the enemy of supplies. Within two weeks, they'll start to run critically short of munitions, fuel, and food. At that point, it won't matter how much ground they'll have captured, they won't be able to hold it, and we'll begin to roll them up and push them back across the border."

The VP nodded in approval. "You said the other option was a political one—what do you propose?" he asked.

"Since this UN force just tried to decapitate our government, I propose we hit them back and try to do the same thing," Tibbets suggested.

Powers couldn't believe it had all come down to this—a tit-for-tat attack on each other's political and military leaders. Had it not been for the death of more than two hundred congressional leaders early in the day, the very idea would have repulsed him, but the pundits and talking heads on TV and the American people at large were screaming for blood. They wanted him to retaliate.

"Fine, General," he consented, crossing his arms. "You may proceed. But make sure you hammer them mercilessly. I want a strong political message sent to them. Make sure it hurts. If these nations want to wage war against us, then I want them to know that while the battles may be taking place in America, that doesn't mean we can't or won't hit them back in their home countries."

With the decision made, it was now only a matter of time until their response was felt around the world.

****

North Sea

For the past twelve hours, the crew of the USS *North Dakota*, a *Virginia*-class attack submarine, prowled the North Sea as they shifted to get into position to carry out the first offensive military action of the war against the nations that had attacked their homeland.

Walking into the communications room, Captain John Barry asked a simple question. "Any additional updates to our orders?"

He was still uncertain about the orders they'd received, but they had been verified and authenticated, so he had to implement them. However, that didn't mean he couldn't check in every few hours to see if they had been canceled or modified.

The two enlisted personnel and one officer manning the communications room turned and looked back at him. "No change to our orders, sir," replied the lieutenant. He handed the captain a folded piece of paper. "We did get a brief SITREP from back home that you should take a look at."

Captain Barry took the note. Seeing the concern on his LT's face, he remarked, "I take it you already read it."

They all nodded and shared some grim looks. "It's pretty bad, sir," said one of the petty officers.

Captain Barry unfolded the paper. As he read its contents, his heart sank. Then his anger grew. He shook his head in disgust.

Seeing the captain's reactions, one of the petty officers commented, "Yeah, that's pretty much how I felt."

"The freaking Pentagon and Capitol Building?" the captain blurted out, speaking to himself more than anyone else.

"Read the rest of it," said the communications officer grimly.

He looked back down at the message. He felt his fist tighten as he read.

The lieutenant in the room couldn't contain himself. "I can't believe they bombed Washington and killed the President. I mean—what the hell were they thinking? Do they really think we're going to take that sitting down?" He smacked his hand on a nearby table.

"Now I understand our orders," said Captain Barry. "It's retaliation."

He paced back and forth for a moment as he thought. "OK, guys, I need to get things ready. We're nearly to our launch point. Keep me apprised of any changes in our orders or anything new that comes across the wires. Oh, and this should go without saying, but keep this information private for the time being. I'll make an announcement to the crew following the launch. Right now, I want them focused on our task at hand, not what happened back home. All right, guys?" The captain had asked it as a question, but it was really meant as an order.

Seeing their nods, he closed their door and headed back to the control room. When Captain Barry entered the room filled with computers and highly trained men of war, he saw his XO waiting for him.

"Sir, we've reached our launch point. We're ready to begin the launch procedures when you're ready."

Captain Barry nodded, then turned to his weapons officer. "Let's get this going, then," he ordered. "We have a lot of missiles to launch, and I want to do our best to get the hell out of Dodge. God only knows who else is out there waiting for us to make a peep."

He felt a bit nervous about the possibility of a German or French sub lurking about. They all knew a German sub had sunk the *Truman* after slipping past the lead two subs escorting it out to sea. Captain Barry was a bit anxious that his own submarine's technology might not be as advanced as he'd once thought.

During the next ten minutes, the crew of the *North Dakota* launched their twelve Tomahawk cruise missiles at targets in Paris, Brussels, Germany and the Netherlands. Their sister ship, the *John Warner*, also joined the fray to send a message to the UN European partners.

When the missiles had launched, Barry let out a sigh of relief. Under his breath, he muttered, "If you want to invade America, attack our capital, and kill our President, we can do the same right back at you, and hit you a lot harder."

The Vice President's Operation Payback was now in full swing. Soon the Europeans would be reminded of American might and global reach.

****

40,000 Feet Above Beijing

Aboard the *Spirit of America* B-2 bomber, Lieutenant Colonel Joe Beckman checked their position one more time to make sure they were still on course. Starting about four hours ago, they'd been experiencing some navigational problems. It had all made sense when they'd received a message alerting them to the possibility of Chinese or Russian interference with the military's GPS system. Fortunately, they had a few other ways to make sure they made it to the target and could guide their bombs to their destination.

As they ran through the final checks on their bomb, his copilot, Reggie, asked, "You really think the President's dead?"

"I don't know. It sounds like he is. We'll probably never know for sure. Even if they can get inside the bunker, I heard the bomb pretty much incinerated everyone in it."

There was a moment of silence. "So, you think they'll get *our* message after we drop these bombs?" Reggie asked.

Turning to look at his copilot, Colonel Beckman replied, "Does it matter? We're about to drop ten bunker-buster bombs on the civilian and military leadership of China."

They rode in silence for another five minutes before their targeting computer told them they were nearly to the drop zone. As they approached the point of no return, they readied their bombs and prepared to unleash America's response to the attack on their government.

Beckman saw that they'd reached the drop zone and signaled to his partner to release the bombs. Reggie hit the button that opened the bomb bay doors, and one by one, the ten 5,000-pound GBU-28 bombs fell toward the earth below. They would gain speed with each passing second of free fall until they impacted against a variety of military and government targets across the city of Beijing.

Their sister bomber, the *Spirit of Texas*, also released their ten bombs, adding to the shock and awe the government of China was about to receive. Unlike previous bombing campaigns against countries like Iraq and Afghanistan, this bombing raid was taking place in broad daylight. With their bombs released, the two bombers turned and headed back for home and the waiting refueling tankers off the coast.

****

28,000 Feet Above Pittsburgh, Pennsylvania

Major Clay Williams of the 11th Bomb Squadron looked at the map and saw they were nearly to their launch point. Looking to his right, under the wing, he saw the two pods of three AGM-158 JASSM-ER or extended range joint air-to-surface standoff missiles, ready to be released.

This was their second bombing mission of the new war. Their first mission had been to deliver a series of cruise missiles aimed at the Canadian ports being used to offload equipment and supplies from Europe. This next round of missiles was being aimed at the Canadian airbases across the province of Ontario. Their squadron was going to hammer the bases at Kingston, Borden, and North Bay and the Trenton facility, as well as the smaller bases nearby at Canadian Forces Detachment Mountain View and Canadian Forces Station Alert. This would effectively cripple the UN's forward air bases closest to the US border.

The bulky B-52H bomber rattled a bit from some turbulence as they flew into another bank of gray clouds. Looking out the windows, Major Williams saw water molecules forming on the window and hit the windshield wipers.

"Systems check," he announced over the internal communications system.

A flash of lightning off in the distance nearly caused him to jump out of his seat. For a brief second, he thought it was an enemy missile or tracer fire from a fighter plane. He took a couple of deep breaths as he waited for his crew members to go through their checks.

A second later, the weapons officer replied, "All weapons show green. We're ready for weapons release."

Captain Tim Lee, his copilot, looked nervously at him before returning his gaze to the sky around them. "This storm might be more dangerous than we thought," he commented.

Major Williams nodded, then turned to look at his copilot. "Just keep watching the radars, Lee, and make sure nothing unusual shows up. We're almost ready to head back home and get out of this soup we're flying in."

His copilot turned to look at him. "I keep envisioning an F-35 popping up out of nowhere and jumping us," Lee said.

Major Williams shook his head. "After this mission's done, I don't think we'll have to worry about that."

"I sure hope you're right. I still can't believe *four* of our bombers got nailed by a single F-35 yesterday."

"It's war, Lee—we're going to take losses. We aren't fighting the Taliban or the Iraqis; this is a modern air force that knows what it's doing. Why do you think we're using the ER version of the JASSM this time? It will give more distance between us and the front line. Just stay focused on your tasks and I'll get us home," he explained confidently.

Another minute went by before their weapons officer came over the intercom. "We've reached the launch point. Unless you say otherwise, sir, I'm going to begin releasing our weapons."

He smiled. *About time*, he thought.

"Begin weapons release. I want to get us out of here."

Seconds later, the ground-attack cruise missiles dropped from their wings and internal bomb bay.

As each missile was released, its small wings immediately popped out just as the engine ignited. Then it would race on its journey to its preprogrammed target.

In the span of a couple of minutes, Major Williams's B-52H bomber released twenty missiles. The eleven remaining bombers in their squadron also released their own JASSM-ERs, adding to the volley of death being hurled at the UN peacekeeping force. It was time to bring the hammer down.

****

The four bombers of Zebra Flight were doing their best to evade the many Russian and Chinese surface-to-air missile systems, not to mention some former NATO-allied SAMs for good measure, like the venerable Patriot III system. If two squadrons of F-16 Vipers and F-22s hadn't flown ahead of them—along with a massive cruise missile attack against the enemy air defense systems—they probably wouldn't have made it this far into Canadian airspace, especially given how heavily the Russians and Chinese had saturated the area with SAMs.

As it was, their warning systems were almost continually going off. New threats would be identified, and then as their countermeasures kicked in or the SAM site was attacked, that threat would disappear.

The pilot, Major Banks, or "Bang-Bang" to his friends, banked hard to the right, hugging the side of another forested area, using the trees and ground clutter for cover.

"How did we get stuck being the ones who'd have to overfly the damn runway?" asked First Lieutenant Rick "Ricky" Porter, for the third time. Apparently he hadn't been satisfied with the first two answers that had been given to him.

Major Banks groaned. *Why did my previous offensive weapons officer have to go and get appendicitis the week before a war started?* he asked himself. Ricky had been temporarily assigned to the plane until his other crew member was healthy enough, and he was getting on Banks's last nerve.

"Just do your job, Ricky, and get the weapons ready," Banks retorted. "We're nearly to the target. When we come around this next bend, I'm going to slow down a bit as we rise up to 2,000 feet to give us enough room to drop the bombs. Make sure to yell out when they've all been released because I'm going to light up the afterburners to get us the hell out of there once you've released them all."

Ricky grumbled to himself but began to get the weapons ready. He was really green, and he'd only finished offensive weapons officer training a month ago. He hadn't been assigned to a crew yet. Under normal circumstances, he would have flown with a crew on a series of training missions to gain a better understanding of the types of missions he'd be flying, but sadly, that wasn't in the cards he'd been dealt.

Their squadron had flown a mission last night, mostly doing this same mission over Ontario, but their bird had been taken out of the mission at the last minute because of a mechanical error. Having missed out on the first mission, Major Banks had been eager to get in on the action. When their squadron commander had asked for two volunteers to carry out the riskiest part of the mission, the cratering of the runways, Major Banks had volunteered. He'd figured the other guys had already flown one dangerous mission without him, and it was only fair that his crew fly one of the riskier missions this time. Of course, he hadn't told the rest of his crew that—he'd tell them after the mission was complete.

"OK, here we go," Banks announced over the intercom as he lined them up for their pass over the base.

As soon as they leveled out, the whole world around them suddenly filled with red and green tracer fire as thousands upon thousands of projectiles sought them out.

"Holy crap! That's a lot of AA!" shouted Marty, the defensive weapons officer. He swiftly did what he could to make sure none of the radar-guided anti-aircraft guns got a solid lock on them.

Many lines of tracers crisscrossed the sky, flying at nearly every possible angle like a spectacular laser show. Intermixed with the strings of enemy fire were small flashes of explosions that kept happening at a higher altitude.

"We're coming over the runways now!" shouted Banks to Ricky.

Ricky hit the weapons release button, and the bombs in the internal bay released. All eighty-one Snake Eyes strung across the entire runway of the base, their four-pointed high-drag tailfins opening up to slow the bombs' fall and help angle them to land at just the right position to inflict maximum damage on the concrete slabs of the runway.

"All weapons released!" shouted Ricky.

In a fraction of a second, the four 30,780-horsepower engines thrust to maximum power and the bomber banked hard to the left as Major Banks tried to put as much distance as possible between them and the target they'd just bombed.

Without warning, the scope in front of Ricky shattered. Sparks flew out and blood was all over him. Frigid cold air suddenly swirled around inside the cockpit.

"We've been hit. I need a damage report!" shouted Banks.

"Hydraulic levels are dropping. Engine one appears to be on fire!" his copilot exclaimed.

"Shut down the engine. I'm going to try and get us some more altitude in case we have to ditch. What's everyone's status?" Banks asked.

Everyone called back that they were OK, except Ricky. Banks called out again, but there was no response.

"I think Ricky's dead," said Marty.

There wasn't too much time to think about that at the moment. The two small holes in the windshield brought in more and more cold air, making it uncomfortably frigid in the cabin. Tracer fire still swept toward them, although it seemed that the bulk of the tracers were still focused back at the airfield. Those targeting them seemed to be oblivious to the fact that they'd already gotten out of the area.

Then the alarm bells blared, warning them that they'd just been acquired by radar. Seconds later, a string of bright objects flew directly at them. Before Banks could take evasive maneuvers or Marty could get the radar jammed, a string of 30mm projectiles plowed right through the cockpit of the bomber, tearing it apart and killing the entire crew in the process. Moments later, the Lancer blew apart into a massive fireball, its wreckage strewn across several hundred yards of a nearby forest.

****

Canadian Forces Base Cold Lake

The crew of the SA-19 "Grison" sat there for a moment, transfixed as they heard what sounded like the end of the world happening not more than five or six miles away at the large Canadian airbase. Dozens upon dozens of anti-aircraft guns fired constantly while the air raid sirens blared, letting everyone know the base was under attack.

Sergeant Kvetsinsky didn't waste a moment. "Get your radar turned back on and start scanning the horizon for possible threats!" he yelled.

A few minutes went by as they watched the fireworks show. Strings of red and green tracer fire filled the night sky, intermixed with smaller explosions. The defenders were clearly doing their best to throw as much shrapnel and projectiles into the air as possible in hopes that one or more

250

pieces would connect with the bombers, missiles or whatever it was that was headed toward the base.

Then a much brighter amber burst lit up the base. In quick succession, before they even felt the ground shake or heard the sound of the first explosion, what seemed like hundreds of orange fireballs popped up all across the runways, hangars and parking ramps of the massive airbase. Soon after, their senses were utterly overwhelmed by the sheer noise of the thunderous explosions, and the ground shook violently from the blasts.

"Get ready, here they come!" shouted the radar operator inside the vehicle. He steered the turret in the direction of the enemy plane he was tracking.

The corporal manning the 30mm machine gun depressed the fire button and sent a barrage of fire in the direction the radar operator had indicated as the source of the threat. No sooner had he fired his first barrage of bullets than they were rewarded with the sight of a massive bomber flying practically straight for them.

Sergeant Kvetsinsky watched as the first string of rounds flew right into the nose section of the big bomber. As the first tracer round hit the nose, he knew instinctively that the next six rounds would likewise be walked right up the nose of the plane and into the crew compartment of the aircraft.

The front part of the aircraft began to disintegrate from the sheer speed at which it was traveling and the fact that the cockpit was no longer aerodynamic. Seconds later, the bomber exploded, breaking apart as it crashed into the ground.

With his eyes wide as saucers, Sergeant Kvetsinsky realized the burning beast of a warplane was now careening right for them. Before he could yell at the driver to move them out of the way, a wave of debris and fire mixed with fuel engulfed their vehicle and everyone in it. His crew had succeeded in shooting down a B-1 bomber, but they'd also perished in the process. In that last flicker of existence, Kvetsinsky saw a prophetic flash of all of the honors and awards they would receive posthumously in Russia for their gallant efforts.

****

From the *Washington Examiner*:

Nearly two days after the UN army attacked Camp David and the Pentagon's alternate command post at Raven Rock, it still has not been confirmed if President Jonathan Sachs is dead or alive. Spokesmen from FEMA and the Army Corps of Engineers have stated that they have a team of specialists working to gain entry into the bombed-out bunker, but it may be days before they are able to confirm if there were any survivors.

With the President either dead or incapacitated, Vice President Luke Powers has taken over as acting President. Powers said in a statement to the press that "the sneak attack on Washington, D.C., and the assassination of more than 200 congresspersons and senators, was a barbaric act that won't go unpunished." He went on to express that he had ordered retaliatory strikes against Russia, China, France, Germany, Belgium and the Netherlands.

Acting President Powers also asked the remaining members of Congress to issue a formal Declaration of War against the nations who are participating in this UN invasion of America. The minority leader, Democratic Congressman Jesús Perez, introduced a war declaration within an hour of that request and has publicly rallied for his caucus and the Republicans to join him in pushing it through Congress.

Powers continues to urge people to remain calm across the country, saying, "The American leadership had planned for these types of contingencies, and we do have a plan in place. We are still functioning as a government; services will continue to be provided, and our brave men and women in uniform are doing everything in their power to defend our great nation. As acting President, I'm asking that all Americans continue to go to work and do their best to carry on with their lives. Please continue to support our law enforcement officials and our men and women in uniform."

Powers added, "The Pentagon has announced a plan to increase the size of the military by three million servicemembers. If you are physically able and willing to join, I ask that you step forward and help us defeat these foreign invaders."

****

From the *New York Times*:

> New Yorkers are torn between their support of President-Elect Marshall Tate and his government in exile in Canada, and the Sachs administration in Washington, D.C. After the sneak attack on Washington, and the killing of more than 200 congressional leaders, nine of which were from the state of New York, many are uncertain if they still support Senator Tate's decision to involve the UN. Even now, UN military forces are less than 100 miles from New York City. Many who do not agree with the UN mission have begun to flee the city ahead of the advancing army.

****

From the *BBC News Online*:

> The world stands collectively aghast at the cruise missile attack carried out against the French capital of Paris during the morning rush hour. At approximately 8:32 a.m., air raid sirens were heard throughout the capital as many Parisians were on their way to work. Without warning, two American Tomahawk cruise missiles struck the Élysée Palace, causing immense damage. Fires raged out of control in the building for nearly two hours before firefighters were able to contain the blaze. It is reported that the President was not at the palace during the attack, though his wife was, and is presumed to have died in the missile strike.
>
> Four additional cruise missiles struck the Ministry of Defence, often referred to as the French Pentagon. The ports of Marseille, Le Havre, Cherbourg, and Brest were also struck by dozens of American cruise missiles, rendering much of the port facilities useless.
>
> According to French defence officials, the cruise missile attacks originated from American submarines operating in the Mediterranean and the North Sea. A massive hunt is currently

underway to find and sink these submarines before they can do further damage.

British defence officials confirmed that the cruise missile attack carried out by the American submarines was not directed at France alone. American stealth bombers also hit targets in Belgium, bombing the ports of Antwerp and Bruges. Several bombs also hit the Belgian Ministry of Defence building.

In the Netherlands, the port facilities of Rotterdam and several railheads were also hit by American stealth bombers. These facilities may have been targeted due to their efforts in support of the UN peacekeeping operations in North America. Germany was also not spared in the overnight raids by US forces; the ports of Bremerhaven, Kiel, and Hamburg saw immense damage. Fires are still raging there as of the time of this publication.

American stealth bombers carried out a bold daylight raid against the German, Russian and Chinese capitals. In Germany, American stealth bombers destroyed the Reichstag and Ministry of Defence buildings. They also hit the Chancellor's residence, thoroughly destroying it. In Russia, American stealth bombers hit the Kremlin and two dachas where the Russian president's family reportedly often stay. It is unclear if he or his family were killed, though it is clear they were the intended targets of the raid.

In China, Beijing was rocked by a total of twenty strikes. It has been reported that the Great Hall of the People has been thoroughly destroyed, along with the August 1st Building and Zhongnanhai government residence complex adjacent to the Forbidden City, where President Chen lives, along with the senior leaders of the Chinese government and their families. It is unclear how many of the leaders of China were killed.

One thing has been made abundantly clear by these coordinated strikes—the United States is retaliating for the UN attack on Washington, D.C., and the presumed assassination of President Jonathan Sachs and more than 200 of their elected officials. Nearly one-third of the American federal government was killed during the early morning raid on Washington, D.C., nearly 30 hours ago. Much of the American government is still hiding in their bunkers, unsure if it is safe to return to their normal functions.

****

From *Der Spiegel*:

Norwegian military units under the command of the United Nations have succeeded in capturing the US state of Maine. After some brief fighting with American ground forces in the area, Spanish, Italian and Belgian troops have succeeded in capturing the states of Vermont and New Hampshire. UN forces have also entered the state of Massachusetts, though they are facing fierce opposition by American Marines stationed nearby.

Canadian Forces have seized control of the northern half of New York state, and have succeeded in isolating the few American forces that were still fighting in Massachusetts and Connecticut. It is believed the UN will capture New York City sometime today as the American government has declared it an open city to spare it from the fighting.

In the Midwest, the elite Dutch-German Division Schnelle Kräfte have broken through the American lines north of the city of Detroit in the state of Michigan. A Russian Army group also punched through the American lines in Detroit after heavy fighting within the city. The Russians have now progressed beyond Detroit and captured the city of Toledo along Lake Erie in Ohio. Russian forces are now moving to capture the city of Cleveland as part of their army group splits off to drive on the capital of Ohio, Columbus.

The Schnelle Kräfte division is currently engaging the American 1st Cavalry and 101st Airborne Division at Battle Creek, Michigan. When they break through this last line of defense, it is believed they will move to liberate the city of Chicago, Illinois, before expanding further into the center of the country. Fighting between the German and American forces is reported to be fierce and bloody, with little quarter being given to either side.

In the West, Russian and Canadian forces have been stopped at the city of Kent, halfway between the cities of Seattle and Tacoma in the western state of Washington. The West Coast states of Oregon and California have announced that they have officially broken away from the United States government, swearing their loyalty to President-Elect Marshall Tate, whose government continues to operate in exile in Ottawa, Canada.

California's Civil Defense Forces, the state-controlled militia force, attacked and overran Beale Air Force Base, seizing control of much of the federal government's surveillance and drone equipment and capabilities in the process. Heavy fighting is being reported outside Travis Air Force Base in Fairfield, California, just west of the state capital of Sacramento and east of San Francisco.

In Southern California, the US Marines have sealed off control of everything from the Mexican border to just south of Los Angeles. It has been reported that there is heavy fighting between the various militia units and renegade California Army National Guard units and the Marines stationed in the area. With critical naval facilities in San Diego and the Marine base at Camp Pendleton, it is no surprise that the federal government has sought to secure the area.

Chinese forces continue to arrive in Mexico, threatening the entire southern border of the US. It is expected that Chinese forces will begin attacking within the next couple of days.

****

From the *Toronto Star*:

Canadian citizens are appalled at the most recent American attack on Canadian soil. Last night, the Americans carried out a daring deep strike raid, destroying the Canadian Forces Base at Cold Lake. It is estimated that over 4,000 military and civilian members were killed during the early morning raid.

The previous night, the Americans raided the province of Ontario, destroying all four air bases in the process. The Ministry of Defence reports the casualties have now risen to over 7,000 UN forces killed and more than twice that number injured since the start of hostilities. It is unclear at this point how much of the UN's air force is still operational after two days of heavy aerial fighting.

American Special Forces carried out a series of raids, destroying more than a dozen rail bridges connecting Eastern and Western Canada. Meanwhile in Mexico, the Chinese ground forces are preparing for a new offensive aimed at capturing Southern California along with the border states of Arizona and New Mexico. With the death of President Sachs by a daring raid on his command bunker, President-Elect Marshall Tate has once again made an impassioned plea for acting President Powers to end the bloody fighting and leave office.

Chapter 15
Stunned

Annapolis Junction, Maryland

It was a cloudy morning—the sun had been unable to burn its way through the thick overcast that threatened the city with snow. Colonel Zaitsev of Spetsgruppa A smiled—it was the perfect weather for what they were about to do today. There was really no better way to impair the abilities of an aerial search party.

As they drove down the parkway in his Chevy Suburban with blacked out windows, Zaitsev made sure to stay approximately three vehicles behind their blacked-out thirty-passenger bus. He checked his rearview mirror. Their second Suburban was still a few cars back, ready to act as their backup should they need it.

"What do we do if the Americans have a checkpoint at the business park?" asked Lieutenant Kanakin nervously. He scanned outside the passenger window continuously for any possible threats.

Casually turning to look at the young officer, Zaitsev saw that Kanakin's anxiety was increasing with each passing moment. His hand was fidgeting with his AK-15K assault rifle. This was his first real mission with them, and it was showing.

Zaitsev shook his head slightly as he returned his gaze to the traffic on the road and the passenger bus they were following. "Lieutenant, you worry too much," he said nonchalantly. "Please, calm yourself. You're going to miss things happening around us if you're too edgy. We have driven this route several times. The Americans have never had a checkpoint to enter the business park, and they will not have one today. Just make sure you don't forget to monitor the business park for electronic jammers that might interfere with the remote detonator."

"*Da*," Kanakin replied. He resumed his vigilant gaze out the passenger-side window.

It was now 0928 hours. They were catching the tail end of the morning commute, so the traffic was relatively light compared to what it would have been ninety minutes earlier. When Zaitsev saw the sign for Jessup Road, he turned his blinker light on and pulled onto the off-ramp, following the bus as it did the same.

As they left the parkway, they seamlessly slid into the remains of the morning commuters and drove the short distance to the intersection of Jessup and National Business Parkway. As they stopped at the red light, Zaitsev reached down and grabbed the black balaclava mask and placed it on the top of his head, ready to pull down and cover his face when the time came. When the light turned green, Lieutenant Kanakin also placed his balaclava on his head.

After their vehicle passed the large blue water tower on the left-hand side of the road, they entered the traffic circle and headed down the home stretch to their target. At this point, Colonel Zaitsev turned to his nervous partner. "See? I told you…no checkpoints," he said.

The young officer sighed, and then he seemed to calm down a bit. After they rounded a bend in the road, they saw a cluster of three-to-eight-story-tall office buildings, intermixed with trees and parking garages for the army of contractors that worked in these secretive buildings.

To the untrained eye, this was just a typical American business park. However, these were no ordinary office buildings. These structures were secured compartmentalized information facilities that belonged to companies that managed nearly half of the National Security Agency's workload. This army of contractors and government service employees managed the offsite data management, storage, analysis, and intelligence capabilities for America's electronic warriors. The main NSA building sat just across the highway.

When the blacked-out passenger bus turned onto NSA Technology Drive, Zaitsev turned to his partner. "Be ready in case there's trouble. When Starshina Dyachenko stops the bus, he will secure the door and get into our vehicle. Then we'll race over to link up with Viper One."

Kanakin nodded, seeming much more prepared for the moment now.

Checking his rearview mirror one last time, Zaitsev saw the BMW that carried his four other team members pull off to take up position at the next target. Looking back in front of him, the bus slowed down as it approached the pulloff in front of the Eagle Alliance building. There were no large-capacity commuter vans or buses ahead of them or behind them, so it looked like they'd be able to make the drop quickly and then get out of there.

Starshina Dyachenko, the operator driving the bus, pulled into the specially designated spot and parked. As he turned the vehicle off, Zaitsev pulled his Chevy Suburban just in front of the bus and stopped. He depressed the unlock button on the door just as Dyachenko rounded the front of the bus and jumped into the SUV. Before anyone in the immediate area knew what had just happened, they sped off through the rest of the parking lot as they raced to get in position near the Booz Allen building a couple of blocks away.

"When we round the next corner, I want you to detonate the bus," Zaitsev ordered as he continued to hit the accelerator. "We need to get the other buildings to start evacuating their people for the next phase."

They whipped past nearby vehicles and the few pedestrians who were still straggling into the office. Zaitsev wanted to put as much distance as possible between them and the bomb they'd just parked. A few more seconds went by before they rounded the next corner, placing one of the large buildings between them and the bus.

"It's time," Colonel Zaitsev announced.

Starshina Dyachenko had a devilish look on his face. He moved his right thumb over the detonator button and depressed it, almost flinching at what was sure to be the loudest boom he'd ever heard.

Unexpectedly, their worst fear came true. The bomb didn't explode.

Knowing something had just gone drastically wrong, Zaitsev slammed his foot on the brake, causing the Suburban's tires to screech and the front of the vehicle to dive forward. They slid across the asphalt, nearly fishtailing in the process. When the Suburban came to a halt, he turned around to face Dyachenko.

"What's going on? Why is it not going off?" he yelled.

After frantically hitting the button a couple more times, Dyachenko just shook his head in frustration and confusion.

Lieutenant Kanakin pulled a small electronic device out of his pocket and hurriedly turned it on. His eyes went wide as he realized what the problem was. "They have the frequencies jammed. That's why it won't detonate."

Turning his wrath on Kanakin, Colonel Zaitsev screamed, "You had *one* job, Lieutenant! How could you have forgotten to check to make sure the Americans were not jamming the RFID frequencies when we got near the target?"

Lieutenant Kanakin hung his head in shame. Had they known the frequencies were being jammed, Dyachenko would have initiated the manual fuse, which would burn down for three minutes before detonating the charges within the bus.

Not wanting to waste any more time disciplining the inexperienced member of his team, Zaitsev threw the SUV into reverse, slamming his foot on the gas pedal. This threw the vehicle into a rapid, tight turn as he swung the vehicle around so they faced the road they had just raced down.

"Starshina, when we get back to the bus, you know you need to go back inside and set the manual fuse, but *don't forget* to relock the door. We can't afford any more screwups!" he yelled. He slowed the vehicle down just enough to make the final turn that would bring them back to the bus.

The Russian sergeant cursed at the young lieutenant as he readied his own AK-15K, knowing all too well he'd probably end up having to use it in another minute.

"I sure hope you haven't screwed up the mission for us," he muttered.

As they pulled around the corner, they spotted a federal police vehicle parked behind the bus with its flashing lights on. A couple of police officers were examining the bus when they looked up at them, their eyes wide as they realized the vehicle that had just roared around the corner was heading right for them.

Sensing immediate danger, the two police officers moved to a defensible position near the open doors of their car and drew their sidearms. Zaitsev saw one of them reach for a radio.

Pop, pop, crack!

The front windshield of the Suburban took a couple of hits as Zaitsev and Kanakin instinctively ducked a bit to avoid getting hit. When they were maybe twenty meters from the police officers, Zaitsev slammed the brakes, bringing the vehicle to a hard halt.

In the blink of an eye, Lieutenant Kanakin was out the door with his AK-15K in hand. Using the passenger door as a shield, he flicked the safety off and let loose a string of shots at the two cops. His 7.62mm rounds punched right through the driver's-side door and the police officers' body armor.

While Kanakin was hammering the officer near the driver's side of the vehicle, Colonel Zaitsev fired three well-placed shots into the other officer on his side, aiming two to the chest and one to the head, just as he'd done countless times over his twenty-eight years in the Russian Special Forces.

Dyachenko darted past them and ran up to the bus. He fumbled with his keys for a second as he found the right one and proceeded to unlock the bus. He then dashed inside to set the manual fuse.

Zaitsev turned to the front entrance of the building nearest the bus just in time to see half a dozen armed security guards burst out the front entrance. Moving his rifle to the new threats, the colonel let loose a long burst from his rifle as he attempted to rake as many of them with bullets as possible. The guards all dove for cover behind anything they could, but the barrage still struck a couple of them.

Spent shell casings rained to the ground around Zaitsev's feet, clinking and clanking as they hit the pavement. The rapid staccato reports of his rifle barked loudly in comparison to the guards' pistols. The noise echoed off the buildings around them, adding to the chaos of this surreal scene.

"Reloading!" Zaitsev shouted. He dropped his now empty magazine to the ground and grabbed for a fresh one from his front ammo pouch. He slapped the new magazine in place and charged the bolt, seating the new round in place.

"Switching!" Kanakin yelled in reply. He advanced around the front hood of the Suburban, then proceeded to empty the rest of his magazine at the security guards to cover Zaitsev while he reloaded.

"Reloading!" Kanakin then shouted as he dropped his own empty magazine to the ground, essentially swapping positions with his colonel.

With a fresh magazine slapped in place, Zaitsev resumed firing on the guards.

Ping, crack, ping, crack!

Bullets flew back at them, hitting the Suburban and shattering several of the vehicle's windows. The bullets zipped past Zaitsev's head like angry bees.

Dropping to a knee, Zaitsev emptied his second magazine at three of the attackers who were trying to bound forward toward him. He hit two of them while the third one ducked behind something and shot back at him.

Dyachenko finally finished with the fuse and emerged from the bus. He stopped just long enough to close the door and relock it. Their only hope at this point was to prevent the guards from getting inside long enough for the charges to go off.

Dyachenko turned. As he took his first steps back toward his comrades, he was hit by half a dozen bullets from a new set of security guards that had appeared out of nowhere.

Crap! They've flanked us, Zaitsev realized.

The colonel grabbed one of the hand grenades from his vest and tossed it toward a group of guards that were hunkered down behind another police vehicle that had pulled forward to help provide them with some cover.

"I've got two more security vehicles heading in our direction!" shouted Kanakin as he fired off a series of shots toward the new targets. The police cruisers swerved and came to a screeching halt a hundred meters away from them. The officers got out and returned fire.

"We have to get out of here!" Zaitsev yelled before uttering a stream of particularly vulgar obscenities.

The colonel jumped back into the Suburban, closing the door just as the driver's-side window shattered in his face, hitting him with tiny shards of plexiglass. Kanakin also jumped in. Before the lieutenant could even get his door closed, Zaitsev had the SUV in drive and floored it. He sped down the road they had originally started down and raced to link up with the rest of his team, which was currently sitting in the other office park nearby.

"Kanakin, keep shooting at them!" Zaitsev yelled. He tried to make himself small behind the wheel while still trying to see where he was going.

All around them they could hear police sirens, angry shouts in English, gunshots, and the metallic crunching of bullets hitting their vehicle.

Suddenly the radio crackled to life in his ear. "Viper Six. What's going on?" asked Major Zlobin, his second-in-command.

"Finally. At least the radios are working," Kanakin muttered to himself as he swapped out a half-spent magazine with a fresh one.

"Viper One, Viper Five is down," he said, depressing the talk button. "They must've had a warlock turned on somewhere near the buildings. The remote detonator wouldn't work, so we had to go back

263

and set the manual charge. Our cover's blown, so go ahead and start the party. We're on our way to your position."

"*Da!*" came the reply.

Zaitsev blew through the intersection as they raced to the next set of office buildings. As he rounded the next corner, he heard the loud ripping of a machine gun opening fire, followed by a small blast.

He spotted the Suburban parked in the center of the road and gunned the engine toward them. One of Zaitsev's soldiers had just finished placing another RPG round in his launcher. Zaitsev watched as the man aimed it at another one of the office buildings and fired. The RPG launched itself toward a glass window on the third floor of the nearby building, exploding in spectacular fashion and throwing shrapnel and glass in all directions.

Another one of his soldiers had the bipod of his PKP MG set up on the rear trunk of a car. He proceeded to fire the machine-gun rounds into the ground level of one of the adjacent buildings in an attempt to kill as many of the people inside as possible.

Zaitsev pulled his Suburban to a halt just to the side of the matching SUV. Colonel Zaitsev and Lieutenant Kanakin jumped out of their vehicle and joined the fray, shooting up the buildings all around them. They pumped as many rounds into the various buildings as they could, trying to kill or maim as many of the people working inside as possible.

Glancing down the block, Zaitsev saw several police cars racing toward their position when suddenly he heard the loudest explosion of his lifetime. The earth shook and they all fell to the ground.

As he sat on his butt, momentarily dazed, Colonel Zaitsev looked up and saw a massive orange-and-black fireball growing in the sky. Debris fell back to the ground like rain. As his eyes drifted below, Zaitsev saw that the explosion had been so massive, it had blown out all the windows of the buildings and vehicles around them.

Zaitsev, who had now fully recovered his senses, yelled to the others. "Time to go! Head to the rally point and let's swap out our vehicles. It's time to get out of here!"

With that, the soldiers of Spetsgruppa A climbed back in their vehicles and sped out of the corporate park. The men raced down the road at a high rate of speed in the two shot-up SUVs with blown-out windows, jumping onto the Baltimore-Washington Memorial Highway. They rushed along until they came upon the next off-ramp and speedily exited the freeway. Then they pulled into the parking lot of a Total Wine, where the next set of drop vehicles was waiting for them.

The six surviving Russian Special Forces soldiers jumped out of the two Suburbans, grabbing their bags filled with gear—extra magazines, grenades and other supplies they might need. They swiftly threw the equipment and weapons into the new vehicles. Then Lieutenant Kanakin and one of the other soldiers pulled the pins on a couple of thermite grenades and tossed them into the shot-up remains of the SUVs, jumping into the new cars and speeding off.

In the rearview mirror, Colonel Zaitsev watched as the thermite grenades exploded. They would start an intense fire that would eventually burn the vehicles all the way down to the frame, eliminating any forensic evidence they might have left behind.

Now that they had their new rides, they pulled out onto Laurel Fort Meade Road and headed west. Their next goal was to get out into the countryside of Maryland and the next rally point, where they would once again change out cars before heading off to their safe house to prepare for the next mission.

****

24 Hours Later
Washington, D.C.
White House, PEOC Bunker

Acting President Luke Powers was typically a calm, mild-mannered man. He seldom lost his cool or even appeared angry in public, but after being stuck in the belly of the PEOC for nearly four days, his patience was running thin. The war was now entering its fourth day, and while some aspects of the conflict were finally breaking in their direction, others were not.

It was nearly time for the impromptu meeting his generals had called, but before he left his sleeping quarters, Powers wanted to review the intelligence summary of the last few days to get caught up on all that had transpired. It was almost dizzying to think of how quickly the battle lines had changed; he'd never realized the fluid nature of a complex conflict before.

By the end of the second day of the war, the UN forces had captured Maine, New Hampshire, Vermont, Massachusetts, Connecticut, and most of New York. By the end of the third day, they'd captured half of Ohio, all of Michigan, the upper half of Indiana, northern Illinois, and the upper portion of Wisconsin.

Yesterday was one of the few bright spots. In the upper Midwest, the UN force had been soundly defeated in a massive running tank battle along the North Dakota-Montana-Canadian border. The battle had gone on for nearly three days before it broke decidedly for the Americans. The 4th Infantry Division, which had been deployed to the upper Midwest, had officially crossed into Canada and was even now advancing on Winnipeg. They'd then move to capture Regina and Calgary as they sought to remove the UN forces in the west and threaten to divide Canada.

In Washington state, a joint Canadian-Russian force had been stopped just south of Seattle. Unfortunately, the 2nd Infantry Division lacked the manpower and resources to push them back across the border until additional help could arrive. Sadly, two of the National Guard divisions that had been slated to come to their assistance had to be diverted to deal with the uprisings in Oregon and California—the two states that had broken from the federal government and were actively working to support the UN force any way they could.

In the Southwest, the Chinese continued to marshal their forces in Baja California and the Sonora Desert. While they hadn't crossed the border or engaged the few National Guard and active duty forces along the border, they'd been hitting US forces with a number of cruise missiles, making air operations nearly impossible.

However, the primary reasons for the impromptu meeting that would be happening in a few minutes were: to discuss the damage assessment from the attack on the NSA yesterday, and to strategize regarding how to respond to the large concentration of Russian, Cuban and Venezuelan forces being assembled in Cuba.

There was a soft knock on Powers's door. Rick, his lead Secret Service agent, announced, "Sir, it's time to head over to the briefing room."

The acting President nodded, placed the report on a pad of paper and took it with him as he stood and exited his private quarters. The two of them walked through the hallway in silence.

As they made a turn to walk down another identical hall, Luke Powers couldn't help but feel like he had been down in this bunker for weeks. He'd already made two televised addresses to the nation from down there. It was starting to feel a bit claustrophobic.

However, while he desperately wanted to go back to the residence and show the American people that it was safe to return to work and their daily lives, the Secret Service was having none of it until the Navy felt reasonably sure there were no enemy submarines lurking off the coast of Virginia that could hit the capital with submarine-launched cruise missiles. The country was still reeling from the loss of President Sachs and more than two hundred congressional leaders. They couldn't risk losing the Vice President as well.

As acting President Powers entered the room, the small cadre of military generals and senior advisors all rose. He waved at them to take their seats and made his way to the empty chair at the center of the table, which faced the two TV monitors. The outstations were already up and waiting for him.

Before he spoke, Powers surveyed the room. The looks of concern were evident on the faces of the men and women before him, but he could also perceive their determination and strength.

He looked up at the monitor that displayed the feed from NORAD. "General Tibbets, what's the damage report from the NSA?" he asked.

With a grim expression, the general replied, "It's pretty bad, sir. The hit on the business park was made by a Russian Spetsnaz team. They drove a bus to the one building that housed our cyber-warfare analytical cell and blew it up. EOD estimates the bus had to have been packed with probably close to 15,000 pounds of high explosives. They're still putting out some fires and sifting through rubble as they continue to search for survivors, but presently, it's looking like around 1,740 people were killed. Probably around twice that many were injured."

Powers shook his head in disgust. "Was there anything we could have done to prevent this from happening?" he asked.

Letting out a short sigh, General Tibbets replied, "Yes and no. I mean, we could have closed off the business park and essentially turned it into a controlled military facility, but it wasn't designed for that, so it would have created a disorganized jumble when people tried to come to work. There weren't specially built entry control points like we have on a military base to accommodate people coming and going."

The general paused for a second as he searched for what to say. "Since 9/11, the DoD's had to outsource a lot of our missions to various government contracting companies. The scope and scale of the intelligence mission, data collection, and analysis of said data was just too big for us to handle on our own—so we outsourced it. We could scale up or scale down depending on our needs at the time. It made economic sense to do so. The problem was it also meant we had a lot of important work being done at facilities that aren't nearly as hardened as some of our critical military bases."

Jumping into the conversation, CIA Director Marcus Ryerson added, "During the Cold War, the Russians had specialized Spetsnaz teams operating inside the US and NATO countries that had trained to carry out this exact type of operation should a war break out. I think we grew a little complacent over the years and failed to account for the fact that they probably still had this type of operational capability within our borders. I recommend we task the FBI and JSOC to specifically hunt down this unit and any others that might be out there."

FBI Director Polanski nodded in agreement, and so did General Tibbets.

"OK. Make it happen, gentlemen," Powers ordered. He took a deep breath and let it out. "Now let's switch topics and talk about this force down in Cuba. What the heck is going on down there?"

Signaling for a slide to be brought up on their shared screen, General Tibbets explained, "The Russians have been busy using their transport ships to move a lot of Venezuelan troops and military equipment to Cuba. Although most of their equipment is old and outdated and these soldiers are poorly trained and led, they can still kill and cause us some problems. We believe they're gearing up to try and land some ground forces in Florida or the Caribbean to try and stir up some trouble. They know most of our combat forces are in the Midwest and Northeast. With the Chinese looking like they were going to invade through the Southwest, we've unfortunately left the coast of Florida and the Caribbean wide open."

"If that's the case, what are we doing about it?" asked Powers.

Admiral Chester Smith had stayed silent but jumped into the conversation at this point. "We've moved several of our submarines to a few positions around Cuba. They've been given orders to pretty much sink any ship they come across that isn't American. We also moved a small task force of two *Ticonderoga*-class cruisers and three destroyers to the Gulf of Mexico. They're going to work with the Coast Guard and either clear or sink the remaining freighters still in the Gulf.

"We've been slowly and steadily hunting down those merchant raiders that hit us during the first day of the war. That task force in and of itself is more than enough firepower to prevent those forces on Cuba from being able to cross the straits to Florida. We'll keep them bottled up and useless on Cuba."

Smiling, the acting President responded, "Thank you, Admiral. One less thing to worry about."

General Markus, the Air Force Chief of Staff, interjected, "The ground forces on Cuba aren't the real problem, Mr. Vice President—it's those SAM nests the Russians built up across the island. They make it nearly impossible for us to carry out any sort of air operations across Florida, southern Georgia, and the rest of the Gulf coast. We need to retask some of our air assets from up north to deal with this threat so we can regain our freedom of air movement."

Powers grunted. He knew the Air Force had been annoyed at him for not allowing them to marshal the needed air assets and bombers to go after the Cuban SAMs. While it was an enormous inconvenience not being able to effectively operate aircraft across the Southeast and Gulf states, the more significant threat had been in the Northeast. Not to mention there had been a considerable need to support the 4th ID in the upper Midwest. However, with the 4th ID now on the way to victory, it might be time to finally deal with this problem in Cuba.

Looking at General Tibbets, acting President Powers asked, "General, do you believe you can detail off enough assets to deal with the Cuban threat without disproportionally affecting our ground operations in the Midwest or the Northeast?"

There was a short pause as the general assessed the situation. "I'll get with General Markus and we'll figure something out," he replied. "We can probably spare some of the air assets he'll need for a few days, but not much more. I don't know that we'll be able to fully remove the SAM threat on the island, but we can probably reduce it."

Powers nodded. "Generals, what I'd really like to focus on right now is figuring out what we're going to do to stop the enemy from capturing more of the Midwest," he said. "Are we going to be able to stop them from capturing Indianapolis, Columbus or Pittsburgh?"

General Pruitt chimed in. "We sure as hell are, Mr. President. The 35th Infantry Division, one of our National Guard divisions, has finally advanced into place around Columbus. They're going to start moving to contact later today. The 36th Infantry Division has just made contact with the enemy around Indianapolis. They're linking up with elements of the 101st Airborne and the 1st Cavalry Division. Their added firepower and tanks will be enough to stop those two German-Dutch divisions that have been giving us fits.

"As to Pittsburgh…we've repositioned the 82nd Airborne near the city, along with two brigades from the 42nd Infantry Division. Now that we have air support, we're going to start making short work of these Russian airborne brigades that were trying to make a move on the city—"

Interrupting the general, the acting President asked, "Isn't the 42nd Infantry Division from the Northeast? Didn't most of those units desert us?"

Pruitt grimaced at the question. "Yes, sir. We did lose roughly twenty percent of the division due to desertions. This is a National Guard division, so a lot of the folks in these divisions have loyalties to their state and communities. I had doubts about the division prior to the surprise attack on D.C., but after it became known that the President had been killed, along with more than two hundred congressional leaders, the remaining soldiers rallied to defend their country. I'm confident they will remain loyal and they will fight to liberate our country."

If the generals are happy with their loyalty, then I won't second-guess them, thought Powers.

"OK, gentlemen. Let's continue with the rest of the brief, then."

Secretary of State Haley Kagel, who'd only been brought to the PEOC that morning, cleared her throat. "If I could speak, Mr. President, I think I may have a solution to our problem with the Chinese forces on our southern border."

While the acting President was stuck in the PEOC, the Secretary of State had been picked up by one of the Looking Glass planes and had been circling somewhere over the country now for two straight days. They'd done several midair refuelings to stay aloft. If the war continued to stay conventional for another twenty-four hours, then they'd look to stand down the Looking Glass and TACOMO missions.

"OK, Haley, what's your idea on how to handle China?" Powers inquired.

Smiling, Haley leaned forward in her seat. "India. *That* is how we handle China."

Powers raised his right eyebrow. "You're going to need to be a bit more specific than that, Haley."

The generals looked perplexed as well. Then General Pruitt smiled mischievously. "What do the Chinese fear more than America?" he asked rhetorically.

Secretary Kagel nodded. "The Chinese are obviously looking to supplant us as the global hegemon by attacking us and participating in this global conspiracy," she explained. "They don't care about democracy or whatever crap Secretary-General Behr is spouting off about. They just care about removing us as a Pacific power and as a threat to their 2049 plans.

"The *only* other country that can threaten China is India. Over the past thirty years, the population of India has doubled. They've now outpaced China in population because they never had a one-child policy. They aren't facing a critical shortage of women for the hundreds of millions of young men coming of age like China is right now."

General Pruitt interjected, "The Indians also have nuclear weapons and the fifth-largest army in the world. I think the Secretary is right. If we could get the Indians involved, it could cause the Chinese to pause."

Smiling at the compliment, Kagel added, "That's exactly what I'm saying, sir. If we can get the Indians to come to our aid, to pose an immediate threat to China—we could potentially get the Chinese to back off."

Acting President Powers steepled his fingers as he looked down at the table in front of him. This was an interesting proposal. *It just might work*, he thought.

He returned his eye contact to the Secretary of State. "OK, Haley. You've sold me on it. So how do we get the Indians to agree to this?" he asked. Before she could respond, he added, "Also, one other question—suppose we do get the Indians to go along with it and the Chinese do back down—do we really believe they're going to pack up and move their two army groups back to China from Mexico and Central America?"

271

"I don't know how we get the Chinese to pack up their army and go home, but I believe we can work out a deal with the Indians," Secretary Kagel replied matter-of-factly.

Admiral Smith chimed in. "The Chinese force in Mexico will, in time, be completely cut off from their logistical support system. When that happens, it won't take them long before they run out of supplies."

"But they could just live off the land and the local economy," Kagel responded. "Central America has enough resources to support them, plus a few friendly nations in South America could continue to supply them."

"Sure, with food and fuel, not munitions," General Pruitt admitted. "But if they opt to fight, they'll run into the same situation the UN force is about to in another week. They're all going to run out of ammunition and then they'll be toast."

"So that brings us back to India," interjected Powers, trying to regain control of the conversation. "What are we going to offer them that will get them to want to risk a war with China? It's not like we can assist them militarily in that endeavor right now."

General Pruitt shook his head in disagreement. "That's not entirely true, Mr. President. The Chinese have committed their navy, air force, and ground force to this UN mission. The bulk of their tier one combat power is in Mexico and Panama, not in Mainland China. They're currently about as weak and vulnerable as they've ever been at home. This is perhaps the one and only chance the Indians will ever have at truly being able to threaten the Chinese in any meaningful way. We could encourage the Indians to make a move on Tibet or some of their other territorial disputes if the Chinese don't withdraw from this fight."

Leaning forward in his chair, General Markus, the Air Force General, added, "I think we should go one step further, Mr. President. We should threaten to use tactical nuclear weapons on them if they don't withdraw."

Powers did a double take and so did a few others in the room. "You can't be serious, General Markus," he remarked. "The situation isn't bad enough that it warrants us using nuclear weapons, is it?"

General Markus held a hand up. "I'm not saying we should use them on our own soil or in Mexico. Hear me out," he said. Then he rapidly pulled up a map of Mainland China and pointed to a particular spot on it.

General Pruitt recognized the position immediately. "You can't be serious," he retorted. "That would devastate their country."

Powers looked back and forth between the two generals, perplexed. He didn't understand what they were talking about.

Secretary Kagel jumped back in. "He's proposing that if the Chinese don't back off and leave this UN force and go home, we'll nuke the Three Gorges Dam."

Powers crinkled his forehead in surprise. "*How* would that help our cause if we did that?" he asked, almost sarcastically.

General Tibbets took up the answer. "It would flatten a large portion of their military that's stationed in the region below the dam—but more importantly, it would devastate the city of Wuhan. Wuhan is like their version of Silicon Valley. It's also home to several of their defense manufacturers, including one manufacturer that's responsible for producing the microprocessors used in nearly all of their missiles. Destroying the dam would wipe out a huge part of their defense industry, in addition to probably four or five divisions' worth of troops and equipment."

"The loss of life would be catastrophic, though," Kagel interjected. "I'm not sure it would be worth the political fallout it would create."

"With all due respect to Secretary Kagel, the invasion of the upper Midwest is already devastating *our* economy," General Pruitt countered. "If the Chinese open a second front in the Southwest, they could gut our country and further destroy our own economy. This isn't the 1980s—we don't have a multimillion-man army that can fight and win on multiple fronts. We have to pick and choose where we deploy our forces."

"You're advocating for the killing of probably more than ten million people, General," admonished Secretary Kagel, her voice rising to a near yell.

"And if the Chinese open a second front, we may lose the entire war," General Pruitt retorted angrily. "We may lose the entire country. It won't matter that we spared a few million peasants in China if we lose our nation in the process. No, I'll gladly sacrifice ten million Chinese if it means we hold America together."

"That's not your call to make, General," Powers shot back. "It's mine, and mine alone."

Acting President Luke Powers shook his head. He needed time to think about this. He couldn't just unilaterally decide the fate of millions of people like that, even if they *were* the enemy. The room grew quiet as all eyes turned to look at him.

After a moment, he looked up at Secretary Kagel. "Pursue something with the Indians. Let's see what kind of bargain we can strike with them…and let's *tell* the Chinese that if they do invade, we won't rule out the use of tactical nuclear weapons on their army."

The generals sat a little taller in their chairs at that comment. Secretary Kagel nodded solemnly. "Yes, sir. I'll reach out to the Indians and see what we can work out. I will also speak with the Chinese Foreign Minister and convey the potential threat."

****

North Atlantic

Vice Admiral Paul Totten stretched out his back as he surveyed the scene before him in the CIC of the USS *Gerald Ford*. He had wanted to spend a couple more days amassing his naval forces before he made his move to deal a decisive blow against the UN naval forces, but after the attack on Washington, D.C., and the apparent dire situation on the ground, he'd been ordered to attack ahead of when he wanted to.

Despite the loss of the *Truman* and the *George Washington* still undergoing refueling and a complex overhaul, Task Force 100 was still comprised of the carriers *Eisenhower*, *Lincoln*, and *Ford*—more than enough combat power to deal with the joint European-Russian naval force sailing toward the US East Coast.

With eighteen destroyers and six guided missile cruisers, along with over two dozen submarines, Admiral Totten felt reasonably confident of enforcing a blockade of North America. Soon, his ships would be in range of their Tomahawk cruise missiles. Then they'd let the subs advance and finish them off. If anything survived that onslaught, they'd handle them with their aircraft. For now, the doctrine of the day was stay at arm's length and rely on the Navy's strength—its Tomahawk missiles and its fleet of attack submarines.

Captain Rory walked up to him and got his attention. "Admiral, the enemy fleet has just passed the tip of Greenland. They'll be in range of our missiles shortly," he informed him.

"Very well, Captain. Send a message to the fleet that they are to begin engaging their assigned targets as soon as they're in range," replied Totten. "Any further ASW reports?"

Captain Rory nodded. "Yes, sir. The *Mitscher* got a probable hit on a German sub, roughly one hundred miles in front of the enemy fleet. The *Forest Sherman* believes they have a probable hit on at least one Russian sub. They're still working out what class, but based on its noise signature, they say it's definitely Russian."

Admiral Totten grunted at the report. *I knew they'd advance with their subs in the lead*, he thought.

"It's a good thing we didn't take the bait and try to get in strike range of our aircraft," he said with a half-smile.

"It would seem so, sir," Captain Rory replied with a smirk. "It was their best option—hoping we'd come charging right into their submarine trap so they could spring it on us."

"Tell the destroyers I want them to keep up the good work," Totten said. "Find and sink those enemy subs. We can't lose another carrier to one sneaking past them. Also, any word on the possibility of more merchant raiders? That last group kind of caught us by surprise."

Captain Rory shook his head. "Not yet. We spotted a couple of suspicious freighters a few hundred miles away, but they check out. The last satellite pass over the area doesn't show any freighters within a four-hundred-mile perimeter of the fleet. If more missiles are headed our way, we'll have plenty of warning."

Admiral Totten walked over to the digital map display on the side of the wall. Arrayed before him was a massive fleet of American warships and a joint European-Russian fleet. In the next ten minutes, the first salvos of the second battle of the Atlantic would begin.

****

The winds around the USS *Vicksburg* had finally died down a few hours ago, and while it was still cloudy, it appeared the worst of the winter weather had moved on. The seas, however, continued to churn, creating some deep troughs and swells that were going to make it challenging for them to carry out their upcoming mission.

Captain Ian Troy called out to his weather operator. "Chief, any idea on whether these crappy seas are going to level out? We're going to have to delay our attack if it doesn't."

Chief Ailes turned to look at the captain. "Yes, sir. I was just sent the latest weather report from the *Ford*, and it would appear we'll be dealing with some rough seas for at least another twenty to thirty minutes before things will start to calm down. I suspect the *Ford* will send out a message shortly, postponing the attack until we start to hit some calmer seas."

Frustrated at the news, the captain grunted. "Very well. Keep me posted of any changes."

Getting up from his chair in the CIC, Captain Troy figured he'd make his way to the bridge. If things weren't going to happen for a little while, then he wanted to get out of that dark, cramped room and go check on the bridge crew.

As soon as he entered the bridge, Captain Troy realized that the crew was alert but also apprehensive. They had their flak vests and helmets nearby, ready to don at a moment's notice. Two of the seamen had their binoculars out and were actively scanning the horizon and the waters around the ship between the rising and falling of the waves.

Many of the crew knew sailors on the *Truman* and the *Stennis*, along with the other destroyers that had been damaged or sunk during the first day of the war. Things were personal. In the last week, the Navy had had more sailors killed and wounded in action than they had since World War II—a fact that wasn't lost on the crew of the *Vicksburg*.

"Mornin', Captain," said one of the petty officers.

"Mornin', guys. How's everyone doing this morning?" asked Captain Troy.

Most of them responded that they were doing well. Some said they were nervous but itching to get this fight going. They all knew they were supposed to start attacking the UN naval force soon—they just hoped they'd be the ones getting in the first punch this time.

Twenty minutes went by in relative silence. Everyone did their best to stay alert and keep busy in front of their captain as he sat silently brooding in his chair, waiting for the seas to calm so they could initiate their attack. While a supercarrier might not feel the effects of a turbulent sea, their guided missile cruiser sure did. Trying to launch a salvo of cruise missiles in twenty-foot swells was not the best idea. They'd wait until things calmed down—it wasn't as if the enemy wasn't stuck dealing with the same weather they were.

Eventually, the size of the waves did begin to shrink. Steadily, the seas were starting to calm as the winter storm traveled further away from them.

What crappy weather to wage a war in, Troy mused.

One of the petty officers who was manning a communications terminal suddenly called out, "Captain!"

Troy walked toward the young man. "What do you have for me?" he asked.

The young sailor held out a printed message from the *Ford*. Grabbing the paper, Captain Troy promptly read it over. They had a slight change in their orders. Now they were to hold off on attacking the enemy ships for two hours until the seas had more fully calmed down. The admiral wanted the fleet to launch their attack as a united front and not individually. This way they could more efficiently overwhelm the enemy's ability to respond to the attack.

"Send a message back," Captain Troy told the communications officer. "Orders acknowledged, standing by to begin attack."

"Yes, sir," the petty officer replied.

Troy turned to look at the bridge crew. "Well, boys, it looks like we're on hold for at least another two hours," he announced. "Stay alert, but you all can breathe a little easier while we wait for the seas to continue to calm."

Looking at his watch, Troy saw he'd been awake for nearly twelve hours. He hadn't slept well, tossing and turning, so he'd given up on sleep and toured the ship. Then he'd spent a few hours talking with many of the sailors and just checking in on them. When the attack was initially delayed, he'd figured he would stay awake for a while, but now that it was going to be at least two more hours, he decided to head back to his stateroom and lie down for an hour.

Before he headed back, he got the attention of his XO. "I'm headed back to my quarters. Wake me in an hour unless something important happens."

"You've got it, Captain," replied the XO.

When Captain Troy entered his cabin, he made his way over to his rack. He took his shoes off but kept his blouse on, staying in uniform while he stopped for a quick catnap. Being a ship's captain, he had to take little bits of sleep when he could.

As he drifted off, Troy's mind began to race. He had this horrible vision that his ship was under attack by a swarm of cruise missiles. He kept yelling to his crew to engage the enemy missiles, but everything they threw at them either missed or didn't stop them. They kept closing in on his ship and his crew. Just as they were about to hit his ship, he was startled out of sleep by the buzzing sound of his phone, which was right next to his bed.

He swung his feet off his rack to allow himself to sit up, then felt his forehead. He had been sweating profusely. The phone continued to buzz as he shook off the nightmare. He hit the button to pick up. "This is the captain."

"Sorry to wake you, sir," said his XO apologetically. "We just got a message from the helo. They have a probable underwater contact. Bearing 324, forty-six kilometers from our current position."

Whoa, that guy is close, thought Captain Troy.

"Thank you for waking me up, XO. I'm heading down to the CIC now. Have the helm steer us toward that contact. Get our other helo airborne to go assist them in locking down his position and alert the other DDGs of what we found."

With his initial orders given, he hung up the phone and slipped his feet into his shoes. Then he walked over to the water basin. Turning it on, he cupped his hands to collect up some of the cold water. He splashed his face a couple of times to rinse the sweat off and wake himself back up. As soon as he'd dried his face with the hand towel, he headed out the door to the CIC.

As he made his way to the nerve center of the ship, he could tell by the lessened rising and falling of the ship that the seas around them had really calmed.

Amazing what twenty more minutes can do, he thought.

When he walked into the darkened CIC, Captain Troy saw several people standing next to the underwater threat desk. He made his way over and a few of them cleared a path for him.

"What do we have, XO?"

"They think it's an *Akula*," said his XO. "They're moving the dipping sonar now to try and get a better bead on him." His voice was low and tense.

"Are there any other underwater contacts?" Troy inquired. "The Russians like to operate in wolf packs. If there's one, chances are there are others nearby." The tension in the room increased palpably.

Before anyone could answer the captain's question, one of the lieutenants flagged him down. "Sir, the *Porter* and the *Laboon* are moving to our position to help track this guy down. They're sending their helos over to help as well," he explained, relaying some message traffic.

Captain Troy nodded, then leaned down next to the petty officer manning the underwater threat desk. "ST1 Klein, if this is an *Akula*, what's the effective range of his torpedoes?"

The sonar technician thought about that for a moment. As an ST, he was supposed to be the resident expert on underwater threats. He, along with four other STs on the ship, was responsible for assisting the captain and the crew in identifying and prosecuting any possible enemy submarines.

Klein's forehead scrunched up a bit. "He's already in range. The *Akula* has four 533mm torpedo tubes and four 650mm torpedo tubes. The 533s are wake homing torpedoes with a range of fifty-three to sixty-two kilometers, depending on how fast they're going. The 650s have a range of fifty kilometers if they cruise at maximum speed."

It was clear that Klein felt pretty proud of himself for a moment as he almost instantly recalled the details of the Russian weapons capabilities, but that abruptly soured when he saw the looks of concern on the faces of those around him.

They were well within the range of those torpedoes, and that was definitely a bad thing. In the game of anti-submarine warfare, the goal is to keep the enemy subs outside their weapons range. When two boxers with unmatched arm lengths compete, the guy with the longer arms can prevail as long as he doesn't get in too close—the Russian sub had a shorter reach, but now they were well within their weapons range, and in grave danger.

Captain Troy turned to look at the helo commander. "Tell the helos to engage the contact *now*," he ordered. "I don't care if they don't have a solid lock just yet. If they drop a torpedo where they think he is, and he is in fact there, that sub'll spin up his engines to try and get away. Then we can get a better lock on his location and get more torpedoes on him."

The lieutenant, a helo pilot himself, reached over and grabbed for the radio handset that would connect him with his boss, the lieutenant commander and senior pilot on the ship. He hastily relayed the captain's message.

****

Captain Adrian Petrunin was feeling a bit anxious to get things rolling. He and the crew aboard his *Akula* had spent the better part of eight hours trying to get into position to deliver a blow against the outer perimeter of the American strike group. When they'd come across a *Ticonderoga*-class guided missile cruiser, Petrunin couldn't believe his luck. At their stalking speed of just six knots, it had taken a bit of patience to get within range of their weapons, but their perseverance was about to pay off.

"Torpedo in the water! Torpedo in the water!" shouted one of his sonar operators unexpectedly.

"What?!" Petrunin shouted. "Where did that come from?"

"Sir, it must have been dropped from a helicopter or plane."

"Helm, increase speed. I want us above thirty knots yesterday!" Captain Petrunin ordered. "Create a knuckle and eject a noisemaker!"

Everyone clung to whatever they could to steady themselves as the *Akula* lurched to the side, creating a cavitation in the water that would hopefully confuse the torpedo.

"Noisemaker away!" confirmed one of the petty officers. Now that the cylinder had been released, it would spin and create bubbles and other noise in the water, which could draw the torpedo off its path.

As soon as they'd completed their hard turn, Captain Petrunin screamed, "Get some distance between us and the noisemaker and turn to face the American warship!"

Once the sub had leveled out a bit, the captain turned to his weapons officer. "Engage the American warship now!" he yelled.

"Yes, sir, obtaining firing solution!" the officer responded. A few tense seconds passed before he announced, "Firing solution obtained!"

"Release two wake homing torpedoes and one of our advanced heavy-weight torpedoes," Petrunin ordered.

"Yes, sir!" came the reply. Seconds later, three torpedoes were in the water, rushing toward the American ship. Two of them would skim the surface and rush toward the back of the boat, while the third would aim for the hull.

For a couple of minutes, their torpedoes sped off toward the Americans, and they seemed to have escaped the attack from the helicopter above. Just as Captain Petrunin was about to breathe a sigh of relief, he heard the sound of a helicopter's dipping sonar ping right off their hull.

Petrunin swore under his breath.

"Torpedo in the water! Torpedo in the water!" shouted the sonar technician. "This one is much closer!"

"Helm, create another knuckle and release a second noisemaker," Petrunin ordered, grabbing something to steady himself.

This time, even though they broke in a new direction at flank speed, the incoming Mark 54 torpedo didn't fall for the trick. It blew right past the noisemaker and reacquired its target.

"Sir, torpedo is still incoming," announced his sonar technician nervously.

"Brace for impact! Brace for impact!" blared the warning alarm on the sub.

Everyone aboard clutched to anything they could find as if it would miraculously stop the incoming projectile; however, seconds later, the entire *Akula* lurched forward, and many crew members were knocked to the floor.

"Damage report!" bellowed Captain Petrunin.

"Sir, the torpedo hit the rear of the sub and fractured its outer hull. The inner hull is also damaged. We're taking on water."

At that point, Petrunin knew they were in trouble. If they didn't do an emergency blow and attempt to get to the surface, there was a good chance they'd sink.

I'd rather save my crew than continue to race away at our current depth, he decided.

"Bring us up!" he shouted to his helmsman. The sub rapidly angled toward the surface, bringing them closer to the air above and a chance at survival.

When the *Akula* was less than two hundred meters from the surface, his sonar technician screamed, "Torpedo in the water! Torpedo in the water!"

Before the captain could respond in any way, the new projectile had slammed into the bow of the ship. The sub's forward movement and its rise to the surface were violently blunted.

"Sir, the hull's got a massive gash. We're taking on too much water!"

That was one of the last things Captain Petrunin heard. Moments later, the power to the sub went out as the engine room was submerged beneath the cold liquid. Then the *Akula* began its long and slow journey to the bottom.

****

ST1 Klein still had his headphones attached to his head when he jumped up and shouted, "Torpedoes in the water! I count three torpedoes, heading 221, thirty-four kilometers and closing fast. I estimate their speed to be somewhere around fifty knots."

Captain Troy reached for the phone that would connect him with the helm. "Bridge, CIC. Bring us ahead to flank speed, heading 115," he said before he hung up.

"Deploy the Nixie!" he ordered.

"Should we deploy the CAT?" asked ST1 Klein.

The captain turned and advanced toward Klein. When he reached the sonar technician's chair, he leaned in and asked, "Do you really think that thing will work? It's failed all of its tests so far."

Klein looked at the captain as he stuck his chin out. "I think it's worth trying, sir. Two of those torpedoes racing toward us are wake homing torps. The Nixie isn't going to stop them."

Captain Troy cringed at the comment. He knew his sonar technician was right. The Countermeasure Anti-Torpedo, or "CAT" as it was called, was still somewhat experimental. The system had been in development with the Pennsylvania State University Applied Research Laboratory since 2013. Thus far, it had been tested with mixed results. Three out of five times it had worked, but the other two times it hadn't, which was the reason why it wasn't trusted among the skippers of the ships it was deployed on. Skippers generally like weapons systems that have a proven track record of working, one hundred percent of the time—a sixty percent success rate wasn't exactly something you wanted to count on when your life depended on it.

Looking at the young man, Captain Troy saw that Klein felt confident it would work. He sighed, then nodded. "Do it. But don't miss, Klein. We only have two of them."

Smiling, Klein went to work. He spun the computer control system for the torpedo warning system or TWS up so it could guide the CAT to the target. As the computer system warmed up, he called out to one of his sonar techs near the rear of the ship. "I need you to get the TWS deployed behind the ship ASAP!" he shouted. The TWS would essentially be dragged behind the ship as it searched for the Russian wake homing torpedoes. When it found them, it would feed the targeting data to the two CATs, which would then be fired at the incoming threats.

The challenge with the CATs was that they were small torpedoes themselves, built for the sole purpose of destroying the Russian-made wake homing torpedoes. Like a ballistic missile interceptor, it was almost like shooting a bullet with a bullet. If the CATs missed the incoming torpedoes, there wouldn't be a second chance. Considering the many failings of the system, the Navy had a self-destruct function built into the final product. The logic was that if the CAT missed, then the sonar technician manning the CAT could detonate its warhead in hopes that it might still be close enough to the enemy torpedo that it would take it out.

It took Klein and the other sonar tech a couple of minutes to get the TWS deployed behind them and for the initial targeting data to start filtering in. To their horror, the enemy torpedoes had closed the gap on them faster than they had thought possible.

"Give me an update, Klein," demanded Captain Troy.

"Sir, the enemy torpedoes are now less than six kilometers away and closing quickly," he explained. "On a good note, one of the torpedoes did go for the Nixie—now it's just the wake homing torpedoes we need to worry about."

"That still leaves plenty of worrying left," Troy mumbled.

The torpedoes had now positioned themselves behind the *Vicksburg* as they maneuvered in for the kill. The TWS had locked on to the incoming threats and fed that data to the two CATs. A soon as Klein saw he had a positive lock on the enemy torpedoes, he shouted out, "Engaging enemy torpedoes now!"

Captain Troy, along with everyone else in the CIC, watched as the CATs shot out and went right for the enemy torpedoes. The first CAT collided with its target and blew up. Cheers and hoots of joy rang out in the CIC at the first confirmed kill. The second CAT was headed right for its target when all of a sudden, the Russian torpedo made another zigzag

283

in its race to hit the *Vicksburg*. This unexpected maneuver by the enemy torpedo enabled it to slide right past the CAT before it could hit it.

Klein saw in a fraction of a second what had happened and jabbed the self-destruct button on the CAT. Praying it was still close enough to take the last enemy threat out, Captain Troy watched the explosion and geyser of water spring into the air less than two hundred meters behind them from the rear-mounted CCTV camera mounted on the exhaust tower.

Everyone in the CIC shouted with excitement and joy when they saw the explosion, believing it must have come from the destruction of the torpedo. Captain Troy held his breath as he waited to learn if the torpedo had really been destroyed. Just as he was about to join in the celebration, the enemy torpedo suddenly appeared on Klein's targeting scope. The torpedo was now less than one hundred meters from the rear of the ship, and he had no more CATs to fire at it.

In that instant, Klein shouted, "Brace for impact!"

The crushing, thunderous boom reverberated throughout the ship as the rear portion of their ship flew upward and then landed back in the water. The lights briefly flickered off and on before they completely went out. The blast had impacted near the engine room and the ship's power plant.

Seconds later, the emergency generators kicked in and the lights turned back on.

"Damage report!" shouted Captain Troy as he walked over to Klein.

Turning to face the captain, Klein sheepishly said, "I thought we had that last one, sir." He hung his head low in defeat. It was his responsibility to protect the ship from an underwater threat, and he had failed.

Before the lieutenant commander in charge of the ship's damage control functions could respond, Captain Troy looked down at Klein, placing a hand on the man's shoulder. "You did all you could, Klein. You stopped two of those torpedoes from hitting us. This wasn't your fault."

Klein nodded, but it was clear he didn't feel any better.

"Sir, we're dead in the water," announced the lieutenant commander. "We've lost contact with engineering. The machine shop just phoned in and said the lower decks are taking on water fast. They tried to get over to engineering, but the corridor was flooding fast. They had to seal it off."

"Get more damage control teams to the rear of the ship. We need to seal off the lower decks and the rear half of the ship or we're going to go down," the captain ordered.

"Someone get a message out to the *Ford* that we've been hit by a torpedo. Tell them we sank a Russian *Akula*, but we're dead in the water and in need of assistance ASAP," Troy ordered next. He needed to get some help on the way. He knew his crew wouldn't last very long in the freezing waters of the North Atlantic in January.

"Sir, I just got a message from the *Porter*," announced the lieutenant manning their coms system. "They're five minutes out from our position and coming to assist. The *Laboon* wants to know if they should head our way to assist or stay out on ASW patrol."

Captain Troy thought for a moment; the *Vicksburg* had a crew of 330 sailors. They wouldn't all fit on the *Porter* if it came down to it. He looked back to his coms officer. "Tell the *Laboon* to make best speed to our position. If we have to abandon ship, I want to make sure our people aren't stuck in the lifeboats for any longer than is necessary."

The next five minutes went by in a blur. Everyone did their best to handle the fires that had sprung up on the rear of the ship and seal off the various corridors and decks that were rapidly filling with water.

"Someone, give me a casualty report!" demanded Captain Troy as he looked at the clock mounted on the wall. It was now noticeably slanted at an angle. They were taking on too much water. The rear of the ship was settling lower and lower into the water, pulling the rest of the vessel downward.

Walking over to him with a clipboard, his XO showed him the numbers thus far. Thirty-eight were unaccounted for, another forty-three listed as injured. Shaking his head, Troy looked at the XO. "I want our wounded picked up by the helos and transferred over to the *Ford* if they have the fuel and ability to do so. We need to start getting them off the ship ASAP, in case we can't stop the flooding."

The XO nodded and moved over to the coms section to start getting that going. Meanwhile, the captain walked out of the CIC and made his way to one of the lower decks. He needed to see the flooding firsthand and try to talk with some of the guys stopping it.

As he traveled down a deck, Captain Troy heard a lot of orders being shouted. When he reached the bottom of the deck as he made his way down the next stairwell, he saw there was already at least three inches of water.

Crap! If we have water on this deck, then it's already overwhelmed the other deck below, Troy realized.

"How bad is it, Chief?" he asked of one of the chief petty officers who had just finished shouting some instructions to one of the damage control parties.

"Not good, sir," he admitted. "We're going to have to seal off the deck below. It's like each time we seal one section off, we discover there's another leak somewhere else that allows the water to get behind each of the sections of the ship we close off."

"Did we get everyone out of the lower decks before we had to close them off?" asked Captain Troy.

A look of frightened uncertainty spread across the man's face before he responded, "I don't know, sir. We tried our best, but the lower decks flooded so rapidly. We tried to compartmentalize them by sealing up that rear section of the ship from the bottom deck all the way up to here. Somehow, some way, the water found a way around those sealed compartments and flooded the next open section. I think the blast may have ruptured some of the water mains or the HVAC system, and that's how the water's moving from section to section."

Captain Troy shook his head in anger and frustration. If that was the case, then there was little hope they'd be able to save the ship. The only way they could stay afloat was if they could successfully compartmentalize the leaks and seal those sections off. Once they got the ship stabilized, then they could work with some divers to see if they could get some of the outer holes sealed up and begin to pump out the water.

While the captain was contemplating how to handle the situation, an explosion rocked the ship. Captain Troy grabbed for something to keep himself from falling. When he'd steadied himself, he grabbed for the phone near the ladder well and connected to the CIC.

"This is the captain. What the hell just blew up?" he demanded.

The officer manning the damage control section responded. "Sir, the fire on the rear of the ship helicopter hangar bay has spread to the ship's internal JP5 fuel tank, and that's what exploded."

While the damage control officer was explaining the situation, Captain Troy looked down and noticed the water had risen another inch on his legs. It would appear this added catastrophe was speeding up their demise.

"Hold on a moment," he told the damage control officer. Then he turned to the chief, who was still standing by him.

"Chief, that explosion we just heard was one of the helo fuel tanks blowing. It would appear the fire in the rear of the ship got to it somehow. Do you think it may have opened another hole in the ship?" he asked.

The chief thought about that for a second. "I think so, sir. Those fuel bladders are placed between the inner and outer hulls of the ship. If one blew, then it probably just ripped another gash in the hull. If we weren't already taking on so much water, I'd say we could seal off the affected compartments and portions of the ship and sail back to port, but we're already in trouble as it is. Another large hole in the hull is beyond our ability to salvage."

I can't believe my ship's going to go down before we even fired a shot off at the enemy, Captain Troy thought angrily.

He shifted the telephone handset back to his head. "Tell the XO to order 'abandon ship.' We need to get as many people as we can off the ship before we go down. I don't want our people dying of hypothermia in the water because we waited until the very last minute to make the call. Send a flash message to the *Ford* that we're going down and ask the *Porter* and *Laboon* to come fetch us out of the water."

Having just given the worst possible orders a captain could dole out, he turned to face the chief and the damage control party standing near him. The water was still rising; now it reached their knees. "You all did what you could. Now it's time to save ourselves. Everyone, drop what you're doing and get to the lifeboats."

Ten minutes later, Captain Troy sat in one of the lifeboats, bobbing up and down in the five-foot swells as he watched their home, the USS *Vicksburg*, begin to sink. The rear half of the ship, which was fully engulfed in flames, slowly slipped under the water while the bow of the ship remained raised out of the water, slowly being pulled skyward as the rear of the ship continued to fall deeper into the water. It only took a few more minutes before the rest of the ship followed the stern beneath the waves.

As the USS *Porter* came near their lifeboat, Captain Troy saw the sailors of the other ship on the deck, ready to help pull them aboard. For the sailors of the USS *Vicksburg*, their part in this operation was over. Now they'd have to find another way to get back into the action to get their revenge. Captain Troy's only solace was knowing they'd sent that *Akula* to the bottom.

Chapter 16
Partisans

January 16, 2021
Near Bolton, Vermont
Camel's Hump State Park

Tony hid under a winter-colored camouflage blanket as he watched the latest convoy of military vehicles travel down I-89, past the small town of Bolton. He felt a slight shiver pass through his body as he fought against the cold temperatures and the biting wind. Within twelve hours of setting up his little position, he'd realized he was not adequately equipped for this.

They always make sniper operations look so easy in the movies, he thought.

When the invading UN army had captured his state a couple of days ago, Tony knew he had to do something to stop them, but he wasn't quite sure what. Then, when he'd heard on the news about the naval battle in the North Atlantic and how the ship his older brother Paul had been on had been sunk, he'd been devastated. He had no way of knowing if Paul had survived or died because mail from the rest of the country wasn't making its way across enemy lines. The occupation authority sure as heck didn't know, and even if they had, they wouldn't have cared less. After brooding about the loss for a day, a plan on how to get the enemy back began to form.

Tony was an avid *Call of Duty* player. It was a way he and his brother had continued to stay in touch and interact—they'd play online together whenever he was in port or had access to his online account. In the game, he'd always been a sniper. Not quite the same as real-life experience, obviously, but in real life he did hunt and sport shoot with his older brother and friends. Even while attending college, he'd still found time to go hunting. Tony had talked to a couple of his college buddies, and they'd decided to take their hunting rifles and do something.

That was twenty-eight hours ago. Now, sitting under his winter camouflage blanket in the freezing cold, he was beginning to have his doubts.

What in the world were we thinking? he wondered.

"Tony, that convoy is getting closer. Are we going to shoot at this one?" asked one of his friends over their walkie-talkie.

They had let the previous two convoys pass without firing a shot. The first convoy had a couple of tanks with it and some other armored vehicles they had never seen before. The second convoy came through several hours before dawn, and they couldn't properly see the vehicles to really know what they were, so they waited for the sun to come up and figured they'd hit the next one they saw.

Looking through his scope to find the vehicles traveling down the interstate, Tony spotted the new convoy. He grabbed the walkie-talkie, depressing the talk button. "Yeah, this looks like a good one. I don't see any tanks or other armored vehicles," he answered. "So, here's what we're going to do—I'm going to shoot at the lead vehicle to try and kill the driver. You guys shoot at the drivers in the other vehicles. If we're lucky, the vehicles will lose control and it'll hurt or kill some of the soldiers in the back. The ones that do survive, we can snipe at when they get out." He paused for a second before he depressed the talk button to add one more thing. "Let's fire off three or four shots and then run back into the woods, OK?"

With their impromptu plan decided on, he returned his gaze to his scope to find the lead vehicle. He sighted in on the driver's-side front windshield and saw the silhouette of the man he was about to kill.

"This is for you, Paul," he whispered. He flicked the safety off his rifle, let out a breath and squeezed the trigger.

Bang!

The shot rang out, but Tony stayed focused, waiting to see if his bullet had hit his mark. In the flash of a second, he saw a splash of red appear on the windshield of the vehicle, which swerved into one of the guardrails on the side of the highway. He immediately pulled the bolt back, ejecting the spent round as a new one slammed back in its place. He looked through the scope again—soldiers jumped out the back of the disabled vehicle. They had their rifles raised but seemed to have no idea where the sniper fire had come from.

As Tony was aiming at another soldier, he heard several loud cracks as his two friends also fired at the soldiers. Tony aimed at one soldier who was shooting in their direction; he placed his red dot on the man's chest and fired.

Bang!

He saw the man drop like a switch had been turned off. Quickly now, he worked the bolt, ejecting the spent round and preparing to fire again. Now the enemy fire was getting closer to their position. He heard some bullets whizzing over his head. A few rounds hit the dirt and rocks in front of him, causing him to flinch a bit. Steeling himself, he took aim at another soldier and fired one more time. His third shot missed.

"Tony! We need to get out of here!" one of his friends shouted in a terrified voice.

Now he heard the rhythmic thumping of a helicopter's rotor blades approaching. Panicking, Tony jumped up, grabbed his camouflaged blanket, and ran like the wind back into the woods. The sound of the approaching chopper continued to get louder and closer.

Minutes later, chunks of dirt, tree branches, and rocks were kicked up all around him as a gunner from the yet-unseen helicopter shot at him. Diving for cover behind a tree, Tony hoped he'd be able to elude the chopper that had been sent to hunt them down. He turned and saw one of his friends running toward him, panic and fear written all over his face. Then, in the blink of an eye, his friend practically disintegrated before his eyes as he was torn apart by the large-caliber machine gun in the sky.

In anger, Tony aimed his rifle at the helicopter, which had to be no more than five hundred yards away. He fired a round, certain he had hit his target, only to see the flying Grim Reaper turn toward him. Before his mind even had time to register what had happened, he saw something fly out from under the helicopter's wing pilons toward him. Then everything went black.

****

Detroit, Michigan

Chief Warrant Officer Trent "Punisher" Lipton of the 1st Battalion, 5th Special Forces Group, had just crawled out of the manhole cover in the center of the now dark and empty street. He looked around him with his weapon at the ready position. The snow was still falling rather steadily, which aided in covering his exit but also made it harder for him to ensure the area was clear of roving patrols. He did a quick three-sixty to make sure the coast was clear, doing his best to look for things out of the ordinary and listen for any voices or sounds that didn't belong there.

The only thing he heard was the steady stream of truck traffic moving across the bridge not far away. When he saw no visible threats, he looked down into the sewer from which he had just emerged and signaled that it was clear to exit. A few minutes later, the rest of his six-man team emerged and dashed to the now-abandoned Great American Truck Driving building on West Fort Street, roughly twenty feet away.

The team had just spent the last six hours crawling around the city's sewers, placing an ungodly amount of C-4 near the support structures of the Ambassador Bridge. The busy suspension bridge, which had been a fixture since 1929, was the key link between Canada and the United States across the Detroit River, and it was vital to keeping the UN forces supplied as they continued their advance into Michigan, Indiana and Ohio. They'd managed to accomplish their task despite the roving patrols of enemy soldiers, who were intent on preventing someone from doing exactly what they'd done.

When the 1st Cavalry Division had been forced to withdraw from the city, several Special Forces units had stayed behind to try and wreak as much havoc with the enemy logistics and rearguard forces as possible. Lipton's team had been assigned the difficult task of trying to drop the critical bridge.

The Air Force had already tried to bomb it twice and had failed on both accounts. During the first attempt, a bomb had hit the span, but it hadn't destroyed it. The enemy had merely placed a patch over the hole in the center of the roadway and continued to use it. When the UN force had realized how close they'd come to losing the critical piece of infrastructure, they'd placed a significant number of air defense assets near it. Those additional SAMs and missile interceptors had enabled them to stop the Air Force's second attempt at destroying the bridge. Since the Air Force was already stretched thin, they didn't have the resources to effectively complete the mission, so the task had fallen to Special Forces.

Once Chief Lipton's team had successfully scurried into the defunct trucking company building, they did a quick assessment of the situation. Looking at his map, Lipton announced, "We still need to travel at least two more blocks before we can detonate the explosives and be sure to escape."

"Ugh. This whole area is crawling with roving patrols," muttered Tiny, one of his soldiers.

Lipton grunted. He wasn't wrong. The fact that they hadn't been discovered yet was only due to their training in stealthy movement and good teamwork.

"I want us to move through this field here and try to make our way down to this pallet and packaging facility just off of Fort Street, on Vinewood Street here," Lipton announced. He pointed to the path he wanted them to travel on the map.

His soldiers looked at the path. Hawkeye crossed his arms. "Sir, that's a lot of relatively open area to cross with little in the way of tree cover and daylight about to break."

Another soldier, Ski, nodded. "Yeah, it doesn't help that it looks like the snow is starting to let up. Our tracks are going to show up pretty easily in the fresh snow."

Lipton thought about that. They were right, of course, but they also couldn't stay in their current location. They needed to get some distance between them and the bridge so they could blow their charges. The longer they left the charges in place, the better the chances were they'd be discovered by one of the roving patrols before they could detonate them.

"I know it's not ideal, guys, but we need to move. We can't stay here," Lipton explained. He paused for a second before looking at their resident sniper. "Shorty, I want you to cover our rear. Do your best to brush over our tracks. Crispy, you take point—try to find us some cover when you can, but move us quickly to our next rally point. We need to blow this bridge before our charges are discovered."

With the decision made, the group moved as a unit to the rear of the building. After doing a quick search of the area, Crispy, their point man, quietly announced, "I think we're clear."

He opened the door slowly and stepped out into the parking lot behind the building. The snow was still falling, but not nearly as heavily as it had been while they had been placing their explosives.

Advancing cautiously through the couple of inches of fresh powder, Crispy kept his rifle at the ready, continually scanning the area as he did his best to dart from the back of the building to a pile of snow at the end of the parking lot. When he reached the mound of plowed snow, he crawled up the top of it and checked his surroundings. Seeing that the coast was clear, he waved for the others to follow him.

Four of them dashed to his position, while Shorty, their sniper, walked backwards slowly, using a piece of burlap to brush over their tracks. While Shorty did his best to cover their rear, Crispy moved from the back of the parking lot down the side of West Jefferson Street toward the railroad tracks. When he reached what he thought was a defensible position, he stopped and did another quick scan of the area. He signaled for the others to follow him again, and Shorty once again did what he could to try and cover their tracks.

It took them close to ten minutes to travel the two blocks. Fortunately, they hadn't spotted a roving patrol, although they did hear at least two vehicles drive past their previous position along Fort Street.

When they reached the pallet packaging plant, they moved inside and searched the building, making sure it was clear. Then they identified possible egress routes should they need to hastily escape the building.

"OK, Punisher, I think we're reasonably safe in this location, at least for the time being," said Shorty. "I suggest we blow the charges now. It'll cause all the roving patrols nearby to rush to the area, so I also suggest we try to find a nice dark closet or room to hide out in."

Crispy nodded. "I concur with Shorty, but I have a better hiding place. I found a staircase that leads to a small storage room on the roof. I suggest we place a few of our mini-cameras down here to keep an eye on the place and relocate up there. We can lock the door, so if a patrol comes to the building and wants to search it, they'll see the door's locked and hopefully think it was left locked by the previous owners before they bugged out."

"Nice find, Crispy," replied Lipton. "Let's do it. Go ahead and get the cameras set up. We'll see if we can operate out of this locale for a few days."

The team immediately went to work on getting their remote cameras set up. It was vital that they know what was going on both inside and outside the building if they were going to make it a temporary home. God only knew how long they'd have to try and hide out in the city before help arrived or they were ordered to try and evac out.

Once they had everything in order, they went up to the roof to admire their handiwork. It was now 0530 hours—still another hour or so of darkness left. At that point, the snow had mostly tapered off, giving them a good view of the bridge.

Pulling the remote detonator out of his pocket, Crispy turned it on. The red light activated, letting him know it was ready. He lifted the safety lever on the button up, then depressed the detonator with his thumb.

BOOM.

A series of explosions ripped through West Fort Street at the base of two of the support structures for the bridge. The blast shook the ground like an earthquake. Chunks of road, rebar and cement flew hundreds of feet into the air throughout a several-hundred-foot perimeter around the blast site. In a fraction of a second, a twelve-foot section of the bridge collapsed to the street below, crushing several abandoned cars and blocking the road beneath it.

Looking at the mess they had created, the ODA team smiled, knowing that they had just dealt a critical blow to the UN force invading their country.

****

Northwest of Muncie, Indiana

First Lieutenant Trey Regan looked through the sight extension of his commander's scope as he scanned the area for signs of Russian armor. His platoon, which was part of the 155th Armored Brigade Combat Team, had been directed to head to a small area called Reed Station, near I-69. The surrounding area was relatively flat farmland, intermixed with a few small copses of barren trees. It was ideal tank country, and their battalion had determined that they'd make a stand in this area.

Their reconnaissance unit had spotted a Russian column of tanks and armored personnel carriers driving down the interstate toward the small Indiana town of Anderson twenty minutes ago. Unfortunately, their recon's communications equipment was being jammed by the Russians, so their unit had been unable to get an idea of how large the enemy force was, or what type of armor they were facing.

With only a company of tanks and another company of light infantry in the area, their company commander had deployed a platoon of tanks to either side of the interstate, intermixed with their infantry brothers, who would bring their own anti-tank guided missiles to the fray for added punch.

"Spotted them!" Sergeant Miller shouted out. Miller was his new gunner. He'd just been promoted to sergeant E-5 a couple of months ago.

"Crap, Miller—call out what you see and where!" Lieutenant Regan shot back. He was a bit angered by the vagueness of the report.

"Sorry, sir. I got a little excited. It's a T-90, nine o'clock, 4,000 meters."

The crew was nervous. This was the first time any of them had seen any combat or faced an enemy tank. The last time the battalion had deployed was three years earlier, and that was to Kuwait. They hadn't seen any enemy tanks or been shot at during that deployment, so they were eager to engage the Russians, as well as nervous at facing a real enemy.

Once Regan spotted the enemy tanks, he responded, "Got it. Load Sabot."

Sure enough, a column of tanks started to appear from around the bend in the interstate. Two BMP-3s were in the lead, followed by at least five tanks, and then eight BTR armored personnel carriers and more tanks following behind them. There had to be at least two companies' worth of enemy vehicles heading toward their position, and that was just what they could see.

Regan wanted to get his report in before they began their attack. He depressed the talk button on his radio. "Dixie Six, this is Dixie Two-Six. We've spotted an enemy column heading toward our position. They're just now passing through 4,000 meters. I count at least twenty-two armored vehicles, five T-90s in the lead with another five pulling up the rear. There may be additional vehicles further back behind the bend. How copy?"

A second later, the SINCGAR radio beeped, letting them know their encrypted radio had synced. "Dixie Two-Six, that's a good copy," replied his company commander. "I want you to wait to engage the enemy vehicles until the last vehicle in the column is no more than 3,000 meters. Have your infantry engage the rearguard with their Javelins. I want you to take out the tanks first, then work your way down to the BMPs before you engage the BTRs. How copy?"

"Good copy. Stand by for contact," Regan responded.

The column of vehicles continued to get closer, moving deeper into their trap. Regan switched over to the platoon net and the coms their infantry counterparts were using, and he relayed the plan to them, making sure everyone was on the same page.

The next five minutes moved at warp speed and slow motion all at the same time. If felt like an eternity waiting for the enemy vehicles to get within range. At the same time, it felt like the BMPs and tanks were starting to get too close, and they worried they would spot them.

"Firing now!" shouted one of the infantry officers over the platoon net.

Looking through his commander's scope, Regan saw four Javelins fly out from their hidden position in the woods and head straight for the rear vehicles in the column.

Depressing the talk button, Regan shouted, "Engage!" to his tankers.

Boom!

His gunner fired their cannon. The tank rocked back on its track. The spent aft casing dropped to the floor and the loader hit the ammo locker door button with his knee. He reached in and grabbed another Sabot round and slammed it home, hitting the locking arm into place before yelling, "Sabot up!"

"Identified! Tank, 1,500 meters to our nine o'clock!" replied Sergeant Miller as he found them their next target.

"Fire!" shouted Regan. Miller fired the gun for a second time in less than ten seconds.

Boom.

Looking through his scope, Regan saw the round fly flat and true as it slammed into the front armor of the BMP-3. It ripped right through the armored vehicle, causing a massive secondary explosion.

"Keep firing!" Regan exclaimed, giving his team the go ahead to keep finding targets without him. He needed to try and make sure the rest of the platoon was engaging their targets and try to keep track of what was happening around them.

Zooming out and away from the target Miller was tracking next, Regan saw his platoon had already blown all the tanks up and were making short work of the rest of the enemy's armored column. The few vehicles that hadn't been blown up yet were both popping smoke grenades to try and blur their vision, or at least mitigate the threat from the Javelins, while the remaining Russian vehicles did everything they could to get off the interstate and seek better cover from his tanks.

BAM!

Suddenly, their tank was jarred hard, nearly throwing Regan from his commander's chair. His arms flailed about to grab for anything that could prevent him from falling.

"Tank to our three o'clock. Twelve hundred meters. Firing!" came the quick and calm voice of Sergeant Miller. He was clearly now in the automated zone a soldier gets into when his training takes over and he just reacts mechanically to the situations happening around him.

As soon as Regan was able to get back into his seat, he immediately turned his commander's sight extension to where Miller had found the enemy tank. He caught a quick glimpse of it just before the turret of the tank was entirely blown off by Miller's shot.

BAM!

Their tank was suddenly plastered with rocks, dirt, and other debris from a nearby explosion.

"Find where that other column of tanks is coming from!" Regan shouted over the platoon net as he sought to figure out where this new threat had materialized from.

"We've got another column of enemy vehicles moving down McGalliard Road. They're approaching from the east right now!" came a voice from one of the infantry soldiers assigned to help protect them.

Crap, how did another group of tanks and vehicles sneak up on us? thought Regan, trying not to panic.

"Blue Three is down," announced another one of his tankers over the platoon net.

"I count ten enemy tanks heading toward us, 1,100 meters!" yelled Miller. He quickly fired the cannon one more time.

"Back us up to the next firing position!" Regan yelled to their driver.

Their tank lurched backwards just as an enemy round impacted right where they had just been, exploding harmlessly in front of them.

Damn, that was close! realized Regan, his palms now sweating.

"Pop the smoke!" he ordered. His driver deftly moved them backwards and then turned them to the left, making sure he didn't give the enemy tankers a good side shot at them.

With the smoke grenades out, the area around them was steadily filling up with infrared-inhibiting smoke. Another tank round hit a tree or something near them, showering their armored cocoon with more debris and shrapnel.

"Tank to our one o'clock!" yelled Regan to his gunner as the tank he'd spotted stopped briefly and appeared to be aiming right for them. A split second later, the Russian tank belched fire and Regan flinched, expecting the round to hit them. Instead, it sailed near them and slammed into one of the Stryker vehicles next to them.

The explosion of the vehicle next to them still jarred their tank, and they were slapped with flame and more shrapnel.

"Firing!" yelled Miller. The tank rocketed back from the recoil of their main gun.

"Dixie Two-Six, pull your force back to Rally Point Bravo! You're about to be flanked!" came an urgent call from their company commander.

"Good copy. Falling back to Rally Point Bravo," Regan replied. He promptly relayed the order to his remaining tanks and infantry soldiers.

The next five minutes were a desperate struggle as Regan and his platoon of tanks and Strykers did their best to try and disengage from the enemy and fall back to the next line of defense. As they passed through the next two platoons' worth of tanks and Stryker vehicles about two miles to their rear, Regan saw he'd lost two of his four tanks and three of his four Stryker vehicles.

The rest of the day was mostly spent exchanging shots with the enemy tanks as they continued a fighting retreat to the outskirts of Anderson, where the rest of the battalion had rallied up and was waiting for them to arrive. They were now less than ten miles from Indianapolis.

By the end of the day, First Lieutenant Regan was the senior officer left alive in his company and had effectively taken command of what was left of their mauled unit. As they began their humiliating retreat around Indianapolis, he vowed he'd get his revenge on the enemy for killing so many of his comrades.

Chapter 17
Desperate Plea

January 16, 2021
Ottawa, Canada
Lord Elgin Hotel
President-Elect Marshall Tate's Office

Marshall sat in the kitchen of his makeshift home in the Lord Elgin Hotel, reading over the latest intelligence summary that had been put together for him by his national security team. What he read was sickening. The country he had sought to lead, to become President of, was being torn apart.

Will there even be a country to lead after all of this is said and done? he wondered.

Page Larson, his National Security Advisor, interrupted his train of thought. "The Ambassador Bridge connecting Detroit and Windsor is still temporarily down. We've had to move all vehicle traffic across the Detroit River to pontoon bridges. It slowed us up for about a day, but the logistics train is back up and running again—"

General McKenzie interrupted. "The bigger challenge we have right now is dealing with the loss of our airfields."

Page Larson grunted. She didn't like being interrupted, but then again, she was glad to see the general above ground. McKenzie had finally emerged from his own bunker complex once he'd felt it was reasonably safe to do so. He still didn't stay in one place for too long for fear of an airstrike, but he did feel secure enough to visit Senator Tate.

McKenzie continued, "We anticipated the Pentagon attacking our airfields, but I'll be frank—I didn't think the acting President would've ordered such a brutal and thoroughly destructive aerial attack on my country as he has. We don't have a single military airport left in operation in the entire country. Once we relocated some of our military assets to the civilian airports, the Americans went after them as well. Heck, even our ports that aren't frozen over are completely destroyed. Sir, we're going to run into a serious problem in a few more weeks if we aren't able to get resupplied from Europe, Russia or China."

"I think your attack on Camp David and then that airstrike on Raven Rock turned the American population decidedly against us," Marshall said pointedly. "Couldn't you guys have done something a little less provocative?" He was still pissed that the UN had unilaterally decided to go after Sachs. The brutal attack on Camp David and the subsequent attack on Raven Rock and the capital had soured any political support he had in Washington and across much of the country.

Chafing at the comment, Guy explained, "It was a military decision. We had an opportunity to cut the head of the snake off, and we took it. We seriously hurt the Pentagon leadership and the military apparatus with that strike. We killed the Secretary of Defense, along with many other senior generals, so it wasn't a complete loss."

Marshall Tate shook his head in frustration.

This is spiraling out of control faster than we can handle it, he thought.

Marshall looked back and forth between his Secretary of Defense, Admiral Hill, and General McKenzie. "Can we still win this conflict?" he asked. "Can we still remove the Vice President from office now that he has taken over, or are we done for?"

There was a short pause for a few seconds before they said anything. McKenzie spoke first. "It depends. We have enough fuel, food, and munitions for at least three or four weeks of hard fighting, but if we can't thin out the American air forces, they're going to pick us apart. The Russian and Chinese surface-to-air missile systems are effective, but we only have a limited number of them. We're also going to run out of missiles at some point if we can't get a resupply."

Marshall let out a breath in a huff. "The battle in the Atlantic was supposed to break the blockade. What happened?"

Letting out a sigh, McKenzie looked at Admiral Hill for support. Hill nodded and proceeded to answer the question as best he could. "First off, you must understand this was a long-shot attempt, trying to break through the blockade. Our goal was to bloody the US Navy up and convince them that the cost of stopping the convoys would be too high—"

Interrupting him, Marshall retorted, "Well, that clearly didn't work. I read the German summary and it sounds like it was a turkey shoot—a horrific military loss for us."

Admiral Hill grimaced at the comment. "It wasn't an entirely one-sided affair. I've read the German report as well—they primarily focused on the UN naval losses and didn't expound upon the losses we inflicted on the US Navy. The Germans lost three of their submarines in the engagement, but they also sank three *Arleigh Burke* destroyers and managed to hit the carrier *Lincoln* with a torpedo."

"Yeah, but they failed to sink the *Lincoln*," Marshall responded. "It's still combat-effective—at least that's what the report said."

Admiral Hill shook his head. "That's not entirely true. The ship did take a hit, and while it was still able to launch its strike fighters, the carrier is going to have to go to the shipyards for repairs. That means the ship will be out of commission for several months, maybe longer, depending on how bad the damage is. That, Mr. President-Elect, is a huge victory for us. It means the Navy only has two operational carriers in the Atlantic, and *that* is going to make it easier for our supply ships to slip past the blockade.

"The Russians managed to sink two *Ticonderoga*-class guided missile cruisers and three additional *Arleigh Burke* destroyers for a loss of nine subs. They also managed to sink four American submarines in exchange for five of their own. These losses are going to hurt the US's ability to run an effective blockade of Canada. We'll be able to start slipping more supply ships through as the Russian and EU navies continue to hunt down the Americans' remaining submarines and surface ships."

Growing frustrated with the losses, Marshall shot back, "Let's not forget, Admiral Hill, that when this conflict is over with, this navy we're talking about hunting and destroying is the same force we'll be in charge of. This is *our* military force we're currently destroying, along with men and women who we'll be demanding loyalty from when I'm sworn in as President."

Admiral Hill paused. He looked out the window briefly, deep in thought, before turning back to face Marshall. "I agree, and you're right, sir. I don't want to kill them or sink our ships any more than you do. We're going to need a military and navy when you become President— but let's not forget that these men and women have also picked a side. They chose Sachs over you. When this is all said and done and we've won, and you are our President, we'll rebuild."

The group sat there in silence for a moment before McKenzie cleared his throat. "Mr. President-Elect, I'd like to discuss the ground operations," he said.

Marshall looked at McKenzie and nodded for him to proceed. He'd taken up enough of their time with his questions. They had a lot more to discuss.

"With regard to the ground operations, we've surprised the American Army and grabbed a lot of land quickly," McKenzie explained, in a voice that was not as optimistic as the news he was sharing. "While we suspected we could grab territory fast, they're getting themselves organized to respond, and now they're starting to get proper air support. What I'm trying to say is they're going to start pushing us back soon if something doesn't change. What we need is a greater popular uprising to take place in the major cities in your country. We need the people to rise up and take up arms against the government, and in particular, we need them to start attacking the military. If they can attack supply convoys, fuel and ammo dumps or even military bases, it'll force Powers to divert troops to deal with them that otherwise would have been sent against us."

Admiral Hill interjected, "We had hoped more ground units would cross over to our side than what did. I had believed we could get some of the Air Force units to side with us and help us out, but sadly, that has not been the case. As to a popular uprising, McKenzie—yes, I agree that we need to stoke those fires and try to get that to happen, but the attack you launched on Washington, D.C., really hurt our chances of getting a plurality of the country to support us.

"Then there were those yahoos who went and gruesomely murdered several high-profile conservatives and their families in California. Those two attacks had the opposite effect of what their intentions were. Instead of rallying to our side, people have become appalled by the violence and are now seeing us as the aggressors. They're siding with the Vice President in this conflict because *you* took things too far." Admiral Hill was clearly frustrated and disheartened at how things were turning out.

Page shot back, "It's not *that* bad, Admiral. We just need to start organizing more people in the major cities to join our cause, especially in California, New York, and Illinois. We have to give them targets to take their rage out on and get them organized into effective militia units."

Admiral Hill held a hand up. "I agree, Page, and we're doing that, but you have to have some patience. This new war is only a week old. It's going to take a few weeks to get things organized. Plus, it's freaking

303

winter. It's hard to hold massive rallies, marches and demonstrations when it's below thirty degrees out."

Marshall shook his head in dismay. "This would have been a much easier task in any other season," he said rather glumly.

"Agreed. But we don't get to choose when these conflicts happen," replied General McKenzie. "We just have to adapt to the situation and make it work to our advantage. Speaking of advantages—I'd like to go over the results of the Chinese missile attack in the Gulf of Mexico."

Marshall nodded, happy for any shred of good news. He signaled for the general to continue.

"Several years ago, the People's Liberation Army Navy converted a number of their large freighters into floating missile platforms. They're calling them *Long Qiwi*, which translates to *Dragon's Breath* ships. They haven't told us how many of them they have, but we know of at least nine. Seven have been sunk by the US Navy, but there are still another two left that we know of, and they made a beeline to Cuba. The Russians, for their part, have built up a plethora of SAM sites all over Cuba in addition to boxing in the Marines at Guantanamo Bay." McKenzie paused for a moment; he had a concerned look on his face like he had some bad news but didn't know how to say it.

Sensing his hesitation, Admiral Hill pounced. "What is it, Guy? Spit it out."

Sighing, McKenzie announced, "I think we have a problem with the Chinese. As much as they've helped us out by attacking the Navy and Air Force bases with their merchant raiders, their ground army in Mexico still hasn't started their offensive. Each day they delay gives the Pentagon more time to get forces moved over there to deal with them. They should have started their offensive two days ago. I'm concerned they may be getting cold feet after that daytime raid on Beijing at the start of the war."

Standing up, Marshall indicated that the others should stay seated. He turned his back on them and walked over to look out the window for a second, trying to think about what he wanted to ask next. Outside, he could still see the charred remains of the Ministry of Defence building and a few other smoldering ruins from previous air attacks. The war scars marred the beautiful city that had so graciously allowed him to set up his government in exile. He felt terrible about all the suffering the war was causing the people of Canada. They didn't deserve this, to be caught in the crossfire of an American civil war.

Turning to look at his staff sitting around the large table next to the kitchen, Marshall asked, "If the Chinese fail to launch their invasion of the Southwest, how badly does that complicate things for us?"

Leaning forward to answer that question, Admiral Hill explained, "It would be the end of our efforts. We need the Chinese to open that second front so it diverts reinforcements that would be sent against our northern front to the south instead. If that doesn't happen, then Powers will be able to move those divisions he's deployed to Texas, New Mexico, and Arizona to face our forces in the Midwest and Northeast. They'll also be able to suppress the uprising that's happening in California and Oregon with the Marines. We need that uprising to be successful. It could generate thousands of new militia members to help us defeat the Marines and give us a few states where we could freely operate."

Marshall nodded. "Then let us hope that doesn't happen," he said. "Let's try to reach out to the Chinese Foreign Minister and remind him of our deal. If China wants access to America's West Coast ports and a guaranteed source of oil and natural gas from my administration, they'd better hold up their end of the agreement."

****

Washington, D.C.
State Department

Secretary Haley Kagel stared at the Indian Ambassador for a full thirty seconds as she tried to discern what he was thinking. His face had remained stoic, devoid of emotion, although she was sure his mind must have been working overtime, running through the calculations and second-and-third order effects of the offer she'd just presented.

After what felt like an eternity for Secretary Kagel, Ambassador Singh crinkled his forehead, breaking his flat expression. "To clarify what you're asking—acting President Powers wants China to believe that we're going to invade and seize control of Tibet and position our forces to appear that we may push deeper into China if they invade America?"

Smiling, she nodded. "Yes."

Singh leaned back in his chair and thought about it for a moment.

Asaf Singh had been the ambassador to the US now for five years. He had gotten on well with President Jonathan Sachs, and it was well known that he had been deeply saddened to learn that Sachs had most likely died at the outset of this terrible war.

Indian and American relations had grown strong these last four years. The US had increased its purchasing of specific Indian products, and India had reciprocated. Both nations were doing well as they sought to right the economic world that China had been exploiting for their gain for so many years.

Secretary Kagel realized that, despite all this positive will between their two nations, the offer she had presented was a huge risk. Ambassador Singh might not even be able to get his country to go for it. However, the reward if it were to work was certainly something she felt must be very tempting.

Leaning forward in his chair, Singh looked Secretary Kagel in the eyes. "And in exchange for this military action—"

Kagel corrected him. "Perceived military action. It may not have to happen if they back down."

Smiling, Singh cleared his throat. "Yes. In exchange for this *perceived* military action and follow-through if it does have to happen, America will pay off India's national debt, and we'll secure a ten-year firm fixed price on natural gas. If prices go down, we pay less—if they go up, our price is already fixed and will stay that way for the next ten years?"

Secretary Kagel nodded. "That is the deal." She saw him hesitate for a moment, so she added, "Ambassador Singh, we both know China is a problem. They're only going to become a worse problem if they aren't dealt with now. If the US is torn apart, if we're broken into fragments—which is what's going to happen if the Chinese invade through Mexico—it may be the end of my country. While I'm sure many in the world will cheer at that, let's not forget the progress our two nations have made together. Let's also not overlook the position India will be in if you have to face China alone. I'm not saying you *should* follow through with the military action, but if India did, you wouldn't find China in a weaker position than they are right now."

"My concern, Madam Secretary, is that I don't believe you or your government fully appreciates the level of casualties or losses the Chinese are willing to sustain if they believe victory can be achieved," Ambassador Singh stated. "Even if we did carry out our attack, the PLA still has all the units in the Western and Southern commands they can draw from to fight us with. The force they sent to Mexico came from the Central and Northern Army Groups. That means they still have more than one million soldiers in the two military districts near us. It would be a bloody fight if we came to blows."

"Mr. Ambassador, how much worse would that fight be if those forces weren't in Mexico?" asked Kagel. "How much graver will that conflict be when those forces return home, battle-hardened and flush with victory? You won't have America to rely on or help you."

Ambassador Singh grimaced. "I get it, Madam Secretary. America is in a bind. You guys are in a tough spot. We know that. I'm just not sure it will help if we get involved at the moment. Even excluding the Chinese threat of invasion, your country is being torn apart from the inside out. How do we know your nation won't split apart, even if the Chinese don't invade?"

She bit her lower lip as she tried to formulate a proper response. "I agree, Ambassador. Our country is in the process of fracturing. However, the UN's attack on Washington, the murder of two hundred legislators and the probable death of President Sachs have also coalesced our people around the Vice President like no one could have imagined. Our country has some serious political divides, but at the end of the day, we're still Americans.

"People are horrified by what's happening—the politically motivated killings, the occupation of several major cities by foreign troops—all of this has stirred the patriotic passions that run deep in our country. The Vice President has just announced a military draft, and even now, our military is in the process of tripling in size. We're going to get through this tough spot, and when we do, Mr. Ambassador, we're going to emerge stronger and better than ever before."

"*Or*, you may emerge incredibly weakened and unable to be of much help to the rest of the world," the ambassador offered as a counterpoint.

Kagel chuckled. "Maybe, but I doubt it. When our domestic troubles have been sorted, Mr. Ambassador, you can bet your job that we're going to be coming for our pound of flesh against those nations who attacked and occupied our country. We've already delivered a powerful message to the governments of Europe. Don't think our attack was a one-off event. If they continue to invade and occupy our country, we're going to rain death and destruction on their cities like they haven't seen since the last great war."

She paused for a second, letting her last comment hang there for a moment with a wicked grin on her face. Sensing that he was still wavering, she leaned in to add, "One more thing, Mr. Ambassador. What I'm about to tell you must stay strictly confidential. You may share this with the key members of your government, but otherwise this needs to stay quiet."

She stopped long enough for him to acknowledge what she said before she proceeded. "It was Chinese H-20 stealth bombers that carried out the attack that may have claimed the life of our president and killed our Secretary of Defense and many of our senior military leaders at Raven Rock. If those bombers could penetrate *our* airspace, they will change the dynamics of a future war between India and China."

She paused for a second while he digested that piece of intelligence. "The bombs that hit the facility the President and our Secretary of Defense were in were Russian-made thermobaric weapons, but it was the Chinese bombers that delivered them. As such, we've warned the Chinese that if they do invade our country, we will respond with tactical nuclear weapons."

Singh raised an eyebrow at that but didn't say anything right away. "You would use tactical nuclear weapons on your own soil?" he asked skeptically.

She slowly shook her head. "No, not on our soil. In China."

"What? Where?" he stammered in response.

"The Three Gorges Dam," she replied nonchalantly. "We've already told them that we'd hit the dam and destroy the economy of an entire region if they attempt to invade our country."

Singh looked almost sick at the thought. He opened his mouth, then closed it as he thought about his response. "You realize such an attack could kill tens of millions of people, right? The political cost of such an attack globally would be worse than what you're already having to deal with from your attacks on Paris, Berlin, Moscow, and Beijing," he said. His voice crescendoed as he spoke.

Slamming her hand on the table and startling Singh, Kagel spoke through gritted teeth. "Those bastards got caught red-handed rigging our election! Then they bombed our capital. They killed hundreds of our legislators and then assassinated our President. French and German soldiers just captured New York City last night." She spoke with vitriol and venom dripping from her voice.

Kagel then leaned forward, closing the personal space between them. "If I were the President, I'd have already nuked these countries back to the Stone Age. As it is, acting President Powers is showing far more restraint than I or our military believe he should."

She paused and then sat back in her chair, noticing how visibly uncomfortable Singh had become. "Ambassador Singh, destroying the Three Gorges Dam achieves a number of military and political objectives. The hydroelectric power produced there accounts for ten percent of China's entire electrical output. It provides fifty-six percent of the electrical power to the province of Hubei as well as thirty percent of Zhejiang Province's power and twenty-four percent of Shanghai's. The loss of this much electrical generation at one time, along with the inordinate amount of infrastructure damage to the region, will force the Chinese to reevaluate whether they're willing to pay that high of a price to continue with their invasion. We have demanded that they withdraw and go home; however, if they choose to still invade, then we'll hit their army with tactical nukes on our own soil if necessary. But one way or another, we *will* stop them."

Singh clearly wasn't quite sure how to respond to what he'd just heard. Seeing the pained look and uncertainty on his face, Kagel quickly added, "Our goal is not to do this horrible thing, Ambassador Singh, but make no mistake—our country has been savagely attacked and invaded. We will use any and all means necessary to win. If we're going to go through an internal civil war, then we'll handle that internally, but we won't allow outside forces to shape our country or its future by supporting one side over another.

"Right now, we're hoping that if India makes a serious threat of intervening in Tibet, it will give the Chinese pause. If they do invade, then we don't have much choice other than to make the price of invading America too steep for even them to pay."

Singh reached for his glass of water, his hand shaking slightly. "When do you need an answer by?" he asked.

"We need to know as soon as possible, Mr. Ambassador. This isn't a decision that we can wait to hear from you about in a week or two. The

Chinese could launch their invasion anytime. If they do, we'll be forced to hit that dam."

"I'll bet the Chinese Air Force is doing everything they can to make sure you aren't successful now that they know you intend to blow it up," Ambassador Singh countered.

She smiled and nodded. "They are. Our satellites show a massive increase in defensive measures being set up around the dam. In the end, though, it won't matter. They know they can't stop us, and the B-2 stealth bomber isn't the only way we have of delivering our response to their invasion. If they do decide to cross that Rubicon, I can assure you, China won't survive."

Grimacing at the ominous statement, Ambassador Singh responded, "I just hope the rest of the world will survive whatever may come next."

From the Authors

Miranda and I hope you've enjoyed this book. We are currently working on the fourth book of the Falling Empires Series. We also recently released two children's books about PTSD—if you know someone who struggles with that battle, we hope that they might be able to use these books as a resource.

While you are waiting for our next book to be released, we do have several audiobooks that have recently been produced. All six books of the Red Storm Series are now available in audio format as is our entire World War III series. *Interview with a Terrorist* and *Traitors Within*, which are currently standalone books, are also available for your listening pleasure.

If you would like to stay up to date on new releases and receive emails about any special pricing deals we may make available, please sign up for our email distribution list. Simply go to https://www.frontlinepublishinginc.com/ and sign up.

If you enjoy audiobooks, we have a great selection that has been created for your listening pleasure. Our entire Red Storm series and our Falling Empire series have been recorded, and several books in our Rise of the Republic series and our Monroe Doctrine series are now available. Please see below for a complete listing.

As independent authors, reviews are very important to us and make a huge difference to other prospective readers. If you enjoyed this book, we humbly ask you to write up a positive review on Amazon and Goodreads. We sincerely appreciate each person that takes the time to write one.

We have really valued connecting with our readers via social media, especially on our Facebook page https://www.facebook.com/RosoneandWatson/. Sometimes we ask for help from our readers as we write future books—we love to draw upon all your different areas of expertise. We also have a group of beta readers who get to look at the books before they are officially published and help us fine-tune last-minute adjustments. If you would like to be a part of this team, please go to our author website, and send us a message through the "Contact" tab.

You may also enjoy some of our other works. A full list can be found below:

Nonfiction:
Iraq Memoir 2006–2007 Troop Surge
Interview with a Terrorist (audiobook available)

Fiction:
The Monroe Doctrine Series
Volume One (audiobook available)
Volume Two (audiobook available)
Volume Three (audiobook available)
Volume Four (audiobook still in production)
Volume Five (available for preorder)

Rise of the Republic Series
Into the Stars (audiobook available)
Into the Battle (audiobook available)
Into the War (audiobook available)
Into the Chaos (audiobook available)
Into the Fire (audiobook still in production)
Into the Calm (available for preorder)

Apollo's Arrows Series (co-authored with T.C. Manning)
Cherubim's Call (available for preorder)

Crisis in the Desert Series (co-authored with Matt Jackson)
Project 19 (audiobook available)
Desert Shield
Desert Storm

Falling Empires Series
Rigged (audiobook available)
Peacekeepers (audiobook available)
Invasion (audiobook available)
Vengeance (audiobook available)
Retribution (audiobook available)

Red Storm Series
Battlefield Ukraine (audiobook available)
Battlefield Korea (audiobook available)
Battlefield Taiwan (audiobook available)
Battlefield Pacific (audiobook available)
Battlefield Russia (audiobook available)
Battlefield China (audiobook available)

Michael Stone Series
Traitors Within (audiobook available)

World War III Series
Prelude to World War III: The Rise of the Islamic Republic and the Rebirth of America (audiobook available)
Operation Red Dragon and the Unthinkable (audiobook available)
Operation Red Dawn and the Siege of Europe (audiobook available)
Cyber Warfare and the New World Order (audiobook available)

Children's Books:
My Daddy has PTSD
My Mommy has PTSD

Abbreviation Key

1MC	1 Main Circuit (shipboard public address system)
AA	Anti-aircraft
AFB	Air Force Base
AFN	American Forces Network
AG	Attorney General
AI	Artificial Intelligence
AKA	Also Known As
AMRAAM	Advanced Medium-Range Air-to-Air Missile
AOR	Area of Responsibility
APC	Antipersonnel Carrier
ASAP	As Soon As Possible
ASW	Antisubmarine Warfare
ATGM	Antitank Guided Munition
AWACS	Airborne Warning and Control System
AWOL	Absent Without Leave
BMP-3	Russian infantry fighting vehicle
BTR	Bronetransporter (Russian armored vehicle)
CAG	Commander, Air Group
CAT	Countermeasure Anti-torpedo
CBP	Customs and Border Protection
CCTV	Closed-circuit Television
CDF	Civilian Defense Force
CFB	Canadian Forces Base
CFS	Canadian Forces Station
CG	Commanding General
CIA	Central Intelligence Agency
CIC	Combat Information Center
CICO	Combat Information Center Officer
CIWS	Close-in Weapons System
CNO	Chief of Naval Operations
COB	Close of Business
COG	Continuation of Government
COSCO	China Ocean Shipping Company
C-RAM	Counter Rocket, Artillery, and Mortar
DDG	Guided Missile Destroyer
DEFCON	Defense Readiness Condition

DHS	Department of Homeland Security
DoD	Department of Defense
DOJ	Department of Justice
EOD	Explosive Ordnance Disposal
EU	European Union
FBI	Federal Bureau of Investigations
FEMA	Federal Emergency Management Agency
HARM	High-Speed Anti-Radiation Missile
HEMTT	Heavy Expanded Mobility Tactical Truck
INDOPACOM	United States Indo-Pacific Command
IR	Infrared
ISK	Islamic State of Kosovo
JASSM-ER	Joint Air-to-Surface Standoff Missiles, Extended Range
JG	Junior Grade
JLTV	Joint Light Tactical Vehicle
JSOC	Joint Special Operations Command
KSK	Kommando Spezialkräfte (German Special Forces)
LE	Law Enforcement
LT	Lieutenant
MOAB	Mother of All Bombs
MOS	Military Occupational Specialty
NCIS	Naval Criminal Investigative Service
NMCC	National Military Command Center
NORAD	North American Aerospace Defense Command
NRO	National Reconnaissance Office
NSA	National Security Agency OR National Security Advisor
NSC	National Security Council
NVG	Night Vision Goggles
NY CDF	New York Civil Defense Force
ODA	Operational Detachment Alpha (Special Forces)
OS2	Operations Specialist
PA	Public Address
PEOC	Presidential Emergency Operations Center
PKP MG	Pulemyot Kalashnikova Pecheneg (Russian machine gun)
POTUS	President of the United States

QRF	Quick Reaction Force
REBS	Rapidly Emplaced Bridging System
RFID	Radio Frequency Identification Device
ROE	Rules of Engagement
RPG	Rocket-Propelled Grenade
S2	Intelligence Group
SAM	Surface-to-Air Missile
SAR	Search and Rescue
SEAL	Sea Air and Land (Naval Special Warfare Unit)
SecDef	Secretary of Defense
SIGINT	Signals Intelligence
SITREP	Situation Report
SO1	Staff Officer 1
SOCOM	Special Operations Command
SOF	Special Operations Forces
ST	Sonar Technician
ST1	Sonar Technician First Class
TACAMO	Take Charge and Move Out
UAV	Unmanned Aerial Vehicle
UN	United Nations
VAB	Véhicule de l'Avant Blindé (French armored frontline vehicle)
VBL	Véhicule Blindé Léger (French light-armored vehicle)
VLS	Vertical-Launch System
VP	Vice President
XO	Executive Officer

Printed in Great Britain
by Amazon